The Goddess who rides a Tiger

Visit www.booksurge.com to order additional copies.

ED MOOLENAAR

THE GODDESS WHO RIDES A TIGER

STRANGE WORDS AND
NAMES IN HINDUISM, USED IN
THIS NOVEL, ARE EXPLAINED
IN A LIST AT THE BACK.

2007

The Goddess who rides a Tiger

ACKNOWLEDGMENTS:

- Many thanks to "father Francis" (Baartmans), who gave me hospitality in the slum of castless people in Varanasy, where he lives and works, and who told me very much about the people he works for and with.

- and I owe many thanks as well to Mrs Kate Hood, who proof-read the text of this novel and did this very well.

Ed Moolenaar

.

CHAPTER 01

The catered dinner had been abundant. Smiling air-hostesses collected the trays with propylene cups and plates with left over food. Tables were stowed in the backs of the chairs. Lights were switched off. Thirty thousand feet above the Black Sea, Tom Corda dozed off in an Air India Boeing 747. He slid slowly into a restless sleep.

Only after a hostess asked him to fasten his seatbelt did he wake up. It was one o'clock in the morning. Some passengers quickly looked for something in the overhead luggage bins. Others stared vacantly out of heavy eyes. Stewardesses checked if everything was okay for the landing.

At the passport check-point, Tom was reminded that his life rhythm was not attuned to the world he was going to, and the customs men's time appeared to be unlimited.

After two hours he was routinely told by an official that he could go through, and he sighed with relief. Outside the airport, a blend of indefinable odors penetrated his nostrils deeply.

He took a cab. Traffic lights diffused a scanty light. Some vehicles were illuminated, but the majority loomed up without lights. The streets were dimly lit, and there were more holes and cracks than asphalt. At four o'clock in the morning, Delhi turned out to be a ghost town consisting of rake-lean donkeys, cows and goats, and a rickshaw wallah in rags who was standing on the pedals against a light slope. The taxi driver overtook all and pushed senselessly on the horn. He considered the wailing a panacea for the countless knots in traffic.

About three o'clock in the morning they arrived in the city center. There was already a swarm of vehicles, vendors, cows, buffaloes, goats and dogs. Horns of Bajaj-scooters tried to drown each other out by crying like suckling pigs. Indignation and impatience sounded in the blowing horns of the Ambassadors, the Indian cars that hadn't undergone any development for ages. It was a pandemonium of ghost drivers who had an unlimited faith in the brakes of their vehicles. Rickshaw wallahs, pedestrians and donkeys were ruthlessly forced off the road. Cows and buffaloes lay somnolently ruminating in the middle of the road, not at all concerned with the chaos. Tom found accommodation in a lodge next to an extensive slum. The toilet bowl leaked. The cistern didn't work. The bolt on the door was broken off. The electric switch yielded no power. Greyish-yellow water dripped from the showerhead. The noise of the fan in his room made sleeping impossible; and the apparatus produced a smell of soured piss.

Lying on his bed, Tom listened to the wailing of scabby dogs in the slum.

Early in the morning, the wailing was taken over by nasal and dissonantly recited calls to prayer by Muezzins that issued from the overbearing speakers of the neighboring minarets.

As an easily recognizable, well-to-do stranger, Tom knew he was a target for beggars, vendors, and unemployed young people. Nevertheless, he decided to take a walk through the slum next to the lodge. Structures of cardboard boxes, rusty sheets, plastic and other rubbish were supposed to protect people against sun, rain and cold. Tom smelled a rubbish-dump as he walked by. He heard the whining buzzing of mosquitoes and saw dark clouds of flies swarming everywhere. Ulcerated children's bodies looked black with flies. Dingy children with never-combed hair relieved themselves between the ramshackle covers with no more embarrassment than the skeletal dogs with ulcerated skins that also made their contribution to the choking stench in the murderous heat of forty degrees. A scraggly horse scratched itself by rolling in the sand. People sat in dull apathy on their heels. A man aged between thirty and sixty years old gazed into nowhere.

Tom wondered if the human beings with their empty eyes saw him. But when somebody talked to him, he could not bridge the two worlds. He could not respond to the ruthless misery. He walked foolishly, as in an unreal dream, between the apocalyptic beings. With his heavily weighted wallet he felt himself a misplaced joke.

The next day, as he walked through the living dump again, he began to perceive something human in the warped beings living there. In spite of a faint sense of shame, he dared to look in some people's eyes. Women with faces on which a smile seemed unimaginable kneaded cow dung into round flat cakes and let them dry in the sun. They then carried the cakes on their heads elsewhere in town to sell them for a quarter of a rupee each.

In a second-class compartment Tom could not expect the privacy he was used to. Nevertheless he decided to take a second-class ticket for his trip to Benares. He had come to India, had he not, to get to know the land and the people, and not to see it all through a tourist's eyes?

He tried to read a novel; his co-passengers were hardly understandable. A betel chewer with dark red-rimmed teeth stumps fencing a dark cavity, produced only unarticulated sounds. The betel had done its destructive work. Tom could not distinguish consonants in the man's chatter. A man opposite him with a beedi, a cigarette of leaves, between his lips, was keen to make conversation in his pigeon English as soon as Tom looked at him.

Tom did not look at him.

It must have happened in the darkness during one of the senseless stops between Lucknow and Allahabad. Everybody knew a reason for the stop, but as usual nobody knew what was going on. Only afterward was it revealed that someone had pulled the communication cord.

The lights in the train were switched on again. The two seats opposite Tom turned out to be empty; the betel chewer and the beedi smoker were gone. Tom felt something was wrong, and then saw that his luggage from the upper sleeper had disappeared. His backpack, his bag with his plane ticket, train ticket, passport, traveller's cheques, money, keys. Everything was gone. The shock was so sharp that he couldn't even say he had been robbed. His enjoyable trip had fallen to pieces.

Nobody in the compartment had noticed anything. Everybody was cosily chatting. "Chai! Kafi! Omelette!" The man with the hawking voice who came along for the twentieth time did not improve Tom's mood.

Going back home, his first impulse, was out of the question. How could he, without money, without papers, without an identity? He felt himself a nobody. A looming hangover pointed his anger at himself. How could I could I have been so stupid? His first reasonable thought came later, just before Varanasi, the town called Benares in English. He got off the train and headed to the police office.

He was politely referred to the full waiting room. The whole world appeared to have been robbed, and thieves did not seem to be interested in a specific nationality. There was a Briton, two Frenchmen, two Germans, an Australian, a Spaniard and four Indians. They sat all gazing sadly around in the waiting room. Only after an hour were the first stories told, but none of the victims were able to share compassion for the misery of the others. After half a day a police-inspector, who continually asked what had been stolen in the trains to his town, received Tom. The man did his task in a friendly, if bureaucratic, way. Tom could not expect any compassion from him.

When he finally came out with his official report, there were already new victims with sour faces at the door to register their misfortune.

To let off steam, Tom cursed whole-heartedly at the thieves. As though he had provoked heaven, the first monsoon rain began, which drowned him in no time in a heavy shower. He was ruthlessly thrown back into himself, as a drowning person on a raft in a sea of distress. He went on fostering his vengeful feelings, his anger and his hangover.

After some time, this senseless fostering eased and an endless numbing mist of grey desperation loomed. What can I do? kept running through his head. He looked for a spot where he could grieve, free from the world, where he could sink into numbing self-pity. He found a wall, a metre high, as grey as the cloudy, opaque downpour. He waded through the dirty water. Immediately a woman with a child on her arm appeared before him, appealing to him with a raised hand. She made him angrier still, as she didn't allow him rest or privacy.

When he got his bearings, he saw the words "Tourist Office" on the front of ramshackle building. He waded towards it. The building turned out to be closed. A passing woman told him it was Holi Phagua, New Year's Day.

He found a young man who would take him to an office of the British consulate.

But nobody was present there either.

Darkness closed in quickly. Tom wandered aimlessly on. The rain had stopped. The water in the streets began to drain away. Tom came to a narrow lane. Slalomming between the droppings of cows, goats, and dogs, he found a little spot in a corner where he could pass the night, more or less protected against the cold. There was no shit. There were only the rusty spots of dried betel saliva. Tom sat down on his heels and made himself small. A few metres away there was a litter of young, scabby dogs. The head of the mother was all despair. Despite his own feelings Tom felt compassion for her. It was dusk. Within a couple of minutes it would be full darkness. Tom took comfort in thinking that for a possible thief there was nothing more to steal.

He awoke with a start due to the concerned voice of a woman.

"Wouldn't you rather come with me? It's wet and cold here."

Tom looked up into a delicate woman's face which was radiating warm interest. The woman wore a light blue sari. Tom took her to be about forty years old. Rigid with cold and from sitting uncomfortably, he got up with great effort.

A quarter of an hour later, he sat cross-legged on a mat in a hut in the slum opposite the woman.

She introduced herself as Satori. "I am a nun; I work in this quarter with three other nuns."

By the warm sound in her voice and her subtle, heartening smile Tom felt himself unconditionally welcome.

Satori had deeply shaded eyes. Her face was delicate. Her sari left the black silky gloss of her long hair uncovered. Her calm and self-confidence impressed him most of all.

Another nun, who had introduced herself as Soedjata, promised to prepare Tom a meal. He had not yet eaten that day.

Satori asked nothing; she left him free to tell her how he had come to be in that dark corner in their quarter.

Before realizing it, Tom was telling his story.

The nun reacted with great concern. "You look tired. After eating, you can sleep in our guesthouse next door."

Soedjata, who came in with a plate of food, was just as attentive. The atmosphere was so relaxing that Tom wasn't surprised by the confidence of the nuns. He finished his meal quietly.

Both the guesthouse and the nun's hut looked like a chicken house. Soedjata spread a sheet and a blanket over a sleeping mat and hung a mosquito curtain over it. "I hope you are already used to mice and cockroaches. You may have faith there will be, with the sunrise, an outlook on your life again." With the Hindu-greeting of hands up to her chin, she wished him a good night; a night that almost had gone by.

At about three o'clock in the afternoon, Tom woke up. He felt peaceful and serene, as if recovering from a heavy fever. He experienced a merciful, almost dreamy, cosmic emptiness in himself. He could even look at his problem detachedly; he felt it was going to be manageable. The indeterminate feeling of being stuck in a swampy fate had faded away. The pulp of anger, revenge and guilt had not been further aroused.

In the nun's hut there was a meal for him, and a note with the announcement that they had been called away. Tom ate the unleavened chapatis with baked eggs, and after that he went out scouting the quarter. Immediately, children came from all corners and stared curiously at him. A little girl hung on his arm. A boy begged with a raised hand and great, pleading eyes. The children chattered in their strange language and laughed with bare white teeth. A woman looked curiously at Tom, but she covered her face with her sari when he looked back. He walked on, followed by the children.

The next day, he awoke early in the morning in the nun's guesthouse. Men outside were gargling and rattling near the water pump, cleaning their stomachs and lungs of dust, dirty air, and the remainders of betel juice. Tom decided to get up. When he came out, women were washing themselves and their children. On their heels, their bottoms some centimetres from the ground, they washed themselves from top to toe. Then they deloused each other and their children. It was cosily busy around the water pump.

Satori had worked in an Algerian desert area for three years, and for six years after that she had worked among Berbers in North-West Africa. After living for a couple of years among gypsies in the south of France, she had come back to Benares. "If I stayed too long in the same place, life would be too routine," the nun said, explaining her wanderings.

A question wrinkled Tom's forehead.

"Every day's certainties could switch my feelings onto the automatic pilot."

"I can imagine," Tom answered. "My life also threatened to become automatic." He told Satori that he was studying economics, but wondered if he had chosen the right direction. "I decided to make a trip to India to get a better view on my life."

"Sometimes it's good to get some distance," Satori said. "By the way, how could you learn to know yourself without crossing the frontiers of your own safe world?"

Tom went on telling her about his life. There was an almost inaudible knock at the door. A woman entered. She was so skinny that her face appeared childish. She snaked her way, with an apathetic, almost animal gaze, as shy as a dog, to a corner of the room. Satori took her hands and invited her to come to sit with them.

The woman assessed Tom with a volatile look, a cross between fear and curiosity. Satori smiled reassuringly.

Deeply bending and silent, the woman sat next to Satori and opposite Tom. He bowed his head to prevent the woman from being inconvenienced by his curiosity. Satori placed an arm round the woman's shoulders.

Soedjata came in and brought food. She and two other nuns came to sit with them in a circle.

Tom saw the hungry desire on the face of the woman who was still bending over. Encouraged by a nod from Soedjata, the woman, using the fingers of her right hand, took some rice between a piece of chapati and then sopped it in the lentil sauce. With the first bite, she overcame her wavering and ate her food as a hungry animal.

No one felt the need for words.

The poor woman, who was intent on her food, appeared to Tom to be just one of the many shadows in rags; one of the countless, anonymous underworld beings who gazed with dead eyes out of their eye-sockets. He had a vague feeling that she had, unconsciously, come here to become a little more human; to become more than a possession, a uterus, and a source of work. He imagined her to have been driven to this place blindly by a primeval drive for development.

Satori said something to the woman in Hindi. The woman got up, bent deeply, and greeted her with joined hands under her chin. She then shuffled shyly backwards towards the door.

"Asha was married off as a girl of thirteen. When she got married one year later to Sanjay, she joined his family. There she had to do domestic work and to take care of the children in the family. Sanjay and Asha had four children. One girl and two boys died young. They still have one daughter; she is twelve years old. This was the first time that Asha had come here. I had expected her to come."

Satori had started her story spontaneously. Reacting to Tom's quizzical look, she continued. "We know the people in this quarter. We know Asha as well. After her son died from pneumonia at the age of one, and still more after the death of her two other children, she was treated badly by her husband and his family. Without a logical reason, the man seems to hold her responsible for their children's deaths. She works herself to death from early in the morning until late in the night, to attend to her husband and daughter, provide them with food, keep their hut clean, collect water, and earn some rupias by selling toffees. But Sanjay can't see any good in her. His perception is confused without his being aware of it. Sanjay has been programmed; I mean, certain ideas from his youth are basic and self-evident in his thinking. For example, the idea that outcasts are untouchable is for him as natural as a hereditary disease. In his experience, outcasts have no rights—they are as low as curs. This way of thinking, as far as it is thinking, is actually meant to conceal the territorial drive of rich and mighty people, but Sanjay hasn't an inkling of that. He didn't learn to feel. His feeling, his intuition, is not important to him because he is not important himself."

"I suppose Sanjay is not the only victim of this prejudice?" Tom asked.

"Definitely not! Asha has the same conviction, along with everybody in this quarter and also elsewhere. There are rich people as well who don't think otherwise. They think their position and their wealth are justified. They probably don't even think at all as they take for granted that outcasts have to take the blame on themselves. The Hinduism reincarnation doctrine has been deformed over the centuries under the influence of men in power and of submissive people, as well. It became in fact a festering fatalism. Poor people may only hope for a better lot in a next life. This is also an excuse for the distressing differences between wealth and poverty. Rich people can also suffer from avidya."

"Avidya?"

"The hundred and eight upanisads in Hinduism contain the essence of the Vedas. In one of the most important Upanisads, the Mundaka Upanisad, the concepts of 'vidya' and 'avidya' are distinguished. 'Vid' means spiritual knowledge, knowledge of the eternal truth. In vidya," Satori explained, "a person thinks and feels from his authentic being and from being united with creation. By developing vidya, a person can experience truth in himself, in his being connected with other people, and in being a part of the cosmos. If Sanjay was able to develop vidya, he could discover his faith as no more than a faith from hearsay. And he could discover that what he feels in his heart is much more authentic than the axiomatic truths instilled in him by other people. If he should learn to see after this truth, after what people believe for convenience, he could experience how much of great value he has in himself. Vidya makes personal development possible, even without richness or by making a career in society. But Sanjay lives with the feeling absorbers of avidya; he sees everything through the blinkers of prejudice."

"Why does he stay with his wife if he doesn't respect her?"

"He could not repay the dowry."

"So, if he had money, he could. . ."

"Sanjay needs his wife for homework. He is dependent on her. He could not take the responsibility for the child and the housekeeping. Like most boys in this quarter, Sanjay learned by hanging around with his friends. Girls must work from the age of six or seven. They learn cooking, washing and caring for children, so that they later can be married off as hard-working labourers at the lowest possible price. Female work is beneath a man's position; and he should not have to do it. That dependence forces men, unconsciously, to convey obedience and discipline to their wives and daughters to keep them dependent. When the girl is young, the father disposes of her. After her marriage, she is at the mercy of her husband. And when her husband dies, and his family doesn't need her for housework, she can be sent away. The constitution of 1950 dictates full equality between men and women, but nothing has changed."

"Are all men here like that?"

"Most men are good. They work hard, if they have work. Sanjay is not bad, either. He is a rickshaw wallah. He contracted a loan for his rickshaw at a high interest rate. Because of that he is left with almost none of his earnings, although he works hard. Besides, he is seriously worried about the dowry for his daughter."

"So Sanjay is repressed as well."

"Sanjay is at the mercy of a ruthless usurer, from whom he can rather expect contempt than compassion. Repression is ingrained in the system, with a long historical development in which there is no room for respect or compassion for the poor outcasts, and still less for their wives. This is a coercive system which passes a life of scanty poverty on from generation to generation. Sanjay had to marry and get children, especially sons, to fancy himself recognized as a man. Deep in his heart he must be afraid of losing his pretended rights as a husband and a father, which means he would not be a real man any more. He has no idea what he could win if he gives up his compulsively defended superiority over his wife."

"If one is not aware of avidya, how can he release himself from it?"

"By overcoming his fear of losing his illusions and by learning to experience reality with all sincerity."

"Illusions?"

"Who likes to see himself as he is?"

"Did Asha never rebel against her husband?"

"For rebellion one must be someone."

"Do you teach her to become someone?"

"She can only learn that herself."

"By rebelling?"

The nun produced an open laugh. "A vicious circle. We can perhaps help her to break through that circle. We are here for the people who can't manage their lives. Furthermore, we want to offer them rest and respect, hoping that they will bud and flourish on their own. We are here, with empty hands; that's all. We hope that people discover here something in themselves."

"And what are you doing to get people so far?"

"It doesn't matter what we do. The point is: what happens around us? It's what Mahatma Gandhi thought, and I agree with him. We are like gardeners who provide for good circumstances and stay expecting the result. We only invite people to freedom by granting them respect and confidence and by leaving them rest and time."

"And the reward?"

"Their smiles are worth much to us. Some of them can't smile anymore."

After a short silence the nun said, "I invited Asha to come back tomorrow. I would appreciate it if you could be here again. Experiencing a man respecting her will do her good."

"I should like to come."

The poor woman, less shy but still with a submissively bent head, now had a name and a history. To Tom, that made her life a living problem. Before, the misery of all those innumerable shadowy beings had no hold over him. Actually he had remained indifferent to it, even when he had seen all the anonymous figures in the slums. They had been beings of a faraway, strange planet. Only now that he knew the name and the life story of this woman, did he begin to feel for her. The miserable woman had a face…and a soul.

Threefold subordination; as a poor person, as an outcast, and as a woman, sat there crouching on the mat.

Satori felt the woman needed warmth and time to shake off the repression of an endless chain of generations. She knew how to choose the right moment for a caress or a warm-hearted word.

Asha's fear began, bit by bit, to thaw in the face of the cordiality of the nun. Encouraged by Satori, she brought her crockery cup with chai to her lips. The tea seemed to warm her a bit. For one moment Tom saw her dark, fierce eyes; still gazing, carefully surveying him. For a while he felt himself too pointedly present. He drank his tea and succeeded in relaxing until he heard a coy voice whisper, "Dhanyavad" (thank you).

The nun reacted with an encouraging smile. Asha rose to leave.

"Asha must prepare a meal for Sanjay and her daughter," Satori explained.

"Are there many women who come to see you?"

"Sooner or later all of them come here. None of the women has a comfortable life."

"Do you never make an appointment?"

"I can't make them understand that they are welcome if they only come at certain times. Besides, they have no clock; they've got the sunrise and the sunset."

"And if there more women come at the same time?"

"They know each other's problems. There are no secrets in this quarter. Besides, we rarely talk about problems; they come mostly for some warmth, or rest, or comfort, or if they are hungry. If the situation at home is too tense, they can stay here for a couple of nights in the guesthouse."

"There is still a lot of work to do for you."

"We aim our care at the people who come our way."

CHAPTER 02

In a ten-year-old two-door vehicle, a "2cv", Tom Corda drove over a wide climbing avenue to the main building of the pharmaceutical concern Medimarket, usually named "The Concern." Mighty beeches on either side made it appear as if he was driving through the middle of a cathedral built by God himself.

In the main building of The Concern, the board of governors resided; the board of managers, with their secretaries, typists, telephonists, counter employees; and the archivist with his co-operators.

Tom was on his way to a third and last application interview. The following hours would be crucial for his future career. He didn't really feel prepared for the world in his old-fashioned vehicle, which he had bought from a fellow student after his last stay in India.

After about three hundred metres he saw the Medimarket building, with its tight horizontal and vertical lines and abundance of plate-glass windows. It appeared as a chilly, capital monument. Tom thought the architecture rectilinear and starchy. In the glaring sun, at that moment straight in the south, it made him think of a colossal square block of granite. He valued the breadth of the front to be about forty metres, with three floors above ground. He thought the building was at least ten metres high.

The grand square in front gave the building the great air of a presidential lodging. The square was paved with flagstones of different colours, and in the center there was a fountain that squirted a tangle of splashing water twenty metres into the air.

Tom parked his old vehicle discretely in the shadow of a tall oak.

Walking across the square, he saw a black limousine sliding

past. The car stopped before a building with a flight of steps leading to an impressive main entrance with double doors. An aged chauffeur dressed in a black uniform with red piping, got stiffly out and walked, rigid from sitting or his age, to the right back door of the car. He held it open for a man who appeared to be about fifty years of age.

The younger man, inscrutable in his tailor-made, pinstriped suit, got out of the car. His impeccable white, ironed dress shirt and black polished shoes impressed upon Tom that the man could have a high place in The Concern. He carried an attaché case in his right hand and a mobile phone in his left. He had a powerful chiseled jaw; his eyes were intently directed forward. He went resolutely to the main entrance, where the chauffeur greeted him with his right hand at his cap.

The man nodded absently and went to the double doors that automatically swung open.

Tom was too early for his appointment with the principal of the General Management of Medimarket, so he strolled to the chauffeur for a chat.

The man came to meet him and began compatibly to talk, as if Tom was an old acquaintance. "I drove Mr. D to his office."

"Mr. D?" Tom asked.

"His name is Drover, but everybody calls him Mister D. Mr. D is the president of the board of governors and the general director of The Concern.

"So he is the big boss."

"Mr. D works night and day," the chauffeur went impassively on, "and it looks as if he works harder the more The Concern grows."

"What do you mean by growing?"

"There have been a lot of mergers and takeovers in the last years. When there is a merger at stake, the meetings are unending. I learn these things from other people; Mr. D doesn't tell me anything, he only gives me orders. And he uses every second in the car for his work."

Tom looked expectantly at the chauffeur.

"It's nice work," the man went on. "It is lovely driving in a high-speed car like that, and in this way I earn a little extra in addition to my little pension. Only the waiting during the long meetings is sometimes difficult. But I am a widower; otherwise, I would just be at home alone."

"Driving the boss is the only work you do?"

"Driving and keeping my mouth shut."

"What do you mean?"

"Well! Sometimes I overhear things," the man sidestepped.

Tom looked at him uncomprehendingly.

"One day you'll understand." The old man smiled at him.

"When did your wife die?"

"Four years, three months and five days ago." The man took a photo of his wife out of his pocket. "I keep her with me still," he smiled, with nervously quivering lips. "We've been together for more than fifty-four years."

Moved by the strong bond the man felt with his deceased wife, Tom could not immediately find any appropriate words. Then he stammered, "It must be quite difficult after so long together."

"Very difficult! I am no more than half a being since..."

Tom hesitated, not knowing how to react. He shook hands. He held the old man's hand for a few seconds. Then he mounted the steps to the main entrance.

He rang the bell and one of the two doors was cautiously opened. "Good afternoon. You are...?"

Tom told the janitor who he was and his reason for being there. The janitor showed him in.

Tom didn't need more than a couple of minutes to acclimatise a little to a world where everything displayed importance. Meeting the chauffeur had showed him to see things in perspective; that's why he didn't feel overpowered by the wealthy atmosphere. He gazed upon long passages with deeply gleaming, marble-tiled floors and panels of rosewood where figurative paintings hung at eye-level on the walls. Two mosaic works were built into the wall next to the main entrance, one above the other. A beam of light shone from the ceiling, and the works seemed to be composed of little jewels. "Human Being" was engraved in a bronze sheet underneath the upper mosaic. The figure had a globe in his hand. The lower mosaic turned out to be an abstract image of "Nature".

A young woman with bleached blond hair, in a black dress, came towards him. "Mr. Corda? I am Mrs. Hooghuis." Smiling, she greeted him with a well-manicured hand adorned by a lot of rings and trinkets. "Would you follow me, please? Mr. Lak is waiting for you."

For every two high-heeled steps of his escort, Tom took one. He tried to keep time with her.

They stopped before a heavy door. The light over the door was green. Mrs. Hooghuis knocked.

A voice which sounded as though it came out of a deep well called, "Come in!"

Mrs. Hooghuis opened the door to a chamber before them.

"Mr. Lak, Mr. Corda is here to see you."

At the back of the room, in front of a high window, was a heavy oak writing desk. Mr. Lak was quickly finishing some paperwork. His head was covered with pomaded hair, precisely parted into two unequal areas. He wore rimless eyeglasses on his shiny face. His tailor-made suit forced Tom for a while to delay his decision on an adjective, a choice between robust and corpulent. A silk tie came out of a blue-white, ironed collar and was secured on a clean shirt by a pin with three little diamonds.

"Good afternoon, Mr. Lak. I am Tom Corda."

Mr. Lak absentmindedly took his glasses from his nose. He looked as if he was wondering what his visitor had come for. He greeted Tom with a mousy handshake and fell immediately back onto his chair.

He pressed a button and, as though she had been waiting for it, Mrs. Hooghuis came out of a side door.

"Would you bring me, please, Mr. Corda's file?" Then he motioned casually to a chair in front of his desk.

"Mr Lak's time must be valuable," Tom thought.

The file was respectfully handed over to Mr. Lak. Looking at Tom's letter in the almost-empty file, Lak began to explore the territory. "You are applying for the recently created position of assistant manager in the Department of General Management of Medimarket. You understand the new functionary will be my assistant?"

"Yes, I do, Mr. Lak."

Mr. Lak described the most important tasks related to the new function. "The new official will have to organize management conferences. He or she will also look after the correspondence of the Department of General Management. And he or she will be in charge of the appointments in the lower positions for this section."

Tom waited.

"And you know," Mr. Lak said, after a short silence in his monologue, "the new functionary will play an important part in our relations with a pharmaceutical company in Benares, India."

Tom's interest was heightened. "Imagine if they send me to Benares…"

Mr. Lak kept looking in the applicant's file, as the applicant began to wonder whether he could feel at home in this perfect setting.

"I see you have travelled a lot."

"That is right. I have been in some Asian countries, and I have been in India as well. The first time I stayed there for a year."

"Yes, I see that." Mr. Lak kept looking in the file, without saying anything. Then he said, as though talking to himself, "It is a very responsible function. My future assistant will have a finger on the pulse."

Meanwhile, Tom's attention and thoughts wandered throughout the interior of the office. A copy of a "Mondraan" in a tight frame behind the manager's chair challenged his imagination to make some mental leaps in his perception of Mr. Lak.

In the corner, behind Mr. Lak stood two subtropical plants. On the desk were two telephones, a button for ringing Lak's secretary, a button for the red and green lights over the door, an intercom device, a paperweight, some piles of paper, and a photo of a happy family, with Mr. Lak in the central position as the head of the family.

The potential finger on the pulse was called to order. "This is your third interview for the job, Mr. Corda?"

"Yes, Mr. Lak. I've had a conversation with the personnel manager, and before that I talked with one of his co-operators."

Mr. Lak took no notice of Tom's answer and followed his own thoughts. "I selected two people out of the candidates for a last interview. Both of them are university graduates. You are one of these two people."

Leaning on the high back of his chair, his fingertips to each other, it looked as if Mr. Lak noticed his applicant only now. He looked searchingly at him, in tight-lipped triumph. "I already told you that it is a function with a high measure of responsibility. We make, therefore, high demands. You must expect to work fifty to sixty hours per week. And if required, you must be willing to travel for The Concern to other countries. On the plus side, there will be a high salary. Are you willing to do that?"

"Of course!" Tom snapped out his response. He had let himself to be taken aback by the man's pomposity.

Mr. Lak smiled affably at Tom's reaction. He rose and held out his hand. "You will hear from us."

He then rang Mrs. Hooghuis, who kindly showed Tom to the exit.

Tom Corda's first working day started with disillusionment. At ten o'clock he rang the doorbell, and the same janitor opened the door. "Good morning. You are...?"

"My name is Corda. I am employed by Medimarket."

"Well! Come in. Where are you going to work?"

"General Management."

"I'll call somebody for you." The man went to his lodge that was separated from the hall by a glass wall. He dialed a number. He waited, nodded, and then came out of his lodge. "Mrs. Hooghuis will come to pick you up."

Waiting near the door, Tom felt himself a visitor. His suit, which he had bought before his first interview, strengthened that feeling in him. In one of the passages, at a distance of about fifteen yards, he observed a feverish, screaming excitement, slowly dying away in the noise of the absorbing space. He tried to imagine the anonymous figures there, who henceforth would be his colleagues. In another passage, more in the forefront, he saw an anonymous colleague moving through the space, speed-walking like an ant, a pile of papers in his hand and a look of pompous seriousness on his face.

From afar, Tom heard the clicking of a woman's heels on the marble tiles. A few seconds later, he saw Mrs. Hooghuis hurriedly arriving. He went to meet her. Her red dress was strikingly pretty.

"I bid you heartily welcome, Mr. Corda. I hope you are going to work here with pleasure." She offered him her well-manicured hand.

"Thank you, Mrs. Hooghuis. I hope that we'll cooperate pleasantly."

Mrs. Hooghuis smiled sweetly.

"I'll take you to Mr. Lak's room, and after that I'll show you your own room." She went off, clicking her heels on the marble floor. Tom followed her.

Mr. Lak's welcome was smothered in his hurry. "Unfortunately, I've no time for you. Mr. D needs to see me. But Mrs. Hooghuis will, meanwhile, take you up to the building and introduce you to your colleagues in the other departments. In the afternoon, I shall introduce you to my fellow managers. But now I've got to go." With a routine look at his watch, he collected some files and left the room.

The agitation of his new boss had a soothing influence on Tom, but he knew himself well enough to know that he soon would be infected by the sense-of-duty virus, and would soon feel a part of the system.

Mrs. Hooghuis showed him to the room that would be his. The room was beside Lak's, with a connecting door, just as at the other side, between Lak's room and that of Mrs. Hooghuis. The most elementary inventory was present: a writing desk and an adjustable desk chair, a telephone, a computer, and a metal filing cabinet. Two copies of etchings hung beside the filing cabinet on the back wall. The rest of the office was bare and smelled of beeswax.

"I suppose I may change the room to my own taste?"

"In a way," Mrs. Hooghuis said cautiously. "That is to say, regarding the rules about it. I shall give you a copy."

Tom didn't feel the need to stay any longer. He looked at Mrs. Hooghuis. She understood his gentle hint, and proposed that they go and see the several departments where she would introduce him to his colleagues.

She knocked first at the door of the typing pool, where at that moment a heated discussion was going on. A blond woman of about fifty years of age spoke in an indignant, gossipy tone. Her sharp green eyes accentuated her willingness to fight. The sardonic lines round the corners of her mouth attracted Tom's attention.

When Mrs. Hooghuis and Tom came in, there was a sudden hush. Twelve women's faces looked up from behind their computers. By intuition, they knew that there was "a new one" again.

The new one was silently observed.

"Who is that blond woman in the forefront, in the middle?" Tom whispered.

"Mrs. Vinnie de Haas," Mrs. Hooghuis answered. "She is Mr. Huls's assistant; she does her typing work here."

The chief of the typing pool, a man with a half-bald skull, rose with difficultly from behind his desk that sat in front of the twelve women. He buttoned his light blue tweed jacket. Seeing the thumbed, orange-green decoration on the left lapel of the man's jacket, Tom thought he had already had a jubilee. He took it for silver.

The man came hesitatingly toward them. "Good morning, Mrs. Hooghuis."

"Good morning, Mr. Rutjes."

Mr. Rutjes seemed to expect the introduction of the new colleague to come from Mrs. Hooghuis.

"Mr. Rutjes, may I introduce Mr. Corda? Mr. Corda is Mr. Lak's new assistant."

The man gave Tom a slack hand. "Rutjes."

"Are you the chief of the typing pool, Mr. Rutjes?"

"Yes."

The silence of the ladies was somehow suffocating. Tom wondered if Rutjes would introduce him to the women. Mrs. Hooghuis put an end to that question. "Shall we go?"

They visited six other departments, where actually no one had time for the new colleague.

In the end, Tom made the acquaintance of the receptionist and the central telephone service clerk.

"This is the nerve center of Medimarket," Mrs. Hooghuis told him. "I know," she asserted, "I worked here for two years on the telephone. The female telephonists and the women behind the counter are the buffers who intercept the shocks from outside."

"How do you mean?"

"I mean the problems and the criticism of the management from outside. It's heavy work, as the employees behind the counter and the telephonists are addressed about unpleasant measures. The Employee's Council raised this problem last year to the Managers' Board. The personnel manager, Mr. Bot, addressed this in a memo, in the name of the presiding director. He was of the opinion that the time of managers was too precious for them to be engaged in complaints from outside. He decided then to raise the quality of the counter and telephone operators by sharpening their selection."

"But anyone calling from outside has to go through the funnel of the automatic answering machine first."

"That is right. Mr. D wants the Medimarket system to run smoothly," Mrs. Hooghuis explained.

"He succeeded well in this."

Tom told Mrs. Hooghuis about his attempt to make contact with The Concern when he wanted some information about the job he was applying for. "You are connected to the automatic answering machine for Medimarket. All lines are occupied at this moment. Would you wait for a moment, please? The woman's electronic voice was very kind, but having a say in it was quite impossible. 'There are currently eight people in the queue ahead of you,' she said. And when I got through in the end, a woman told me that Mr. Bot could not be disturbed. 'Perhaps you could call another time?' she suggested. I decided then to risk the application without the information," Tom said.

"It can be difficult for people from outside to make contact with the responsible functionary," Mrs. Hooghuis answered kindly. She looked back once more at her former colleagues; one, with therapeutic patience, was holding an interview with a caller.

After lunchtime, Mr. Lak had a half-hour at his new assistant's disposal. The half-hour began twenty minutes later than planned, but Tom was already in a waiting mood. He didn't feel sucked into the collective hurry. Nevertheless, he was sorry that he didn't have his morning paper with him.

He sat in the same chair before Lak's desk as when he had had his job interview. Lak quickly read through some papers. Tom's eyes were caught again by the Mondraan-labyrinth on the wall behind Lak's back.

"Mr. D made an interesting announcement," Lak started, while his eyes flew along the last lines of a report. Then he looked up, little stars of triumph in his eyes and a tight-lipped smile on his face.

Tom looked at him expectantly.

"Still in confidence," Lak added, with a mysterious sound in his voice. "Medimarket will possibly need you."

Tom wondered if Lak was playing a joke or ragging him. He could not imagine that the financially supreme Medimarket would need him; but on the other hand, he could not imagine Lak playing tricks on him. Or did I assess the man wrongly? Tom wondered.

Lak remained serious.

Tom waited silently for Lak to go on.

"Once more, in confidence. The information can not leak out before Mr. D has formally made a decision, and that could still not be for some weeks."

Tom had no idea of what to think.

"You know," Lak went on, "that Medimarket is a worldwide company."

"Yes, I know."

"Medimarket also maintains relations with a pharmaceutical company in Benares, in Northern India."

Tom began to get nervous and warm as his blood pumped rapidly through his veins. He felt tension along his back and neck at the thought of a possible adventure. He had a foreboding that they would send him to Benares. But the question burning on his lips stayed stuck there.

"If you would like me to do so," Lak went on, "I'll recommend that the general director assign you a part in this business."

"Do you mean...?" Tom's voice sounded hoarse.

"We will not rule out the possibility of sending you to Benares for an exploratory investigation."

Tom tried to bridle his enthusiasm. I must make a businesslike impression, he thought, and I must drum into my head that The Concern will need me...although I can't imagine that.

"What would that actually mean?" Tom asked casually, as though this was part of his daily experience.

"I can go no further on that matter," Lak answered carefully.

"When you can tell me more, I will certainly consider it."

Don't forget: The Concern needs you! Tom said to himself once more. He rose to his feet.

The door to his room opened and a man entered Lak's office; a man almost a head taller than Tom, with a big head, chubby cheeks, a whiskered double chin, and a solid stature. His pin-striped chalk suit strained tightly. From his collar hung a dark red tie, which was stretched tightly round his neck. He looked self-confidently at Tom. "You must be Mr. Corda, my colleague's new assistant." His affected words were forced through his collar.

"Yes, that's right."

"Huls," the man said. A full, strong hand clasped Tom's. The handshake and the man's confidence kept Tom from making further conversation. That wasn't necessary, as Huls took the initiative. "I learned from my secretary, Mrs. Haas, that you already made the acquaintance of the people in my department."

Lak joined in the conversation. "Mr. Huls is the manager of the Finance Section; one of the most difficult posts in the company."

Huls radiated a discreet pride and rewarded his colleague with a compliment. "General Management should not be underestimated."

The two managers smiled kindly at each other.

Tom looked, embarrassed, from one man to the other.

"To the point!" Huls stated, as he addressed Lak. "I came here to tell you that I am going to celebrate my twenty-fifth jubilee next month. I consider this also as an opportunity to inaugurate my new house."

"Two good reasons for a party," Lak answered.

"During all those years, I've dedicated my forces to The Concern," Huls went on. "That is to say, I entered into Medimarket at the time when it was only a little pharmaceutical concern. With mergers and by takeovers, we grew into The Concern it is now. Without any pretensions, I wonder sometimes whether Mr. D would have got that far without us."

"So do I..." Lak hesitated in agreeing with his colleague.

Huls addressed Tom. "You must know, Mr. Corda, it is not a custom here to plunge immediately into the matter. Anyhow, it is not my style, but I am going to make an exception for my colleague's assistant. May I invite you and your wife to my party?"

Tom was very pleased. "I'll gladly accept your invitation. I do not yet feel fully at home here; your party will be a good opportunity to make it better. And Vera, my wife, can also then make the acquaintance of my colleagues."

"I'll send you an invitation in writing," Huls ended, then he addressed his fellow manager.

Tom seized the opportunity to go to his own room. When he was there, he still heard the two men talking. He looked back and found the door was not pulled closed after him. Lost in his thoughts, he returned back to the door.

Then he heard Huls saying, "Don't worry, Ruud, you will definitely not have any problems."

The plotting sound in Huls's voice held Tom back from pulling the door closed. He had to catch the rest of the conversation.

"That boy is acquainted with the country; that can be useful."

"That may be so, but I staked my position!" Tom heard Lak's timid reaction. "You know the medical recommendation was negative. There is something wrong with his heart. If the Board of Governors learns this, I shall lose their confidence."

Tom's heart thumped.

"Your decision to appoint the man fits perfectly in Mr. D's policy. He assured me personally."

"Appointing a heart patient; how can that fit in Mr. D's policy?"

"Mr. D said something about experimental subjects in a project he is preparing. He wouldn't tell me more."

"So I must have confidence in it," Lak said resignedly.

"You can put confidence in it. Besides, we'd better send this inexperienced young man Corda to India, rather than a clever old stick who would immediately see through the situation. We must be on our guard against dragging our name through the mud, Ruud. Believe me, this Corda is the man Mr. D needs. He will discover nothing there in disorder. In my opinion, he is too trusting for that."

"Can't you go over there yourself?"

"Me? No…that's not for me, the poverty and uncertainties. No, Ruud, you know I am a supporter of development aid, but if it is a matter of doing a job in a country like that, then I would rather delegate it. Besides, I can't be absent from here. Mr. D needs me."

Tom left the door ajar, afraid that the two men would notice he had overheard their conversation. He dropped onto a chair behind his desk, so that he could sit and stare ahead of him.

Something wrong with my heart. Once he had felt a pain in his chest, and he had periods when he was a little short of breath. But knowing now that he had been medically rejected gave him a mental punch so severe that the rest of the conversation between Huls and Lak only scarcely got through to him. With the voices of the two men in the background, he came slowly to a sense that he had been appointed in spite of the medical rejection. That didn't put him into a cheerful mood. So, I am disabled, he realized, and I am being simply set up as a pawn, not cunning enough to discover their dark trap. I am curious to know what sort of job this is.

CHAPTER 03

After overhearing the conversation between Huls and Lak, Tom went to pieces.

True, he had already earlier suspected something was wrong with his heart, but it had been a piece of cake to reason it away and forget the pain in his chest after it had eased off. His shortness of breath had been inconvenient, but he had pushed it aside as something not to be worried about. Nor had he discussed it with his G.P. Now, in retrospect, Tom realized he had been afraid of a medical examination, and of a negative result.

His world had fallen in now; a foggy feeling of monotony came over him, a cul-de-sac in a promising world.

In the afternoon, "the coffee woman," as she was called in corridor chat, Mrs. Sandy Kamat, came in and poured him a cup of coffee. "You don't feel well, Mr. Corda?"

"I got an unpleasant message."

Sandy looked worried. "Probably I can't do anything, but if you want to drop in for a talk, you'll be welcome."

Tom was surprised, but his intuition told him that Sandy had more at her disposal than serving coffee.

"Thank you. Yes, maybe I will…"

Half an hour later, they sat opposite each other.

"I am Sandy. May I call you Tom?"

"Okay, Sandy." Without knowing, Tom was the first person in The Concern who had used her first name.

He felt he could take her into his confidence, and he told her what he had overheard that morning.

Sandy laid her hand on his. She didn't need words to make him feel that she felt sorry for him.

Tom let it happen. He enjoyed no longer being alone with his problem.

"Shall I make a cup of coffee for you?"

"Thank you!"

Tom forgot the time. His work didn't interest him any more.

"So it is a double hangover," Sandy diagnosed. "You just learned straight away something is wrong with your heart, and in the same breath they degraded you to an instrument. You must feel ghastly."

"In such a situation it is good if there is someone who can make you feel back in the picture."

Sandy sat down again. "Tom, of course I can do nothing for your heart; I hope there are people who can help you. But for your work in The Concern, I will tell you this: this is the first time you feel misused here, but it will not be the last time. And you are not the only misused person here."

"You know that feeling as well?"

"I know it very well. The first day I worked here I made up my mind. I said to myself that I would be the one to decide whether I would allow them to use me or not."

"And if you decide no?"

"Then I shall let them know."

"There is nothing left to decide now anyway". Where else can I apply with my heart?"

"If you show them who you are, they will respect you."

After half an hour in a traffic jam, Tom drove his old 2CV into the drive beside his house. He switched the engine off, removed his seat belt, and got out.

He kissed his wife, Vera, and his ten-year-old daughter, Rose. Then he disappeared into the bedroom to release himself from his working clothes: his suit, shirt and tie. "A noose (as in his view his tie was) is, in Hinduism, a symbol of earthly attachment," Satori had told him. But for Tom the tie had rather a claustrophobic sense; tying it in the morning, in front of the bedroom mirror, could make him feel that he was confining himself to a small world, a world of having faith in careers. During the day this feeling of constraint usually dissolved into a faint communal sense; then it felt nice not to be out of tune. But driving back home after his work, the tie felt like a strange organ that had to be rejected as soon as possible.

In The Concern there were no regulations about working clothes; but in jeans and a sweater, Tom realized, he would expose himself to unspoken, critical glances. That afternoon, he had asked Sandy Kamat if he could allow himself to come in in jeans and a sweater. She had looked at him, weighing it up for a while, before giving her opinion. "A strong character doesn't lose his identity by leaving his suit at home."

However, Tom had decided to fit in for the present with the unwritten rules of The Concern.

While Vera washed the vegetables and Tom peeled the potatoes, he told her about his experiences of that day.

The shock came hard for Vera. "So, it's worse than you thought."

"Yes. I've to attune my life anew."

"And I've to attune my life anew to yours," Vera answered.

"At any rate, it is good to know that I am not alone."

"We should talk about this with our G.P."

"I already made an appointment."

"We 'll go together," she decided.

"Okay!"

"And that experimental subject Huls talked about? What can that mean?"

"I've no idea. Even Huls didn't know."

"And you cannot ask Mr. D?"

"I hardly know The Concern; but what I know is that one can't approach Mr. D as though he were a normal person."

"And if it concerns you?"

"Don't forget that conversation was not for my ears."

"That's true. "Do you know what sort of job it is they will use you for?" Vera asked.

"It must have something to do with their contacts in Benares that Lak had told me about earlier."

"And you may not discover there anything in disorder?"

"It looks like."

"Can you travel to India with your heart problems?"

"I shall discuss this with the G.P. It is a soothing thought to know, isn't it? Soedjata has a friend who is a physician."

"You mean Sudhir Varma?"

"Yes. And if he can't help me, there will probably be someone else in the clinic he works in."

Tom and Vera had met each other eleven years before. Walking on a sidewalk, Tom had seen her sitting in an outdoor café. She was alone.

He knew immediately that she was the one, the woman he would spend his life with. And she knew as well; he saw it in her open mind.

He chose a table next to hers. They looked at each other and didn't know what to say. He offered her a drink.

Three hours later they were still sitting there. They had told each other about their lives.

They had walked away, hand in hand.

The next day they made an appointment with the register official in the municipality Vera lived in.

Two months later they were married.

They went on a honeymoon to France. There they found themselves lost in a little old mountain village, where old men with prematurely lined faces played jeu de boules on the square in front of the church. Old women watched the jeu from old benches.

The church and the square formed the center round which the village was built, the center of village life.

The village had one shop, next to the church. It was the village's pub, as well. Everything they needed was on sale there, and the news of the village was passed on there too, sometimes as silly gossip.

Tom and Vera drank a Pernod in the pub every day and then they enjoyed a simple plat du jour. They listened with respect to the talk, carried out with religious seriousness, about the coming thunderstorms. In hot summers, thunderstorms were always expected.

They danced in the evening on the square in front of the church. These were timeless and spaceless hours. United in music and motion, their dancing together was like eternal freedom, like being freed from earthly attraction. Fatigue was strange to them; in music and dance, primeval forces were set free in them, as though their souls, united, had released them from earthly reality.

After their honeymoon, they went on to live timelessly and in the clouds.

Seven months later, Rose announced herself.

Vera decided to stay home. She loved her work, but loved her baby more. Her work was counselling students who were not in tune with their surroundings, and often not with themselves, and who had therefore lost perspective on their studies.

While Vera was recovering from the effects of childbirth, the students with the worst problems came to their home. Every working day, she spent two hours with them.

Tom did administrative work for a project developer. During the twelve years he had worked there, he had never asked himself why he had applied for that job. His life revolved around his free time and Benares.

Finally, an advertisement for Medimarket made him realize that he had to change.

Now, after the conversation between his boss and Huls, he came to realize that he had not applied for another job during all those years because he had unconsciously been afraid of a medical examination.

That night, he lay on his back and glared at the dusky ceiling. The conversation between Huls and Lak dominated his thoughts to the point that it made falling asleep impossible.

Vera slept quietly beside him.

Tom realized that his life was no longer a matter of course. He had, naturally, known he was a mortal being; but in his ambitions, a healthy earthly life had always been taken for granted. That life now showed its limits. The 'why' of my life has only scarcely occurred to me, he realized. I've always seen myself as a dynamic person who was used to looking forward, being goal-orientated, planning. I was a manager, in heart and soul. I was invulnerable. But actually I've become stuck in a flat image of myself. What did I actually do in the years that have passed by? I had a good job; that is to say, a well-paid job. I worked hard...I was pretty successful. But what happened around me? And what happened to me? I've got a wife I love very much and a daughter who is much more important than my own life. And I scarcely enjoyed it.

Quieted by his astonishment at the questions singing through his head, Tom lay glaring at the vaguely visible ceiling. Why does the 'why' period of a child move so quickly past? he wondered. Why does it move past at all?

CHAPTER 04

Tom Corda had been working for three weeks for Medimarket when, in the morning on his way to his room, he felt an unfamiliar tension in the building. He looked around and saw colleagues from other departments hurrying through the passages of the building. Hurrying wasn't actually unusual, but it was different from what he was used to.

A young man looked shyly around. A woman typist with a sheaf of papers in her hand appeared to rein in her steps. A man with little spectacles that increased his clerk's aura passed Tom without looking at him. It was almost palpably silent in the building.

Tom didn't know what to think about it; he only understood there was something unusual afoot.

He shrugged it off, looked around once again, and went to his room. He took the mail from his desk.

But before he had opened an envelope, Lak appeared in the doorway. He looked anxious. His face was bloodless.

Disaster, Tom thought.

"Minutes passed and disappeared without a trace…minutes of the utmost importance."

"What sort of minutes?"

"The minutes of a meeting of the Boards of Governors and Directors. An extraordinary meeting," Lak emphasized.

"And there is no copy?" Tom realized immediately that his question would not throw any new light on the matter.

"Of course! That is not the point. The point is that the discussions in that meeting must remain secret and not be leaked. Mrs. Van Dam had copied the minutes yesterday afternoon, and had sent a copy to all the participants in the meeting. Then she went to the library adjoining her room for a while, and when she returned, her own copy had gone. She has gone through everything; her desk, her filing cabinet, the wastepaper basket, everything. It could not be found in Mr. D's room, either."

"Is it really so serious if anybody else reads the minutes?"

Lak looked with disdain at Tom.

A question too far, Tom understood.

"And now?" he asked, to break the silence.

"There will be ample investigation," Lak answered. "These minutes must not turn up in the wrong hands. We conferred yesterday until late in the night about the question; Mr. D, Mr. Huls and myself. If the minutes fall into the wrong hands, this would turn into a disaster."

There was silence for a while. Lak stared woodenly forward.

Tom got a little nervous, as the problem was dished up to him without anything that could be used as a handle. He understood that he had to manoeuvre carefully when looking for a solution.

"What can I do, if I don't know what the matter is?"

"These minutes are strictly confidential," Lak answered.

"How will the investigation be carried out?"

"Everyone who has been in Mrs. Van Dam's room or in Mr. D's will be interviewed."

"Are there people other than managers who go into that room?"

"Mr. Huls and I have already been interviewed."

Which other people went into the Holy of Holies?" Tom wondered. *Typists don't. Mrs. Van Dam types everything for her boss. Ah! Sandy, of course! She brings coffee there. But who else? I don't know. That means Sandy will be interrogated. I could just drop in on her this afternoon.*

"I think it disagreeable, Mr. Lak, but I can't do anything. What could I do, I know so little?"

"I advise you not to talk about it pending the investigation. Perhaps I shouldn't have told you." Lak looked indecisively around for a while, then went back to his room.

"I paid a visit to the big boss this morning," Sandy began, when Tom sat facing her.

"So?"

"He invited me personally."

"That honour isn't reserved for everyone."

"I feel exceedingly honoured." With a sad smile, Sandy raised her cup to her mouth. "They were particularly kind. His secretary, Mrs. Van Dam, was with him. I go there every day a couple of times, and he has no time for even a quick look at me. But this morning I was received as an important guest. If they invite 'the coffee woman' for an interview, it must be quite important indeed."

"The minutes..."

"You know about it?"

"Yes. But I can not talk about it. Besides, I only know that the minutes are lost. Mrs. Van Dam had left a copy on her desk. somebody took them while she was away in the library."

"That's exactly what I understood from their friendly interrogation."

"What did they ask you?"

"They started with a general talk." Sandy plunged into relating her conversation with Mr. D.

"Mrs. Kamat, we would like to have a talk with you. How do you like the work you do for Medimarket?"

"Well, it's excellent!" I answered. "I've already been here for twelve years."

"You will understand, Mrs. Kamat, we sometimes fail to take sufficient interest in our employees because of the enormous pressure; at least we don't show it enough."

"You have too much to think of to take personal care of your employees; I understand that very well. So if I know you appreciate my coffee, I'm content. And I've never had any complaints about my coffee, so..."

"Your coffee is excellent, Mrs. Kamat, there may be no misunderstanding about that!"

"Thank goodness!" I said. "I was afraid you would have my head on a platter about it."

"Absolutely not! I've nothing but praise for your coffee. No, Mrs. Kamat, it is quite another thing."

"Then," Sandy said, "he exchanged a look of mutual understanding with his secretary, and went on:"

"We invited you in to ask you some simple questions."

He said this as though he would set me at ease beforehand, so that the questions should not pass beyond my comprehension. I nodded to make it clear that I was ready to be interviewed.

"Mrs. Kamat," he wheedled, "you were in Mrs. Van Dam's room yesterday afternoon?"

"Of course!" I said. "I go there at least four times a day, to bring coffee and tea and to collect the cups."

"Did you see anything unusual yesterday afternoon?"

"Unusual? No..., I don't know what you could mean."

"Did you see anybody else? In Mrs. Van Dam's room, or in mine, or somewhere hereabouts?"

"No. Why do you ask?"

"Mrs. Kamat, some documents have been stolen."

I had no idea what he was talking about.

"The minutes of a meeting. The papers were on Mrs. Van Dam's desk. Yesterday afternoon, at ten minutes to four, the minutes were discovered to be missing."

"Are you sure they just haven't been misplaced by accident?"

"No. We have searched high and low. They must have been taken by somebody."

"And you did not leave them at home?" I asked Mrs. Van Dam.

"Mrs. Kamat, believe me, we've thought of everything. The minutes have not been taken by either myself or Mrs. Van Dam. That is a fact."

"And now you are asking me if I saw someone who may have taken the minutes away? I saw no one."

"Are you quite sure?"

"My mind is still okay. And so is my memory."

"And then," Sandy said, "Mr. D cleared his throat before uttering the crucial question:"

"I feel obliged to ask you a disagreeable question, Mrs. Kamat."

He looked for a moment at his faithful companion, then they looked both at me. At that moment I realized that I was the suspect.

"Mrs. Kamat, did you, yesterday afternoon between a quarter to four and ten minutes after four, take a document from Mrs. Van Dam's desk?"

That direct question hit me like a stone against my chest. I needed some seconds to recover. Only then was I able to react.

"Mr. D, you are accusing me."

"No, Mrs. Kamat, I am only asking you."

"It sounds like an accusation."

"I had to ask you this question."

"But not in this way."

"I was very kind."

"There are various sorts of kindness."

"You have not yet answered my question."

"As long as you see me as a suspect, I shall not. You have hurt me deeply."

"As long as those minutes are lost, everyone is a suspect."

"Then you should interrogate everyone. I am not willing to answer this question. And if you do not like it, then you should dismiss me."

"After saying this, I ran away angrily," Sandy finished.

"I hope he will not dismiss you," Tom said after her lively account.

"I am not afraid of that."

"You can't say anything you want."

"Indeed. He who will survive here must hold his tongue."

"You've survived here for twelve years."

"Mr. D is convinced that I know too much."

"Is that your weapon against him?"

"That is his weapon against himself." Sandy bestowed a disarming smile upon Tom. "Tom, if they believe I took the minutes, they also believe I know the contents of them, so they will think I know something that could give them a lot of trouble."

The next morning, Sandy waited for Tom at the entrance of the Medimarket building. She looked quite sad.

"Sandy, what's the matter?"

"They searched my bag."

Tom's mouth fell open.

CHAPTER 05

"Mr. Maya is here. He wants to have a word."
Sudhir Varma was panic-stricken when his assistant, Sarásvati Arora, brought him the news. He had never met Amal Maya. But Maya was known as a very rich man. And Sudhir knew Maya was the man who decided who might pull the strings. Amal Maya had influential connections, and had strived to make sure that he had more influence than anybody else in the region.

"Mr. Maya wants a word? You mean Amal Maya?"

"Yes. Amal Maya."

"Show him in immediately!"

Sudhir tidied up the papers on his desk. He straightened his *kurta*. He smoothed his hair and went to the door. He looked for a moment, mesmerized, at the door before opening it. There he was: Amal Maya, in person.

Sudhir greeted him, deeply bowing his head. "*Namaskar*, Mr. Maya. Your visit is a great honour to me."

Maya smiled. "I thought it time for a little chat, Dr. Varma."

"Of course, Mr. Maya! May I offer you a cup of tea?"

"That's a good idea."

Maya sat down in one of the three armchairs which were situated around a little table in the corner of the room.

By now, Sudhir had rung the telephone on his desk to ask his assistant for two cups of tea.

He hesitated before sitting down. "Do you allow me...?"

Amal Maya nodded, with the air of a man who knows the world is at his feet. He took out a cigarette. "Do you smoke?" He held out a golden case to Sudhir.

"No, thank you, Mr. Maya."

Maya took a look around. "You've got a nice office. How is your practice?"

"Excellent, Mr. Maya."

"Your wife is not here?"

"No, my wife is at home."

"If I'm well informed, you can't do your work well without her."

"That is right, Mr. Maya." Sudhir would not contradict his famous guest.

There was an ironical gesture round Maya's mouth.

Sudhir tried to break the silence. "My wife solves many problems, if that is what you mean."

"Yes, something like that. I will not be unkind, Dr. Varma," the mighty man smiled, "but I've been told your medical and surgical skills are better than your management qualities."

Sudhir became a little uncertain. *What does he know about me? And what does he want?* He moved uneasily in his chair. "I don't know what you mean, Mr. Maya."

Amal Maya waved away what he had said with a smile.

Sarásvati Arora came in with the tea. She was dressed in a dark red, silk sari and had silver toe-slippers on her feet. She waited for a moment at the door.

Maya motioned to her to come closer with a jovial gesture.

Sarásvati composed her face instinctively. With the tray in her hands, she walked elegantly to the table between the two men. Something in her braced itself. She sensed a sort of danger.

Amal Maya looked inquisitively at the young woman, who remained polite. Putting the cups on the table, she ignored the assessing look of the visitor. Then she greeted him, by slightly bending her head.

"I am looking for a secretary," Maya remarked airily when Sarásvati had closed the door after her.

Sudhir felt uneasy. "I wonder if she will change; she really enjoys her work here."

Maya took a sip of the tea. "I am not here for your assistant. But I must compliment you on her; a charming young woman." Maya smiled kindly.

Sudhir looked at his visitor. Only now did he take the time to examine him properly; the small, gleaming eyes set in a smooth face contrasted with a raven-black moustache, and a head with hair of the same blackness, receding a little.

"Two months ago you transplanted a kidney in one of my friends."

The casual remark came at Sudhir like a sledgehammer blow. All of a sudden, there was a tense, sticky silence in the room.

After a while Sudhir broke the silence. "I don't know what you mean, Mr. Maya. Besides, I am bound by my official oath of secrecy, and may not talk about this."

"I know. You don't need to say anything. I'll tell you what I know. My friend's father had found a poor devil in one of the slums in the south of the town who was willing to sell one of his kidneys."

"I know nothing of this," Sudhir whispered timidly.

"You picked that kidney out, didn't you?"

Sudhir's face was deathly pale. He wasn't thinking of his patient confidentiality anymore, but he couldn't say a word. It was some seconds before he could control himself sufficiently to reply, "That man was brain-dead."

"That brain-dead man is cheerily back on the scene; he bought a rickshaw with the money he got for his kidney." Maya smiled kindly at Sudhir.

"The man had a donor codicil," Sudhir defended himself.

"Donor codicils can be signed by anyone."

"And someone assured me that the man was my patient's cousin."

"You didn't check that, I suppose," Maya answered quite calmly.

"No, I didn't."

"And you had no permission from the donor's relatives either?"

"I didn't even know who the man was. And I don't know that now."

Sudhir knew he had broken the Organs Donation Act of 1994. And he realized, as well, that the act had set the penalty for organ donations on a commercial basis as imprisonment.

"Your wife is not aware of this?" Amal Maya supposed, sympathizing.

"My wife knows nothing about it. Nor does my assistant," Sudhir answered with a tightened throat.

"I understand," the other man nodded. "However, Mrs. Arora assisted with the operations, didn't she?"

Sudhir wondered how Maya knew Sarásvati's surname.

"But she knows nothing."

"She is also bound to secrecy, I suppose," Maya answered. "So she is not supposed to sound the alarm."

"Who else would do so?"

Maya ignored Sudhir's question. "I can release you from your troubles."

"How do you mean?"

"If you'll do a little job for me, I'll make this donation legal after all."

"How could you do that?"

"A friend of mine is a member of the Authorization Committee of the state Uttar Pradesh. As you know, this committee can decide, on the basis of the 1994 act, that non-relatives of the patient may dispose of organs as well, provided that they have a particular reason."

"What sort of job do you want me to do?"

"A transplant."

"A transplant?"

"Somebody asked me if I could fix him up with a kidney."

"And you can?"

"I can procure him a kidney; the kidney of someone who is in my debt. I need someone who would be willing to transplant the organ."

"I must examine first, if…"

"Of course you will have to examine whether it is possible or not. Apart from that, the transplant is on the same order as the one you did for my friend."

"But you know, a doctor must see if everything is okay."

"Of course! Exactly as you did before with the operation of my friend." Maya smiled amiably at Sudhir.

"May I think about it for a couple of days?"

"Shall we say one day? I want to know before tomorrow at four o'clock."

I am at the mercy of Maya," Sudhir knew. *If I refuse, he will make me to go to jail and my name as a doctor will be worth nothing anymore.* Though Sudhir had been acquainted with the man for less than half an hour, he understood that Maya did not have a spark of compassion in him.

"Your wife and Mrs. Arora need to know nothing."

"I cannot operate without her."

"You must have removed someone's kidney before. She will not get suspicious if that happens again."

"But implanting the same kidney into somebody else?"

"Must she know it's the same kidney?"

"No, I suppose not."

"Well! Call me tomorrow before four o'clock. Then you can tell me if we have a deal." Maya handed Sudhir his visiting card.

"I shall call you, Mr. Maya." Sudhir tried to hide his uncertainty.

Maya scented it. "You've a good reputation, Dr. Varma!"

Sudhir wondered if there was any threat in Maya's friendly voice.

Maya rose to his feet. He greeted Sudhir and went to the door.

Sudhir was too confused to reflect on what had happened. *Mr. Maya knows everything, and he has prepared his case very well. I had better do what Mr. Maya wants.* He began to look for a safe way out.

Sarásvati showed Mr. Maya politely to the door. She had made up her mind to parry even the least kindness with a neutral reaction.

"I had an interview with Dr. Varma about a kidney transplant," Maya said on the way to the exit.

"I am sure he will tell me if he thinks it necessary, Mr. Maya."

"The interview I had with Dr. Varma could have consequences for you."

"I don't understand what you mean, Mr. Maya."

"I don't know how much Dr. Varma informs you about the identity of his patients. You write this up in the administration, I suppose?"

"You don't need to worry about the administration, Mr. Maya."

"I understand. But maybe you are unaware that the interview I had with Dr. Varma concerns a tricky case."

"Dr. Varma will tell me what I need to know, Mr. Maya."

Maya hesitated, not knowing for a moment how to go on. Then he decided to change tactics.

"If you ever get into trouble, you can always get in touch with me."

"I don't expect any trouble, Mr. Maya."

"It might happen that you would have to look for another job."

"I have no reason to leave Dr. Varma!"

"And if you should have a reason?"

"Then I would see."

Amal Maya hesitated again. Then he whispered, "I advise you to think about my offer."

"Which offer, Mr. Maya?"

"I am looking for a secretary."

Sarásvati did not react.

Amal Maya greeted her courteously, if somewhat detachedly, by touching his fingertips against each other under his chin.

Sarásvati shut the door, closed her eyes, and leant against it. She shuddered. At the same time, she was glad she had been able to keep control. *That man will go on dogging me,* she realized.

She went to Sudhir's room, to learn how the interview with Amal Maya had gone.

Sudhir sat behind his desk, staring ahead.

Sarásvati waited for him to speak.

When it dawned on him that Sarásvati was there, Sudhir began to talk to himself. "I've not yet made a decision; I will quietly consider and discuss everything."

As Amal Maya walked to his car, he had an idea: he could have a word with Mrs. Varma. He could learn from her whether she knew about the illegal transplant carried out by her husband, or not. Or if she had any suspicions. In that case, he could use her help to force Dr. Varma's cooperation. He gave the driver an order to take him to the Varma's house.

Shakti opened the door. She took the man before her to be about fifty years old. She saw that the front part of his skull was as smooth and shiny as his round, white face. A full and perfectly groomed black moustache appeared to be meant as a compensation for the bald part of the skull. The round belly under his *kurta* seemed to her to be a mark of complacency. The man was dressed expensively. Shakti recognized the quality of the silk of his trousers and the overhanging *kurta*. His friendliness alerted her to be cautious. Outside the fence, she saw a gleaming American car and a chauffeur keeping guard over it.

A *mighty man*, Shakti guessed. She acted somewhat reticently.

"I am sorry, but I don't think I know you."

"My name is Maya, madam, Amal Maya." He bent courteously, without removing the affable friendliness from his face.

The name was vaguely known to Shakti.

"Well, Mr. Maya, come in." She motioned the way to the living room on the ground floor. She showed him to a seat. "Would you like a cup of tea?"

"Yes, please, madam!" Maya answered courteously.

"I'll give orders to my servant." By intuition, Shakti behaved more importantly than she was used to doing.

She disappeared into the kitchen and asked Ragu to invite Maya's chauffeur in, and to bring tea to the living room. Still, before she sat down in front of Amal Maya, a shadowy image from a vague past loomed up in her memory. Some years ago his name had been connected with the kidnapping of an eight-year-old girl out of a slum in Kanpur. Shakti remembered the picture of the girl in the *Indian Times*. The affair had caused a big row, as the kidnapper had mentioned Maya's name. The next day, the indignation had bulged out of the papers. A politician spoke about a ghastly punch below the belt to one of the most respectable businessmen in India. The kidnapper had been arrested. The next day, the papers had reported that the man had hung himself in his cell.

"My husband once spoke about you," Shakti began politely. "I hope you will not blame me if I say I cannot now recall what it was in connection with."

"On the contrary, madam! I highly appreciate that you still remember me. However, there are probably not many people who do not know me."

"Would you please aid my memory and tell me why you are so well-known?"

"Of course, Mrs. Varma! You know, I have much influence on the course of business inside and outside the town. And there are many people who owe me something."

A feeling of discomfort seized Shakti. A thought: *What does this man want from me?* flashed through her mind. She could not immediately get control of herself. The smooth, friendly face of the man made her feel nauseated. *He sees in my face that his words have hit me. How can I relax?*

Ragu came in with the tea. That relieved her; now she could focus her attention on him. "Thank you, Ragu. Did you ask Mr. Maya's chauffeur to come in?"

"Yes, ma'am," Ragu answered.

"Will you and the chauffeur drink tea in the kitchen?"

Ragu knew Mrs. Varma well enough to understand what she meant. He signalled reassuringly with his eyes, and when he went back into the kitchen, he left the door ajar.

"You are very kind to have my chauffeur called inside, madam, but you need not have done so. He can wait near the car; that is part of his work."

By this time, Shakti had recovered. She reopened the conversation.

"People who owe you something. Do you mean people who are in your debt?"

"Those are not the words I would use, madam."

"I hope you will not think me impolite if I ask you what purpose brings you here." Shakti realized her words didn't sound hospitable. It was not customary for her, far from it, to ask a guest the purpose of his visit to her house. And she knew the chilliness in her voice sharpened further her lack of hospitality.

Amal Maya understood as well. His face showed a painful grimace, but he recovered his balance quickly. He was aware of his power; it gave him confidence. He also enjoyed the fact that he had found in this woman an opponent of stature. In the games he played nearly every day, this was a rarity. The fact that he usually had his pawns where he wanted them in the shortest possible time sometimes decreased the pleasure of the game. That sometimes made his work boring. He preferred to be among the circles of practised politicians or mighty businessmen who could offer him some resistance. They made his work thrilling.

And now he sat before a woman whose husband he had just check mated with some simple moves. This enthralling woman, whom he had thought to entrance with only his charm, was found to offer resistance. Maya had even forgotten Sudhir Varma's assistant. Now all his attention was focused on Varma's wife.

Shakti was not aware that she had become a provocative target for her opponent. Nor did she realize that Maya, who usually needed no more than a nod to get what he wanted, only appreciated the game if he experienced some opposition.

"You inquire after the purpose of my visit, my dear Mrs. Varma. I'll tell you with pleasure. An hour ago I paid a visit to your husband."

Shakti's heart thumped. She wondered if Maya could hear this.

But, using an ordinary tone of voice, he went on to say, "We had a cosy chat. I think, madam, your husband and I may be working together on a little matter in the near future. Your husband will tell you something like that, I suppose." Maya took a sip of tea and then took on a chatty posture, with his right knee over his left and the fingers of his hands against each other under his chin—a posture that said he had all the time in the world.

Shakti would have liked to scratch his calculating smile from his face, but decided to use his own weapon: his wheedling friendliness. *His Achilles' heel is in his head,* she realized, *he overrates himself immoderately.*

"Your husband and I had a talk about his work, and especially about his kidney transplants. I must say, Mrs. Varma, your husband is quite a reasonable man. And he realizes that I covered his back."

"You covered his back?" Shakti felt overwhelmed. She already suspected that something about her husband's work was wrong. Some months ago, she had also wondered where a certain kidney had come from. This vague suspicion now took on, following Maya's words, a more distinct form. But what worried her most was that Maya should perceive something was confusing her.

"I have important sources of information, Mrs. Varma."

"Information about what?"

"You understand what it is about. But I already told you that I covered for your husband."

"Then I suppose you will go on covering for him," Shakti replied composedly. She was aware that she must tread carefully.

"Of course, madam! That is why I am here."

"Can you explain to me why, exactly, you are here?"

"I asked your husband to render me a service. You could make it clear that he can render himself a service, if he does what I ask of him."

Amal Maya's friendliness had gradually become colder and harder. He looked now expectantly at Mrs. Varma.

A chilling threat, hidden in a kind politeness, kept Shakti from showing him the door.

"What do you mean?"

"I don't want to use more words than necessary."

Shakti realized she wouldn't get an answer to her rather vague, non-committal question. She moved back. "How can I make it clear to my husband that he will render himself a service, if he does what you ask of him, when I don't even know what you ask of him?"

Maya would not go further into the matter. He tried to lay a red herring. "I had hoped you would trust me, madam."

"If you want my trust, you have to do something to earn it."

Amal Maya could not remember if he had ever been driven into a corner where he didn't see a way out. He looked at Shakti without any sign of understanding; but he realized that Mrs. Varma was not willing to take what he had proposed. Amal Maya, a master in playing cat and mouse, was aware that he had underestimated his opponent.

Shakti waited quietly for a reaction. Her eyes held his.

That troubled Maya. Eye contact was unusual to him; it was something he had never learnt to deal with. But now, in front of this charming woman, who in no way showed that she was impressed, he didn't know where to look. He changed knee over knee, smoothed his moustache and searched for words. "Madam, your husband will undoubtedly tell you what you don't know."

"My husband is bound by his official oath of secrecy."

"I am sorry, madam, I can't tell you anymore either. But I hope you will follow my advice."

Maya rose. He gave Shakti his visiting card. "If you have problems, you can always reach me by dialing this number. I'll be pleased to have another talk with you." He tried to conceal his confusion from her. He greeted her by bending his head and went to the door.

His chauffeur ran round the house to open the car door.

"What does Maya want from you?" Shakti stood before her husband and looked at him.

Sudhir had just put a bite of food into his mouth. When he had emptied his mouth, he asked, "How do you know?"

"He was here."

"Amal Maya?"

"Yes."

"And?"

"I don't trust him."

"I am afraid I'm not yet rid of him."

"So am I," Shakti answered, "but I wonder if you should enter into his proposal."

"I got the impression that he can protect me."

"Amal Maya will protect you as long as it is in his own interests."

Sudhir did not know what to say. He was aware of the fact that he needed Shakti's help. Sarásvati had told him she honoured his wife's name, the name of the goddess Shakti, who is the source of female energy and sense and vital strength. But Sudhir's problems clouded his own thinking, sense and vital strength.

CHAPTER 06

P arvati relaxed on a cane settee on the veranda. She had decided to lose herself in her reveries. Amal, her husband, had gone. Otherwise, he wouldn't have allowed her a nap in the afternoon.

As she lay there, the memory of her mother-in-law's passing came into her memory. This event had marked a break in her life; she had received then, as the eldest son's wife, the charge of the family household.

But first she had had to point out to Amal, who had been sleepwalking in his grief, that he should do his duties. He should make an arrangement with the leader of the cremators. She, Parvati, had, with Amal's youngest sister, Bindu, washed the dead body of her mother-in-law and swathed it in red bandages. That same day Amal and his brother, Kumar, and Kumar's sons had performed the dire duty on the river Ganges. The body had been strapped on the roof of a van, and the men had ridden to the Marnikarnikaghat, where the cremation would be done. Amal had shaved his head before he, as the eldest son, set fire to the pyre.

Parvati had known that this event would affect her husband terribly; half a year earlier, he had also set fire to the wood under his father's body. Amal had then woodenly sat staring, without being aware that he would have to take over the helm.

After her mother-in-law's death, Parvati had taken over the housekeeping and the administration of the family's finances. It had taken her a couple of hours to get a good understanding of the bookkeeping. Bindu had helped her. Although the young woman was only sixteen at the time, it had turned out that she perfectly controlled the organization and administration of the family. In the few days of Amal's absence during his mother's passing away, and in the time of the cremation on the river, Bindu had made the decisions that had to be made. Parvati had discovered that she had to deal with the personality of a young woman who knew who she was and what she had to do. After being married to Amal, a spontaneous friendship had developed between her and Bindu. Bindu made her marriage more or less endurable.

Parvati's eyes didn't close as she relaxed on the settee. For a short moment, there was pain on her face when she thought of the fact that she and Amal had no children. She would eagerly have given him a son, to set a fire under his mortal remains after his death. She did not think this important, but Amal was convinced that his reincarnation would only go well if his own son set fire to his dead body. In the beginning of their marriage she had wondered why her husband had not made love to her. After a week he had expelled her to another bedroom, and she had obeyed him with relief. Soon after that she suspected that Amal had tried to get a son with another woman.

She had never loved Amal, but in the first weeks of their marriage she had still presumed that the marriage, arranged by their fathers, would, in the long run, lead to love. Now, after twenty years, she saw that their marriage had degenerated into a complex of daily patterns and rituals, formed by matters of course. Their personal contact had entirely crumbled. They were strangers to each other. She knew that he lived a double life. And she knew as well that he had become rich at the cost of other people. But she suppressed that knowledge, because it hurt her too much.

She recalled the grandly organized wedding. Amal had been brought to his bride on an elephant. There had been three hundred guests. They had eaten from banana leaves.

She and Amal had seen each other twice before. Although she didn't want to be exposed to a strange family, and her father was against it, Amal's father had arranged a viewing so that the members of the Maya family could see, before the wedding, the woman who was coming to join their family.

Before the wedding ceremony, her female friends had smeared her with henna and ochre. They had been at work on her for three hours, and had not kept their mouths shut. She, Parvati, had felt unhappy. Then she and Amal had sat there on thrones, side by side, like nineteenth century maharajahs. They had not looked at each other during the ceremony. She had not shown any emotion at seeing the man she would share the rest of her life with.

She knew she had to be grateful to her father, as he had found a good match for her and had paid a high price for her marriage. She still felt a little guilty at her lack of gratitude to her father.

But, thinking of her husband, she felt nothing.

The wedding feast had lasted three weeks. In those weeks she had learned much from Amal's grandmother, Durga Devi, about the work she was supposed to do and about her duties as a wife. From Durga Devi she had also taught Amal a little.

Durga Devi had told her the boy had been brought up as a child prodigy. "In this country," the old woman had said, "boys are pretty often prodigies. My daughter-in-law stayed home, to take care of her son. His father sacrificed one hour of his time every day to teach his son what he had to do, and still more what he was not permitted to do. No school was good enough. And the boy did what his parents expected of him. But he did not see, as little as his parents did, that he had to fill a hole in their lives; a hole they tried to fill up with money, a splendid house, ornaments, and...a child. But the hole grew greater and deeper. The boy was protected like a precious diamond. And they waited on him hand and foot. But he lacked somebody who was there just for him; he had only educators. When he was twelve or thirteen years old, the model child wanted to break out of his dependence. He no longer needed anyone else. He looked for warmth in a debauchery of drinking and dreaming. As his rights over his own emotional life never had been respected, he screened it. He never learned to trust anyone else, or even to trust in himself."

"But you gave him warmth, didn't you?" Parvati had asked.

"In the first years, the boy hardly came round to see me; and later he felt ashamed to be cuddled by his grandmother. A boy doesn't need an old woman for this," she smiled sadly.

The contact with Durga Devi had reconciled Parvati more or less to her new life. But the old wise woman's death three years after Parvati's marriage had distressed her very much.

After her marriage, Parvati prepared the tea and the snacks for her and her husband. For the rest, they ate in the family kitchen. She looked after his clothes. She cleaned their rooms. And when there was a party for Amal's connections she took perfect care of it. Parvati was a model wife. When Amal ate, she served him, and after the meal, she cleaned up as he watched TV. During that time, there was always a sweet love movie from Mumbay or a macho movie from Hong Kong.

But she and Amal had never talked about personal matters.

She knew that Amal didn't like his work, nor could he manage it. Once, when they still lived in his parent's house, he had said something about it. In one of his restless hours when he couldn't sleep, she had heard him crying, "That work doesn't suit me!" At that moment, she had hoped that he would at last tell her what he had on his mind. She had gone to his room and had proposed that they look for a solution together. But he had shouted that he could solve his own problems.

The next day he had told her that he had conferred with his brother about building a new house on the river Ganges. Sunar Chand, a police chief inspector, had promised to arrange a concession for him. Chand had asked him for a service in return. "That's just the way it works with friends," he had said.

And Parvati, who was a stranger in the web of services of important men, had not seen a problem then.

CHAPTER 07

The night after he had talked to Ruud Lak about his trip to India, Tom had lain awake for hours; hours filled with memories of the nuns, Satori and Soedjata, and of the poor residents of the slums he had over the years become more or less familiar with.

Now, after a sleepless night, Tom and Vera were on the way to the party James Huls had invited them to. After half an hour of walking over a patchwork quilt of fields, pastures and heartlands, they passed through a black cast-iron gate into a huge, high-fenced garden which had the air of a park. Amazed, they walked over a broad asphalt path to the Huls family's new house.

The house had been built on the outskirts of a forest. The garden was still expecting the planned overgrowth. The landscape architect had accentuated the differences in levels in the slanting plane with rockwork, erratic boulders and sleepers. Halfway along the garden were flowerbeds, not yet overgrown, around a pond with two spouting fountains. In a separate corner was a greenhouse. On either side of a swimming pool, a open and covered terrace had been erected. A sunroom was under construction at the back of the house.

Before Tom and Vera arrived at the house, a great, black, gleaming car passed them, followed by a smaller, light green car.

A man in his late forties stepped out of the black car. He wore a dark blue suit, smoothly pressed and sharply creased. A sea-lion's moustache, two empty eyes, and hanging shoulders gave him the submissive air of a person who is in the long-lasting, tiring process of getting old. The man went round the car to the passenger door and opened it for a richly embellished woman. The woman was just a little too made up. She showed a strikingly sound set of teeth between red lips. Her face had been tanned on the sun-bed. Fair hair waves betrayed a recent stay under the dryer. She wore, under an open scarlet coat, a white jersey with a deep décolleté, and below that a tight skirt with a hip-high slit. Vera, used to comparing her age with that of other women, took her to be about fifty.

The man with the sea lion's moustache introduced himself and his wife as Charles and Mirabelle Bot. "Mirabelle is the sister of the hostess," Charles added to the introduction.

Mirabelle, acting a little, extended her hand conventionally and greeted Vera and Tom with a prefab smile.

The couple who were in the smaller car came out of the shadow of a tree.

"I told you about Bill Mocker," Tom said. "But this is first time I have met Bhikni, his Indian wife."

Charles Bot shook hands with Bill Mocker and embraced Mocker's wife.

Mirabelle bent the upper part of her body forward as she greeted Bhikni and placed her head circumspectly on either side of the other woman's cheeks. Then she admired Bhikni's dark green sari with a little exalted sigh and with something stately in her voice. Bhikni appeared to be shy about the compliment.

Bill, sturdily built and inconspicuously well-dressed, kept to the background and looked shyly at the scene.

When he noticed Tom and Vera, he shook hands and introduced Bhikni to them.

Bhikni's sleek, agate black hair undulated playfully over her bare shoulders. Although she was a little tense, she gave the impression of being spontaneous. She smiled modestly. She had dark skin and somewhat sunken, darkly shaded eyes. A red dot, a *tica*, was stuck on her forehead. She had simple, black-silver ornaments on her fingers and around her neck that looked like they had been made for her.

Charles Bot mounted the steps and rang the bell. A jovial James Huls opened the door. James proved himself to be experienced in the shaking of men's hands and the embracing of women.

Tom and Vera looked on at the greeting ritual. After that, in the spacious reception hall, Huls shook their hands and paid Tom, as an experienced host, a compliment on his charming wife.

Tom hung his and Vera's jackets on one of the bronze horse-heads in the hall. Then they looked, a bit flabbergasted, at three beautifully framed, abstract paintings which had been painted in the seventies of the last century. They didn't, however, get the time for a serious look, as they were invited to come in.

In one of the two rooms, more or less separated from each other by a fireplace and a bookcase, they saw three sitting areas, a sideboard, a huge chest, and a lot of antiques.

While they were admiring an old chandelier with countless crystal globules, James' wife came to greet them. "Annelize," she introduced herself. "I hope you will enjoy the evening." The greeting had a formal character and was uncertain on both sides. Annelize led her guests to a table, where they were served coffee and cake, then said she must excuse herself, in order to welcome other guests.

Stirring their coffee, Vera and Tom looked around to see if there were people they knew present. A young woman saw them looking and went over to them. She introduced herself as Fleur Huls and asked them who they were.

Smiling at her spontaneous behavior, Tom told her that he was a new colleague of her father's. He explained how he had met him, and how her father had invited him to this occasion.

"My father did not mention you, but he talks mostly about himself."

Vera switched to another subject. "You are still at school, Fleur?"

"Yes. The final examination is next year. Then I am going to study at university and live on my own!" she declared firmly.

Ignoring Fleur's ambition for independence, Vera changed the subject to another matter. "Fleur, we understood that this party is also meant to launch a development project. Can you tell us something about it?"

"Of course! Some months ago, Mr. D launched the idea that Medimarket should go in for development aid. Mr. and Mrs. Bot and my parents were immediately enthusiastic. They have already decided to collect money and to send that money to a poor country."

"To a poor country?" Vera asked.

"Yes. In my opinion, they haven't even noticed that there are also people with huge pockets in poor countries."

"But there should be a purpose for that money, shouldn't there?" Vera supposed.

"They realize that now. They conferred about the problem, under the leadership of Aunt Mirabelle. Mr. D invited her to take up the presidency of the foundation because none of the managers of The Concern had time for it. They have decided to spend the money on education and to cooperate with the Maya foundation."

"The Maya foundation?" asked Bill Mocker, who had caught the last words and joined them, with his wife.

"The Maya foundation is a foundation in the north of India that is funding education for poor children," Fleur answered. "Medimarket will start a foundation here under the same name."

"Mirabelle has just asked me to join the foundation as an adviser," Bhikni told her, with an almost apologetic smile. The Indian woman held a glass of red wine in her right hand. She didn't seem to feel at ease in the rich environment. Her dark, dreamy eyes reflected timidity, now that she knew the attention of the other people was focused on her.

"And what do you think?" Fleur asked her.

"I advised Mirabelle to be cautious with money," Bhikni answered. "There is a great need for money in my country, to give poor people a chance to improve something in their situation, but a lot of money there also sticks to bureaucratic and corrupt fingers. There is a need for knowledge and experience to get money for development aid to the right place. And everlasting attention!" Bhikni did not really seem free when choosing her words. The tone of her voice pointed out that she looked for harmony between herself and the situation she had found herself in. The staccato of her diction and the perfect pronunciation of her words betrayed the fact that she did not speak her native language; she lacked the naturally casual accent of people who have grown up in the country. But she spoke her new language surprisingly well; better than her husband, who produced a mixed lingo that sounded Texan.

An elder lady joined the group and laid an arm round Fleur's shoulders.

"You don't still know my grandmother, do you?" Fleur asked, changing the subject. "Grandma, may I introduce you to Mr. and Mrs. Corda? And to Mr. and Mrs. Mocker?"

The elderly woman shook their hands. "I am Mrs. Sturing, Annelize, Mirabelle and Frank's mother."

Mrs. Sturing wore a snowy white silk blouse with a stiff collar and sharply starched light grey trousers. Around her neck hung a gold chain, and on her fingers she wore three gold rings. It was all too new for her old, wrinkled skin. Her hair, ever natural and living, had been modelled by a hairdresser into a silky wig with a glazed wave of lacquer, grey with gleaming light blue shades. Her appearance was that of a distinguished, expensive world. But the expression on the older woman's face did not match with that world; she was playing a part that did not suit her.

Vera felt sorry for the woman. She told her what they had been talking about.

"Yes. Mirabelle told me about a foundation and that she had been made president of it. I advised her to get a look at the country. But she did not think it necessary at all. Besides, why should she follow the advice of an old woman?" she added, with a sad smile.

Annelize, who had been eavesdropping, caught her mother's words. She joined them. "The world is not the same anymore as it was in your day, Mum. We live in a world of efficiency. If Mirabelle went to that country first, it would not only cost a lot of money but a lot of time as well. We cannot let the poor children wait still longer, can we?"

"You are right, dear child. After all the centuries of poverty and wretchedness it really is time to do something now."

Fleur put an arm on her grandmother's. "Do you feel well, Grandma?"

The woman reacted with a gentle, wistful gleam in her eyes. An unwrinkled confidence shone from her old face. She was clearly fond of her granddaughter.

"Wouldn't you put on anything comfortable, Grandma? And you could take that gold off too; it doesn't become you at all!"

Mrs. Sturing's face cleared. "I've got no other clothes here, dear child, but you may free me from the gold."

Fleur didn't need to think about it. She took her grandmother's arm to lead her to her own room.

Annelize looked worried. A vague laugh revealed faintly quivering wrinkles at the corners of her mouth. Her head didn't really sit on her shoulders; it sank a little into them, as though she was cold. Lips pressed together in long lines and coquettishly beseeching eyes marked her kind face. She thought it advisable to explain her mother's and her daughter's behaviour. "Mother is pretty easily influenced by Fleur. I can, of course, understand the frivolity of a young girl; but an elderly lady should understand that she can't do anything she wants. That's why I keep an eye on it when Fleur and my mother are together. This morning, I took my mother to my hairdresser. An ideal opportunity to make it clear to her that she may love her granddaughter, but she must remember that a seventeen-year-old girl does not always know what is becoming."

"Worrying about your mother and about your daughter, cannot be easy for you," Vera answered.

Glad to meet someone who understood her, Annelize looked at her gratefully. "It causes me a lot of trouble, Mrs. Corda, our daughter enjoys a model education. But when a girl comes to a certain age, her parents can't control everything."

"That is quite true," Vera assented. She fancied that Fleur, in her childlike enthusiasm, must have bumped against a wall of rational arguments. And how, after discovering the first fine cracks in the parental perfection, she had developed the necessary verbal arsenal in her struggle for independence, to be able to resist her parents in their attempted molding of her.

Fleur and her grandmother returned. The elder woman enjoyed being free of her gold.

Annelize thought the story about her mother needed some addition. "Mother lives in an elderly people's apartment half an hour's drive from here. I go and fetch her twice a week. She stays for an afternoon and an evening with us. Mother also goes for two half-days to Mirabelle. So she doesn't need to be alone too much. We bought that easy chair at the fireplace for her. Sitting there, she is the center of the family. But she preferred to walk around this evening. She doesn't sufficiently realize how such a party can fatigue her. Well, it is up to her to decide, isn't it?"

The elderly woman had not made the impression that she was overly fond of the central place in the precious house where feelings were muffled with arguments.

"We know what is good for mother!" Annelize assured proudly. She spoke kindly, at the same time about and to her mother. "Mum likes to be coddled by her daughters, isn't it true, Mum? We take care of her clothes; we bring her to the hairdressers; and when she is here or with Mirabelle, she is enormously spoiled. Isn't that true, Mother?"

"Yes, my dear." Mrs. Sturing seemed to resign herself to the carefulness of her daughters.

"You may not complain about a lack of care from your daughters," Bhikni supposed cautiously. Bhikni had also noticed that Mrs. Sturing patiently suffered the perfect, competitive care of her daughters, as she was not a match against their watertight arguments.

"I feel like a human being now," Mrs. Sturing confided to Vera, "like in former days, when my children were still children."

"Fortunately you've a granddaughter."

"Yes, she treats me like a woman. But as for my son, my daughters, and sons-in-law, I am an object of care. They see me as a figure from the past, with different interests and no understanding of modern times. I may enjoy the welfare they offer me, but they expect me to leave the real life to them."

"Grandma has fashionable daughters, pompous sons-in-law, and a son who knows everything," Fleur explained.

Vera offered Mrs. Sturing an arm. "You have a terrific granddaughter," she whispered heartily.

"I couldn't wish for a better one. But Tineke understands me as well. Tineke is my son Frank's wife. She picks me up occasionally, mostly as a surprise. Then we drink coffee. At such moments I can forget my cosseted life and enjoy the cosy gossip of my daughter-in-law. Those trips are also sort of a tacit conspiracy against the rest, which gives me pleasure."

"I believe you are enjoying yourself, Mum," Annelize said as she saw her mother chatting away.

"Yes, dear! I hope you are too."

"To me it is enough that you and the guests enjoy themselves, Mum."

After a moment of silence, Annelize asked Tom how he felt about his work for Medimarket.

"I like it very much; particularly this evening. I am happy to receive your invitation," Tom answered kindly. "A party like this gives me the opportunity to make the acquaintance of other people, much more than just by working together."

"You are absolutely right!" Annelize replied. "James thought so as well; in The Concern he only comes in contact with the members of the board of governors, his fellow directors, and his own subordinates, so he is glad to meet other employees here."

"I hope to get better acquainted with him as well," Tom answered.

Actually, he knew James Huls in no more than profile. He saw him now out of the corner of his eye: an impressive head with a conqueror's look, a padded belly that liked good eating and drinking, and a tie laying draped over it. There was a royal decoration on the lapel of his. Tom had not yet been able to get a good idea of the man as a person. Fleur had given him an impression of her father with her carefree remarks, but he knew from experience that he should not rely too quickly on other people's opinions, and especially not Huls's own daughter.

Annelize, who saw Tom stealing glances at her husband, appeared willing to add to her husband's profile. "There is no committee or advisory body James doesn't participate in," she whispered with repressed pride.

"I hope to meet your husband at one of the committees."

"He told me something about a committee Mr. D had asked him to participate on. Actually, James would have refused, as he already takes part in so many committees. He is so terribly busy!" she emphasized. "But if Mr. D needs him, and his abilities, he just cannot refuse. But I am happy that you are going to get to know him better now." Annelize looked at her husband, who was talking seriously to Charles Bot.

Tom knew Charles Bot as a man with iron standpoints. When people debated in meetings, Bot usually sat with a blank look, somewhat hunched up, recovering from a lack of sleep. But Tom knew that the man could suddenly wake up and offer his debating colleagues the final judgment. What Mr. Bot said was true.

"What do you think of the wine, Mr. Corda?" Annelize intruded on Tom's reflections.

"A delicious wine! You have good taste, Mrs. Huls!"

"My husband chose the wine. He is a connoisseur."

Fleur overheard her mother's final words. "Father never drinks wine; you know that!"

"You are right, my dear child, but that doesn't mean that he doesn't know a lot about wine."

"You think Father knows about everything."

"He understands many things. When you get older, you will see the qualities your father possesses."

Annelize asked Tom, with a knowing glance, for solidarity in her view with her still inexperienced daughter.

"The qualities of my father...You're making me laugh! Don't you see how he...?"

Tom felt a painful scene threatening the air. Without thinking, he took Annelize's arm. "Mrs. Huls, we tried to have a look at your paintings in the hall when we came in, but unfortunately we had no time for it."

"I will gladly show them to you, Mr. Corda." Annelize showed Tom into the hall. She had forgotten her daughter.

"This moon landscape drew my attention when we came in."

"It's a very precious piece, Mr. Corda."

"I see. The frame alone is worth a fortune."

"Actually it's impossible to express the value in money."

"In what way do you think the value should be expressed?"

"How do you mean?"

"What does the painting mean to you?"

"I think it's splendid. Everybody does. James said a museum would give a fortune for it. James is an expert."

Tom closed his eyes. He imagined his hostess in the painted landscape, as a conjugal shadow in the moonlight of her husband's glory. He wondered what she would have to hold on to, if she ever lost the Icarus faith she had in her husband.

Sympathizing and feeling a little sorry for her, he looked at her. "It is splendid indeed!" he assented. "But I am not an expert; I can only say whether I think it is beautiful or not..., and whether it has something to tell me."

"Does it tell you anything?"

Tom hesitated. "Yes, it does, but I am missing something; I don't know what it is."

Annelize looked anxiously. "You are missing something in the painting? Nobody has ever said that. James certainly didn't. James thinks it's a perfect painting."

"It is indeed perfect." *That's it,* Tom realized, *it is perfect. It is as perfect as The Concern is.* "Yes...it's perfect," he said, to soothe Annelize's anxiety. "I hope you enjoy it very much."

"It has already brought us much pleasure. It also fits very well in the hall. When people come in, it always draws their attention.

And everybody speaks of it with such high praise. You're the first person who has hesitated."

"I told you, I am not an expert. Besides, I would like to take some time and sit here for a while to see it better."

"James sees such things immediately."

"Is it not dangerous to have it so close to the front door?" Tom embarked on a new course.

"It is well-guarded and fully insured. It has to be; it is such a precious piece."

CHAPTER 08

Kailash Anand knocked at the door.

When he heard somebody shout "Yes!" he edged shyly in, as though he was afraid he would desecrate the floor with his bare, unwashed feet. Without looking at the man behind the great desk, he bowed deeply.

Amal Maya sat looking in a colour magazine. He did not react to the timid figure in front of him, who was dressed in a grubby white *dhoti*, a loincloth, and a dirty shirt.

Kailash remained standing at the door, bowing his head.

It was a few minutes before Amal Maya looked at him. "What do you want?"

"I heard you're looking for somebody who can clean your house, sir," Kailash answered.

"What sort of work have you done before?" Amal Maya kept looking at his magazine.

"Cleaning, sir...and preparing meals...sir, and I helped for a while in a restaurant, sir."

"Do you know how you should behave with people of a higher caste?"

"Yes, sir."

"I am a member of the Vaishya-caste. Do you know what that means?"

"No, sir."

"I suppose you do not belong to a caste."

"I am only myself, sir."

"What do you mean?"

"I don't belong to a caste, sir."

Kailash was an outcast. But he had no idea, that his far forbears had violated certain caste rules and had therefore become outcasts and untouchables. Over the years they had found work in maintaining graveyards, in cremating bodies, and in sweeping streets.

Amal Maya shrugged his shoulders and looked bored. He signified, with a scornful touch round his tight lips, that he didn't want to spend more of his time on this conversation, and he focused his attention back to his colour magazine.

Kailash didn't know what to do. If he asked, the man would probably get angry.

Fortunately, a woman entered. The woman greeted Kailash with the palms of her hands joined together under her chin and bowed her head lightly. She asked him who he was and what he had come for.

Kailash answered the greeting and made an obeisance. "I am Kailash Anand, ma'am. I've been told that you are looking for a servant to clean your house."

Parvati looked at her husband.

"It is up to you to settle this; running the house is your department."

"Please follow me," the woman said as she nodded encouragingly.

Kailash followed behind her through tiled passages with red carpets and big windows that admitted much light. He hardly dared to plant his bare feet on the floor. He really felt untouchable in this splendid house. In the hotel he had worked in, his plot had been staked out. There he had swept the corridors and put fresh sheets on the beds. Later, he had assisted the cooks. But after three months, the head chef had told him that his services were no longer needed. That was a week ago now, and he had not earned one rupee since. Now he followed the kind woman. He thought her beautiful. The mysterious haze and the dark, natural shadows of her soft, sad eyes, outlined by a snowy white, intrigued him. The vividly contrasting, darkly gleaming pupils radiated a soul-warm compassion, which moved him.

Arriving in the kitchen, the woman smiled sadly at him. She introduced herself as Parvati.

For a moment, Kailash had the feeling she had chosen him of all people for her heavenly smile. But he realised also that the world of this woman was not his. Not a word could pass his lips.

"Take a seat," he heard her whisper.

Kailash saw six chairs, half-pushed under a table. He did not feel himself becoming in this house and in this kitchen. He sat in his hut on a jute mat on the loamy floor, squatting or crossing his legs under his bottom. He did not dare to take a seat.

Parvati felt his embarrassment. She sat down and invited him to a chair in front of her. Then she started to talk to him, "Three years ago, my mother-in-law passed away. She cooked for the family. From then on I had to prepare the meals. But it has become too much work for me. Moreover, my cooking is not really good. My sister-in-law, Bindu, who helped me in the kitchen, will now keep the books for my husband. That's why we are looking for someone who can keep the house clean. But if that person can cook, I would prefer that. Do you think you can prepare a meal occasionally?"

Kailash fancied himself in a dream world. He could not understand why this captivating woman from an inaccessible world talked to him so commonly and confidentially. She addressed him as though he were equal to her, as though he was a human being as she herself was. He had never experienced this before; out of her world he knew only orders, often snarled orders; but he was mostly ignored. And now he sat in a splendid kitchen with precious furniture in front of a woman who told him with respect and warm affection about her life.

Parvati saw that Kailash was embarrassed. She encouraged him to answer her question.

Kailash began, stammering, "I have worked for two years in the Ganesh restaurant. Initially I did only cleaning jobs. But one day the kitchen help got sick. There was much work to do in the kitchen. I saw the cooks could not manage it. I told them I could prepare chicken. I'd always carefully observed how they prepared meals. I prepared Tandoori chicken for twenty-two guests that day, and the days after I prepared two meatless dishes. The cooks were happy with my help, especially as the assistant was sick for three months. But when the assistant came back and was told that I had taken over his work, he got angry. He went to the boss and told him that an outcast had cooked for the guests. In his opinion, the boss should forbid me access to the kitchen; otherwise, the guests would stay away, knowing that their meals had been prepared by an untouchable man."

Kailash only now began to realize that he was openly and honestly talking about his experiences to a woman—moreover, to a strange woman. He had never talked like this, not even to his best friend, but he felt he could be honest. Actually, he couldn't do otherwise; the words came of their own accord.

"I can certainly use someone who is enterprising."

Kailash looked questioningly at her. Enterprising; he had never heard of that, but he understood that he might start here. It would not, however, dawn on him that he could work for this kind woman.

"Do you think you can handle it?"

"Yes, ma'am!"

"Will you work for me?"

"Of course, ma'am! I'll do everything you want."

"And you don't even know what you're going to earn," she answered, sadly smiling.

Kailash hadn't even thought about his wage, although he needed it very badly for his wife and their three children. When the woman mentioned an amount higher than his last wage, Kailash could not comprehend it.

The next morning, before the sun rose on the other side of Gangama, of mother Ganges, he stood at the door of the kitchen. When the woman with the sad eyes opened it herself and invited him in, only then could he believe that he had found a job nicer than he had been able to dream of.

Parvati asked him to start his service by making tea. She showed him the things he needed, and he started his work ardently.

When he had finished, she invited him to take a seat at the table and drink tea with her.

Kailash didn't understand what had happened to him, but he did what she asked.

"Kailash, I want to discuss something with you. I want to talk about a secret job that I want you to carry out for me, and you may not speak to anybody about that job."

"A secret job, ma'am?"

"Yes. Kailash, I engaged you yesterday for household work. But would you do something else for me as well? It's a job not without danger."

"Ma'am, I told you yesterday I would do anything for you."

"Will you promise me then to keep this secret from anybody else?"

"From your husband as well?"

"Yes."

"I promise."

"Kailash, I want you to be my courier."

"Your courier?"

"You will be charged with carrying special messages."

"You can rely on me, ma'am."

CHAPTER 09

Amal Maya felt satisfied when he looked back on the thirty-eight years of his life. A fermenting self-satisfaction left him with the conviction that great happiness would come to him shortly. In the mirror of his daydreams he saw himself admired by beautiful women. Love was a gift of the gods, he mused, a gift that would fall into his lap; the only thing he needed to do was wait for the perfect woman.

The goddess Durga played a crucial part in his love dreams. As far back as his memory reached, Amal had performed a ritual in the temple every Tuesday, with the most extreme care and in the minutest detail. And on the other days of the week, he didn't forget the goddess. He visited her often in the temple, and had ordered a room be decorated in his new house at the river Ganges as a temple for his beloved goddess.

For Amal's father, Lakshmi, the goddess of welfare, had been the most important goddess. And he, Amal, had worshipped her for a long time too. But since the time his feelings had been stirred up by mysterious forces, and had been less in step with his parents's ambitions, Amal had created another goddess in his dreams: a dreamy creature who had a great influence on his life. He dreamed of a goddess who looked every bit like a good friend of his wife, Parvati. This woman, named Durga, lived in the south of India and was married to a merchant in electronics. Amal had met her once, at the beginning of his marriage to Parvati. He had been seventeen and Parvati sixteen.

Ever since, he had idealized the woman more and more, and in the end he had come to identify her with the goddess Durga. Actually, the goddess Durga had become his favourite goddess, as a result of his devotion to Parvati's friend. Amal's religious experience had taken on an erotic nature which was embodied in the worldly Durga.

The goddess Lakshmi had taken second place, after Durga. But when there was any important business to do, he went to Lakshmi's temple as well. Actually, it was also self-preservation that made Amal to approach the goddess of welfare with rituals and prayers. Lakshmi might be important, but Durga was the central point in Amal's religious life.

The first night after his wedding, he had slept with Parvati and had discovered that his nude wife left less room for free fantasy than Durga did. Durga, dressed in a splendid silk sari, with silver bracelets round her wrists and silver rings on her fingers which, with her silver anklets, suggested a dreamy nimbleness. Durga had eyes that possessed the inscrutable depth of mountain lakes in the silvery light of the moon.

Since their wedding, Amal saw Parvati as his property. And what is deadlier to fantasy than possessing?

Amal was very devout and religious. This should yield a better life after his death than he had now. He knew he had made good karma in his past lives. And deep in his heart, he was glad that he had inherited a pious character from his father. The gods who had traced out his path of life were apparently well disposed to him.

On Tuesdays, Amal Maya got up at four o'clock in the morning. Other nights of the week, he went on quietly sleeping through the summons to prayer of the muezzin. His house was only five hundred yards from the nearest mosque, and the whiny singing voice of the muezzin coming from the huge speakers from this and other minarets could be heard by everyone for miles around. But Amal had quickly become used to it, and after three nights he had not heard the summons anymore. It was as though a mysterious being in his subconscious had concluded that the calls to prayer were not intended for him. The muezzin didn't have a hold on him anymore, in his sleep or during the day. Amal Maya had over the years become so familiar with the waves of racket of the big city that an electronic voice more or less was no longer of any importance.

But on Tuesdays Amal's natural alarm reacted to the voice of the muezzin. On Tuesday nights he awoke at the first call from the speakers, and before he had opened his eyes he knew that day was dedicated to his beloved goddess. The voice of the muezzin, swelling up in the thin, dark depths of his sleep, penetrated his mind more than on other nights. Amal had wondered if his goddess secretly had called upon the god of the Muslims to be helpful to her on Tuesday nights, and to let the sound of the summons to prayer into her worshipper.

When the building plans for his new house at the river Ganges, which he had lived in now with his wife and servants for seven years, had been under discussion, he had hinted that a temple in honour of the goddess Durga should form the center of the house; the hearth where the religious fire would burn.

After a long, uncontrolled hawking up from the bottom of his stomach, Amal spit the phlegm into the washbowl. He dressed himself. Parvati had, before going to bed, made ready a clean *kurta* of brocade silk. He was used to wearing this coat on Tuesdays; it was part of the weekly ritual. Amal spent a lot of time shaving. Then he took a bath and cleaned his teeth with twigs of the neem tree in his backyard. He perfumed his black hair and his huge and carefully trimmed black moustache with a lotion. He sprinkled his face with a matching scent. After a strict inspection before the mirror, he judged himself worthy for the weekly ritual in the temple.

Parvati was still asleep in the adjacent room. Through the door that was ajar he saw his sleeping wife. For a moment, it flashed through his mind that he hardly knew the wife to whom he had been married now for more than twenty years. They spoke rarely to each other.

Amal went to the kitchen on the ground floor. Kailash had prepared a breakfast for him. Amal didn't see his servant when he came in. He never did; he only gave him orders, or he criticised him.

It was nothing unusual for Kailash that Amal Maya didn't greet him. Kailash knew there was an unbridgeable gap between the Vaishya caste the Maya family belonged to and his own family that was part of the masses at the bottom of society. Kailash was used to being seen as part of the furniture by his boss. Apart from his criticism and his orders, Amal Maya had only once spoken to him. That was when he had come to offer his services six years earlier. But Amal Maya had never yet addressed him by name. Amal Maya had never even wondered if his servant had a name.

After six years, Kailash knew his boss liked delicious food and a lot of it, so he had scooped a considerable quantity of rice on his plate. He had put three *chapatis* on it. Along with these pancakes of unleavened bread, he had baked two eggs for his boss. As Amal Maya smacked with an open mouth, Kailash knew it was good.

When he had eaten enough, Amal belched passionately and cleaned his chin with his napkin. He washed his hands in a bowl held before him by the invisible servant. He left the kitchen without a word.

Outside the kitchen, he pressed the palms of his hands together before his chin and strode with dignity to the house temple. Deeply bowing his head, he greeted his favourite goddess, Durga. He closed his eyes and murmured one of the *Vedic* texts he had learnt as a boy from his father. He had muttered that text so often, in his droning memory that he never was aware of what he was praying.

Besides, his thoughts were somewhere else. The day before, his younger sister, Bindu, had tidied up the wage-records. She had discovered that sixty-four people, most of them children, did not receive any wages. Amal had lain awake for half the night. Bindu must not discover why these children didn't get wages. He needed to discuss this problem with his partner, the police inspector Sunar Chand.

"An Ambassador is not a car for a man in my position," Amal thought, with a sense of satisfaction, as he sat behind the wheel of his car. A month earlier he had traded in his Indian car for a new one, an American car. This American car had a cylinder capacity of two hundred and forty bhp and better matched his social position. He had got a substantial amount for the ambassador. "It's a pity that my father didn't witness this; he would have been proud of me. He was a sharp negotiator, a quality I've inherited from him."

Amal remembered the negotiations his father had carried out for his marriage to Parvati. He mused wistfully on the patience and perseverance his father had used to get the dowry: golden ornaments, a scooter, and a piece of land.

Later, after the wedding, Parvati had protested when she had had to take over the care of him from his mother, but he had put her in her place. With his friends in the streets, he had always been more agreeable than with his wife. Besides, he had learned English there. He had not needed a school for that.

He and Parvati had met after an announcement in the Sunday edition of the *Indian Times*. A man had recommended his daughter as a young woman with a good education, who was religious and intelligent. Amal's father had thought these qualities matched his son's, and had proposed that he reflect on the announcement.

During their first meeting Parvati had not reacted to his advances. "Actually, she was conceited," Amal mused, "she wasn't aware that she might enter into a rich family. I never noticed any sign of appreciation. Looking back, I wonder why I asked my father to continue the negotiations. But, on the other hand, he got all that was possible out of it. I'm glad I inherited his feeling for business."

Amal's feeling of self-complacency was reinforced by his noiseless new car. Hanging below the rearview mirror was a picture of Durga sitting on her tiger. By pushing a button in the car, he closed the door of the garage. That made him feel proud; he felt like a master of his surroundings. He drove slowly through the gate from his home ground to the Durga *mandir*, the temple of Durga. Amal felt so content that he didn't even get angry when a shabby rickshaw-cyclist impeded him. The man had difficulty climbing a steep slope and was pushing his rickshaw with two passengers to the verge of the road.

A hundred yards further Amal gave way to a cow; the animal didn't know where to go. Amal, however, did not let this spoil his humour. Besides, he had respect for cows. He was also used to the blocks in urban traffic. He had never yet driven the seven hundred yards between his house and the temple in less than twenty minutes.

He parked the car in front of the temple and bought a garland for the goddess. The flower sellers in front of the temple had years earlier raised their prices, as they knew Amal Maya always bargained to the limit. So he paid more for the garland than other people, and for the feeling that he was slyer than the merchants.

In the open space before the pink and light blue painted temple, Amal took his slippers off and rang the bell. He went in and strode to the precious and richly decorated statue of Durga. As soon as he crossed his legs and sat down on his bottom before the familiar statue, he started to dream. As usual, he thought again of the earthly Durga with the splendid sari, who knew how to leave the enchantment to the imaginary game of suggestion. The mysterious tension had remained intact. Dark, slim feet in silver-coloured toe-slippers and a pair of dark silver anklets had accentuated her natural female beauty. On her hands, which were lightly folded on her belly, she had worn some well-chosen jewels and bracelets of the same dark silver round her wrists. The bracelets and anklets had intrigued him, and in his darkly clouded subconscious had taken on the meaning of possessing and being possessed. A white veil over her mouth had confused him most of all. The veil reinforced the mystery and the bewitchment, like in a fairy tale. Out of a couple of dark eyes that sparkled with a mysterious fire radiated an open-minded astonishment. A downy-soft, pearly skin testified to youthful health and an almost supernatural strength of mind. Her face and attitude spoke a clear language, natural and self-conscious and, in spite of the veil, open and herself. She had smiled at Amal when she greeted him with her finely lined hands before her chin. And he had only stared, tongue-tied, at the miraculous figure.

Amal had hardly slept the week after meeting her. He had not been himself for one moment. *What does she think of me?* That question had mastered his body language the week after he had met her. That question mastered his whole life.

On the last night, before being awoken by the muezzin, Amal Maya had had a dream. He had been standing on a bridge, and had seen the eyes of the goddess Durga in the fickle, elusively waving water. He had looked for his image in her eyes, but had only discovered emptiness in their deep, dark, silent emptiness.

Now, in the temple, Amal laid the garland at the feet of the goddess, and let himself glide away in his daydreams. "Beloved goddess," he prayed in a whisper, "why did you let me down last night?"

But the goddess didn't answer him.

He stayed on, looking at the statue. "Why don't you help me? I come every week to see you. And I bring you flowers every week."

The goddess kept silent. It was now not the dark emptiness of the past night that haunted Amal; it was an empty, indeterminate feeling deep down in his heart; a feeling of uncertainty. At the back of his mind he hoped to lose his uncertainty and to get a sense of security from his goddess.

When he had muttered his ritual texts, he fled from the temple. There, watched by the flower merchants, he started his powerful car. The tumbling traffic didn't leave him time to think about the visit to the temple. He didn't like to think anyway.

He drove the car into the garage and went into the house. He saw his wife in the kitchen, discussing the evening meal with Kailash. The familiar way she had of dealing with the servant irritated him for the umpteenth time, but he continued on without saying a word. Fortunately, Kailash could cook very well; otherwise, Amal Maya would have fired him a long time ago.

Amal had been glad that Bindu had been willing to take over the bookkeeping. Deep in his heart, he knew Bindu could easily do this work. She had been pulling the strings more and more. He saw this, but didn't see it. He was the leader, wasn't he? A leader can't do everything, can he? A real leader delegates, and if he has a good employee for bookkeeping, he makes use of this person. Which great leader can oversea everything?

A week after that Amal sat cross-legged on his prayer mat. Durga kept silent, like her statue. Amal had given up his deeply bent attitude. He saw now the petrified look of the goddess and noticed that she would not release him from his empty, woeful feelings. He rose, and after a quick ritual greeting he left the temple in a bitter mood. The flower-sellers laughed goodnaturedly at him. "Another garland wasted," Amal muttered.

CHAPTER 10

You removed a kidney from a healthy man to implant it into a sick person. Why didn't you tell me this?"

Sudhir's face sallowed slowly.

Shakti remained, looking sad, in front of him.

His eyes looked for a refuge on his plate; he evaded her look. He would have preferred her to get angry; her sadness paralysed him. His mouth hung half-open. He couldn't remember when he had ever felt so nasty. He had no defence against her words. And he had to face the confrontation.

His thoughts wandered back to the moment it had begun.

A man had addressed him in front of the temple of Ganesh.

"How is your practice, Dr. Varma?" the man had asked.

"I can not complain," Sudhir had told the man. "There is a lot of work to do."

"Is it true that you are looking for a kidney donor?"

Sudhir had been surprised. "How do you know?"

"Dr. Varma, I know somebody who had an accident and who is being kept alive artificially. As you know, the kidney must be removed before the heart breaks down."

Sudhir had looked at the man without understanding him.

"Perhaps you can save your patient's life with the kidney of this person."

Sudhir had wavered between hope and disbelief. "Can you be more clear?" he had asked.

"Of course, Dr. Varma!"

"What is your name?"

"Ajay Khosla."

Although there was something in Khosla's eyes that alarmed him somewhere in the dreamy depth of his consciousness, Sudhir had not deemed it necessary to think further. He had only thought of the stroke of luck; his patient urgently needed a kidney, and there were few donors. And now a case of cerebral death had come forward, exactly what Sudhir needed.

"It happened more or less by accident," Sudhir told his wife. "That man, Khosla, took me to a man who had had an accident. The man was on a heart-lung machine. A physician told me the man was brain-dead. I didn't check it. That was a mistake. That physician told me that I did not need to remove the other kidney too, as it had been damaged by the accident. The kidney of the brain-dead man appeared to match my patient, and I removed that kidney and implanted it into my patient. My patient recovered quickly and is still doing well, although he needs medicines to prevent rejection. I was very happy with that kidney. Only later did I hear that the donor hadn't been in an accident at all; they had merely anaesthetized him. The man was later discharged from the hospital. Now, in retrospect, I wonder if the man in the white overalls was actually a physician at all."

"Why didn't you tell me this then?"

"I did not want to tell you more than was necessary; perhaps because I didn't trust it deep in my heart."

"What didn't you trust?"

"When my patient had already gone home, I heard a rumor that the kidney donor could have been an outcast who lived in a slum. They had offered him money for an experiment. The man had accepted the offer. They had sedated him. I made inquiries, but didn't get any information...until..."

"Until Amal Maya came to see you." Shakti had immediately seen the link.

"Maybe. I can't prove it."

"But now he is forcing you to make a contribution to his lucrative business."

"I promised him my cooperation."

"You've already promised him?"

"Yes. I'm supposed to call him within twenty-four hours."

"Yóu have to call hím? Within twenty-four hours?"

"Yes. I thought it better to do what he wanted of me; otherwise, I could lose my good reputation. And there is a chance that I would go to jail, if I..."

"And you think you will be rid of him after that?"

"I hope so."

"If you transplant that kidney, he will have even more of a hold over you. That first time you can plead ignorance, although you worked rather carelessly. But if you do it again, knowingly and willingly, you can't defend yourself anymore. Amal Maya will not stop there; you had better count on that. Why didn't you talk about it earlier? Then perhaps we could have found a way out."

In a way, Shakti was relieved that her husband was more a victim of his own naivety than an accomplice to the misuse of innocent victims. But he had fallen for it very easily, hadn't he?

Shakti was aware that she would have to use her female charms in the fight against Maya, which she knew was a powerful weapon, especially when she flattered his vanity as well. She thought the self-humiliation was horrible. Thinking of having to praise the man she despised intensely was beyond bearing for her. It had already cost her a superhuman effort to make use of his offer. He had told her that if she ever got into trouble, she could always find him by dialing the number he had given her. She had a problem now. There was much at stake, for Sudhir and herself, so she decided to phone Amal Maya.

"Unfortunately, Mr. Maya is in a meeting again."

This was already the third time Shakti had tried to get in touch with Maya.

The next day she phoned again.

"I beg your pardon, madam, but Mr. Maya may not be disturbed."

Maya's secretary promised to call her back.

The secretary did not call her back.

Shakti called again. This time, she succeeded.

"Will you hold the line, please, madam? Mr. Maya will be with you presently."

She wanted to scream and throw the receiver back onto the cradle, but she had to speak to Maya. She couldn't see another way out. She had to prevent Maya from giving publicity to Sudhir's illegal operation, as this would mean he would lose his good reputation and his medical qualification, and perhaps even go to jail. *I must take care,* she thought, *and hope that Maya will not force my husband to keep his promise. And for the future, it is necessary that Sudhir not be forced to use the kidneys of healthy people for his transplants again.*

"Here is Mr. Maya for you, ma'am."

"Good afternoon, Mrs. Varma. Will you excuse me, please, for making you wait? I couldn't really free up any time."

Shakti again felt inclined to throw the receiver on the cradle, but she knew Sudhir's future depended on Maya. She knew that Maya knew this too, and that he felt she could not defy him. She realized that self-restraint was necessary.

"I understand that you are busy, Mr. Maya, but you promised me your help in case we got into trouble. So I took the liberty of pressing for a talk with you." She compressed her lips and pinched her eyes shut. She felt an almost physical pain at the humiliation she was heaping on herself, but knew by intuition that she would only get somewhere with Amal Maya by using ego-massage.

"Do you have a problem, madam? I think it extremely annoying to hear that. Tell me; it would be worth everything to me if I could help you in any way."

"I can't discuss this over the phone."

"Oh well! I'll gladly invite you for a conversation. Is there any rush?"

"The sooner, the better."

"Okay! I'll put you through to my secretary so you can make an appointment. I hope to receive you as soon as possible. *Namaskar,* Mrs. Varma."

After she had made an appointment with Maya's secretary, Shakti put the receiver down. She was trembling all over.

At the gate, Shakti was stopped by a policeman, who asked her politely for the purpose of her visit.

"I am Mrs. Varma. Mr. Maya expects me."

The man entered his watchman's box, phoned, and asked if he might let Mrs. Varma pass.

Shakti walked along a long drive between palm trees, cypresses, neem trees, tamarinds, fig trees and all sorts of plants, toward a residence like a palace with a lot of marble. She saw the Indian flag on the roof and next to it, a flag with stars and Amal Maya's initials in Hindi characters.

"He is at home at least," she concluded grimly.

She ascended eight white marble steps and pulled a heavy bell. She heard deadened footsteps inside approaching from afar. A heavy door was opened. A man with an abundant moustache, a blood-red turban on his head (decorated with Maya's family arms) dressed in white trousers and a white *kurta*, ornate with red *galloons*, his hands in white gloves, bowed deeply. After that he stared at her feet.

She negated his hint to leave her slippers at the front door.

The man asked her if she would follow him. His face looked serious.

They went through a long corridor paved with marble tiles, the walls of which were ornate with paintings of gods and goddesses. Walking through other corridors, Shakti saw three identically-dressed servants.

They ascended broad flights of stairs with marble steps and meranti wood banisters. Halfway, above a platform where the stairs made a U-turn to the right, hung a two-meter-high portrait of Amal Maya, so dominantly present that a visitor's eyes could not evade him.

Upstairs she saw two other men in Maya's uniforms.

Her companion led her into a waiting room and showed her a seat. He knocked at a door and went in.

Shakti heard the man ask if he might announce her.

"Mr. Maya will receive you as soon as possible," he said when he came out. Bolt upright and motionless, he remained standing before the door.

A thick woollen carpet invited Shakti to let her slippers slide from her feet. She enjoyed feeling the downy-soft wool on her bare soles. She could see by the weaving work that the carpet had been woven by childrens' hands, possibly by the hands of little debt-slaves or kidnapped children. Nevertheless, she decided to enjoy the relaxation it offered to her feet.

Perfectly calm, she took in the interior of the waiting room. It consisted of dark brown panelling and richly coloured paintings of the goddesses Durga and Lakshmi. A great picture of Amal Maya hung in the middle of the room.

For a moment she was impressed by the opulence she found herself amidst. But she soon saw that wisdom and taste were missing in the collection; it appeared to her to be an exhibitionistic display of vulgar wealth.

After a quarter of an hour she heard a bell.

The uniformed servant before the door sprang into immediate action. He knocked, entered, and came back promptly. "Mr. Maya will receive you now, madam."

She shoved her feet into her slippers, rose and went to the door. Inside, about ten yards from her, she saw, Amal Maya sitting behind a great walnut desk. The high back of his chair suggested dignity and power; a suggestion strengthened by his family arms high in the back of the chair. Nearly behind it, the Indian flag hung passively down.

Amal Maya looked up from a paper that was before him. When he saw her, he rose, came from behind the desk, and went to meet her. He approached to within two yards, then greeted her with praying hands before his chin and bowed. "*Namaskar*, Mrs. Varma, I praise myself happy that I may at last receive you here."

"And I praise myself happy, Mr. Maya, that you could make some time free for me."

He offered her a seat in front of his desk. He sat down behind it.

From her seat, which was a little lower than his, she looked up at him.

"May I offer you a cup of tea, madam?"

"Yes, please, Mr. Maya."

He pushed a button.

Shakti looked casually around. The pomp annoyed her, but she had not forgotten to caress Maya's vanity. "You have a splendid house, Mr. Maya, and you have decorated it gorgeously."

Amal Maya smiled modestly. "I consider your compliment a great honour, madam."

"How did you do all this?" Shakti emphasized her admiration.

"There are many people who wonder how I did it, unfortunately they are not always free from jealousy. Therefore, I appreciate that you are so honest in your admiration."

Shakti was frightened. She wondered if he saw through her praising words.

But Amal Maya appeared to be happy with them. "With all due respect, I agree with you that it is a splendid house. I decorated it with great care. Apart from the considerable amount of money I bestowed upon it, I also spent a lot of time on this project—four long years. And that is not yet everything, madam," Maya said. "Without great expertise, good organizational skills, and a select network of connections, I could not possibly have achieved this. So I dare to say that I am proud."

"You may be proud; I have never seen so many beautiful things before."

Amal Maya rose from his seat, came from behind his desk, and started to give an explanation about some of the valuables. He forgot that he was a busy man. "I commissioned a great bronze statue of the goddess of welfare, Lakshmi, as I owe her very much. And I wished to honour Ganesh, the elephant headed god, with a painting. But Durga, the painting that is in the huge frame in front of my desk, is the most important goddess for me."

The enormous dimensions of the painting had already attracted Shakti's attention as she entered. The artist had rendered the divinity's winsomeness in colours as sweet as honey. The goddess rode her tiger. Shakti wondered if Maya understood the meaning of it: controlling ego and arrogance.

But before she had taken a good look at the goddess and her tiger, Maya called her attention on to the next object d'art. With growing enthusiasm, he told his guest about the enormous collection in his office and in the rest of the house.

After showing Shakti all his art in his study, Amal Maya suddenly remembered that Mrs. Varma hadn't come to view his art alone. "I beg your pardon, madam. I've let myself go on about my love for art; that is my weak point. I hope I have not annoyed you with my explanations."

"On the contrary!" Shakti protested with careful indignation. "I've rarely enjoyed art so much as I have just now."

"But you came here with a problem. I feel myself a bad host, because I didn't immediately give my attention to it. Tell me about your problem."

At that moment there was a knock at the door, and after Maya's "Yes!" a man in a uniform, with his hands in white gloves, came in with a silver tray of tea and sweets. He served them silently, then waited stiffly at attention until Maya signalled by slightly waving his right hand that he could go.

Carefully sipping the tea, Shakti told Maya how Sudhir, without being aware of it, had brought trouble upon himself.

"Quite a nuisance for your husband, Mrs. Varma!"

"I hope, Mr. Maya, that you will not make it still worse by asking from him to use the kidney of a healthy person for a transplant."

"I told your husband that I will help him; I only want to prevent him from getting into further troubles."

"The problem for my husband will not be resolved if he complies with your request."

"The problem will naturally not disappear; but I can offer your husband my protection." Maya smiled suavely.

"What do you mean by protection?"

"I mean that your husband will not encounter problems if he does what I ask of him." The smile on Maya's face was now somewhat calculating.

"And if he doesn't do what you ask of him?" Shakti looked Maya straight in the eyes.

Maya's gaze wandered away. He took time to formulate his answer. "Your husband would be stupid if he did not accept my offer."

"Offer?"

"He will be paid very well."

"But it concerns the kidney of a healthy person."

"That person offered his kidney entirely voluntarily."

"Forced by poverty, I suppose."

"That is not my problem. Besides, I can assure you that I put no pressure on them."

"You put pressure upon my husband."

"Your husband is free to say no."

"What will happen if he says no?"

"Then I can't offer him my protection."

"What will happen then?"

"Mrs. Varma, I can't see why your husband would refuse his cooperation, as he did exactly the same thing before."

"Mr. Maya, what will happen if my husband refuses to cooperate with you? You said that he is free to say no."

"He is free indeed to say no."

"What are you going to do if he says no?"

"Then I shall withdraw my protection from him."

"Does that mean that there will be a leak that my husband carried out an illegal kidney operation?"

Maya began to see that he could not avoid an answer. He looked outside for a moment, where he had a magnificent view of the park that surrounded his villa. Then he said softly and carefully, "It would be a nuisance, Mrs. Varma, if it should somehow get out." A subtle threat sounded in the tone of his voice, and the smile that should have reassured her made that threat only more inauspicious.

"And you can make that happen."

"Mrs. Varma, what do you think of me?"

"If he did cooperate, there would be no leak?"

"Who can guarantee that there will be no leak? But if your husband cooperates he can be assured of my help."

Shakti realized that Maya held them in his power. She asked herself how she could reduce the damage.

"Mr. Maya, suppose that my husband does what you ask of him. Will you promise me then that it will be the last time you ask such a thing of him? And do you promise me too that you will never make public what you know about him?"

"Mrs. Varma, my power is great, but I can't foresee the future. I can only promise you that I shall do everything to prevent a leak."

Shakti could not remember when she had ever felt so dependent or ever been so powerless. She had never found it so difficult to control her anger, either.

"Mr. Maya, such a vague promise doesn't offer me any guarantees."

Maya seemed upset. Convincingly upset. "Mrs. Varma, you misjudge my sincerity, if you don't take my promise seriously."

Shakti doubted herself for a moment. She wavered between anger and guilt. For one moment, she felt helpless against the moral indignation in Maya's voice, as she doubted the honesty of his meaning.

Maya scented her doubt and made instinctive use of it. "Mrs. Varma, if you trust me, you can be sure that I am going to protect your husband to the best of my abilities."

"Mr. Maya, please don't doubt my trust in you. But as a businessman, you'll probably not take it ill if I adopt a businesslike air as well. I ask you, therefore, for a solid guarantee that you'll never take the information you know about illegal kidney transplants and make it public."

Maya would not, however, make her any promises. By doing so, he would not only lose his power over her husband, but also his power over her. He was convinced that he could win her over with his charm, his influence and his wealth. And as long as he had a good card up his sleeve she wouldn't cause him too much trouble. He would not play that card yet. "Mrs. Varma, I still have to arrange a number of important matters today. So I propose that we discuss the problem of your husband over a delicious dinner."

Shakti knew that Maya, smiling now like a man who is convinced of his superiority, held her and her husband in his power. She was, however, also aware that he wanted something from her. *As long as Maya believes that he can win my love, and as long as I can keep him on a string, I shall be able to keep a balance, however unsteady, in the relative power. I shall throw my charm on the field of battle, as a weapon against Maya's power over my husband. But I'll have to run the gauntlet.*

"Mr. Maya, I feel honoured by your invitation, but I wonder if I, as a married woman, may accept it. I am afraid that my husband would notice this."

"You can leave safely this to me, madam. Nobody will have an inkling of it. I promise you a careless and pleasant evening."

Shakti thanked him with a charming smile, although she almost choked on her anger. She was angry because of her powerlessness, but still more by the mealy-mouthed voice of Maya and his condescending kindness. She felt humiliated by his conviction that she saw something in him, and by his undervaluing her intelligence.

"I shall think about it, Mr. Maya."

That night, she lay on her back staring into the darkness.

Before visiting Maya, she had already tossed and turned in her bed for three nights. For the umpteenth time she shivered with the recollection of that afternoon. She couldn't banish his look from her mind. That look had been paralysing, like the unfeeling eyes of a vulture. Now, in the darkness of her bedroom, she saw the beady eyes of the beast that mastered her before falling on her with its sharp, crooked nails. The weak laugh round his mouth had been a confusing camouflage. Her powerlessness made her desperate. She didn't know how to control her choking anger. Besides, there was still her husband's naivety; a brewing annoyance to her and a threatening explosive for her anger. She could not imagine a person having any confidence in Amal Maya. Sudhir kept hoping that if he did what Maya wished, he would spare him for the rest of his life.

Staring into the darkness, she fancied herself dependent on a ruthless predator playing a game with her, a game in which he left her seconds to live, but who, in the final reckoning, would leave nothing of her intact.

Shakti dreamt that night that she had been caught in a smooth, slimy web. If she managed to free one hand, the other became stuck in the web. This kept going on, with one limb after another being freed and then trapped in its turn in the sticky spider threads. A huge bird spider with plate-glass eyes in a smooth face leered greedily at her fierce efforts to free herself. The images of the spider's head and the web moved and broke as if through a lightly waving watery surface. The spider went on turning around her with endless patience. At the moment he stretched his hairy paws to her face, she awoke frightened and soaked. The feeling that she still swayed along in the waving web went on stirring her for some minutes.

CHAPTER 11

Mr. D had invited the managers of Medimarket to a special meeting.

While they were waiting for Mr. D, who was late, their uncertainty about what to do increased with every passing minute. And nobody seemed to be able to think of anything to talk about. This inability and the tension caused by waiting made the atmosphere a little oppressing.

James Huls, who never felt timid in the least, found, in the oppressing atmosphere round the meeting table, no subject suitable for a discussion. He looked now and then at the door Mr. D and his secretary, Hélène Van Dam, would come through, and from there at the precious watch his wife had given him on the occasion of his professional silver jubilee. "I hope he will not be much longer," he said, breaking the silence. "I need my time very much. I have already clocked up seventy hours this week."

Nobody responded to Huls's stock comment. Some people made no secret about how many hours they worked. Outpourings about working hours were usually infectious, but the Huls's remark now choked to death in the oppressing silence round the table.

Huls's assistant, Vinnie de Haas, didn't think it becoming to break the silence, although she could never usually hold herself back in her own familiar world of female colleagues. Vinnie was slightly addicted to droning on about mistakes and abuses; her face had even been modeled on it. By her unrestrained ability of association, she knew how to cause a disastrous confusion with her side ways comments, and in discussions she could ruthlessly force congestion. Foolishly looking for an understanding ear and for someone to listen to her point of view of the moment, she could fight like a lioness.

But now, in this company, Vinnie sensed that her words would be shrugged off.

Bill Mocker was staring ahead. There was a vague, timid smile on his face. The American and Tom Corda had exchanged words before. As usual, the man had spoken his native language, loaded with words he had gathered in the two years he had been in his new country, and those words sounded as American as the rest. But Tom liked the man, and with him his abuse of the language.

Next to Bill sat Charles Bot, with his sea lion's moustache and the empty look of a brood-hen. Everybody knew that the chronic workaholic had worked until past midnight.

Ruud Lak was excited. He thumbed agitatedly through his file, looking for something, or perhaps looking for nothing. Lak's nervousness worsened the tense atmosphere in which the people waited for redemption from outside.

The redemption came. As Lak heard footsteps, rhythmically accompanied by the quick clicking of stiletto heels, in different metrics but keeping time, he rose quickly to open the door.

Mr. D nodded casually and went straight to his chair.

His secretary, Hélène Van Dam, followed him.

Two unknown men of about forty years of age came in after them.

Hélène showed them their seats, one to the right of Mr. D, the other to the left of Ruud Lak, who would preside over the meeting. Hélène sat down between her boss and Lak. She had pen and paper ready in order to take notes of the meeting.

Ruud Lak rapped a wooden hammer on the table, although it was already uncomfortably silent. "Ladies and gentlemen," he started tensely, "Mr. D invited you to this meeting to make an announcement of the utmost important. But before he passes on to this, I'll introduce to you two gentlemen we invited here as well."

Lak cleared his throat, and then looked to the right. "Next to Mr. D sits Mr. Colin Sharpe, presiding director of the British biotechnical enterprise Pigor. And next to me," Lak looked at the man to his left, "sits professor doctor Derek Pump. Professor Pump is scientific manager of this enterprise."

Lak addressed himself to the two managers of Pigor. "Mr. Sharp and Professor Pump, I'll now gladly introduce the members of our managing board to you."

He looked to the man who sat at his right. "Mr. Huls leads the Financial Department of Medimarket. He is undoubtedly willing to give his opinion about the information the president of the board of governors will offer us."

Huls, who was clearly surprised by the presence of the two gentlemen, could only keep silent.

"The woman next to him is Mrs. De Haas." Lak looked kindly at her. Vinnie de Haas nodded hastily, with a sweet smile. "Mrs. De Haas is Mr. Huls's assistant and an indispensable help to him."

Vinnie blushed.

"Mr. Bot is the personal manager of The Concern. He will certainly be an important cornerstone in working out the new plans relating to what Mr. D is going to tell us. I cannot, however, run ahead of his announcement. But I can tell you this: Mr. Bot is a competent reorganizer."

Mr. Bot let the introduction go resignedly across him. Nothing of him stirred more than was strictly necessary.

"Mr. Mocker manages the Department of Public Relations. He makes himself useful to our consuming market."

Bill Mocker laughed timidly.

"And last, my assistant Mr. Corda. Mr. Corda possesses great management capabilities that will certainly come in handy too."

Lak's compliment surprised Tom. He didn't know how to react. He couldn't help feeling that the faces of his colleagues demanded an explanation from him.

"May I ask Mr. D, the president of the board of governors of Medimarket, to address the meeting?"

Mr. D rose, looked for a moment at the two guests, and started his speech.

"Ladies and gentlemen, you wonder maybe why we invited the gentlemen Sharpe and Pump." The supposition sounded like an observation. Mr. D looked around before going on. "Mr. Sharpe and

Professor Pump represent a highly particular enterprise. Both of them play an important part in the British biotechnical enterprise Pigor." Mr. D inserted a short pause again, by which he kept the group in suspense. "Pigor researches the possibility of xenotransplant." Mr. D looked around again, and perceived only inquisitive looks. "That is to say: Pigor inquires into the possibilities of implanting animal tissues, and even animal organs, into human beings."

There was now a question in the air that was not, however, verbally expressed by anyone.

"You know there is a shortage of donor organs. The waiting lists of patients needing a new organ grows longer and longer." Mr. D looked for a moment at his secretary, who recorded every word her boss uttered. "Scientists within Pigor and those of other scientific institutions all over the world have, for a long time, been looking for possibilities to help these people in one way or another. Professor Pump will presently give you an explanation about the phenomenon of xenotransplant, and will inform you about what's going on under his leadership at Pigor."

Mr. D now took a long pause to give his listeners the occasion to digest his words. But the digestion flagged, waiting for further elucidation. The faces round the table remained focused on the big boss of The Concern.

"Ladies and gentlemen, six months ago Mr. Sharpe applied to me with a request for financial help. Pigor needs a lot of money in the next ten years." Mr. D took a sip of water. "Medimarket has a wide scientific interest, as you know, but our concern also pursues interests in science. Long and intensive discussions between Medimarket and Pigor have been held. These discussions resulted in the conclusion that a takeover of Pigor by Medimarket was the most desirable option."

Charles Bot was awake now. He realized an important task was awaiting him.

James Huls looked on critically.

"Ladies and gentlemen," Mr. D went on, "the board of governors of Medimarket decided, therefore, to take over the splendid

British enterprise Pigor. You'll understand that this decision will have far-reaching consequences for The Concern. With our new daughter, Pigor, we will aquire a new activity: scientific research for xenotransplant. This research will cost us a lot of money, but we think this takeover is entirely economically safe in the long term. Therefore, we are very happy about this takeover."

Mr. D waited for a moment before going on. "Ladies and gentlemen, you'll understand that we will have a lot of work to do to effect this takeover. I hope and expect that I may rely on all of your cooperation."

James Huls, more or less in a trance after his boss's words, nodded in a stately fashion.

Charles Bot sat upright, as though he would like to start work immediately.

The other members of Medimarket seemed to be too impressed to express their surprise.

"Ladies and gentlemen, I thank you for your attention." Mr. D sat down.

Mr. Lak proposed ringing for the coffee. The boss concurred.

"Good morning, ladies and gentlemen."

Besides coffee, Sandy Kamat usually brought a relaxing atmosphere with her.

"I thought," Sandy said in her own, familiar way, "the ladies and gentlemen would certainly like a tasty cup of coffee, so I made fresh coffee for you."

Mr. Lak looked pityingly at his colleagues.

Mrs. Van Dam's look was disapproving.

Mr. D heard nothing.

Bill Mocker looked desiringly at the pot of coffee Sandy went round with.

Tom Corda admired Sandy, as she didn't care a jot about the oppressive silence, and went on without letting it suck her into the treacly atmosphere. She was not impressed at all. And she was always surprising; she held none of the supermarket opinions of the day. She said what she thought. She didn't let herself be tempted to show formal politeness, and she wasn't interested in what other people thought of her. A luxuriant head of loose hair and tiny mocking lights in her eyes gave her an air of defiance. Everyone stealthily respected her.

The two guests were surprised to see how she proudly went around the long meeting table.

"I couldn't survive without your delicious coffee," Bill Mocker remarked.

His colleagues looked at him surprised and kept silent.

When Sandy had disappeared, Ruud Lak looked at his watch. "Ladies and gentlemen, after the important news you received from our president you'll undoubtedly have questions. Therefore, I invite you to reply to his announcement."

Huls was the first one who came up with a question. "Mr. Chairman, may I ask the president of the board of governors if the board has already developed any ideas with reference to the credit facilities for the new project?"

Tom, knowing that democracy in The Concern was a seriously played game, was surprised that the man responsible for the financial management was not involved in this aspect of the decision-making.

Huls himself seemed to see this as a matter of course.

Mr. D smiled condescendingly. "Mr. Chairman, as Mr. Huls knows, we've worked for the last fifteen years with all the means we have at our disposal to accomplish acquisitions, mergers and reorganizations. And we have succeeded very well, by economizing and by clearing the working floor. With our strong management, by good acquisitions, and by huge profits, we have achieved an enormous financial strength and a prominent position in the market. This position may not, of course, be weakened. Creating a new market should be a challenge to all of us."

Mr. D, the motor of common thinking in The Concern, had for a moment showed some emotion, but nobody noticed that he had answered a question nobody had asked.

"Do you think," Bill Mocker asked in his Texas accent, "that xenotransplant will be accepted by society?"

Mr. D showed the shade of a lenient smile. "We'll have to wait and see, Mr. Mocker, but promoting this new possibility that science has procured for us is first of all a task for you. So I hope that I may also rely on your unconditional dedication."

"Xenotransplant is, for the time being, an unknown domain," Bill Mocker answered. "I hope we shall have some information on it."

"Mr. Mocker, Professor Pump will serve you hand and foot; presently he will inform you about his work and about the state of affairs in this area." Mr. D looked at his watch. "I am sorry, Mr. Chairman, unfortunately I must leave now. But I expect that I can leave the direction of the meeting to you."

"Of course, Mr. D! It is a pity that you can't stay any longer, but we understand."

Lak pressed the bell for a second cup of coffee.

Tom Corda strolled to the window. Bill Mocker came to his side. Looking down, they saw Mr. D leave. His walk was goal-directed. Without paying any attention to his surroundings he moved on, his attaché case in his right hand and his mobile phone at his left ear. They saw him get into the limousine.

Meanwhile, Sandy had returned. "You've earned another cup of coffee, haven't you?" she said in her tuneful voice.

None of the people round the table seemed to have heard her words. Vinnie de Haas gazed neutrally ahead. Ruud Lak searched hastily through his papers. James Huls studied his nails. And Hélène Van Dam had no time for a look at 'the coffee woman.'

"You are an oasis in the burocratic desert," Bill Mocker confided to her, when she poured him his coffee.

Sandy rewarded him with a warm smile.

After the five-minute coffee break, Professor Pump was invited to relate his story.

ED MOOLENAAR

The professor adjusted the microphone to mouth level and started. "If you'll allow me, I'll start by telling you our history of testing xenotransplant," he began. Then he paused, coughed, and went on with the automatic tone of someone who has already told his story hundreds of times. "Ladies and gentlemen, for some decades scientists have been able to implant the organ of another human being in people who have a sick organ. The donor has always been a brain-dead human being. I don't need to tell you about the heart transplant, carried out in the 1960's, by the South African physician Dr. Barnard. We call this form of transplant, from human being to human being, allotransplant.

Xenotransplant means the transplant of an animal's organ tissue or of an animal's organ into a heterogeneous being. In practice, that is to say: in the near future, it concerns transplanting an animal's organ into a human being. And to be still more concrete, Pigor is looking into the possibility of implanting a pig's heart in a human being. You'll understand that it concerns people with a sick heart who otherwise should die."

Tom's mouth fell open in astonishment. And when the impact of the words of the professor had penetrated, his whole body became tense. He felt his heart thumping. He tried to imagine how it would be...

But the professor brought him back to reality by continuing his speech. "Implanting the organ of an animal into a human being carries great problems with it. Innumerable scientists all over the world have already fought for years to conquer these problems. I am going to tell you something about these problems, and explain how we try to resolve them.

"The immune system of the human body, that already has difficulty accepting the organ of another human being, doesn't accept the organ from an animal at all."

The professor took another drink of water, and then explained how he and his team had succeeded, by means of a process of nuclear transplant and genetic adaptation, to breed a pig that would be more suitable as an organ donor for a human being. After concluding that

102

the possibility of the rejection of a pig's heart by the human body would be strongly reduced by this, he took another sip of water.

Huls and Bot nodded with serious and understanding looks. The others remained neutral.

The professor knew that most people couldn't follow him as he told this, and he was used to it. He waited for a moment, to mark a transition in his story. "We are frightened of virus infections after a xenotransplant." Professor Pump looked at the faces round the table, to see how his listeners perceived this allegation.

The faces asked for further explanation.

"We are especially afraid of unknown viruses, which are dormant in the animal, but which might be activated in the human body. A comparison with the HIV virus that caused the epidemic of AIDS forces itself upon us here. In the case of the HIV virus, there was also talk of an infection of one sort or another. Pigor breeds pigs under the strictest sterile conditions. Only when we get this danger—the danger of an eventual virus infection—sufficiently under control, can we believe the implantation of a pig's heart into a human body to be justified. Ladies and gentlemen, I thank you for your attention."

While the professor was talking, a word came into Tom's mind, a word that now began to churn in his head: *experimental subject*. He could not, would not imagine, that he...

Curious to know what his colleagues thought about a pig's heart in a human body, Tom looked around. He didn't, however, perceive any confusion or doubt on the other faces. Only Bill Mocker seemed somewhat embarrassed; it seemed that he did not know what he should think about it.

They think it perhaps less abnormal than I do, because they have a healthy heart; it is an academic problem for them. But for me...oh, I cannot think of it! A pig's heart in my...?

Vinnie de Haas proposed asking for the coffee woman.

Lak, however, stopped her. "We've already drunk two cups of coffee." He looked round the table. "I propose we take this opportunity, to ask Professor Pump any questions you may have."

Huls had a question. "When do you think scientists will be able to implant a pig's heart into a human being?"

"In five to ten years," Pump answered resolutely.

"May I suppose then, that research will go on for that time?"

"Research will be necessary forever."

"And that research will cost a lot of money, I suppose."

"A great deal of money. That was the reason why we appealed to Medimarket for help."

"That money is, in my humble opinion, entirely justified," Huls said, "for if it wasn't, the president of the board of governors wouldn't have come to this decision."

"Your boss has made the right decision."

Tom gestured with his hand for attention. "Professor Pump, why did you choose a pig, and not another animal?"

"The reason is simple," the professor answered. "Organs of pigs look most like that of human beings."

Tom wrinkled his forehead. The words of George Orwell escaped, barely audible, out of his mouth. "Some animals are more equal than others."

Vinnie de Haas looked at him as if he were deranged.

Professor Pump smiled shyly.

There were no further questions.

Lak thanked the professor, then proposed that his colleagues spend the next Monday morning meeting on the takeover of the British enterprise.

He got an approving mumble for an answer.

After the meeting, Tom went to the room of his boss to discuss a problem. "May I have a word?"

Lak looked up from his work. "Yes." Lak was usually a little stiff when switching the focus of his attention. "Yes. You come as if you've been sent for. The point is, we are thinking about sending you to India. To Benares."

"To the pharmaceutical company Medimarket is trading with?"

"Yes. Mr. D wants an evaluation of the deliveries of this pharmaceutical company to Medimarket. For three years, we have obtained products produced by that company. Mr. D will get a better view of the whole business, such as the production line, the means of production, and the administration. And they may have other interesting products to offer us. In brief, you're going there to look after the interests of Medimarket."

Tom was glad that he could go to Benares, where he could see his friends again. But he hadn't forgotten the whispered talk between Lak and Huls on his first work day at The Concern.

A deep frown appeared on his forehead. "You surprise me, Mr. Lak. When would I go?"

"Six weeks hence. You need some time to apply for a visa, you need vaccinations, and I must apply for your ticket. You will travel business-class, of course."

Tom, who had forgotten the words of Professor Pump, was in a blaze. But at the same time, he was aware that it could become a precarious enterprise; there was something in the Benares business he was not supposed to discover.

"I shall discuss it with my wife. I'll let you know as soon as possible." Tom surprised himself with his sober tone. In his soul there was only music. Even Vera couldn't stop him. He was convinced that she would welcome the trip as well.

"One more question, Mr. Lak: Who is the owner of the company in Benares?"

"We don't know. The only name we know is that of the manager of the company. He is called Majumdar."

"You don't know the owner's name, but Medimarket had done business with that company for three years?"

"No. The only thing we know is that it's somebody who must be fabulously rich. But you could perhaps discover his name. It's not relevant. But if you are there anyhow, you could enquire after the name."

Tom forgot the matter he had gone to Lak to discuss.

Because of the prospect of a trip to Benares, he couldn't sleep that night. The memories of his first trip to India, and particularly his stay in Varanasi, as he called Benares, would not leave him alone. That first trip was already more than twelve years ago now. Then, he had not even known Vera. He had met her six years later. When he met her the first time, he had already been to Varanasi three times. When they married, they had gone there together for six weeks. And Vera was, just like him, deeply impressed. Meeting the people in the slums had made a great impression on them. Tom had often remembered the nuns, and Asha as well. He had got to know Asha better over the years. To be able to talk to her, he had even taken lessons in Hindi. Satori had encouraged him to do so. She had explained to him that the experience of a man treating Asha with respect would benefit her personal development. Asha had flourished more every time he went to see her. And not only Asha; there were other women who had gained more self-confidence as well, although this didn't mean that their husbands always appreciated it.

CHAPTER 12

Sarásvati was a charming woman, and she was aware of it. She had grown up with the admiration of all those around her. Her charm was as self-evident for her as her existence itself. She wore a red and purple sari and silver anklets above red toe-slippers. An aura of innocence from a natural timidity gave an extra distinction to her charm. But in spite of that timidity, she had an aura of strength and an independent spirit. The red *tica* on her forehead, a symbol of spiritual receptivity, seemed to accentuate her independence.

Sarásvati went to the Varma's house in a rickshaw.

Shakti opened the door and saw immediately that her friend came bearing an unpleasant message. She asked Ragu to make tea.

The two women, sitting in the living room of the Varma's home, looked, in several respects, like each other.

Shakti was aware of her charm as well, and she also had a strong, independent character. She had long, black silky hair and she wore a dark blue sari, the end of which was draped over her left shoulder.

Shakti made her friend feel comfortable. "I am glad to see you here again. In the last weeks, I only saw you at Sudhir's practice. I was already thinking of inviting you over. But you beat me to it."

"I've come to talk about work, and I can't stay long. I told Sudhir that I was doing an errand."

"He doesn't know that you are here?" Shakti felt a nasty foreboding.

"That makes my visit still more difficult."

"Tell me!" Shakti said to her friend.

Sarásvati looked at the woman before her, who was seventeen years older. She knew that she could trust her. She started her story. "Three months ago, a man lay in the hospital. He had kidney trouble. The trouble was so serious that he would only live if he received a donor kidney. Sudhir actually had no hope, and he had also told the patient that he didn't see any possibility. The patient was desperate, and he offered Sudhir a lot of money if he could provide a kidney. Sudhir regretted it very much, but he could not help the man. Sudhir told you this at the time, I suppose."

"Yes, he did."

"Two weeks later, a man came into the practice. Sudhir was at the hospital. The man told me he had a message for Dr. Varma. I asked him who he was. He answered me that he could not tell me, and also could not tell me the name of the person the message came from. I asked him what sort of message he had for Dr. Varma, and if he was allowed to pass that message on to me. He answered that he had been ordered to take the message to Dr. Varma or to his assistant. He then told me that the man who had donated a kidney for one of Dr. Varma's patients was not brain-dead, as had been told to Dr. Varma before, but was a healthy man who had sold one of his kidneys."

"I suppose that you told this to Sudhir as well?" Shakti said.

"Yes. But he reacted rather curtly. 'Leave this to me,' he said. Then he went away."

"And the patient who needed a kidney?"

"He's got one."

Shakti could not yet form an image of what had happened, or could have happened; her emotions did not allow a sober weighing of the facts. She looked at Sarásvati. She knew that her friend had spoken the truth. Then she stared sadly and absently outside. She could not utter a word.

"Sudhir has always put confidence in me," Sarásvati said.

"It's good that you told me this." It came softly, but resolutely, out of Shakti's mouth. "I wonder if this has something to do with Amal Maya."

Sarásvati understood what Shakti meant. "You know Amal Maya came to see your husband last week?"

"He was also here."

"Was he?"

"Maya came to see me after visiting Sudhir. He talked about kidney transplants without saying anything concrete. But he did tell me that he would protect Sudhir, and that he would go on doing so. I got the impression that he wanted to know if I knew something and what I thought about it. I did not, of course, commit myself."

"Amal Maya told me that he had a conversation with Dr. Varma about a kidney transplant, and that this could have consequences for me as well. I asked him what sort of consequences he meant. He told me then that it might mean that I would have to look for another job, and that I could become his secretary."

"Amal Maya's secretary?"

"I told him that I had no reason at all to leave your husband."

"So he threatened you with the loss of your job? What does Maya want from us?"

"I've no idea!"

"And now?"

"I don't know," Sarásvati answered.

"I will go to see Maya." Shakti told her friend that she had visited Maya and that he had invited her to dinner.

CHAPTER 13

Ravi lived in a loamy hut on the bank of the river Ganges. As far back as he could remember the hut had already been carried away by the flooding river seven or eight times during the monsoon. And each time he had rebuilt the hut, with his father, and after his father had died, by himself.

The hut consisted of two rooms. In one of them was his sleeping mat. In the other one stood a cooking pot and a bucket. There were four stones between which a fire could be made out of cow dung. There was a broom for cleaning the hut and to take with him to his work. Ravi was a sweeper.

Ravi's wife had died five years earlier after giving birth to their only child. The child had died an hour after that.

Ravi had borrowed five hundred rupees to buy the firewood for the cremation of his wife's body. He had shaved his head bald before he, with an acute pain in his heart, had set fire to the wood stack with his wife's body. The child's body had been thrown into the river. He had shuffled back to his hut, terribly lonely.

Since his early youth, Ravi had cleaned the floors in a factory and the place around it. The people there were used to dropping their rubbish where they went. Ravi had to sweep the same floor three times a day. It was such an old habit that nobody thought it uncommon; Ravi included. He got a meager wage for his work.

In the morning, long before sunrise and without having eaten anything, Ravi went to work. He swept then, with gnawing hunger, for hours. People who came along looked past him. Ravi had more or less gotten used to the hunger, and he had learned to live with his eternal tiredness. He had also known his parents only as poor, hungry and weary people, cut dead or disdained by other people, and without a spark of self-confidence. And it had been no different for his grandparents and great-grandparents. From generation to generation it had been taken in by the children, like diluted milk, that they weren't worth anything and that they should only be submissive and grateful for what other people left them. It was, therefore, quite understandable that Ravi saw himself as a worthless being who was scarcely tolerated by other people.

He lived in this way, hungry and tired, day in and day out, year in and year out. Actually, he didn't realize that he lived. He shuffled to his work, and swept the floors and the place blindly. And after he had shuffled back home in the evening, and had eaten a handful of rice with an unclear sauce of vegetables and herbs, and a piece of unleavened bread, he gave way to a stunning emptiness.

One evening, hunched on his mat as though someone had planted him there in a far past, he saw in a dream a wonderful woman, looking lovingly at him. There was a warm and hearty compassion on her face, and she laid her hands on his shoulders. The touch flowed through him with a warm glow and a sparkling feeling of happiness. The gentle eyes of the woman and her merciful hands made it clear that she esteemed and loved him. This experience awakened an unknown warmth within him.

"Ravi, I am Radha, the inner force of Krishna. I bring you his blessing and his protection. I am the incarnation of perfect love and dedication. God lives in the hearts of all creatures; in your heart, as well. People see you, Ravi, as a poor sweeper, as unworthy, and you have never learned otherwise. But from now on, you'll be free in action and in thought, and you'll see reality as it is; you'll see more clearly than people who only see a poor sweeper in you."

Ravi was drunk with happiness. The warm feeling in him became stronger and he felt an unknown inspiration flowing within him. He saw the world now as he never had seen it: he saw people who were glad and happy, and he felt the sadness of other people; he saw their faces and their hands; he saw a dog lovingly licking her puppy; he saw flowers bursting open. And he experienced all this as a flower that opens invitingly to the sun and contently closes in the silvery twilight of the moon again.

Ravi was surprised when his dream went on after he awoke. He knew that dreams defied the laws of time and space, but he had never had any notion that a dream could survive in the reality of the day.

He wondered at his hands and his fingers. He looked with surprise at his feet that had only shuffled all his life. He felt a rushing life force in his body. It was as if he felt a warm glow in his heart. At the same time, there was a peace in him that left room for reflection. He realized intuitively that he should quietly do justice to the happiness and the energy overwhelming him. If he allowed it, time would mature this new wisdom in him.

When Ravi, the morning after that wonderful night, went to the pump to get water, he saw a woman scouring her pans with sand and rinsing them with water. Ravi knew that the woman, who had lived for a couple of months in the quarter, was a widow.

Asha was surprised when she saw Ravi. She hadn't known him other than with a bent back, hanging shoulders, dim eyes—as an overdriven, bony pack animal. *Is that Ravi? That man with a peaceful smile on his face? As long as I've lived here, I pitied him, but I never felt any human contact with him.* Asha forgot her pans. She filled her lungs full of air so as to come to her senses. *Am I seeing things clearly?* In order to free herself from the hallucination, she shook her head. Then she looked at him for a while and set to work again.

Ravi, who had heartily greeted his neighbour, pumped his bucket full of water and went back to his hut. He laughed, collected his broom, and went off to his work in a happy mood.

On his way, he thought of the face of the woman he had seen at the pump, and who he had never seen before, not really seen before. *I saw something in those dark, mysterious eyes that made me think of Radha. When I come back tonight, I'll look again,* he thought. *Strange that I didn't see it earlier.*

He kept walking. He saw trees and plants and flowers of all sorts, the existence of which dawned on him only now. He let the fresh morning air penetrate into the pores of his skin and he felt younger than his memories could span. He greeted everybody he met, and now and then he began a conversation, so as to share his happy feelings with other people.

Arriving at his work, he enjoyed the astonishment on the face of Bhikoe, his boss, when he greeted him and asked him if he had slept well. Bhikoe was so dumbfounded that he forgot to snap at Ravi.

"Now then, sir, I'd better begin," Ravi said cheerfully. "Shall I give your office a good turnout?"

Bhikoe, who had always seen Ravi as a sweeping-machine, stared to him with an open mouth. As he could not immediately think of an answer, he muttered disconcertedly, "If you think it's necessary."

Ravi did not hesitate, and said, "I'd better start now, for you will have a visitor presently."

He started to clean the desk of his employer, so as to give it a thorough going over.

Bhikoe, used to commanding his sweeper like a dog, was completely upset. Although he thought his desk could very well have a thorough cleaning, he was angry all the same, because his sweeper had taken the initiative and, what is more, turned everything in his sanctum upside down.

What, however, in the depth of his heart, bothered him the most was that the control he had over this creature, as though he was his property, began to slip away from him. Although he had always been irritated by the submissiveness of his sweeper, he could now not bear Ravi's self-assured behaviour. Bhikoe was so surprised that he was speechless.

Ravi cleaned the desk quickly and thoroughly, put everything back in its place, and began to work on the rest of the office. When he asked his boss to move aside for his broom, Bhikoe stepped aside like a sleepwalker. He wondered if he was dreaming.

When Ravi had finished and had asked his boss if he thought it good, Bhikoe could only nod.

"Then I am going to start with the corridors, and after that I'll sweep the place clean."

When Ravi closed the door behind him, he saw a woman arriving. She came every week to see his boss. He had never paid any attention to the woman, who was a being out of a very mundane world. And the woman, on her part, had never seen him other than as a trifling figure that, like his broom, belonged to the factory.

Ravi surprised her then, when he held the door open for her.

The woman entered the office, to discover the man she did business with sitting in his chair, gazing ahead. Her appearance brought him back to reality. Bhikoe, normally a gallant host and full of self-confidence, could not find a beginning for conversation. He would not confess that the sweeper had unbalanced him; not to himself, and still less to his business friend, the charming Gauri. So he muttered, "I didn't sleep well."

Gauri, however, felt that there was something else. "Strange, that sweeper, he has never yet looked at me, and now he held the door open for me."

"This morning that man came into my office and he said what he thought. And he worked as he had never done before."

"Didn't you ask him what had happened?"

"No, I didn't even think of that. Why should I? I can't be concerned about a sweeper's life, can I?"

"Well, I am a little curious," Gauri confessed.

After they had talked for a while about business, there was a knock at the door. Bhikoe called, "Come in!"

Ravi came in. "Excuse me for intruding on you; I have come to tell you that I've finished my work. Have you got anything else for me to do?"

Bhikoe, surprised again, stammered, "No."

"Do you agree then that I can go home? There would be no sense staying here, while there is no work to do."

"Well," Bhikoe stumbled. He would not be narrow-minded in the prescence of his female guest.

"Okay, sir! You'll see me then tomorrow morning at half-past six. I wish you both a happy day."

Ravi left Bhikoe and his visitor flabbergasted.

Ravi, who had an afternoon off for the first time since his early childhood, was determined to enjoy it. Walking toward his hut, he let the lovely warm sun rays act upon him. He enjoyed the nature round him as he never had before. His only remaining desire was to share his happiness with other people. And he succeeded in infecting the people he met.

An old man, greeted by him, continued on his way more upright when he saw Ravi almost dancing along the path.

And a man, who had had financial worries for many years, felt that afternoon the sun more important than his worries.

And a young woman, who had been beaten that morning by her husband, opened her crusty face as she saw Ravi's radiant eyes and his singing mouth.

Ravi's neighbour Asha enjoyed the happy sounds that came out of his mouth. That morning she had shrugged her shoulders, but she saw now that she hadn't been wrong. "Ravi, you are so happy; what happened to you?"

"Asha, I saw myself as I really am." And without giving her an explanation, he went on. "I only now see how nice you are." But he realized immediately that a man could not speak so boldly to a woman who was still in mourning for her late husband.

But Asha laughed. "Ravi, you didn't see me at all."

"You are right, Asha. I am sorry for speaking in this way. I said it before realizing it."

"Why should I blame you for what comes out of your heart? But I hope that you'll look at me better from now on." Then she was startled by her own words, for Ravi might think that she didn't know her place.

But the stars in his eyes reassured her.

Ravi took the bucket out of his hut and went to the pump.

Three young women, who sat there washing clothes, looked up.

"That is Ravi!" one of them whispered.

"Hello, ladies. I will not bother you; I need some water. I've decided to make a delicious meal."

The young women gazed with open mouths and eyes at him. "Is that Ravi?"

Ravi greeted them with a smile and left the young women astonished behind him.

In his hut, he put half a piece of cow dung between the stones and set fire to it.

Ravi's transformation dominated the talk in the quarter for days.

Ravi himself went with pleasure every morning to his work. His boss had adapted himself to the changed behaviour of his servant, well aware that the work was done better than ever before. At Ravi's suggestion, he ordered rubbish cans be put in several places, and he instructed his people to use them. By doing so, Ravi now had an extra two hours every day for enjoying his hut and for a chat with Asha. Bhikoe also agreed to Ravi's request for a small wage increase, as he had no arguments against his pleas. Besides, he could not deny that Ravi, in all his past years of service, had earned more than he had received. Bhikoe even admired this sweeper who he had, until then, hardly discerned from his broom. They sometimes fell into conversation, and Bhikoe became more and more impressed by the simple wisdom of the illiterate man.

Ravi was well pleased with his work. He enjoyed sweeping like reciting mantras; it brought him into a mood of meditation, giving him a feeling of being bonded with the living world.

After some weeks, Ravi and Asha drank tea together.

"I don't know," Ravi said, "how your grief is for your dead husband. Your mourning time hasn't yet gone by..."

Asha smiled. "Sanjay was a good man," she said. "Our marriage had been arranged by my father and his eldest brother. But we weren't in love with each other. The loss of three of our children drove us still further away from each other. One morning I saw him spitting blood. We didn't know what had come over him. I asked the nuns for advice. Sister Soedjata came to look. She told us that Sanjay suffered from tuberculosis. But Sanjay refused any help from her. He preferred a charlatan, who made a deep impression on him with magic words and a stethoscope. He didn't believe that this man used the same, precious potion for all ailments. He kept working, because there must be money earned for redeeming the interest for the rickshaw and for the dowry of our daughter. But he got sicker and sicker. When he died, I was empty-minded. I had no grief. When his body had been cremated, his family didn't need me anymore, and I was sent away. With pain and grief, and with the help of the nuns, I found myself at last. I would distance myself then from my old life and start again in another place. A man from Europe I had met through the nuns sent me some money. My daughter remained with the nuns, so that she could go to school. I go often there to see my daughter and for a talk with the nuns."

"Ashadji, will you marry me?" Ravi asked.

"I would like to do so, Ravi, but you know the laws of Hinduism forbid a widow to marry a second time."

"What do you think more important: our love or the laws of Hinduism?"

"Our love. But…I have no money for a dowry."

"Do you, then, still feel bound by strange obligations?"

"No, I don't think so. I feel free."

"So do I," Ravi answered.

"I already wanted to marry you," Asha said, "since the first time you saw me and greeted me."

Although a man and a woman may only touch each other after they are married, they embraced, for religious and cultural interdictions and obligations shriveled in the warmth of their love.

Their first child was a girl. Ravi took the crying child in his arms and kissed it. The young human being seemed to feel quickly content in the cherishing arms of her father. He felt intensely peaceful, and he softly whispered her name, "Chinky." He then laid the child in Asha's arms.

They were poor; but they were happy, extremely happy. They loved each other intensely. And although denied respect by many other people, they esteemed each other and themselves. They were not blinded by standard judgments.

CHAPTER 14

"Are you looking for anything particular, Mr. Corda?"

"Yes, Mrs. Van Dam, I am looking for an English dictionary."

"It is there, in the corner."

"Thank you."

As Tom turned the pages of the dictionary, a sheet of paper fell out. He picked it up and saw what it was: the minutes of a meeting. It gave him a shock, as though the paper was electrified. He realized that he had the lost minutes in his hand, the ones that had caused so much hullabaloo and that a mysterious taboo still lingered around. Everybody in The Concern seemed to be afraid to know the crux of the problem, as if they, by knowing, could be considered as possible suspects. Tom had not dared to ask anybody if those minutes were ever found; he had only talked about it with Bill Mocker and Sandy Kamat. Bill had told him he was sworn to secrecy. And Sandy kept silent about it because her bag had been searched.

With the minutes in his hand, Tom looked around cautiously. Mrs. Van Dam sat behind a table, reading a magazine.

Tom put the paper back and considered what to do as he looked in the dictionary. *I will not be involved in this,* he decided. More or less reluctantly, he kept the dictionary in his hand. It felt like a time bomb. He would put the dictionary back, but he couldn't decide whether or not to leave the minutes unread in the book.

Then he heard Mrs. Van Dam rise. "Did you find what you were looking for, Mr. Corda?"

"Yes, ma'am. Technical terms in English always cause me some trouble. But I know what I wanted to know."

"Was it for your letter to the pharmaceutical company in Benares?"

Tom wondered how she knew that he was writing a letter to Benares. "Yes, ma'am. You know I am going there, and I want to prepare the manager there for the purpose of my visit."

Tom became, little by little, aware of what it could mean for him if Mrs. Van Dam had seen him with the lost minutes in his hands. She would probably assume that he had seen their contents, and so had become a potential bell-ringer. At least if the contents were dangerous for the leaders of The Concern, in case of a leak. To be wrongly initiated in the secrets of The Concern could put him in a difficult position. As the time bomb ticked dangerously, he put the dictionary back. He greeted Mr. D's secretary and went to his room.

Mrs. Van Dam must have put the minutes in the dictionary, he considered, *lest anybody should read them while she was out of her room. And after that, she must have forgotten she had put them in that book. But if she uses that dictionary again and finds the minutes, then she will know I had that dictionary in my hands. Then she will conclude that I've seen the minutes. After all, perhaps it's better to take them out of the dictionary and destroy them as soon as possible.*

But he changed his mind immediately. *When she remembers that she put the minutes in that dictionary, and when she doesn't find them, then she will know that I had that dictionary, and that it must be me who took the minutes. And then I'll really be a suspect; then I'll be a time-bomb myself. I'd better leave the minutes there.*

When Tom came back from the typing pool, to have his letter typed for Benares, the telephone in his room rang. He picked up the receiver.

"Good afternoon, Mr. Corda. Mrs. Van Dam speaking. Can I have a word?"

"Of course, ma'am!"

Tom felt bad. *She must have discovered it; she will sound me out about the minutes.*

"Mr. Corda, after two weeks you'll leave for Benares, for interviews with the management of the company we do business with."

"That is right, ma'am."

"I should like to exchange thoughts over it, at least if you can make some time for me."

"Of course, ma'am! When do you want me?"

"What do you think of tomorrow afternoon? After the New Year's reception?"

"Okay, Mrs. Van Dam." Tom put the receiver back on the cradle.

She used the dictionary, or she remembered that she put the minutes in it; I must have reminded her as I was using it. And now she thinks, now she knows, that I saw the minutes, that I read them...Who wouldn't come to that conclusion? Now I need to know for certain if the minutes are still in the dictionary; then at least I shall know what she knows. Tom decided to go for a look in the library immediately.

There was nobody in the library. Tom sneaked over to the corner where the dictionary was. He felt like a burglar. He looked around and took the dictionary out of the bookcase. The minutes were still in it. He hesitated.

Then he took the sheet of paper cautiously out of the book, and looked at the door to Mrs. Van Dam's room. It was completely quiet. He read:

Strictly confidential!!!

Report of the extraordinary conference of the Board of Governors and the Board of Directors of Medimarket, with reference to an order for a survey into the situation of general practitioners in the country.

The president, Mr. D, bids Mrs. Van Dam, his fellow members of the Board of Governors, Jonkheer Hoogen-Van der Wal, the gentlemen Jova and Hormans, and the directors Bot, Lak and Mocker, heartily welcome.

He expressly points out that everything, discussed in this meeting is highly confidential and must remain strictly secret.

For the sake of secrecy, he also proposes leaving instructions for performing the survey-project, to be discussed in this meeting, to him, Mr. D...

Tom felt a draught. He looked around. The door to the corridor was open. He put the sheet of paper hurriedly back into the English dictionary. He felt his face flushing. He turned round and saw Vinnie de Haas. He nodded a greeting and went on to look in the dictionary.

"Good afternoon, Mr. Corda. Nice to see you here."

I should have known, Tom thought. *When I am anywhere in the building working at something, there is a big chance that Vinnie casually comes in. And then I know there is something not quite in order.*

Vinnie, a cog in the system, a hurrying cog, was omnipresent in The Concern. Tom sometimes had the feeling that she was his shadow. And Vinnie always had a red pencil standing by in her hand.

"You haven't yet finished the report about the functional effectiveness of the employees of the Department of Sales promotion, Mr. Corda? We're waiting for it." Vinnie said this very kindly.

"Can you wait for two days?"

"Two days? Can't you hurry a little more?"

"I've more to do than just that report."

"Oh well, I thought as you're just reading here? Shall we say tomorrow afternoon?"

"I'll do what I can, but I can't promise anything."

Vinnie went off with a touch of triumph on her face.

Tom waited for a moment. Then he heard a rumbling from Mrs. Van Dam's room. He decided not to pull the minutes out again. *At least I know she didn't take them out,* he thought.

CHAPTER 15

On her tenth birthday, Chinky sat in the sand on the river Ganges near her parents's hut. She was supposed to take care of her younger brother, Naval, and her still younger sister, Devi. She had just given them a bit of cooked rice with *dahl*. The two younger children were now sleeping in the hut.

That morning her father had left for work long before sunrise. Her mother had gone to the market with her handcart of bananas. If her mother could sell all the bananas, she would earn eight rupees. And when her mother was ill, she would earn nothing at all; so, if she was not too ill, she went to the market all the same.

Chinky saw the rickshaw-cyclist arrive. The man had passed his lunch breaks with her once before. She didn't know him. He was not from their quarter, and judging from the way he talked, he was not from this region. The man was very nice. The last time she had even been given a water ice from him.

"*Namasté!*" the man greeted her.

Chinky laughed. She liked talking to strange people. And the man could tell nice stories.

The story he told her now was about a man who was fabulously rich and was living in a splendid house. "He lives along the Ganges as well," the man told her, "and he has a lot of servants. He is very devout and he goes every Tuesday to the temple to pray there. And, what's more important, this man does lots for children. He takes children, who don't get enough to eat from their parents, or who have no home at all, under his wing. He makes sure that these children get work. He has already helped many children in this way."

Chinky was impressed.

At a certain point, the rickshaw cyclist asked, "Would you like to meet this man?"

"Yes, I would like that, but I can't leave my little brother and sister by themselves."

"Your friend could take care of them for a while, couldn't she? If we go in the rickshaw, we'll be there very quickly, and we'll be back before you know it."

"I've never been in a rickshaw," Chinky answered. "It must be exciting."

"Take a seat, then!" the man said. He rose and went to his vehicle.

Chinky was proud to be seen in a rickshaw by her friend. She looked around, less to see than to be seen.

When they went outside the quarter, she had an eye for the houses and the streets they rode through. What she saw was new for her.

After a while, the man stopped in front of a house in a remote, quiet street.

Chinky thought it strange that the house was not on the river; had the rickshaw cyclist not said that it was?

The rickshaw cyclist rang the doorbell.

A man, as old as her father, opened the door. He looked at her. Then he took money out of a bag, which was hanging from his waist, and gave it to the rickshaw cyclist. Then with his thick, fat fingers, he took Chinky's arm, pulled her inside, and shut the door. The rickshaw man stayed outside.

The other man pulled her to the back of the house. He opened a door and pushed her inside. She fell on a concrete floor. The man shut the door and locked it with a padlock.

Before realizing it, she stood in a totally dark den. It smelled fuggy and it was cold. It slowly dawned on Chinky what had happened. She was stiff with fear.

After a while, she felt with her fingers along the walls of the den. It felt moist. She discovered that the space was one yard broad and something more than a yard long. She knocked at the door and waited, but she heard nothing. She knocked harder. The only thing she heard was a dull echo. After that, it was silent.

A moment later, she was startled. Something ran over her bare feet; it felt fluffy. Fear strangled in her throat. She was seized by a desperate panic. She called for her father and mother. Then she began to cry.

Much later, the crying passed slowly into a soft sobbing.

After a long time, she was tired. She was hungry and thirsty, as well. She squatted, with her little feet on the concrete floor, her head in her hands. Now and then she went to sleep, only to be frightened awake again by nothing, for there was nothing—except the little fluffy animal that crept over her feet. Chinky peered into the darkness.

After a while, she heard footsteps coming closer. The door was opened. The light in the corridor blinded her. A hand, the fat hand of the man who had locked her in, caught her arm and pulled her into the corridor. He didn't say a word. The man opened the door to the street and pulled her out. He kept clutching her as he shut the door of the house. He pushed her into a little van and tied her wrists with rope behind her back. With the other end of the rope, he tied her ankles together. A dirty rag was put in her mouth and tied up behind her head. The man pushed her further into the van, where she fell onto the steel floor. There were no seats. There was nothing. The back door was slammed shut.

Chinky felt the van start to move. The man drove fast. Holes in the road surface had never bothered her, as she had never seen a road without holes. But now every hole the van rode through made her fly up and land down on the steel floor again. It hurt dreadfully and it made her desperate, as it didn't stop. Again and again, she was thrown up like a sack of rice. The rag in her mouth didn't allow her to scream. She felt like a wounded animal, attacked from all sides by beasts of prey.

Now and then, the man jammed on the brakes, and then accelerated suddenly again.

ED MOOLENAAR

After a while, the stopping and accelerating ceased. There were also fewer holes in the road surface.

Chinky slipped away into unconsciousness.

But then there were holes in the road again, and she was thrown up again, only to fall back harshly. She felt pounded and wounded all over her body. There was no spot left on her body that did not ache.

Then she sank again into an unconscious, dark emptiness.

She awoke now and then. She had no idea of time. She didn't even know whether it was day or night. From the pain, she had become indifferent to what happened outside. The pain had also tired her out terribly. She couldn't even think of her parents anymore.

Chinky had no idea how long she had been in the van. She wasn't even able to think anymore.

The driver got out and opened the back door. He pulled her out of the van.

She fell on the ground. It was dark; she wondered if she was blind. She had no feeling in her hands and feet.

The man lifted her up and carried her into a great shed. It smelled old and sour. Her nose registered the smell of old batteries, of quick lime, of exhausted oil, of ammonia.

The man pulled the dirty rag out of her mouth and loosened her ankles and wrists. He laid her on a sack on the floor. In spite of the pain and a terrible thirst, she fell asleep.

She didn't know how long she had slept. She had been awoken by thirst and pain. It was completely dark. She couldn't see anything at all. She heard rustling everywhere.

Her mouth felt like bark. Her tongue was a thick, dry, leathery rag. She bobbed for hours between sleeping and a smoldering consciousness. She had no idea of time anymore. The worst of all was her horrible thirst, still worse than the pain.

After an endless, dead silence, a rattling at the door startled her. Somebody came in with a broad beam of light. She became mad as she smelled water. The man who had taken her put a plate of rice and a bowl of water next to her on the floor, and without saying a word he left again. He shut the door.

Chinky tried to sit up, but she couldn't. She shoved, with great pain and effort, her hand towards the bowl of water and pushed against it. Water gushed onto the floor. Some drops fell on her hand. Painfully, she brought her hand to her mouth and licked the drops. Water had never been so delicious. She wanted more, but she was afraid to overturn the bowl. She felt carefully to see if the bowl had a handle. Her hand found only a smooth, round surface. Her eyes glared wildly with fever into the total darkness. Water within reach that she couldn't grasp; it made her crazy. She tried to sit upright, but she fell back, half unconscious. She regained, more or less, consciousness. She tried again to sit upright, but a terrible tiredness pinned her to the floor. She wanted to cry, but she had no tears anymore. Then she fell back into a troubled sleep. She could only think that it should be the last time...

She awoke to the divine feeling of water in her mouth. It oozed through her gullet to her stomach. Never before had she felt the delightfulness of water with each cell of her body. She opened her mouth to get more. She yearned for all the water in the world. As she opened her eyes, she saw the man, who had brought the bowl of water earlier. He was holding her mouth open with a finger and pouring water out of the bowl into it. When the bowl was empty, she wanted more.

No more came.

The man formed a little ball of cold, cooked rice and put that into her mouth. She swallowed the wrong way. She couldn't turn herself and was in danger of choking. Her face and neck became purple and blue. The man turned her on her belly. She vomited and fell asleep with her face in the vomit.

Asha had felt uneasy and had decided to go home, although she hadn't sold all her bananas.

Naval saw his mother approaching with her cart of bananas. He ran to meet her. "Chinky has gone off with a strange man and hasn't come back yet," the boy told her.

Asha suddenly felt a steely bandage enclose her chest, and her throat was pinched off. She stood foolishly staring at her son, while her cart with bananas rocketed on. "A strange man!" The words pounded through her head. With the certainty of a mother animal, knowing her nest has been looted before she has seen it, Asha knew that her daughter had been kidnapped.

In the quarter children had already disappeared—a girl of nine and a boy of six. The parents of the girl had gone to the police office.

"Do you know for sure?" they had been asked. "You should wait a few days; perhaps she will come back."

When the boy had disappeared, Ravi had joined the parents at the police office. He would be less easily put off.

"What do you want us to do?" a policeman had asked him. "Can you tell us where we have to look?"

"But you'll get more complaints about missing children," Ravi had answered. "What are you going to do about that?"

"You must listen to me!" the policeman had replied. "Those children of yours are always roaming about, and when one of them disappears, we get to put it right. You should attend to your children better!" The man had turned on his heels and had disappeared behind a door.

Ravi and Asha had already felt the carving pain of the idea that their neighbours had been sentenced to lifelong, torturing uncertainty about the fate of their child. They would never know what had become of their child. How could they ever voice their grief if they didn't even know where to direct it? Even their sorrow was to be smothered in uncertainty.

The news had sentenced the quarter to a paralysing impotence. The only thing people could do was show their compassion to the parents of the child by searching at random, and by endlessly discussing suppositions of all sorts. The people had tried to fill in the grey hole of sadness with talking. But they hadn't words to tell each other what they felt. They didn't even know what to feel. But they did realize it could have been their own child. And they realized that they could only come up short toward parents with such a terrible grief.

The parents of the girl hadn't noticed all this talking; they had retired and secluded themselves from the outer world. Sorrow and feelings of guilt made it impossible to even talk to each other.

This history flashed through Asha's head before she could admit her thoughts on to the horrible message her son had brought her. She could not ask him questions. She forgot her cart of bananas. She even forgot her son. She went, delirious, to river banks. "Where?" she asked Naval, who had followed her.

The boy went to the place where Chinky had sat with the strange man. He had seen the man riding away with Chinky.

Asha followed her son. "Who was it?" she squeezed out of her tightened throat.

"A strange man with a rickshaw."

"Where did he go?"

The boy pointed in the direction of the center of town. Asha went foolishly in that direction. Naval went after her, with anxious questions in his eyes.

Devi came out of the hut and went to her mother. Asha took her hand and held it firmly, to protect her.

Through a mist she saw Naval's pleading look, and she took his hand as well. "A man with a rickshaw?" she asked him. She had become icy calm. "What did he say?"

"I don't know; I only saw him riding away with Chinky."

Asha went on walking about at the place where Chinky had sat. Terror, rage, disbelief, and sorrow pulsed fiercely through her head.

Then she saw Ravi coming. That meant a new pain; she had to tell him that Chinky had disappeared.

Ravi felt the ground give way under his feet. The world became dark before his eyes. He immediately realized what had happened.

His heart missed a beat and his brain stopped for some moments. He needed this short pause; otherwise, he would have gone out of his mind.

They stood, silently and helplessly, face-to-face.

Chinky's little friend came timidly towards them. As everybody was silent, the girl began falteringly to tell them, "It was a dark man with a great, dark moustache and raven-black, long hair. He wore a dirty white scarf round his forehead. I've seen him once before. He gave Chinky an ice cream. This afternoon he went over to Chinky and began to talk to her. He told her a story about a nice man who was fabulously rich and who took care of roving children and got them work. The man had a new rickshaw, a cycle-rickshaw. He promised Chinky that he would show her something, but I don't know what. I also wanted to sit in the rickshaw but I wasn't allowed."

Nobody reacted. The girl fell silent and looked with a mixture of fear and compassion at her friend's parents.

Asha went to the spot where Chinky had sat and showed it to her husband. "A strange man with a rickshaw," whispered a strange, harsh organ in her throat. Her eyes stared lifelessly at the empty place.

Ravi shivered at the desperate, hoarse sound in his wife's voice. He felt a wild need to hold Asha and the two children tight, but he could not. He felt, half-consciously, that he would shut out Chinky by doing so.

A neighbour had found the cart of bananas and brought it back. Asha didn't see it.

Later, sitting before his hut, Ravi was afraid of touching his wife or Naval or Devi; it would feel as though Chinky didn't belong to them anymore. He turned in upon himself. And so did Asha. They sat with broken spirits before their hut. An oppressive, treacly apathy kept them from doing anything. Death appeared to haunt the hut. Naval and Devi looked anxiously at their parents; they didn't know how to react to their passivity. Neighbours observed them from a distance but didn't know how to approach them. They whispered to each other.

The children's stomachs were growling, but they didn't dare to break the silence. Ravi and Asha, however, didn't feel hunger. When Devi started to cry, Asha automatically struck her shoulders. And when Naval or Devi asked for food, she prepared a meal for them in a trance. The children ate.

Ravi went to his work. He swept the corridors and the factory like a robot.

His boss had heard about the Ravi's daughter kidnap. He didn't know what to say. He had no idea how he ought to react to Ravi's sorrow. But Bhikoe could not concentrate his thoughts upon his work. Since Ravi's surprising change, eleven years earlier, Bhikoe had discovered more and more human traits in his sweeper. He had even started calling him by his first name. Now he could sympathize with Ravi's sorrow. He decided to give him half a wage more at the end of the week.

Asha remained home. She knew that she had to stay with the children. For the rest, she gazed into the gray, ruthless emptiness life had become now. She could not and would not imagine what had happened to her child. A total lethargy swamped her. When Naval or Devi asked for a bit of food, she rose. Something in her guided her, so that food found its way onto the plates.

When one of the children leaned against her, she didn't notice. And when Ravi came home, they hardly saw each other. Now and then they had a bite of rice, but they didn't taste food.

They began to grow thin. Ravi had fallen back into his old apathy, and Asha was not able to encourage him because of her own vacant grief. Since Chinky's disappearance they hadn't touched each other. They didn't allow themselves to do so. They could not experience pleasant feelings. Their eyes and their slumped shoulders expressed only a dull despair.

CHAPTER 16

It was the first time Tom Corda had taken part in the New Year's meeting of The Concern's management at full strength. The council of shareholders, the board of governors, and the board of directors, with their secretaries, were all invited for the yearly event in the imposing meeting hall.

People sat behind tables, which were placed in a long rectangle. Waiting passively made some of them a little uneasy.

Everyone in his own way attracted Tom's attention.

A man, who had been introduced to him as the chief of the Packing department, sat ticking his *biro* on the table.

A man of about sixty who had 'Environment' on his portfolio was arranging his papers.

Bill Mocker's assistant in the department of Sales Promotion, a woman in her early fifties with synthetic blond, freshly made up, hairdryer waves, inspected herself closely in a little round mirror.

Charles Bot, personnel manager, looked at short intervals on his watch.

His secretary, sitting at his side, polished her nose with a rose powder puff.

A cameraman had installed his equipment in front of the still empty, high-backed chair that Mr. D would sit in. A battery of microphones had been placed on the table in front of the chair.

Two journalists observed the preparations. A restrained buzzing was almost palpable.

Ruud Lak, who was supposed to lead the meeting, waited at the door for Mr. D's arrival.

In the middle of the hall, in front of Tom, hung a huge painting: it depicted cloudy heavens, glowing by sunset, and in the foreground a flock of wild ducks. The fiercely contrasting colours claimed his attention and invited him to a palette of dreamy fantasies.

One minute too late, Lak announced the arrival of the president of the board of governors, Mr. D.

The buzzing died away into a silence that was charged with expectation.

Mr. D stepped quickly to his chair.

His secretary, Hélène Van Dam, came after him, swaying her hips on high stiletto heels.

Lak shoved the seat of his boss for him backwards, and then forwards again. He sat down between Mr. D and his own secretary, Marianne Hooghuis. Hélène Van Dam sat to the right of her boss.

Lak rose again and timidly broke the silence. He spoke with a flatly intoned voice. "Ladies and gentlemen, I have the honour of giving the floor to the president of the board of governors and chairman of the board of directors, Mr. D." He confirmed his words with a round of applause that was joined by the people in the hall.

Mr. D rose from his seat and smiled at his audience affably from left to right. His deep-set eyes and thick, dark brows intensified the shadowy inward-directed look.

"Ladies and gentlemen!" His words sounded as a kind of order. His voice, with a touch of moral salve in his undertone, resounded metallically through the room. A smoothly shaved chin and powerful jaw made it clear who was in command at The Concern.

"The most important pillars of our policy are: scaling up and a powerful top management. By this policy we saw a yearly increase in our profits. Medimarket, ladies and gentlemen, is growing and will grow forever."

Lak shot upright to bring the microphone for his boss up to mouth level.

Mr. D took a sip of water.

Lak signalled to Mrs. Hooghuis that the glass had to be refilled. Mrs. Hooghuis rose and filled the glass.

Mr. D took another drink of water, and the glass was refilled again.

By the whining sound in Mr. D's voice and by the painting in front of him, Tom had already dozed off to another, dreamy, world. His eyes were attracted by the painting, by the glowing clouds, the sunset, and the flock of ducks that, collectively or directed by instinct, seemed to change their course exactly at the same time, like in a dance.

Nevertheless he still heard Mr. D's voice:

"An elaborate analysis has taught us that the power of the top management should be maximized. Therefore, we must develop new strategies. Certain traditions of deliberation, for example, will prudently be adjusted in favour of quick decision-making at the top. The board of governors implemented brainstorm procedures about decisions taken by the board. Our available electronic means will help us to mould the people's thinking and acting into patterns, being on the same wavelength of our system of undertaking we developed."

The fifth drink of water seemed for Mr. D a step toward the message that had already leaked out. "Ladies and gentlemen, I can inform you that the research of our daughter company Pigor made so much progress that we shall soon be able to save people suffering from incurable heart disease by implanting an animal heart."

These words made Tom's own heart protest. It thumped harder than he was used to.

For a final time, Mr. D looked round, to scrutinize the impression his words had caused.

When Lak rose and applauded, more applause exploded, and Tom's hands joined in.

When, on a sign from Lak, the applause died down, the latter began to speak. "Ladies and gentlemen, I propose we fill our glasses and toast the scientific achievement of our daughter company."

Six girls in impeccable white and sober black were let in to serve the invited people their drinks and snacks behind a long, white-covered table.

Two girls provided Mr. D with a drink first. Hélène Van Dam, at his side, got the second glass.

With a white port in his hand, Tom began to take in the atmosphere in the hall. He didn't feel like talking with anyone. The somehow solemn atmosphere, the chic clothes of the guests, and the earnestness people discussed, emphasized his feeling of not really belonging to this world. Mr. D's last words made him painfully aware of his heart condition. Heart insufficiency, his GP had said. "Your heart has a lack of pumping power and doesn't supply enough oxygen-rich blood and nutrients. That's why you are somewhat short of breath and why you had a little disorder of consciousness last night." That was two months ago, but time had done nothing to ease his mind.

When he heard Bill Mocker's voice, Tom looked behind him. Bill was talking to Hélène Van Dam.

"Mrs. Van Dam, did the inquiry into the lost minutes have any result?"

Mrs. Van Dam frowned, drawing her eyebrows togther to form a warning. She seemed embarrassed by the question. "No, Mr. Mocker, unfortunately not," she whispered. Then she turned her back to Tom, so that he could not understand the rest of the conversation.

Two hours later, Tom sat in Hélène Van Dam's room in an easy chair opposite her.

"Do you want a cup of coffee, Mr. Corda?"

"Yes, please! I've had two glasses of port."

Mrs. Van Dam phoned the kitchen. "Good afternoon, Mrs. Kamat. Will you bring a pot of coffee into my room, please? With some sweets?" Mrs. Van Dam sat down. She set her right knee over her left.

Tom saw her well-formed legs at a strategic level promisingly disappear under a splendid black silk, tight-fitting gown. Around the woman hung a flavour of a precious, naturally female perfume. Her aura of self-consciousness gave an extra distinction to it.

Tom knew Hélène Van Dam from the meetings where she made notes. Then, she had hid herself in a mist of delicate haughtiness.

Her silence gave her an air of superiority. And when Tom had met her in one of the corridors of the building, she had greeted him with a hardly perceptible nod, as if she looked from the stars at one of the many little spots in the space. Therefore, he had been surprised when she had addressed him; he had not expected that she would ever have a chat with one of the ordinary employees. And now she granted him a warm smile. He wondered if he was dreaming.

But Tom was also aware that the woman could bring all her guns into position to make him confess about the lost minutes he had discovered in the library. The paper, it was true, hadn't been taken out of the dictionary, but Tom was convinced that she had left it there to wrong-foot him, as he might not know that she had discovered him having stumbled onto the minutes. She would want to know now whether he had read those minutes or not.

"How do you like working in The Concern, Mr. Corda?"

"I work here with pleasure, Mrs. Van Dam."

"Your function implies a great responsibility; can you manage it?"

"I haven't had the least problems with it."

"I'm glad to hear that. I can tell you that we are satisfied with you as well."

Tom wondered whether these words of praise were an introduction into an interrogation about the minutes in the English dictionary, or whether she really meant what she had said. Besides, he thought the praise rather strange; compliments were unusual in The Concern, compliments for ordinary people, at least. For compliments, there were jubilees and funerals.

"Thank you, ma'am."

Sandy Kamat knocked at the door and came in with a tray of coffee and chocolates. For a split second, her eyes betrayed her surprise at seeing him there. She put the tray on the round table between him and Hélène Van Dam. "This is what you wanted?"

Mrs. Van Dam nodded kindly. Tom's nod to Sandy had something uncertain in it.

After Sandy had gone, Mrs. Van Dam poured coffee into the cups and invited him to take milk, sugar and chocolates. She smiled warmly. Then she put her fingertips of her finely manicured hands together under her chin. "Mr. Corda, we are sending you to Benares with an extremely important mission."

Tom nodded. He wondered what she meant by "we." *Does she speak for the board of governors? Or for her boss? Or does she run the show in the wings?*

"I suppose that you understand the mission."

"Of course! I'm going to evaluate the arranged and executed deliveries, and I'll see if the Indian company can deliver more interesting products, for attractive prices. And I am going to see how the working conditions are."

"You have grasped it well. I would not have expected otherwise. I do not, however, want to talk with you about the products we buy from them. We shall charge you with still another order, an order that's much more important."

Now she will launch into a conversation about the minutes. Tom straightened his back.

Hélène Van Dam studied her fingertips. She looked at Tom again. "Mr. Corda, what do you think about us having dinner together? I mean, in a nice setting, outside the working atmosphere. We can go through your mission once more. What do you think of that?"

Tom had the feeling that his circulation had ceased. His tongue refused orders.

Mrs. Van Dam waited, smiling, for his answer. When she adjusted her position in her chair, Tom's eyes were attracted irresistibly to her legs. He wondered if it was real; if the woman he had seen in his hazy dreams as a high priestess in the holy of the holies of The Concern had really invited him for dinner. He couldn't believe that she was coming on to him. *She wants something from me,* he knew. *Does it concern the minutes? Has she choosen this roundabout way to obtain her purpose? Are those minutes so important? Or so dangerous? Or will she really just talk about my mission? Or what?*

"Okay," he said, when he was able to look into her eyes, "but I will call my wife first. I hope that she hasn't already prepared a meal for this evening."

"You're called Tom, aren't you? Please, call me Hélène," she ordered, more than she asked. But it sounded like a particular favour, as if she would make an exception for him. "Outside The Concern building we don't need to be formal, do we?" she elucidated her favour.

Tom was too surprised to be capable of an adequate reaction. So he was glad that the waiter came to ask if they wanted to have a drink beforehand.

"What do you think of this red wine, Tom?" Hélène showed him the wine in the list.

Tom could only agree.

When the waiter had brought the wine, Hélène insisted on trying it herself before the man filled the glasses. After a lasting, critical look, her nodding changed slowly from tasting to approval.

After the waiter had poured the wine into the glasses, she suggested a toast to a prosperous trip to India. "Tom, enjoy it; you deserve it."

"I shall surely enjoy it."

Hélène took a sip and rounded it off with a second toast.

A beautiful woman," Tom thought, *quite different than I had imagined. Before today, I saw her as an inaccessible beauty. She has always intrigued me. She has something mysterious. She evokes the suggestion that she has something special, without showing what. Her casual, almost haughty look has something provocative. But I don't perceive any haughtiness now.*

As he looked up, their eyes met. He looked admiringly at her smoothly polished face around which he imagined an aura of distinguished elegance. She looked self-conscious. Her black silk gown contrasted perfectly with her silver blond, softly waving hair. The silver round the wrists and round her Nephertiti neck completed a beauty only accessible to gods. There was something in her that he felt attracted to. Hélène Van Dam knew how to suggest and how to provoke a dim, dreamy presumption, and how to set unrelenting limits where the dream of hidden promises started to get too close.

Tom knew, of course, what he did not see; nudity was for him, from his weekly visits to the sauna with Vera, as natural as for a child. But all the same...

He tried to imagine Hélène Van Dam in a steam bath or in a eucalyptus bath. But he knew that he would never meet her in a sauna. She belonged to another world, a world that did not give itself away.

Her narrow waist, her defiantly rolling hips, and her beige-yellow jersey above a dark brown, close-fitting skirt had reminded him of a dinner with Vera.

The waiter had put the plates, with a lot of fuss, in front of them. Discussing the wine with a serious, smooth face, he had just a little too conspicuously played the game of civilized people. With a conventional subservience the man had at last recommended "Poire Belle Hélène" as the final course. The stylish name of the pear had gone on to sing a note in Tom's head.

La Belle Hélène looked now at him with a heavenly smile. He could not believe it. His happy marriage began to dissolve a little in the warm feelings Hélène evoked in him, like sugar in a cup of hot tea.

Hélène ordered another bottle of wine.

Through a mist Tom saw the swell of her bosom against the fringe of her gown. At the same moment, his eyes caught the warm radiance of her face. Lightly clouded by the wine, he felt involved, with heart and soul.

Then all of a sudden he grabbed at his heart. It threatened to run away with him. He felt a stinging pain. He shut his eyes and let his thoughts of the woman in front of him ebb away.

Little by little his heart became quiet.

Hélène Van Dam looked concerned for him. But when he smiled, she toasted with her glass.

After a short pause she launched into the subject she had used as the reason for the dinner, Tom's mission. "Tom, you wrote a letter yesterday to the company in Benares."

"Yes. I asked the manager there if he could receive me next month."

The minutes Tom had found in the English dictionary had sunken into the deeper layers of his consciousness.

"I suppose you also told him what you were coming for."

"Yes, in summary of course. Mr. Lak had already written to him about the aim of my trip."

"I have already told you that you will have another task to fulfil while you are there. That task is quite important for The Concern. Tom, this is going to be a highly responsible mission. Much will depend on your wisdom and your tact."

The conversation between Lak and Huls flashed through Tom's head: "...*exactly the man Mr. D needs...he will not discover there improper anything; in my opinion he is too trusting for that.*" But immediately Tom's thoughts, swimming in a flush, were diverted by the décolleté of the woman before him.

"Tom, the reputation of Medimarket is at stake in your mission."

Now she is going to tell me about the minutes. Tom's thoughts were suddenly clear. He laid his knife and fork down to concentrate his thoughts on what he would now be told.

"Tom, we want you to collect all possible information about the working circumstances and working conditions in that company. Show the manager there that you are particularly interested in the production process and in the people working there. Take photos if you can get permission. And if not, you should try to get your information in another way. Talk to employees as often as you can. Keep your eyes and ears open. You could eventually, inconspicuously, try to get the name of the owner of the company. But give them no inkling of why you want that information."

"Why I want that information."

"Why The Concern wants that information."

Tom nodded thoughtfully.

"Medimarket wants to get to know the company we have already cooperated with there for three years."

Tom waited for more explanation.

That information did not come. Hélène took her glass and toasted him again.

"You can stay there as long as is necessary to get sufficient information."

"May I decide myself when it is sufficient?"

"We leave that to your judgment. But when you get questions about the mission, you can always phone or e-mail me. In view of the difference in time, you may have to call me in the middle of the night."

Hélène didn't seem to notice the surprise her words had caused; she just went on with her instructions. "And when you come back, I want a comprehensive report from you. And that report is confidential. That's to say, you may not speak about it with anyone in or outside The Concern, only with me."

"I understand."

"Tom, I will rely on you. After reading your report I shall discuss it with you, at a nice dinner of course. What do you think of that?"

"It appears to me..." The word Tom was looking for drowned in his flush.

Hélène Van Dam beckoned to the waiter.

"Was it all as you wished, Mrs. Van Dam?" the waiter asked.

"It was excellent. You can send the bill to Medimarket, as usual."

When Tom sat in the back seat of a taxi next to Hélène Van Dam, he wondered if she had found the minutes; she had not said a word about them. He made up his mind. The next day, he would look in the dictionary. But he would have to be very careful. After all, the library was next to her room.

CHAPTER 17

Sudhir was watching TV after dinner: an assembly line product out of Hong Kong with an inimitable, varying tangle of pistol-shooters. One of the men, now and then to the forefront of the screen, attracted attention because of the mechanical way he killed the people around him. The man lacked the least bit of emotion, and he gave the impression that the playful power was due to him by nature. The man showed himself to be a master of life and death.

Sudhir didn't realize the impression it made upon him, still more the man's juggling of his weapon.

Shakti preferred the historical novel she was reading.

Suddenly she said, "I have an appointment tomorrow night with Amal Maya." She went on reading, as though she had told her husband that she would go out shopping.

Sudhir, however, reacted as if he had been bitten by a viper. "Amal Maya? Why?"

"To discuss your problem." Shakti didn't look up from her book.

"My problem? But it is not up to you to arrange that!"

"To whom else should it fall then?"

"What do you mean?"

"Something has to be done. You cannot run the risk of the publication of a story about your kidney transplant. And if you do what Maya wants and are going to transplant a kidney from a healthy person, you will be completely at his mercy; then you can't plead ignorance anymore."

"I am already at his mercy; I've promised him that I'll do it."

"A promise made under coercion."

"I had only one day to make the decision."

"And if you had refused?"

"Then he undoubtedly would have leaked the story about my illegal kidney transplant. I could have pleaded ignorance, of course; but then I would have the reproach that I had not tested properly to see if the brain-dead man was really brain-dead."

"Still, that would have been much less serious than the charge of deliberately transplanting the kidney of a healthy man."

"You're right," Sudhir sighed, "but do you think you can do anything? And aren't you reluctant to meet that man?"

"Sure I am! Like meeting a rat! But I don't see any other solutions."

Sudhir looked foggily at his hero on the screen. The problem had kept haunting him. "Shall I join you?"

"I'd better go alone. Maybe I can take advantage of it."

"You won't let yourself...?"

"No!" she screamed. "Please, don't worry about that! The idea already holds a nightmare for me."

She had chosen a dark green sari which suited her and showed to herself to her full advantage. She wore the ornaments she had received from Sudhir at their marriage: a simple, dark silver necklace which accentuated her slender neck, and silver bracelets and anklets. Little silver rings decorated the middle toes of her feet. She had stuck a dark red *tica* on her forehead. For her this meant a symbol of spiritual susceptibility. She wondered if Amal Maya would see it as other than a beauty mark. She had painted the parting of the hair above the *tica* with red ochre, accentuating the fact that she was a married woman.

Maya's chauffeur took her to a restaurant, the place where the meeting was to take place. A servant was waiting for her. The man was dressed in white silk clothes: gloves, wide trousers under a long coat with red piping. His head was covered with a red cap. On his feet he wore red slippers with high-pointed tips. He looked quite serious as he showed her to a table.

Shakti saw Amal Maya sitting with his back to the wall, an introverted look at his face.

Maya and the wall will be my view for the rest of the evening, Shakti thought.

He rose and greeted her, bowing his head as he saw her. His balding crown attracted her attention. She saw two precious golden rings inlaid with diamonds on his thick fingers. The waxen smile on his face meant nothing to her, though she knew that subtle touches could give it completely different meanings. Now it was the wheedling smile of a man courting a woman by showing his wealth.

The servant had pulled her seat back. She sat down in front of Maya.

Maya snapped his fingers and asked the man for the wine list. The waiter carrying the wine lists and menus, wearing the same dress as the other waiter, came to offer the wine list to Maya and his guest.

"I am happy, madam, that you accepted my invitation. I thought I had something to make up for, being forced to let you wait last time. That's why I offer you dinner. I hope you will enjoy it as much as I do."

"I appreciate it very much, Mr. Maya, that a man in your position is willing to spend so much time with me. I can tell you that I see this as a great honour." Shakti granted him a bewitching smile.

Maya's face radiated. He foresaw a delicious evening. Then he looked at the wine list. "Madam, I almost forgot my duty as a host. Forgive me, please. Would you like to choose yourself, or may I recommend a special wine to you?"

Shakti, who never drank alcohol, left the choice to him.

"Okay! I propose we order this red wine, as an introduction to our dinner." Maya pointed to a very costly wine.

Shakti wondered if Maya was a connoisseur. "This is an expensive wine, Mr. Maya," she answered timidly.

"Oh, that is nothing!" Maya waved away her objection with a generous gesture of his hand.

Two waiters, dressed in white, with white gloves, served the wine.

Maya insisted on tasting it. "I want to be sure," he explained, "that you will get the very best tonight."

As the waiters, one with the bottle in his hand and a white napkin over his wrist, the other with a corkscrew and a white napkin as well, stood demonstrating their neutrality as silent sentries. Maya took his glass, waited for a moment, and then brought the glass to his nose. He smelled it, looking reverent, and took a careful sip. He closed his eyes, waited again, and tasted with an expert look.

Waiting for the result, Shakti became slightly tense.

After a long pondering, Maya ended the ritual by carefully moving his head in a slight turn from the left to the right and back again. "Yes, I may offer you this wine."

The waiter with the bottle passed behind her and poured her glass half-full, then did the same with Maya's glass. The man didn't move a muscle of his face, as little as the waiter who kept guard standing with the corkscrew.

Maya raised his glass. "May I drink to your well-being, madam?"

Shakti raised her glass as well and smiled encouragingly.

They drank the wine.

She gave a yelp of delight. "What a delicious wine!" Not used to alcohol, she tried to hide the fright of her first drink. *I must be careful,* she realized, *I'm not used to alcohol and I don't know the influence of this wine.*

Amal Maya was proud and glad. "Madam, you'll lack nothing this evening. Only the best is good enough for you." He took a gulp of wine.

Shakti sipped from her glass. "Mr. Maya, I am not as experienced a drinker as you are. You should not see this as a lack of appreciation."

"Absolutely not, madam! I only want you to enjoy this evening." Maya took another gulp of wine.

"Do you think me impertinent if I ask you to call me Amal?" Maya gave her a roguish look; his face didn't show any doubt.

"You are very forward," she said, lowering her eyes.

"It is a little fast indeed, but I have only the intention to make it more pleasant still."

"Do you know, Mr. Maya? It is difficult for me to call a man like you by his first name."

Maya smiled. "I know. There are other people who also find it difficult. That is a drawback of my position, the distance from ordinary people. That sometimes makes me feel lonely." There was an emotional sound in his voice and a shroud of sadness lay on his face.

"Well, if I can do you a favour, I will try." Shakti looked timidly at him.

"You will do me a great favour, madam; or may I say Shakti?"

She wondered how he knew her first name. "It is a great honour for me, Mr. Maya."

"Mr. Maya?"

"It is very unusual for me, Mr. Maya."

"Amal,?" He laughed encouragingly.

"Amal," she said timidly. She bent her head. "I feel honoured that you invited me."

He smiled at her.

Halfway through the rich and varied meal, Shakti mentioned the matter she had accepted Maya's invitation for. "Mr. Maya."

"Amal, isn't it?" He smiled naughtily.

"Amal, I will not intrude upon the pleasant evening, but nonetheless I want to ask your attention about a problem I have not yet found a good solution for."

Now that he smelled business, he was again the Maya she knew. She recognized the sly little glints in his eyes.

"I knew you hadn't found a way, but I am happy that you see it as well." Maya took a gulp of wine and he casually snapped his fingers at one of the waiters.

Shakti noted that this was the seventh time his glass had been refilled. Maya showed this also; his face was red and it seemed more swollen than it was at the beginning of the evening. He had also become more frank with her; he had tried to put a foot against hers, after which she had pulled her foot back while distracting him with a smile. She knew these casual contacts, these risk-free attempts of men who want the enjoyment, but not the chance of a refusal.

Shakti asked herself if the moment, chosen by her, was suitable for launching into her problem. She did not know the primitive drive of Maya's power instinct, and she wondered if this instinct would dissolve in alcohol or rather would become more ferment.

"You are very powerful, and you are the only one who can solve our problem," she said with a flattering sound in her voice.

Touched by her admiration and under the influence of the wine, Amal Maya was swollen with pride. He smiled. "You understand me very well. I appreciate that."

She gave him an admiring look. "You are famous for helping mankind. Therefore, I dare to appeal to you and to ask for your help. You do not wish my husband to lose his practice?"

Maya showed a modest pride on his face, as to a naughty girl who had spoken defiantly. "But I shall protect your husband. You know that."

"Only if he renders you a service..."

"I will help mankind, as you said. I will help somebody to get a healthy kidney."

"At the cost of the health of another healthy person?"

"That person gives his kidney voluntarily and he will be amply paid for it,"

"You know it is illegal, what you are proposing?"

"I do nothing illegal; I only mediate between two people who are both looking for help. One seeks a healthy kidney; the other one needs money. Besides, I shall take care that the donation will be legalized."

"But my husband could get into trouble by doing this."

"I want to prevent him from getting into trouble."

"You can prevent that, if you will not let leak it out."

"A leak can arise without me."

"If you don't want a leak, there will be no leak."

Amal Maya was confused. He beckoned the waiter responsible for the wine, to have his glass refilled, although the glass wasn't yet empty. He took a gulp and tried to restore his dignity by sitting more upright. "Shakti, you are right," he said with emotion in his voice. "If I don't want a leak, there will be no leak. You see that well. I am able to prevent it. I promise you that there will be no leak, but in return I expect that your husband will help me in my efforts to serve mankind."

Shakti felt herself to be in a labyrinth in which she, looking for a way out, arrived for the umpteenth time at the same point. It began to dawn on her that the man before her was convinced of his humanity, and that the thought of making a profit from the kidney transplants was now washed away with alcohol. She asked herself how she could persuade him to be a benefactor without self-interest. Then she had an idea.

"Do you know the story of the poor Brahmin Sudama?"

"No."

"I am going to tell you."

"I like to listen to you." Amal looked tenderly at her.

Shakti told him the story of Sudama, who was very poor. He couldn't even give his wife and his children food and drink. And she told him how badly he suffered as a result of this, especially because his young children had to suffer hunger innocently and he could do nothing about it.

Then one day, a certain Krishna came to the village Sudama and his family lived in. Krishna was hungry and asked for some food. Sudama's wife said to her husband that he should go and help Krishna. And Sudama went to Krishna with a handful of rice, gave him the rice, and asked for nothing in return. When Sudama went back home, his meagre hut had been changed into a great, splendid house, and his family was rich and happy."

Amal Maya smiled. All sorts of images moved through his drunken brain. *What Sudama did, I could try as well,* he thought in a whirl of alcoholic excitement. He controlled his drunken fit with some difficuly. He bent toward Shakti. He cleared his throat. "I shall show you that I can be good as well, like Sudama. Your husband can rely on my protection. I shall take care that there will be no leak."

Shakti rewarded her host with a particularly charming smile. "Mr. Maya."

"Mr. Maya? What should you call me?"

"Amal. I thank you for your magnanimity. I knew you would help us. But I am still happy that I've not been mistaken about you. You are really the man I imagined from the beginning."

Her words worked like massage oil. *This woman knows how to appreciate my qualities,* Amal Maya thought. *Magnanimity! Yes, that's the right word.* Maya was seized by a delicious feeling. *Here is someone who appreciates me; magnanimity, that's it; magnanimity, yes; I am magnanimous...*Amal Maya forgot to drink. He looked at Shakti with a blissful glance. "I am really glad that I can help you and your husband. Do you know that your husband's problem has occupied my mind all this time? I was terribly concerned for him."

Shakti smiled once again and sipped a drop of wine.

Her smile lured Maya a step further. "You should not misunderstand my proposal, Shakti; I hope you don't."

The intimacy in the tone in which he pronounced her name made Shakti close her eyes; but she especially feared what he was going to tell her next.

"What do you think of having a drink and a cosy chat in my house after we have finished our dinner?"

Shakti lowered her eyes modestly. "Oh, Mr. Maya...Amal, I feel honoured by this proposal. But you know that I, as a married woman, cannot go to another man's house without asking for trouble. Actually, I have already gone too far by appearing in public with another man. My husband was very concerned; he knows your charm. I could only convince him by telling him that it would be an innocent meeting tonight. Otherwise, he absolutely would not have consented. Accompanying you to your house? And so soon? No, I can't afford to do this."

"An innocent meeting," Maya's sultry voice whispered.

"It was a wonderful evening and I enjoyed it very much. You were a terrific, generous and charming host. I thought it a privilege to sit at a table with you. And I can assure you that I do not regret accepting your invitation at all. But if I went with you, I would spoil everything."

"Nonetheless I hope that this delightful evening will have a sequel."

"So do I," Shakti answered with a smile. "But I don't dare to promise you anything."

"Then I shall give the order to take you home now."

Maya beckoned the waiter and told him to call his chauffeur, who was waiting in the parking area.

CHAPTER 18

It slowly dawned on Shakti that the sound she heard, from a dreamily vague somewhere, was the sound of the telephone. Her hand groped sleepily for the receiver.

"Can I come to see you?" Sarásvati's voice woke her up.

"Yes, of course!" she almost shouted. "I'll get dressed."

She felt relieved; Sarásvati was one of the few people who was able to sympathize with her. Besides, she and Sarásvati had both been alarmed when Maya had appeared on the stage, and they had tuned their thoughts intuitively. They needed each other, and they knew this.

Shakti took a shower, got dressed, and ate a bit of the breakfast Ragu had prepared for her.

Sarásvati was shocked when she saw Shakti's face. "You are not sick, are you? It seems as though you've got a fever."

"I got sick by sitting for a whole evening in front of Maya," Shakti replied with a faint smile. "I've a terrible hangover; he raised an anger in me I can't free myself from. I've got the feeling that a parasite is devouring me from inside."

Shakti told her friend about her dinner with Maya.

"How could you endure it?"

"I don't know, but I didn't see another way out. And he promised me that he will take care that Sudhir's illegal operation will not leak out."

"That is not a guarantee, though."

"Of course not! But as long as he is convinced that he can make a pass at me, we can feel more or less safe. It's my only trump card."

"How can we fight this man?" Sarásvati asked.

"Smoothness doesn't offer much grip," Shakti said.

"Fighting stupidity is like mud-fighting."

"Unless you know your adversary's vulnerability."

"His self-satisfaction," Sarásvati answered. "Because of his power and wealth people will do anything for him, women as well. He fancies that they fall for his charm. So he thinks himself able to charm me as well. That self-satisfaction is our only chance. Although the thought of it drives demons through my dreams, I shall react to his courtship, up until a certain point…"

Shakti looked questioningly at her friend.

"I have begun to realize," Sarásvati went on, "that Amal Maya's empathy is too limited to allow him to imagine a higher form of intelligence than his own. Is a human being able to imagine other people with a higher developed intelligence than he has himself? As the prisoners in Plato's cave saw the people's shadows as the real people, because they had never seen any thing else than shadows, so can Maya's knowledge not reach further than his own shaded brain; there is in his view no higher form of intelligence than what he can experience. He can't grasp real human intelligence. I mean, he cannot do anything other than value us according to his own standards. If you feel underestimated by him, you value him too highly; you expect too much from him."

Shakti hesitated. "He has got a powerful weapon, hasn't he?"

"We can try to neutralize that weapon with our own weapon."

"Flattering and flirting. But I shudder at the very thought that he imagines I see anything in him."

"Is his opinion important to you?"

"If he did not have us in his power, then maybe."

"We must get him in our power."

"I think you are right."

"As long as he thinks that he can get you with his charm, he will not throw away his chances by causing problems."

"So we must keep him dangling."

"Yes. That is what I am going to do."

"How do you mean?"

"Maya offered me a job."

"What?"

"Yes, he did. I tore his letter to pieces in an outburst of anger. But I've changed my mind. I'm going to accept the job."

"Are you? What sort of job is it?"

"Private secretary."

"The job he offered you before?"

"Yes. I shall be charged with the phone calls in and out. I must take care of the mail. I am going to play hostess when people come to see him. I must take care of personal administration. I shall get a room next to his."

"What?"

"Yes. But I'll keep him at a distance."

Shakti was surprised by the laconic demeanour of her friend. "If necessary, you can rely on me of course!"

"Our friendship should not be too conspicuous; don't forget that Maya has his tentacles everywhere."

"So if I understand your intentions, you are going to spy on him," Shakti said.

"Perhaps I shall get some information we can use."

"I think it heart-warming that you will do this; but be careful, please! Amal Maya will not give you delicate information if he doesn't trust you. And how would you get his trust, if you keep him at a distance? Maya thinks he has a right to everything and to everybody."

"I shall be able to keep him at a distance now that I have control of myself. His boasting and his vanity annoyed me terribly. But I realize now that I was annoyed because I felt, unconsciously, underestimated by him."

"As he supposed that you didn't see through him..."

"Exactly! But now I can laugh about it and feel able not to spoil his illusions."

"Don't forget either," Shakti impressed on her, "that he wants you, and not the reverse. He offered you a job, as he sees you as an attractive woman. Keep that in mind! He needs you. Take care that this doesn't change. If you should agree to his advances—forgive me for saying this—the relationship would fundamentally change. Then you would become an object he could play with at will. Spoiled people think their plaything most attractive as long as it is wrapped up. Keep him believing that you mean a lot to him, and the more he has to do to get you, the more that you will mean to him. Keep believing that he needs you. But be careful; for a spoiled person who doesn't get what he wants may lose his self-control."

"I'll be careful. But do not forget yourself what you have advised me." Sarásvati laid her arm round her friend's shoulders. "And don't forget either that you are named after the goddess who grants you meaningful and vital strength."

"I'm glad with this advice from the woman who is named after the goddess of wisdom," Shakti answered laughing.

A rickshaw cyclist brought Sarásvati up to the gate. She had declined Amal Maya's offer to be collected by his chauffeur.

A police officer in a khaki uniform, a baton in his right hand, commanded the watching policeman to attention. He put his rubber stick under his armpit and greeted Maya's new secretary. Standing at attention with his right hand at his cap, he spoke in a dignified manner, "Mr. Maya ordered me to attend you to his office." He brought his hand down with a rigid motion, took his baton in his right hand and stamped his right foot half a metre away from his left. Then he asked, "Mrs. Arora, would you follow me, please?" He turned by raising his right leg forty centimetres from the ground, swung it to the right, put it down, and put his left leg next to it.

Maya had stationed a police officer to wait for Mrs. Arora at the entrance to his terrain. He would accompany her to his office.

Sarásvati saw the ritual as an introduction to a display of male behaviour. Although stupefied, she nodded her head affably, as though this reception was a daily routine for her. She walked next to the policeman who marched along, his rubber stick in his left hand rhythmically swaying in time with his other arm, all the way along the long drive to the main entrance. She suppressed the inclination to take the rhythm over. *I must remain myself in all circumstances,* she decided. So she walked at ease over the drive between the young neem trees, cypresses, tamarindes, casuarinas, fig trees and all sorts of other trees and plants.

The police officer stood to attention again, put his baton under his left armpit and rang the doorbell.

When a servant in uniform opened the door, he spoke in a dignified way: "Please, go in, madam."

Sarásvati went in.

As she looked around, the policeman preceded her, the rubber baton in his right hand.

So the thing serves not only to hit poor devils; it has a ceremonial function as well, Sarásvati concluded.

The policeman was aware of the importance of his task. He led the way without saying a word. His earnest look seemed programmed.

She had difficulty keeping up with him. Meanwhile, she had an abundance of impressions; the mosaics in the splendid floor tiles, the paintings of gods and goddesses on the walls, the servants with their red turbans, yellow *kurtas* and white gloves, walking about everywhere. Shakti had already told her about the wealth; but it was too abundant to absorb in such a short time. Only the gigantic portrait of Maya halfway up the marble stairs was so overwhelming that her eyes could not avoid it.

The policeman halted in front of a heavy, walnut-brown vanished door, went in and reported to duty, standing at attention and with his right hand at his cap. Then he gave his message. "Here is Mrs. Arora to see you, Mr. Maya." The man remained standing to attention like a statue, his hand at his cap.

Amal Maya rose and came from behind his desk to the door to welcome his new secretary. He put his fingertips together at under of his chin and bowed slightly. "I bid you welcome, Mrs. Arora. I highly appreciate the fact that you have decided to accept my offer. Would you allow me to use your first name?"

Sarásvati needed some time to find a suitable reaction, as she had not expected such a direct confrontation. "Excuse me, Mr. Maya, I am not used to being addressed by my first name at my work." Her answer sounded polite. But she didn't betray anything of her feelings.

"But I thought my friend, Dr. Varma, called you Sarásvati."

"That's right. I was only sixteen when I started working for him."

"You are not yet married; are you?"

"Not yet, Mr. Maya."

"When are you going to marry?"

"My father and my fiancé's father are still negotiating the date."

"Your father hasn't any problems with the dowry, I hope?"

"Absolutely not!" Her tone was flat and formal.

Maya realized that his interference in this question was not appreciated. So he decided not to go on into the matter. He switched to another subject. "You would prefer maybe that I confine myself to the non-personal on the first day in your new job," he said with a faint, uncertain smile.

And then to the policeman, who was still standing to attention with his baton under his armpit, he said, "You may go!"

In his life Amal Maya had not experienced much resistance; he had not learned how to handle it. To the people in his service, his wishes were orders.

But the two women he had met now were different. He thought their attitude stimulating and defiant, but this made him also uncertain. He didn't worry about Mrs. Varma anymore; she had accepted his invitation to dinner and had been deeply impressed during that dinner. He already looked forward to the next meeting. *But I've misjudged this young woman,* he admitted to himself. *She behaves as though she owes nothing to me. I offered her a splendid job. Here she can live like a former maharajah's wife, but she doesn't seem to be aware that she is my subordinate from now on. And if she becomes my wife,* he went on to dream, *she remains my subordinate. Oh, she is still young,* he told his vanity, *she must be impressed by the new situation. It must be a fairy tale, mustn't it? To be the private secretary of such a powerful man, as powerful as a maharajah. And, moreover, to be allowed to work in such a splendid house, in such a palace. She must be surprised; I must give her time. I must be patient. What woman could resist my offer? I shall find out which man her father found for her. And I must make arrangements to interfere; I will not share her with anybody else. But, for now, I must be practical.*

Maya changed his tone. Somewhat chilly, he said, "I'll show you your office and tell you what you will have to do here." He opened a door that was next to his desk. "After you," he said politely.

Sarásvati saw a room, not bigger than a quarter of that of Maya's, but bigger than she was used to. She smelled fresh paint in the air. To her right she saw a small, low table and two seats. On the other side were a desk and an adjustable chair. On one of the walls hung a copy of a picture of the goddess Durga, riding her tiger. A thick carpet covered the floor.

"I've had the room repainted. The colours are now more attuned to a woman with a refined taste. I have also ordered the furniture to be replaced. I hope it will please you. Until last week, it was Mr Shah's room. I gave him another function."

"It could have been my own choice," Sarásvati replied with a controlled enthusiasm. "I think I can work here quietly."

"About your work," Maya said, hooking into her words. "You will take care of the incoming telephone calls, and you are supposed to check the outgoing calls of my other employees. You will look after the incoming and outgoing letters. You will arrange my appointments. And you will manage the personal administration. Finally, I expect you to act as a hostess for important guests. You understand that your function is quite confidential."

"I understand that very well; I am used to dealing with confidential information, Mr. Maya."

"Avih Shah, your predecessor, will give you instructions about your work. You will understand that I cannot concern myself with these kinds of details. But I shall show you the rest of my house. I occupied myself personally with the building, arrangement and furnishing."

Maya preceded her. He showed her the house temple of Durga which was opposite his office. He told her emotionally about his favourite goddess.

Next to the house temple were Maya's private rooms.

The windows in the delightful living area offered a grand view over the river Ganges to the east and to the south.

While her feet sank into the woollen carpet that covered the whole room, Sarásvati looked down at the Holy River, like she had never seen it before. The water, quietly rippling with the rays of the afternoon sun to the north, would have tempted her to a meditative rest if Maya hadn't been there.

Maya enjoyed the magnificent view in the mirror of her admiring eyes. "What do you think of this?"

"I only now see how beautiful the river is," she whispered.

"You have a splendid view from this room, don't you think so?"

"Sure!" Sarásvati said, still a little dreamy from the beauty of the river. "It is also because of the lovely sun shining on the rippling water and of the colourful life along the river. I could look at this for hours."

But as she had no eye for the wealthy furnishing of the room and no ear for the enthusiastic musings of the owner, Maya was slightly disappointed. "We have no time for the river now. I'll show you the rest of the house."

They went into a huge kitchen, where Maya's wife gave instructions to three men. The woman greeted her shyly.

Sarásvati thought she saw a misty glimpse of fear in her shaded, jet-black eyes when she looked at her husband. The precious, purplish-flaming sari, draped over long, straight hair, seemed, in spite of the beauty of the woman, not really to be in tune with her. With her hunched shoulders, she gave the impression of being an oppressed being.

"That is my wife," Maya told Sarásvati. He ignored his wife and directed Sarásvati's attention to the expensive kitchen equipment.

Maya's wife waited in a corner, surveying the scene with sad eyes.

"It would be nice to cook in here!" Sarásvati thought this to be a desirable compliment.

"If you wish to do so, I shall give you the opportunity with pleasure, and I shall place a number of assistants at your disposal as well."

"But I can't cook at all!" Sarásvati laughed. "I should better assist the cook."

"That is out of the question! I can't allow you to assist someone of a lower caste."

When he had showed her all his fine things and she had rewarded him with a compliment, for the sake of the unsteady equilibrium of their relationship, he led her back to her room. He called Avih Shah from behind his own desk to give the man the order to instruct his successor, Mrs. Arora, about her new tasks.

The man reported to him almost immediately and bent deeply. Maya sent him to the room that had been his.

Sarásvati heard a chilly sound in Avih Shah's voice as he greeted her. "Namaskar, Mr. Shah," she greeted him in return. "I am sorry that you have lost your position; I didn't know I was going to replace you."

Avih Shah shrugged his shoulders. "I've got other good work to do: controlling the housekeeping. But your job is the most important one. You'll get to know so much here that I would advise you to keep yourself ignorant of. Being silent is my most important quality. But you've got another quality which any man would lack." His whispering voice had an ironic undertone.

Sarásvati apologized once more and proposed that they start work.

Shah took a pile of letters from her desk. "Each morning, one of your tasks will be to take the letters out of the box, to read them, and to tell Mr. Maya about the contents of them. He will tell you then what you have to answer. So take care to always have pen and paper with you."

Avih Shah explained to her how the central telephone worked, and he told her how to deal with Amal Maya's agenda. "The personal administration and the wages records shall take much of your time. There are twenty-two people in Mr. Maya's service, working in and round his house. Besides those, there are a number of people who work as freelancers. These people—police officers, tax officials, politicians and the like—provide him with important information. Mr. Maya is the only one who knows what they do. There is only a wage list pertaining to these people. And then there is a network of people, who figure on no lists at all. But you'll get to know them, as they often come to see Maya."

CHAPTER 19

After passing through customs control, Tom Corda felt relieved. There were two thousand American dollars in his bag—'development money' from the Medimarket's Maya Foundation for the Maya Foundation in Benares. The customs official had raised a number of inconceivable, bureaucratic obstacles, but he had at last given permission to go on, as Tom had solved the problem with a hundred rupees note in his passport.

Outside the airport building, he felt and smelt Mumbay. The sickening smells of sewers, exhaust fumes and other indefinable things, smothered in the sultry, heavy evening warmth of the town, gave him the impulse to fly back. But he knew he would get used to the numbing smells and to the pandemonium of the innumerable anonymous figures, screaming and fighting for priority in traffic. Animals and human beings all tried to find a path, as though they were swarming around a giant ant's nest.

The taxi driver put Tom's case into the boot of his old Ambassador and started the car. The man zigzagged through the traffic. Tom knew the crazy hurry of Indians in traffic, but he nevertheless felt relieved when they arrived.

In the hotel he was received with kind regards. A boy insisted on bringing his case to his room, and waited there with great questioning eyes for a tip.

Tom stretched the mosquito curtain over his bed. Then he wrapped himself in a sheet. When he felt that sleep would not come, he tried to read. But his eyes registered the words without his awareness of what he was reading. With the book on his chest, he lay staring at the humming fan above him. The apparatus provoked his confused jetlag feeling. He sunk into a dejected mood. He didn't even know whether it was a feeling or the lack of a feeling. His thinking seemed stripped. The room felt like a prison cell. He missed Vera and Rose and he felt the need to call them, but he had already tried and the interference had not left him much hope.

About six o'clock he fell asleep.

After two days in Mumbay seeing friends, the trip to Delhi was successful. Reserving a train journey from there to Varanasi didn't, however, go off as he had planned. He waited for an hour and a half in front of the window in the New Delhi Railway Station.

"The train to Varanasi is fully booked for several days, sir," the counter clerk told him, his teeth fixed together. Tom decided to take a plane.

"The flight for tomorrow afternoon has been cancelled, sir. I can put you on the waiting list for Friday." The man could not guarantee that Tom would get a place even then.

Satori had gained some more wrinkles. Her face relaxed in an open laugh as she recognized Tom.

Later, when he sat on a mat in front of Satori and Soedjata, it seemed to him as though he had never been away.

After they had exchanged their stories, Tom asked after Asha and Ravi.

Satori bent her head before answering the question. She needed a long introduction to tell Tom the news. "The last time you were in Varanasi, you were in their new hut where they lived with their children. They were quite happy. They had developed themselves from submissive beings to people able to feel and think independently. Unfortunately, their happiness was ruined."

"What do you mean?"

"Their daughter Chinky has been kidnapped."

Tom was instantly overrun by smothering sadness, anger and dejection; sadness because of his friends and of their beautiful, open-minded child. The child came vividly to mind. A little girl, promising an eternal beauty. Fresh innocence. Little stars in her sparkling eyes. A child with an unblemished confidence in life and a great susceptibility for new impressions. A child totally adjusted to discovery and astonishment. With little arms created for a close embrace. Perfect velvety-tender skin. Her engaging smile had given Tom a warm feeling the last time he had seen her.

But now he felt anger flare up in himself because of the anonymous, powerful and unscrupulous figures who had casually destroyed every spark of happiness for these poor people.

"How is this possible?" was all he could say at last.

"We don't understand it either." The faces of Satori and Soedjata were as sad as Tom's.

"Can we go to them?" Tom asked.

"Okay. Next week."

The next morning, Tom sat on his mat before Satori again.

"It is good that you have come back," she said.

"My boss had something for me to do in Varanasi. But more than that, I felt the need to get away from work for a while."

"Why?"

"It is rather oppressing to me."

"Would you tell me about?"

"I always have the feeling that I may not make a mistake there. As though everyone is keeping an eye on me and has a red pencil behind his ear."

"People cannot make works of art only using a red pencil."

"Unless it was a massacre," Tom said. "But it is not yet that bad in The Concern."

"Have you spoken about your feelings there?"

"What could I hope to achieve in such a powerful concern?"

"You could find that your position in that powerful concern might become clearer; above all for yourself."

"They should not be grateful for that."

"Do you wish them to be grateful or do you wish them to respect you?"

"I must think about that."

"What had your boss got to do for you here?"

"He wants me to make inquiries in a pharmaceutical enterprise of an unknown rich man from which Medimarket obtains medicines."

"The company of Amal Maya?"

"Is that the name of the rich man?"

"I think he is the owner. Actually, nobody is sure about that. It is, however, sure that Amal Maya controls many enterprises in and round Varanasi, and probably he is also the owner of the pharmaceutical company you are talking about."

"Has the Maya Foundation been called after him?"

"Maya Foundation? I've never heard about that."

"I've got a lot of money with me for the Maya Foundation. The Medimarket people call it development money."

"The only thing I can tell you for sure is that, if the Maya Foundation has been called after Amal Maya, that foundation has nothing to do with helping poor people."

"I am going to make an appointment with Amal Maya."

"I hope that you will succeed; making an appointment with Amal Maya is like asking for an audience with a king."

Life had passed over Ravi and Asha without their being aware of what happened around them. Their feelings were petrified, with the memories of their daughter. They did vacantly what had to be done to keep their two remaining children alive. For the rest, they were squatting in front of their hut, like strangers to themselves and to each other. Dim eyes gazed out of their hollow faces. Nobody addressed them. The people who had tried this after Chinky had disappeared had gotten no reaction. The inhabitants of the quarter had gradually confined themselves to compassion. But also that compassion faded away, as Ravi and Asha faded away themselves. They sat gazing ahead like inanimate strangers, like drugged beings.

Even Satori had not been able to give these two people a spark of life, in spite of all her affection and patience. She came every week. She laid her arms round their shoulders, but she didn't get the least reaction. Sometimes she spoke, but there came never an answer. She had done this for more than two years, and she intended to go on doing it, for she thought these two people were worth it.

Ravi lay as usual on his back staring into the darkness until deep in the night. He had no idea what time it was and it didn't interest him. Then, all of a sudden, there was a bright light in the hut. A radiant being stood before him.

Ravi knew it was Radha, the loving force of Krishna. Radha or Radharana, infinitely more beautiful than the goddess he had often seen in sweet colours on pictures and paintings, radiated a mild love.

Ravi felt attracted by an overwhelming force.

The goddess laid her hands on his shoulders. "Ravi, open yourself to your sadness and your anger."

A soul-warm force streamed then in a healing silence through him and his frozen feelings began to relieve. He felt an agreeable sparkling through his whole body, as in his first dream many years earlier. The rigidity in his shoulders began to ease. In his lifeless eyes began two little stars to glimmer. He felt the tension of his paralysing sorrow flow out of his body. He experienced a relieving feeling; it was as though he, after a long time, could draw breath again. The grief at the loss of his child was still unimaginably smarting, but he realized now that he had to give it a place in the eternal rhythm of arising and going down. His grief was embedded now in a new feeling for what was good and nice.

After the goddess had disappeared, Ravi and Asha woke up.

They lay, silent and relaxed, next to each other on their sleeping mats.

"I had a dream," Ravi said, astonished at the fact that he had talked to his wife.

"So had I," Asha answered. She was also astonished that the words came so easily out of her mouth.

She told him about her dream, and Ravi told her what he had dreamt. They noticed that they were filling up each other's stories; they had had the same dream.

When Ravi looked at Asha, he saw a little spark of the old glow coming back into her eyes. But when he began to say this to her, she was ahead of him. "Your eyes have a glow again."

Their thoughts went out to their daughter, but were no longer locked in frozen memories; now they could think freely of what could have happened to her. They admitted, with a scorching pain, to all sorts of possibilities. Only now they dared to ask themselves where their daughter could be, and in whose hands. The pain cut razor-sharp through their souls, but they understood that they had to go through that pain.

Ravi started to stroke Asha's shoulders and her hands, as he had not yet done before. He felt the tension in her easing. And Asha felt cherished and solaced by her husband's stroking hands. She even began to feel it as agreeable; a sense of guilt kept her from enjoying it completely.

Since Chinky's disappearance, every enjoyment had been taboo; it would have felt as a denial of their child.

But now she could leave room to her grief and her anger. The first tears broke through and trickled down her cheeks, and Ravi encouraged them by embracing her. They started to cry together. There came a beginning of confidence in their life, and with that came a new hope. Had the goddess not spoken about hope? Hadn't she?

Satori and Tom took a taxi. Satori tried to prepare Tom for the sorrow he would be confronted with.

Ravi and Asha sat on their heels in front of their hut. Satori greeted them and sat down with them.

Tom could scarcely recognize his friends. He had heard about what they had experienced, but he had not been able to imagine the changes in them that it would have wrought.

Then he saw Asha with a sad smile looking at her husband and taking his hand. Ravi reacted sadly. Tom felt there was something special on at hand.

After an hour, they looked back and saw Ravi and Asha sitting and holding each other's hands.

"You saw a miracle," Satori said. "Since the kidnap of their daughter they have had no contact with each other; this was the first time they could get back in touch with each other. This is the beginning of their healing."

CHAPTER 20

Tom took a motor rickshaw to Maya's house. The driver drove as quickly as he could.

When Tom was dropped in front of the gateway of Maya's estate, he looked at the man unbelievingly. "Is this the right address?"

"Mr. Maya lives here, sir."

Tom paid the man. He then took the time to attune himself to the new situation. From outside the gate, he viewed the huge building and the extensive park that surrounded it. A long drive across the park came out onto a great square. At the other side of the square, he saw an impressive flight of steps leading up to a huge front door. Long, dark cypresses reached like looming ghosts high into the dusky sky; to Tom they looked like omens of the night.

"I thought Maya was an ordinary citizen," he muttered to himself, as he looked at the two flags on the roof at the head building and recognized Maya's initials. "India doesn't have any sovereigns anymore, does it?"

The policeman who was at guard duty at the gate thought he should do something. He asked Tom what he wanted.

"I have an appointment with Mr. Maya."

"Your name?"

The policeman went to his sentry box and phoned. It appeared to be okay; the man opened the gate.

Tom walked along the drive, crossed the square and mounted the steps. He pulled at a heavy, wrought iron ring. Shortly after that, he heard deadened footsteps approach. One of the two half-doors swung open. A man with a huge moustache in a lackey's uniform greeted him and bowed, his hands praying at his chin. The man looked serious. He beckoned Tom to follow him.

Tom followed the man along a long corridor toward broad marble steps. He tried to distribute his attention between the imperturbable lackey, the beautifully tiled floors, the splendid carpet under his feet, and the gods and goddesses who hung in glorious painted colours and in precious frames on the walls.

Halfway up the steps was a portrait of a man with a black moustache and little, sly eyes in a smooth face. From a great, sumptuous frame, he stared haughtily down upon Tom.

The lackey led Tom to a waiting room. Standing to attention, he knocked on the door. It was a couple of minutes before Tom heard something. Only then did the lackey begin to move and open the door. Tom heard Amal Maya say in Hindi, "Show Mr. Corda in and then wait for further instructions!"

Tom decided that Maya didn't need to know that he understood the language. Maya would then be inclined to negotiate in Hindi, and Tom's fluency in the language was limited. He was too practical to give the advantage to the other man.

Maya came to his guest and greeted him. He introduced himself, kindly smiling. Then he showed Tom to a seat in a corner of his office.

Maya went to his desk and pushed a button. In the room next to Maya's rang a bell.

"My secretary, Mrs. Arora, will be present at our interview."

Tom supposed that Maya involved his secretary in the conversation because of his limited English. He had already noticed that the English language of his host was confined to the stereotypes of the street-traders jargon strange tourists are approached with.

Mrs. Arora entered. She impressed Tom immediately with her natural grace and her heart-warming smile.

Maya hinted to her that she may sit down. Then he instructed her about what her part in the conversation was to be.

Tom pretended that the conversation between Maya and his secretary was not understood by him.

Maya charged the lackey at the door to fetch tea from the kitchen and then to resume his place at the door.

Mrs. Arora addressed Tom and told him in good English what he had already heard in Hindi. "Mr. Maya considers himself fortunate that he may receive you. And he hopes that you will have a nice time in our country. He promises you all the cooperation in your inquiries and he wishes you good luck with them. You may see everything you wish to. And if you then have other wishes, you need only to tell him. Mr. Maya has a reputation to maintain."

Maya smiled in approval, pretending he had understood Mrs. Arora's translated words.

Tom smiled back and thanked his host for his kind words. "I would like to make use of your offer."

Amal Maya's eyes looked to his secretary for help. She translated Tom's words and she was given the order to relay Maya's answer in English. "Mr. Maya tells you that he bought the pharmaceutical company three years ago and that since then the profit has much increased."

"Can Mr. Maya tell me which products, other than those supplied to Medimarket, are prepared and packaged there?"

By means of his interpreting secretary, Maya replied that he would get Tom a list of all the products the company produced.

Tom asked if he might see the company.

"Mr. Maya will arrange this for you."

"Can Mr. Maya introduce me to the manager?"

"If Mr. Maya can make some time free, he will introduce you to the manager."

"I am highly interested in the production process; may I talk to the workers?"

"Mr. Maya says that you had better discuss this with the manager; he is not engaged in the daily running of things. He confines his interference in the enterprise to the financial aspects."

"Would you make it clear to Mr. Maya that I can't stay long in Varanasi? I would like to see the company and to interview the manager and the workers this week."

After a short passage of words, the secretary translated. "Mr. Maya will take your request into consideration."

The knives are already being whetted, Tom thought, *although it happens with a smile. I think Maya wants to control my enquiries. He said that I could see everything I wished; we will see.*

Tom also concealed his thoughts behind a smile.

The servant came in and poured them hot, sweet tea. They drank their tea and they tasted the sweets the man had put on the table before them. Meanwhile, the conversation babbled airily on.

When the pharmaceutical enterprise came up again, Tom asked if Maya would tell him something about the working conditions in his company.

"Mr. Maya asks what you mean by that."

"I mean the wages that are paid, the facilities for the employees, the holidays and the like."

"Mr. Maya will instruct his bookkeeper to inform you about this."

The conversation became gradually less businesslike and their attention was turned more and more toward's Maya's art treasures.

Tom had never got used to the religious painting art in India. Now, however, he thought a compliment on Durga in front of Maya's desk could work as a lubricant for his inquiries. "May I ask you who made this splendid work?"

Maya rose to give his usual explanation. "Durga is my favourite goddess, and therefore I ordered a famous painter to paint her after my own ideas. You see how divinely she rides her tiger."

Tom saw a goddess with a more or less rigid mouth, wearing jewels at every possible spot on her body.

"It has been painted copiously," Tom said deliberately.

"You have a sense of art, Mr. Corda! You see that the goddess lacks nothing; the painter expressed this magisterially. I'll show you some more pieces in my collection. Will you follow me, please?"

Sarásvati Arora joined them to fill the gaps in the English language of her boss.

Tom enjoyed Sarásvati's lively interpreting. But he also realized that the excursion was not without obligations; he saw it as an offer to the gods for the sake of a good outcome of his mission. With the help of Sarásvati, whom he thought prettier than all Maya's goddesses, he larded the abundant religious wealth with admiring comments.

On the way back to Maya's office they saw a woman come out of the kitchen. The woman made a modest, almost shy impression. She had draped a red sari over her long, jet-black hair. She smiled at Tom and Sarásvati. When, however, Maya looked at her, her shoulders hunched into her sari and her eyes lowered. The scene lasted no more than two seconds. But it was enough for Tom to become interested in the woman. *She is not a servant and she is not an ordinary woman,* he thought. *Why did Maya look at her so contemptuously? She is a beautiful woman. Maya doesn't hate good-looking women as far as I know.*

Before Sarásvati could introduce the woman to Tom, Maya had already gone on.

Tom hesitated between Maya and the unknown woman. He decided to follow Maya; he wouldn't know how to explain to the woman why he had addressed her.

The next evening after dinner he suddenly saw Sarásvati before him in the restaurant of the hotel he was staying in. "I want to speak to you without Maya's knowledge and outside his house." As she said this, she looked around, frightened, to see if there was anyone listening. "If Amal Maya knows that I met you, I would not survive." She looked fearfully around.

Then she went on, whispering, "You must know the enterprise Medimarket trades with is contaminated."

"Contaminated? What do you mean?"

"The work is done by children, children who have been kidnapped and who must redeem the debts of their parents. They work as slaves, twelve hours a day or longer."

Tom thought he had prepared himself for the unpredictable and uncalculating character of India, the country full of surprises.

He also knew that India had many children working in all sorts of sectors, often as little slaves. And he realized that the Bonded Labour Act of 1976, forbidding slavery for redeeming debts, had not had much effect. But now he looked at the young Indian woman incredulously. This concrete confrontation impressed him more than all the statistics he had ever seen.

He needed some time to be able to react. "Have you already eaten?"

"Yes, I've just eaten."

"May I invite you for a drink?"

"I like tea. Tray tea, please; I prefer to regulate the quantity of sugar myself."

"Does this mean that Amal Maya lets children work as slaves for him?" Tom continued, after having ordered the drinks.

"Yes. I have seen for myself. When I last left my work for the night, I decided to have a look in Maya's pharmaceutical company; I had never been there before. As I knew that you were coming, I wanted to see the company with my own eyes. So I went there. A man whom I assumed to be the manager was talking there to somebody else. This man and the manager were so absorbed in their conversation that they didn't notice me. Then I heard a child crying. It was the soft, whining and desperate crying of a child that is sick and has been left alone. I got the feeling that something was wrong. And I wanted to know what it was. The two men had not yet seen me. There was a door at the back of the room. I went to it and I opened that door carefully. The men didn't notice it. I saw a corridor leading to a courtyard. Nobody was there. So I went through that corridor and across the courtyard. The place looked quite deserted. The child's crying sounded more clearly. I opened another door. Then I saw six children sitting on jute mats on a loamy floor. Two other children were sweeping the floor. There was a musty, sour air, and it was dirty. I had to get used to the twilight before I could distinguish the children from each other. They were dirty and lean and they looked bad. They stared vacantly ahead. One child sat stirring a great pot; another child was filling little bottles with a yellow mixture; a girl sat at an apparatus blanking pills. I was flabbergasted. Then the man the manager had been talking with came in. I was still numb from what I saw there, but the attitude and the sound of the man made me realize that I had to do something. I ignored him and I went to the children. The children sat there gazing at me with hollow eyes. The man who had come in became nervous and he shouted that I must go away. I asked him who he was. He said, 'I am Ajay Khosla.' I refused to go away. I went to stand in front of him and I told him to leave me alone with the children. He hesitated. Then he went, reluctantly, away. It was some time before I could talk. Then I addressed one of the children, a child with tears on its face. The child did not react. Another child did not either. A girl of about twelve years old, with a half-filled bottle in her hands, began inaudibly to cry. She was the child I had heard before. I went to sit next to her and laid an arm around her shoulders. Then there came a burst of crying. Another child joined her wails, and still another one. A boy of about eight years could feel it no more apparently; he gazed at me with a totally petrified feeling on his face. It was as though I had a ghastly dream. I sat there I don't know how long. As I looked around, I saw, at the back of the room a gate of aluminium tubes through which aluminium strings were strung. An open padlock hung on a bolt. I went there. Behind the gate I saw a dark kennel measuring four by two metres. There was a mat on the floor. And there were some zinc cups with remains of food in them. In the corner lay a child, a skeleton, wrapped in skin, with great, empty eyes. It lay staring into death. I went to the other children. I sat down next to the boy and placed my arm around him. Another child came to me and hugged itself to me. There came ever more children. They would all feel my arms around them. It remained quiet for a long time.

Then a girl said something in a strange language; I think it was Tamil. The girl that had cried said she could not understand two of the other children. But she did know that they had been taken away from their parents. She herself had been kidnapped by a rickshaw-cyclist and had been brought here. She told me that she had not seen her parents and her younger brother and sister for two years. A strange man had lured another girl into his car. The man had brought her here and he had received a handful of money from the manager of the company. This manager is named Ram Majumdar.

"I sat there crying with the children," Sarásvati ended. "It was as though the ground under my feet was sinking away. How is it possible that human beings can do something like that?"

Tom needed time before the story had passed the bottleneck of his comprehension.

"This cannot be true!" he almost screamed.

"I couldn't believe it either," Sarásvati said in a choked voice.

"What did you do after that?"

"Khosla came back with the manager. That man was angry. But he was afraid as well. He had a stick in his hand and he tried to hit me. I seized that stick and threw it away. 'You will pay for this!' I cried. The man did not know what to do. He and Khosla stayed there like statues as I went past them."

"Can't we release those children?" Tom asked.

"If it was that easy, we would have done it. But you cannot undervalue Amal Maya's power!" Sarásvati looked with meaning at Tom. "It is a power that spares nobody and nothing."

"I'll go to the company tomorrow."

"Then you will find no children there anymore. I went to Sudhir Varma's house on my lunch break. He and his wife Shakti are friends of mine. When I had told Shakti what I had seen, she went to the company immediately. The children had been taken away. The kennel they had slept in had been cleaned. Shakti asked Khosla where the children were, but he replied with a grimace, 'what children, ma'am?'"

"So I am too late to make my inquiries," Tom realised.

"When you visit the company, everything will be all right; Maya will take care of that. You must realize," Sarásvati went on, whispering, "that human beings are no more than instruments or playthings to Maya."

"I am glad that you told me this. I already had my doubts."

"You have a right to know this. But, please, be careful! On no account let Maya notice that you know something. My life would be in danger. I'm not sure of my life any longer anyway, since Khosla and Majumdar have seen me in their company. They often come to see Maya. They have never seen me before; otherwise, they would have known who I am. And then Maya would quickly know it was me who discovered the children there. If Khosla or Majumdar sees me with Maya, then my life will not be much worth any more. Maya will eliminate me, to save himself. A sword hangs over my head. I have even thought about leaving Maya."

"Then Maya will have no interest at all in sparing your life."

"You are right. But I must pay close attention."

Sarásvati proposed letting the matter rest, for safety.

Tom seized the opportunity to launch into another subject, one that had occupied his mind for some time. "Yesterday we saw a woman in Maya's house. Who was she?"

"Maya's wife. Her name is Parvati."

"I didn't get the idea that Maya treated her like his wife."

"He treats her as his property."

"The woman made a deep impression on me."

"She is a fantastic woman in every way.

The next day Tom had another visitor. "Mr. Corda, there is somebody who wants to see you."

Tom went to the lounge of the hotel. A man was there waiting. He was dressed in white cotton trousers and a white *kurta* of the same fabric. The man rose, bent deeply, and greeted Tom with praying hands.

Tom introduced himself.

"I am afraid I can't tell you my name," the man answered. "I have come to bring you a message from Mrs. Maya."

"A message for me? Does Mrs. Maya know who I am?"

"She knows who you are and she knows your purpose here in Varanasi." Tom looked at the man astonished.

"Mrs. Maya asks you to come and see her."

"I shall do so with great pleasure."

"Her husband may not know that you are going to see her."

"How can I see her without being discovered by her husband?"

"I shall let you know when you can come."

"Okay! I shall wait for your message."

A week after that, Tom sat in front of Parvati.

Parvati proposed that he call her by her first name. "You are a friend of my friends," she argued.

Tom thought it excellent and asked her to call him Tom.

"Would you excuse me, please, for being so mysterious? It would turn out badly for me if my husband was to discover that I am talking to you."

"He will not learn it from me."

"I know I can trust you."

Tom nodded, with a question on his forehead. He did not understand why he had received this compliment.

"You asked my husband for permission to make inquiries into his company."

"Yes. Yesterday I had a second interview with him, but I am still none the wiser."

"You will not learn from him what you should. There are— there were—eight children working as slaves in that company; Sarásvati already told you."

Tom nodded.

"You must know that Sarásvati will be at great risk, if you write about these children in your report."

"I will not bring Sarásvati into any problems."

"Thank you."

Parvati switched to another subject. "I know about your contact with Satori and Soedjata."

"You know the nuns?"

182

"I knew Satori before I married Maya; but since my marriage I have only had the opportunity to see her three times; my husband has ordered someone to shadow me. So I can't approach the nuns directly. My husband would know immediately. May I ask you to bring the nuns a message from me."

"Certainly, with pleasure!"

"Will you tell the nuns about the children who worked in my husband's company? One of the children, a girl, is now here. She works in the kitchen. I have the feeling that the nuns know who she is."

"Can you tell me something about her?"

Parvati told him what she knew.

"The girl who was brought here was kidnapped by a rickshaw-cyclist?"

"Yes, that must have been about two years ago."

"Near the river Ganges?"

"Yes."

Tom told Parvati what he knew.

"I had a premonition that I had to tell you this," Parvati answered, elated. "Now I know why."

"Shall I warn the police?" Tom replied spontaneously.

"The chief inspector knows about it. If we report this, we'll get ourselves into trouble."

"And if I go to her parents, could they do anything?"

"The parents are outcasts and live in the slums; nobody will believe them if they accuse Amal Maya."

"What sort of country is this?"

"This country is called a developing country. One of the problems in this country is that a limited number of powerful people block every progression for poor people."

"Is the Maya Foundation an invention of your husband?"

"Yes."

"I have money for the foundation which I brought with me."

"Don't give it to Maya!"

"Of course not! I shall tell Satori about the child in the kitchen; she will do nothing precipitately."

"Excellent!"

"How can I stay in contact with you?"

"By means of Sarásvati. Or of my courier."

CHAPTER 21

If Amal Maya had a dream, it was a nasty dream. He thought himself fortunate that he almost never dreamt. That's what he thought, at least; but he had no idea that these uninvited guests from the unconscious are usually erased from the memory after waking. Maya's dreams underwent the same fate as the people who did not fit in his life: they were chased away like awkward insects.

Last night's dream had, however, stayed nestled in his mind.

The goddess Sarásvati had danced over the beach of Gangama. Sarásvati was the personification of science and wisdom, of order and music, and of the rhythm of the universe, created by Brahma. Sarásvati danced the rhythm of the waves of the holy river, a rhythm, alternately opening and closing itself in a natural harmony with creation, as her body spoke a language, admired, but not understood by Maya. Her face expressed a serene emotion.

Maya saw her dance as a tempting game. He tried to grasp her round her waist, but a bag, hanging from his neck, impeded his movements. In that bag was a dowry. Every time he thought he could catch her, she slipped, light-footedly dancing, away.

After some failed efforts to catch her, she disappeared on the horizon into the water of the holy river.

Maya waded after her. He looked under the surface for the dancing goddess. But it became dark in the depths around him; he saw nothing anymore. The water grew syrupy and his hands were red, blood red. Then he heard the silvery laugh of the goddess Sarásvati.

Maya plodded to the riverbank. There, he tried to escape from the dark red water by digging a hole. After digging too deep, he felt the earth cave in over him and he became trapped in the hole. The bag round his neck tore to pieces. The contents, consisting of pellets, fell to the bottom of the hole. One of the pellets burst open. Maya saw little children's hands and feet and eyes, wrapped in a wad of pubic hair. He heard the high, shrill, inhaling whistle of a wailing owl. Cracks wound their way until they were deep in the walls of the hole. Sand was coming down. Maya crept deeper in, on the run from the sand.

When he woke up, Maya floated, heavily shaking, in his own sweat.

Amal Maya was a powerful man. He had powerful connections as well, connections that formed a network of egos. Those egos turned round their own axles and were, like poles as they were inclined to repel each other. They were, however, condemned to each other, entangled in a web of corruption and of merciless jealousy.

But they were powerful. And Maya was the most powerful of all of them.

Chief inspector Sunar Chand admired Maya's secretary who provided him and his guests with tea. He could control his admiration so that nobody could catch him doing so. He tried to get her attention with a smile. He must, however, content himself with her polite, impersonal nod.

Puttilal Kakkar, a leading official in the service of the local community, gazed, openly and without any embarrassment, at the young woman and chewed his *betel* leaf with an open mouth.

Maya and Chand were members of the Vaishya caste. Kakkar was a Thakur. Originally, the Thakurs formed no more than a sect within the caste of the Sudras. But it had become a custom through the years that sects were named castes as well.

The men failed to make any impression on Sarásvati. With her proud attitude, accentuated by her red sari and her jet-black shining hair, falling in long waves over her back, and the fiery red dot on her forehead, outlined against the creamy white complexion of her face, she was an inaccessible beauty. Her politeness was confined to the reserved courtesy required by her position as a hostess.

Amal Maya was proud. He enjoyed the impression his secretary made on his guests. He followed their looks.

When Sarásvati had withdrawn with a subtle nod, he waited for their compliments. It delighted him then that Kakkar asked him. "Where did you get that woman from?"

Maya hinted that Sarásvati had received many offers when her former employer had come into problems. "But," he argued, "I took her boss under my protection; and his secretary chose to receive safety and certainty here with me. And the job I gave her she would not have got anywhere else."

"Is it only the job she chose?" Chand asked, with a faint irony in his voice.

"You should ask her," Maya avoided answering him. "There are more women looking for my protection."

After they had chatted for some time about women, Puttilal Kakkar went to the window to spit the phlegm of his blood-red *betel* outside.

"Shall I keep the window open?"

"No, shut it," Maya answered. "I invited you here to discuss some important matters that are not suitable for open windows."

There was a silence. The two visitors looked at Maya, curious about what he had to tell them.

"Kakkar, have you already looked after a licence for a school in the slum next to my territory?"

"Not yet, but it can be arranged within about six weeks. The procedure was started two years ago. There have been five inspections until now."

"That is what I want to discuss. My man at the bank told me that an amount of two thousand American dollars will shortly be transferred into that school's account. That message came last week."

Maya broke the short silence that fell after his words. "I propose to ask for ninety thousand *rupees* for the licence; that is about the equivalent of two thousand dollars." He waited quietly until the others approved his proposal.

"Ninety thousand *rupees*; that is thirty thousand for each of us. The Europeans will meanwhile make up the money for the school."

Maya, who led the conversation, sounded out the reactions of his mates and concluded, "So we agree." Then he asked, "Who will arrange for us to get the money?"

"I will," Kakkar said. "I'll invite the nun who organizes the building. I will offer her our protection."

"The other matter I want to discuss with you is that of employing vagrant children."

Now it was quiet as a conspiracy in the room. The men knew that they were involved in a risky undertaking.

That undertaking had started three years earlier.

Ram Majumdar, the manager of Maya's pharmaceutical company, had asked him for some children to work in the business.

"I shall see what I can do," Maya had answered.

A week after that conversation, Maya was sitting in a coffee shop at Connaught Place in New Delhi. He had just emptied his plate when he saw three boys of about eight to ten years walking past his window. They looked dirty and they were dressed in rags.

Maya went out and beckoned to the boys. "Hello guys, where are you living?" Maya asked them.

The boys did not live anywhere. At night, they looked for shelter against the rain, the cold, and the police in a corner of a blind alley.

"I can provide you with permanent shelter and permanent work, and food and drink every day."

The boys glowed when hearing that, and one of them answered spontaneously, "With pleasure, sir!"

"Then you must wait here and don't tell anybody about this. I'll be back in a minute."

Maya went back into the coffee shop to pay for his meal.

"Come along, boys!" he said. "Have you ever sat in a car?"

"A car? No sir," the eldest of the boys said. "We have never even sat in a rickshaw."

"Then you may ride with me," Maya promised. He had a feeling of pride at making the children happy.

The car was in the second circle of Connaught Place.

Maya made the boys sit on the back seat and he shut the doors.

"We will take a long drive. What do you think of that?"

"Very nice, sir!"

This was better than the dark corner they were used to sleeping in. The boys enjoyed the ride; they had never experienced speed like this. They went past places they had never seen before. The shop center at Connaught Place and its surroundings had been their world.

Krishna, the youngest of the three boys, had not seen his mother for years; he could faintly remember a lean, sad-looking woman of an indefinite age. He had never known a father.

Nand and Montu were brothers. They had not known their father either. Their mother and their elder sister had earned money by inviting men into their hut to lie next to them. Their mother and sister had never had any time for them. From the age of four, they were sent out to beg for money. Since then, they went home less and less, for if they did, they had to give up their *money*. And when they did not bring enough money home, they were beaten.

They left the town. The boys thought it splendid.

"What a nice man!" Montu whispered. People were rarely kind to them; mostly they were chased away like stray dogs. Now they had met this nice man. They could not believe their happiness.

But when it became dark, a question began to form in their heads: "Where is this nice man bringing us?" The nice man had said nothing more since they had left the town. He had told them that they would take a long ride, but they had not expected the ride would be so long. They didn't dare ask though.

Within ten minutes it was pitch-dark. The boys, who now saw only the glittering of headlights and now and then the light of a street lamp, became sleepy and their eyes soon closed.

Nand was the first to awake. It was already full daylight. They were headed towards the sun. He woke his brother and his friend up. The boys realized that they were very far from their own familiar world. They looked silently at the man who sat sleepily and stuffily behind the steering wheel.

After a quarter of an hour he stopped at a filling station. He told the boys that they should keep quiet and that they were not allowed to talk to anyone. He got out and bought some tea in an earthenware cup at a *chai* shop across from the petrol pump. He also bought baked eggs with white bread. Then he ate the bread and the eggs.

The boys looked at it longingly. "Maybe now he will buy something for us..."

After finishing his food, the man paid and came back to the car. He got in and started the motor. He began to hum a song. Apparently, he felt good.

The boys began to realize that they would get nothing. The man had forgotten them. That strengthened the already gnawing feeling in their stomachs.

After fifteen minutes, Nand dared to broach the subject. "Why didn't we get anything to eat?"

"You must first work before you get something to eat."

"What must we do?" Nand asked timidly.

"You'll see. After about six hours, we'll be at our destination." The man drove silently on.

When the sun stood high in the sky, he stopped again. In a shop he bought half a bunch of bananas and a bottle of mango drink. He came back to the car and the boys' hopes rose again. *One banana,"* Nand thought, *"is enough to appease our hunger; one little bottle of drink for the three of us is actually very little, but it would be very delicious.* Once he had tasted that drink, as someone had left half a glass on a table on a pavement. Krishna and Montu also looked longingly at the bananas and the mango juice.

The man sat down behind the steering wheel, took a drink out of the bottle, peeled a banana and ate it in three bites. He drank from the juice again and then ate the second banana.

While the boys watched with big eyes and open mouths, the man finished the bananas and the drink. He threw the skins and the bottle out of the window. He belched muddily, cleaned his moustache with the back of his left hand, and started the car. Nothing in the demeanour of the man showed any notion that he remembered their existence.

From the droning of the motor, the heat of the afternoon sun, and their empty stomachs—a quite familiar feeling anyway—they fell into a restless slumber. They did not awake until they arrived in a strange town. The uproar was as bad as it was in their native town. The swarming traffic was heavy up ahead.

After one hour of driving, stopping and driving again, the man stopped in front of a white building.

The boys looked at it with a frightened curiosity.

"Stay in the car; I'll be back in a minute." The man went into the building and came back with another man.

The man who had brought them here opened the door and ordered, "Get out!"

They climbed with terror out of the car. Then they were lined up next to each other with their backs to the car.

The man from the building inspected the boys. He smelled them and made a wry face. With a stick he forced them to open their mouths, and he looked inside with the stick between their teeth. With the same stick he pushed their ears forward to look behind them. Then the boys had to show their hands, and with a rap of the stick, the man forced them to turn them over. In the end, the two men greeted each other with praying hands.

The man from the building urged the boys inside with the stick. They went through a great room and came to a courtyard. The man ordered the boys to undress themselves and to throw their clothes into a dustbin.

As they stood naked against a wall, the man ordered another boy he had fetched to pump water into a bucket and throw it over the boys who had just arrived. Then he had to scrub them clean with soap and a brush and wash them off with the same bucket. After that, the man left the boys standing against the wall.

When it got dark, the boys still did not know what would happen to them.

Krishna started to cry. The other boys joined in.

After about an hour, the boy who had cleaned them came back with three sets of clothes. The wide white trousers were too large and had to be kept up with a rope round their waists. The white jackets hung over their knees. The sleeves were rolled up.

"Can you get something for us to eat?" Nand asked the boy who had cleaned them.

"You'll get something to eat tomorrow," the boy said. He led them into a dark room.

In a corner, separated by a fence, lay five mats. On every mat lay a thin blanket.

On a mat at the back lay a girl who they couldn't see very well in the dark.

"We sleep here," the boy said.

The man with the stick locked the fence with a padlock.

Overwhelmed by everything that had happened to them, none of the three boys knew what to say.

Nand told their names to the boy who had given them the new clothes. He introduced himself as Sunar and said his friend was named Rabri.

"We must roll pills and pour drinks into vials, and there are many other chores to do. The boss is named Ram Majumdar. He is very severe. When we don't do our work well, we don't get anything to eat. In any case the food we get is not much and it is tasteless and always the same. But if you are hungry, you will eat it all the same."

"Do you think that we will get some food when it gets light?" Montu asked hopefully.

"We don't get much in the morning," Sunar said. "Maybe a little rice with *dhal* and water."

"And in the evening we get rice with *dhal* and water as well," Rabri said, completing Sunar's story, "and sometimes some vegetables."

"Did you never try to get away from here?" Nand asked.

"Yes. Once," Sunar answered. "The police brought us back, and the boss beat us with a strap. We were not fed for two days. But we've hardly noticed it, as we were only half-conscious from the beating. After that, we had to work longer a couple of times, as we had not worked for three days. Since then we are guarded better. Ajay Khosla sets us to work and he watches over us. Besides, if we could get away from here, we wouldn't know where to go."

It was still night when Ajay Khosla came to wake the children up.

They were given an aluminium plate with a little cooked rice and *dhal* and an aluminium cup of water.

They had just finished their food when Khosla came in. He opened the fence and ordered the children to wash the plates and the cups under the pump on the courtyard.

After that he led them into a close and stuffy room. There were cockroaches everywhere. Lizards sat stuck on the walls. It stunk of sweat and urine.

Khosla ordered the three new boys to sit down on a mat on the floor. "You begin today with packing pills," he said to the three new workers. "Look how these children do it. Take care that you work well and hard. You may only rest when I tell you. Do you understand?"

The boys mumbled anxiously that they understood.

"When the boss is awake, he will come to inspect your work."

When Khosla had gone, Sunar encouraged the other children to work hard. "Ram Majumdar always has a stick with him. If you haven't done enough, you'll get a beating. And when he has drunk too much the night before, he already starts beating before he has even had a look at your work."

It struck the three boys only now how ashen grey the hollow faces of Sunar and Rabri were. There was scarcely any flesh on their arms and legs.

"How long have you been here?" Krishna whispered.

"I have been here for two years; Rabri for roughly one and a half years. I don't know exactly," Sunar whispered, "it is hard to keep up; all days and nights are equal. And we never have a day off. We must always work, and after work we are too tired to stay awake. There were three of us, but three weeks ago my little sister, Giti, got sick. Khosla kicked her to get up, but she couldn't. When we came back to our cage in the evening, Giti wasn't anymore there. Khosla said he would look for a replacement. We don't know what they have done to my sister."

At noon Ram Majumdar came for a look, with Ajay Khosla following in his wake. He had the stick he had inspected the boys with the day before in his right hand. "I have come to see our new acquisitions. And I want to see what they have done. You don't need to stop working, when I am inspecting your work."

Meanwhile Amal Maya had driven home. He was beyond his lack of sleep. He had discovered a new way to earn money. *And I hardly needed to do anything for it. Oh well, it stank in the car; but after opening the window, the stench passed away in no time.*

Since then, each drive to Delhi had increased in amount between a thousand and three thousand *rupees*. He had selected the children well. There was also more and more demand, especially as most of the children did not hold out long.

That was good for my traffic, Maya thought back. *It remains, however, a risky business.*

The affair round the kidnapping of a little girl in Kanpur came back to his memory. *That kidnapper was so stupid to call my name. But fortunately I could smooth everything out and I've taken care that that man will keep his mouth shut forever. That made me more cautious; since then I have my men for picking children up from the street. Khosla especially is a valuable employee. But there is still one thing that's bothering me: who was the young woman who entered the pharmaceutical company and managed at an unguarded moment to get to the back of the building where she saw the children at work? Khosla thought she was a daughter of Dr. Varma, but the Varmas have no children. I hope I can discover who she was, so that I can take action.*

While these thoughts ran through his head, Sarásvati came in after a knock at the door, to supply the men with tea. The silence around the risky subject still hung heavily in the room.

Sarásvati served the men, who thought it self-evident to be served, without granting them any personal attention.

When Sarásvati had left the room, Maya needed a short interval before coming back to the matter.

Then, after he had taken a drink of the hot, sweet tea, he resumed the conversation. "Our rickshaw wallah lured another child away; a girl of eight."

"Out of the slums, I suppose," Sunar Chand thought aloud while he looked in his bag for his diary.

"Of course! But she looks good. Besides, I ordered that the drivers who take care of the transport of the children should be more careful with their loads; tidying up children after the transport costs us a lot of time. By the way, does one of you have any interest in the girl?"

"What is the price?"

Fifteen hundred *rupees*.

"The prices are rising."

"You could call it risk money. With a little luck you can earn it back in a couple of months."

"I could use a child for begging in front of the station," Kakkar replied prudently. "You get a lot of tourists there."

"Fifteen hundred *rupees?*"

"I will pay a thousand," Kakkar answered.

The men agreed on an amount of twelve hundred and fifty *rupees*.

"Who is that rickshaw cyclist?" Sunar Chand wanted to know.

"The less you know, the better it is."

"We need more girls. For prostitution," Chand said.

"I shall take care of it," Maya answered.

"That makes a difference to the fathers of the girls; they don't need to pay for a dowry for them," Kakkar said with a laugh.

"And we make sure that those children are no longer a burden on society," was Maya's opinion.

Chand and Kakkar agreed by nodding.

"There is still another point: an inspector in your office has threatened to give publicity to our work with children; the man should be bothered by his conscience."

"No problem!" Chand waved Maya's remark aside. "I will keep him in control. Two of my men are willing to act as witnesses against him in a corruption matter."

CHAPTER 22

I have a surprise for you." Amal Maya's face was full of expectation. He rose from his seat and went to the man-sized safe in the corner of his office. After he had entered in a numerical code and had opened two other locks with two different keys, he turned a huge chrome wheel, to open a heavy, twelve-centimetre-thick door.

Sarásvati, seeing how Maya opened the complicated lock of the safe, sensed an unknown threat. She knew that only Maya had the keys to the safe and that nobody else knew the code. She also knew that the safe contained a lot of secrets, secrets known only to Maya. She saw, in a flash, high piles of banknotes and caught the sparkling of gold, silver and jewels.

Kneeling and deeply bent in front of his safe, Maya cherished his treasures with his hands and his eyes. Then he took a little parcel out of the safe, closed the door and locked it carefully.

He had a strange sparkle in his eyes as he came to Sarásvati. He gave her the parcel.

Sarásvati could not think of an excuse for a refusal. She hesitated with the parcel in her hand.

"You may open it!" Little lights of anticipatory pleasure flickered in Maya's eyes.

Sarásvati fumbled at the knot of ribbon round the parcel, but the knot did not give way.

Maya could not wait any longer; he looked for some scissors on his desk and cut the ribbon.

Sarásvati took the paper from the little case and lifted the lid carefully. She saw through a mist of anger and fear crimson pearls in soft white tissue paper. She felt the blood in her face sink away. She froze. In her memory flashed the moment when as a child she had played outside her parents's house and suddenly felt the earth under her feet moving due to a faint earthquake. Her hands clasped at the seat before her. She became angry with herself, as she couldn't control herself in his presence. She stood there like a statue, gazing at the case in her hand without seeing anything.

Amal Maya smiled because of the overwhelming impression his present made on the young woman. He took the necklace out of the case and fumbled the little hook open. He didn't notice the wild fear and anger in Sarásvati's eyes. As he hung the necklace round her neck, she screamed hoarsely. Her whole body shook. She felt assaulted. Suddenly, she turned around and ran to her room.

Maya was startled. He didn't understand this. He stood foolishly with the necklace in his hands in front of his desk.

After a short pause, he decided to ask her for an explanation. He sat down behind his desk, with the necklace before him, and phoned her.

There was no reply.

Now he was angry. "If I call her, she must react!" he growled. "She is my secretary."

He rose from his seat and went to her room.

Sarásvati sat behind her desk, her face bent over her arms, shaking and crying.

Curious as to why she had reacted in this way, he controlled his anger for a moment. "Did I deserve your ingratitude?" he whispered with a faintly reproaching undertone in his voice.

"I will not be ungrateful," she sobbed. "I can not accept this. I get a good wage here. I don't want more. This present is much too valuable."

An uncertain smile came, hesitatingly, to life on his face.

It's too valuable indeed, he thought, *I overwhelmed her; I should be more patient. Actually, she is still a child.*

Looking down at her, he said, "You are not yet used to wealth; I understand that. I was perhaps a little silly by forgetting that. Let's forget this and get back to work."

Amal Maya went back to his room.

I am too good to her, he thought, *she is my employee and I pay her well. At least she sees that she gets a good salary and that this present is too expensive. But on the other hand, she demands a lot of patience from me. It would be easier if she came out of the slums; then I could take her just like that. But I can't afford to do that with her. In my position, I cannot afford the fuss that would be the outcome if I should force it. I should have a look at the girl Khosla brought me. She is not a Sarásvati, it is true; but she will be better than nothing.*

Great, anxiously wild eyes looked up from the floor into the fierce light that suddenly was aimed at her. Chinky had not seen any light for days. She closed her eyes to get used to the glare. Then she saw a heavy-set man in a silk *kurta.* She saw precious rings glittering on his fat fingers. It flashed through her head that the man must be more then ten years older than her father.

The man came into the store room and kicked at her upper leg, indicating that she should get up.

She rose, but she remained kneeling. She looked with great dark eyes fearfully, like a young deer, expecting the heavy, hairy claw of the colossal predator in its neck, instinctively knowing that there are no more than a few seconds left, seconds that the animal would use to play with; a sadistic pleasure like an aperitive in advance.

Maya slapped the girl with his stick on her upper arm and forced her to get up.

While Chinky stood trembling on her bare feet, he walked around, inspecting around her. He smelt her sweat of fear and the smell of a body that hadn't been washed for some days. His lips, squeezed together, marked his displeasure. He came in front of her and lifted her face with his stick under her chin.

Great tears rolled over her cheeks.

Maya growled; the tears irritated him. Deep in his subconscious fermented a misty recognition of something human in the shivering creature before him. He closed his eyes and held his breath for a moment to let this intrusive feeling ebb away. Then he lifted her dress with his stick and saw that she wore no knickers. He didn't know that she had only one pair and they were in her parents's hut.

Chinky was embarrassed and pushed her dress down. That brought her a slap with the stick on her hand.

There were more tears.

Maya turned around.

From his living room he called his *hijra*, the eunuch who was also his bodyguard. He ordered the man to get the girl out of the store room and to bring her into the kitchen. The man must order the other girl working there to put the new girl into a bath and to give her clean clothes. After that, the eunuch must take the new girl from the kitchen and bring her into his room.

Lila knew what was going to happen, but she obeyed. She would never forget the anger Maya had rained down on her. She had caught her breath for a moment after she had massaged him for half an hour, from his neck to his feet. Maya had called her to order. She had retched and turned her head for a moment, as he had led her hand to his penis. Maya, disturbed in his pleasure, had lost his self-control. He had grabbed her hair and dragged her over to his bed. Then she had been forced to finish the job.

Two years earlier Lila had been kidnapped in Mumbai, and in those two years she had learned Hindi, the language of the North of India. She knew what she could expect if she refused to do what the boss ordered.

Chinky wore a dirty, worn dress. Lila took it off. She caressed the girl. She didn't know that this was the first kind gesture Chinky had experienced since the day she had gone with the rickshaw-cyclist. She looked half-unconsciously at the other girl who was a little larger than she was and must be about two years older.

"I am Lila," the girl said.

Chinky did not react.

Lila wondered if the girl understood.

Chinky, even though numb, understood the kindness of the other girl. She sensed that she could trust her.

Lila made Chinky step into a barrel of water and washed her clean.

Chinky, who had always washed herself, squatting near the pump in front of her parents's hut or in the river, looked up; but she enjoyed the bath. She did not know how long she had been away from home, as she had been in coma and had lain for days and nights in a deep darkness. After that, she had had to do all sorts of work in a dirty workplace in a medicine factory. There could she wash herself once a week with a bucket of water and a bar of sand soap. In the last few days her body had seen neither soap nor water.

After she had finished in the bath and had been wiped dry, Chinky was dressed by Lila. She was given white cotton trousers and a shirt, and over this a coat with long white sleeves. Paralysed and numb, she let Lila do her business. She underwent it as if she wasn't there herself.

Lila put the girl on a mat on the floor and sat down next to her. She laid an arm round her shoulders. She thought about telling her what was going to happen to her, but she could not. She did not know if the girl would understand her; for she had not yet said a word.

Ten minutes later, the door of the kitchen was thrown open and the *hijra* came in. Lila shivered.

The man inspected Chinky and gave Lila the order to clean up the mess. He took Chinky by the arm and pulled her with him. They went through a corridor, climbed the marble stairs, and went through another corridor.

The unreal situation she found herself to be in worked like endorphins and numbed Chinky's fear.

They came to a door. The servant knocked and opened the door after he got permission. He pushed Chinky into the room, greeted his boss politely, and left.

Chinky didn't dare to look around. Through a haze, she saw the man who had visited her in the store room. He sat on a bed. She recognized, still hazier, a painting of the god Shiva over the bed; Shiva with a deer, a rattle drum and fire. Sister Satori had once explained to her that Shiva's open hand symbolized his bravery, that the deer was a symbol of a capricious mind, that the rattle drum meant creativity, and that the fire represented destruction. Shiva danced on the head of the demon Apasmara Purusha who represented the human ego.

To Chinky it was, however, no more than a shadowy colour game, hiding an unknown threat.

Maya went to the window and closed the curtains. He pushed a button and a dark red light came on over the painting of Shiva. He took his long coat off, kicked his slippers away, and took his trousers off.

Chinky was astonished and looked anxious. She had no idea why the man had taken his trousers off. Then he also took off his undershirt. Chinky saw a thick, black, hairy belly with a great bulging navel hanging over his underpants. The man then removed his underpants, to show a long, flabby penis, hanging between the pubic hair of his upper legs. The man did this as if he were alone in the room; as if she did not exist.

Chinky only really became afraid when she saw him in his awful nakedness coming towards her.

He grasped her by an arm and pulled her to the bed. He sat down on the edge of the bed and he put her before him. He took off her coat and her shirt without looking at her and he pushed her knickers down. Then he rubbed his hands along her legs, first along the outside and across her buttocks, and then between her thighs.

Chinky was rigid with fear.

Then she felt his moustache slowly coming down and sweeping over her chest. Her terror was so intense that only with great difficulty did she manage not to pee.

When the man could drop his head no further, he laid her on the bed and forced her onto her back. He swept his moustache over her belly.

She could not move and she was so contorted that her body felt dead.

His face appeared again. His mouth looked for her mouth.

There were now tears of disgust gliding along her temples.

He laid a cloth over her eyes.

She then felt a hard thing between her labia. It battered at her to get inside.

She cried out in pain.

He hit her with the outside of his hand on her chin.

She tried to keep quiet.

He became angry as he could not get his penis inside. He guided her hand to his stiff penis.

When she felt a sticky snot in her hand, she pulled her hand back.

Then she could no longer hold in her pee.

Maya felt the warm liquid over his hand and had a terrible fit of anger. He slapped her with both sides of his hand anywhere he could hit her.

She fell from the bed.

His rage had, however, not yet cooled down and he kicked her thighs.

She tried to protect herself with the cushion that lay next to her, but he could not stop his striking and kicking.

When he had blown off steam, he opened the door and dragged her by an arm out of his room.

There she remained, lying naked.

Maya called his *hijra*. "Give the girl in the kitchen the order to clean my bed. Then you must take the new girl back to the store room."

Lila cleaned Maya's bed and she went back to the kitchen, where she knew that she would find Parvati.

Parvati felt deeply unhappy and wounded when Lila had told her what had happened.

One and a half years earlier Lila had, after much insisting by Parvati, been able to confide in her that Maya had abused her. Maya had threatened to kill her if she ever talked about it to anyone. "Every day," Lila had added to it, "when he had no other woman at his disposal."

Parvati decided to wait until the evening. Her husband would be in his living room, as she knew. Either with a woman or watching TV. Round ten o'clock he would have drunk some whisky. He would give his orders from his room and he would only come out to go to the toilet. The life of Amal Maya, Parvati knew better than anyone else, elapsed according to a fixed pattern.

Once, when the store room had not been used for some days and the key had been left in the door, Parvati had made a copy of it. She realized that she feel the wrath of her husband if he ever learned of this. Since their wedding, he saw her as his property, as something that had to obey him and go along with his wishes.

His imagination about her before their marriage quickly shrivelled when he possessed her. What Parvati, however, didn't know was that reality didn't always tune her husband's erotic fantasies. During their marriage, he had had sex with innumerable professional women; and the variation had kept his hope for perfect love in shape.

Parvati now had no doubt that he had misused and battered the new girl. She knew him well enough. She also knew that his anger could easily be stirred up by only a shadow of a thought that he could have something human before him. Such a thought must be immediately suppressed. Maya saw a girl he had paid for as something he had the right to do with as he wished. The opinion of such a girl about his behaviour didn't interest him any more than the opinion of a dog. Maya had an enormous need to be respected by important people, but the opinion of a being of a lower sort held no importance to him. He didn't, therefore, have any feelings of shame.

Around ten o'clock, Parvati looked for the watchman.

"I heard some rustling," she said to him. "Would you please have a look round the house? Otherwise, I will not sleep tonight."

"Of course, ma'am! I shall blame myself personally if you do not sleep quietly. I'll get a torch." The man was very kind.

When he was gone, Parvati took a torch and went to the store room. She opened the door and shone the torch on the face of the girl, who closed her eyes against the fierce light. Parvati saw tracks of blood and dried tears and she saw that the child was dirty. When she lifted her up, the child groaned faintly. Parvati carried her outside and shut the door of the shed. She went quickly to her room with the girl in her arms, and once there, she laid her on the bed. She checked to see if the girl had any fractures or serious wounds but discovered only bruises and dried blood. She cautiously washed the girl with lukewarm water and rubbed a sterilized ointment over the crusted wounds and a palliative ointment over the bruises. After she had nursed the girl, she knelt next to her and gently caressed her forehead and cheeks. "I don't know who you are and I don't know where you come from, but I'll find a way to get you home," she whispered to the child. She went on gently talking.

The girl gradually became a little quieter.

"You've not only been wounded on the outside," she continued, "your soul has also been mistreated. And your parents? They must have been torn apart by sorrow and uncertainty. They probably never discovered what happened to you. They must have questions to which they never received an answer. What is worse than losing one's child in this way? And what is worse for you than losing your parents like this?"

The child did not react. Parvati thought she saw a fleeting gleam of tired gratitude on her face. She kissed the girl on her cheek. "I'll treat you as if you were my daughter," she decided, "and I'll protect you as much as I can. But I am afraid I shall not always be able to save you."

The girl's eyelids flashed open and closed. For a split-second Parvati saw her sadly imploring eyes. Then, yielding to an impulse, she whispered, "I promise you that I shall get you back to your parents."

She was surprised by her own reaction. She had made now a promise the effect of which she absolutely could not oversee. But although she was scared to death of her husband, she also felt a strong self-confidence, a feeling she had not known since her wedding many years ago.

The child fell into a deep sleep. Parvati remained sitting with her, and continued caressing her with all the love she had.

At five o'clock in the morning, she put her nightdress on, threw a duster over it and went to look for the watchman.

"I heard it again," she said. "It sounded as if somebody walked under my window."

"I'll have a look for you, ma'am," the man said.

Parvati took the girl back to the store room, laid her on the mat, spread her clothes over her, and shut the door.

CHAPTER 23

After returning from India, Tom was back at work in The Concern. He phoned Hélène Van Dam to tell her that he had finished his report and that he could deliver it to her the next day. After that, he waited for a suitable moment for a quick look in the English dictionary in the library—- to see if the lost minutes were still there. He had intended to look before leaving for India, but hadn't had a chance.

When he got an opportunity to go to the library, he looked carefully inside. Nobody was there, so he picked up the dictionary and saw that the minutes had disappeared.

"The minutes were gone," were the first words he said to Vera when he got home that evening.

Vera was worried. She was aware of the danger he was in; Hélène Van Dam could draw her own conclusions and put him on the sidelines. "Tom, I hope this won't be the end of your career."

"So far, it seems OK."

"They will not allow you to know something that could jeapordise their plans."

"They probably won't."

"That could mean dismissal."

"If I had taken the minutes with me, then..."

"Do you mean that you would then have a powerful weapon against them? But you haven't got those minutes. Besides, bell-ringers are lepers. You could not live there anymore, let alone work there."

When Sandy brought Tom his coffee the next morning, she asked him to drop by and see her in the afternoon. "I've got a surprise for you," she said.

"For me?"

Sandy smiled and disappeared.

Tom drank his coffee and hurried up to Hélène Van Dam's room.

As she sat diagonally across him in one of the armchairs, she gave him a warm smile.

Tom didn't expect her to give any attention to the report he had offered her. *She will of course talk about those minutes,* he thought.

"You have done a great job, Tom." Hélène Van Dam glanced rapidly over the eight pages of Tom's writing. "Tell me. How did you get on?"

Tom coughed. He had to switch his train of thoughts to the trip. "The trip was quite successful. But the investigation into the pharmaceutical company met with great difficulties. I discovered that the owner of the company is a certain Maya, Amal Maya. The man was very kind and he promised me all the information I wanted, but in the end he gave me no information at all. I had three interviews with him. I visited the company where the products for Medimarket are made and packed five times, but I could not discover anything particular."

"Did you see how they work there?"

"When I was there, the production had closed down."

"You were there five times, and you saw nobody else other than the manager, Ram Majumdar? I suppose you asked him about the work and about the working conditions?"

"Of course! But every time he told me I must have terrible bad luck, as there was by chance a public holiday. There are often religious holidays in India."

"And you could not make an appointment for a suitable working day?"

"Of course I did. But when I went back at the time we had agreed, the door was shut."

"And you called Mr. Maya to ask him to account for this, I suppose?"

"Of course I did. I had to make a new appointment with him, but that man is so terribly important that making an appointment alone took me a few days. The appointment for the last interview required eight phone calls and a letter. His secretary did what she could to put me in contact with Maya, but the man has an enormous arsenal of excuses; a normal man would lose heart after the umpteenth time. I tried for eight days to get in touch with him. Then I wrote him a letter. The answer was a visit from his secretary to my hotel; she was desperate. She told me she had read the letter to Mr. Maya and that he had promised her that he would receive me two days later. Indeed, he did that. When I went to him then, his secretary was already there to act as an interpreter. She apologized in English for the behaviour of her boss, who obviously didn't understand this. When I asked him why he had made me wait, as I was a representative of an important business relationship, he denied quite simply that he knew anything of my attempts to make an appointment. He remained extremely courteous. And he promised me quite kindly that he would make sure that I could see the production process in his company. After that interview, I went to the company twice, but again, both times, the company was closed. I am afraid that there is something in the production process that someone was at great pains to hide from us."

"Were there no other sources of information? Mrs. Sarásvati, for example?"

"Mrs Sarásvati told me what she could tell me."

"What is your advice, Tom?"

"Medimarket should break off all connections with Maya. I also gave this advice in my report."

"Without any firm evidence that something was wrong with the working conditions?"

"Indeed, I could not establish solid evidence."

"It will not be easy to convince the board of governors. Maya's company is quite profitable for The Concern."

"I am sorry that I can't produce any hard evidence."

"Tom, I propose this: I am going to read your report. Then we shall discuss it tomorrow night at dinner, with a glass of good wine. What do you think of that?"

Tom saw the seductive smile of the woman before him. But he was now also convinced that Hélène Van Dam must have some idea of the existence of child slavery in Maya's company, a phenomenon from which Medimarket achieved great profit. He had, it is true, not mentioned child slavery in Maya's company in so many words, but he had hinted it well enough.

"I have an engagement with Vera tomorrow night."

"No problem! We can do it the day after tomorrow."

Tom hesitated. "This is already the second time you have invited me, and I can do nothing in return for you."

"But you don't need to do anything in return! You have already made yourself quite useful to The Concern!"

"Okay! The day after tomorrow it is then."

That afternoon, Tom dropped in to see Sandy.

Sandy poured coffee and sat down in front of him. She gave him a sheet of paper. "Look what I found."

It was the lost minutes.

"How did you discover them?"

"Do you remember what you said to me? You said that Mrs. Van Dam had put the minutes on her desk. And while she was away in the library, somebody must have taken them."

"It's possible that I said this."

"So I said to myself: It could be that Hélène Van Dam put the minutes into a book, and that she took that book back into the library later, and she forgot that the minutes were in it. That morning I had seen an English dictionary on her desk. Well, you see, my reasoning was right."

Tom hesitated between admiration and curiosity.

"Well, read them! Then you will understand better than me.

Tom read:

Strictly confidential!!!

Report of the extraordinary conference of the Board of Governors and the Board of Directors of Medimarket, with reference to an order for a survey into the situation of General Practitioners in the country.

The president, Mr. D, bids Mrs. Van Dam, his fellow members of the Board of Governors, Jonkheer Hoogen-Van der Wal, the gentlemen Jova and Hormans, and the directors Bot, Lak and Mocker heartily welcome.

He expressly points out that everything discussed in this meeting is highly confidential and must remain strictly secret.

For the sake of secrecy, he proposes also leaving instructions for performing the survey-project, to be discussed in this meeting, to him, Mr. D...

Furthermore, the chairman reminds the board of governors of Medimarket that it has been judged in an earlier meeting that The Concern's market-oriented approach regarding its extensive arsenal of medicines should be better profiled. He suggests an investigation into the most important target group for Medimarket, the general practitioners, to visualize the market situation; and to tune the Medimarket policy in due course to the results of this investigation. He invites those present to help by giving meaning in this meeting to the investigation project in question.

The meeting takes the following decisions with regard to the investigation project in question:

Researchers should examine:

- *to what extent G.P.'s in their prescribing are more aimed to standard prescriptions and/or to their patients;*
- *to what extent G.P.'s are sensitive to money;*
- *what knowledge G.P.'s have of medicines and how far their knowledge can be refreshed by Medimarket;*
- *how far and how G.P.'s can be influenced when prescribing;*
- *how G.P.'s can be best convinced of the effect of the medicines delivered by Medimarket.*

The meeting proposes:
Informative conferences in pleasant resorts; presents; bonus payments; attractive sales representatives; etc.

Finally, the chairman announces that Mrs. Mirabelle Bot, who, after a partial medical study, and who has been a sales representative for some years, will be invited to care for the subject 'Presentation' in a course for sales representatives.

The expenses for the research will be discounted in the prices of the medicines.

The paper trembled in Tom's hand.
Sandy waited quietly for his reaction.
"This must be destroyed, Sandy."
"Why?"
"If they ever find this…"
"I will not leave it here; just imagine, they could ransack my belongings again."

As they were sitting at the table that evening, Vera told Tom that she had paid a visit to Mirabelle Bot that afternoon. "She had invited me to tea. So I thought, let's go; that woman needs a pat on the back. The idea that someone finds her worth a visit already seemed important to her."

"It's good that you did it."

Tom thought back to Mirabelle's anniversary.

He and Vera had discussed a present. The result was a decorated candle.

Mirabelle had opened the door.

Her mouth had a bitter quality. Her cheekbones stuck sharply out. Faintly sunken cheeks marked a bony lower jaw. A hairdresser had fashioned a cotton candy in artificial colours round her head. The corrections cried out for attention.

Vera and Tom's embraces were tolerated.

Later, when they looked for an opening to a conversation with some other guests, they heard a shrill laugh in the kitchen. It immediately became dead quiet in the house. Nobody moved. All attention was fixed on the kitchen door.

Vera pinched Tom's hand. She knew: their present had been chosen wrongly. After endless seconds, Mirabelle appeared, but was quiet. Her eyes looked broken. As if nobody was home, she went past them to the front door. Nobody had heard the bell.

Bill and Bhikni Mocker then came in.

That evening they saw Mirabelle with her arm hanging from a sagging shoulder. She brought her cigarette agitatedly to her mouth. She tipped the ashes off after each pull. It was as though she was steered on remote control. Her eyes were empty. Her face was ashen, and ugly with dissatisfaction. She breathed hurriedly. With the smoke of her cigarette she seemed to inhale every gleam of attention she could. No mark of feeling. As if a worm had gnawed for years at her soul.

"I feel deeply sorry for her," Tom heard Vera say.

"In what way?"

"She was under the influence of alcohol. I wonder if it was an exception. She told me that she couldn't sleep and that she often got up, perspiring and with a dry mouth. Mirabelle is oversensitive. She is haunted by phantoms about what people think of her. Innocent remarks about her figure or her shoes are carefully weighed in front of an imaginary mirror. She must be found nice. To endure criticism one needs some self-respect."

"I think her haughty."

"She gives that impression. She tries to fill the gap of feeling worthless with the conviction that she is not like ordinary people. That gives her a look of haughtiness."

"So if I knew her better, I wouldn't think her haughty."

"Maybe."

"Did you know that she was a sales representative in medicines?"

"Yes, she told me that. She broke off her medical study after two years; she didn't like it anymore. Then she worked as a sales representative."

CHAPTER 24

Tom stood on a high, steep cliff. His upper body was strapped into the belt of a hang-glider. He shuffled cautiously toward the edge of the cliff. He then looked into the breathtaking depths of the valley. He put one foot in front of the other one. But no matter how often he did this, he failed to get a foot over the edge. He knew that the step over the edge had to be made; only by stepping over the edge and by relying on the wings of the glider would he be free. A mysterious force, however, held him back from taking the decisive step over the edge of the cliff.

It's the hang-glider's fault that I can't step over the edge, he thought, *the wings are too short.*

If I fix the sails on the glider they can pull me over the edge of the cliff.

But the wings appeared to be too long, so that they were jammed on the bottom of the cliff.

I must build a mill under the hang-glider to give more room to the wings.

Old classmates, colleagues and an old neighbour helped him with the building. More people got involved. Working together, they built a mill under the hang-glider.

But the flight was still not sucessful; every time they tried out the hang-glider-mill, something failed.

I want to fly! I must fly!

Before he awoke Tom saw a mouse in a turning wheel trying to climb up toward the mice that looked less grey in the fierce light high in the mill. At a well-chosen moment, the mouse risked the jump from a turning wheel to a narrow ladder that led to a turning wheel higher in the mill. If he had timed it wrongly, he would have fallen back onto the wheel, or maybe even onto the work floor. The smart mouse stayed on the wheel that was moved on by other mice, to risk the jump at the right moment. He then grabbed the tail of another mouse and clambered upward.

At the bottom of the mill, on the level of the work floor, was a little door. That door was open. The mice on the floor could see that door and could leave the dark mill if they wished.

Tom sat apathetically behind his desk recollecting his dream of the previous night. Rags of the memory of his dinner with Hélène Van Dam haunted his thoughts in fits and starts between images from his dream. It had already been two weeks ago. He had wanted to say no, but he hadn't been able to do so. Nevertheless, he hadn't seen it as an obligation; she was a seductive woman, wasn't she?

No, he had enjoyed the meal with this woman despite the fact that she deliberately cooperated in a policy he thought hypocritical. That she had been talking about that policy and he had not been able to say what he wanted to say had made him angry. His promise to Parvati that he would not put Sarásvati in danger, and his lack of hard evidence had made him keep his mouth shut. He had not been able to add more than unfounded advice.

He had seen the high priestess of The Concern as a supernatural being, one who had come down to earth and taken the form of an ordinary woman. The minutes of the meeting about the research into the G.P.'s prescribing behaviour had made it still worse.

"They target on profit, on eternally growing profit. And on their positions. They don't believe in human beings; they only believe in capital and careers."

His interest in Medimarket activities had become colourless for Tom after his experiences with Maya's company and after reading the minutes about the research into G.P.'s behaviour. A hangover in his mind troubled him. And the dizzy atmosphere in his room was soaked with desperateness. A butterfly, who with endless patience tried to reach the free world outside, kept stubbornly bouncing against the window. Tom opened the window and showed the butterfly to freedom.

He paced up and down through his room. He rummaged a little through some papers on his desk. And he glanced for the umpteenth time through the thick innovation report he had contributed to himself. The innovation of policy, and of terminology, gave him the feeling that he was desperately old-fashioned. He could not keep up with the complicated formulations and calculations any more. The gentle reminders of Vinnie de Haas about back reporting pounded already for a while on his feelings of self-esteem.

In a meeting about the report one day earlier he had kept his mouth shut, afraid to say anything stupid. Echoes of beautiful sentences from that meeting had repeated themselves in his sleep. This had been the run-up to his dream about the mice in the mill.

The innovation report, which eight people had worked on for seven months, lay before him. With empty eyes he looked at the voluminous tome. He saw his contribution to it as an action of complicity in a growing madness. He had made an attempt to read it, but he felt dyslexic.

Then, as his empty eyes gazed in front of him, he suddenly felt a pinching string round his breast.

He dropped into an armchair. It was the pain he was afraid of. Since his heart infarction five months earlier he had not been free from fear, although he had recovered miraculously quickly.

Tom decided to call the medical officer.

"Shall we try hypnotherapy?" The physician looked up from a file he had just scrawled some notes in.

As his patient had not automatically agreed with his proposal, a weak frown of incomprehension grew on his forehead. It had not occurred to Tom that the question had to be interpreted as a kind prescription.

He had presented a series of complaints to the physician. "I don't feel able to do my work anymore; the simplest job costs me an enormous effort. Shortness of breath bothers me very much. And sometimes I am tormented by a pain at my breast and in my left arm."

"Your blood pressure is very high, Mr. Corda. And your cholesterol level doesn't satisfy me either. And you are about twenty pounds too heavy."

"Twenty pounds?" Tom replied anxiously.

"You are overweight, Mr. Corda. You should see a dietician. And you need more exercise."

"Exercise?"

"You could walk for an hour every day. Or biking could be good as well."

"Walking? Biking? I am already tired to death at the end of the day without walking or biking. And at night I lay awake for hours. I have always worked hard, but I can't do it anymore."

"You are rather tense. And that is the reason that I mention hypnotherapy."

"What good would that do?"

"You could learn to relax. I am going to refer you to the health service of the New World Therapeutic Center." The physician explained what Tom could expect there. He gave him a pamphlet about the NWTC and a pile of forms. The hall of mirrors of the New World Therapeutic Center where the therapy would take place was displayed in colour on the pamphlets.

"And rest for a couple of weeks!" the doctor said before Tom left the consulting room.

Tom needed three hours to fill in the twelve pages of the registration form. The questions about identity, relatives, past, work and health complaints were, for the most part, formulated in an other-worldly language. Tom's allergy to forms began to manifest itself. "Are they even going to read all these answers?" he asked himself.

A grey, autumnal drizzle isolated him on his first free Monday. It was cold in the house and in himself. He felt only emptiness in and around himself. He was missing something to hold on to, to live for. The future had overexposed the present with inflated expectations. But now he was thrown back upon himself, upon the reality of today.

He now had time for himself; he now could do the jobs he had always been intending to do. But without an ordered schedule, all his plans were adrift. It began to dawn on Tom that he had grown addicted to the rhythm that had been supplied by a hectic working system. His life rhythm had run away with him.

Dragged away from a fixed and safe pattern of living and working, he now had to find his own way. Something in him prompted him to think that he now had to arrange his life by himself. He had to make choices, free from a system of appointments and commitments. But how could he strike out on a new course, as every objective had fallen away? He missed the rhythm of shaving, washing, breakfast, the traffic jams, arriving late at work, the meetings, the coffee breaks. And he also missed, strangely enough, colleagues.

He realized deep in his heart that he had been wrapped up in a system of rules and procedures. His responsibility had been surveyable. He realized that his self-respect had hung by a thread. He had lived on the appreciation, as a matter of fact, that was woven into his position.

He had quickly got tired the last time, but the fear of criticism had given him the force, on credit indeed.

The fear of the pain in his chest had now overwhelmed that other fear, the fear of becoming superfluous. There was now a strange, weakly fermenting emptiness that was in discord with his feelings and that increased his restlessness. He experienced a sort of jetlag. It kept him awake at night and causing unexpected attacks of sleep by day. He dreamt about people with piles of paper. People who infected each other with a sense of solidarity and responsibility.

Tom had never deeply explored the question of the meaning of life and what his purpose on earth was. Now he suddenly stood with that question in front of a grey hole. The organized, contolled life had gone.

And the 'couple of weeks' the medical examiner had made reference to had been a comforting introduction to another life.

The drizzle had stopped. The sun was even breaking through.

Tom fled his house and after a while found himself sitting at the edges of a wood.

Sitting there and thinking, nature slowly began to calm his racing thoughts. An army of red wood ants demanded his attention. Female workers lugged lice, flies and caterpillars. They climbed in a confusing jostle over each other.

Tom tried to imagine the way ants were thinking. *Do they have their own personality? They have their antenae and senses of smell, but I see only swarming egos, an inimitable complicated, endless pattern.* He became mesmerized by the question as to whether it had happened arbitrarily or if they were guided by whom- or whatever. *They go on their way so accurately. What is the purpose of all this? Of all the trillions and trillions of ants in the world?*

The mystery made him more restful and he was afforded the peaceful rest that being at one with nature can offer.

The ants were less bound by their lanes than motorists; they negotiated obstacles more dexterously and changed direction quickly. There were no jams.

Tom cast his thoughts back to the daily commuter traffic jams. *I never became jam-resistant,* he realized. *But I did not find it abnormal, the daily drive to and from my work, with the familiar intersections and crawling traffic; everyone took the car, so.... My colleagues would have thought I was mad if I had taken the train. The daily drive had become an automatic activity, had unreasonably found its way. But otherwise, I would have had to wait fifteen minutes for a connection.*

He sat in quiet astonishment at the edge of the wood. He felt free. Free from wishing to be indispensable, free from believing in a career. It occurred to him that he didn't need to be afraid of becoming unnecessary. He felt the sunlight entering through the pores of his skin and penetrating to his soul. He noticed that he could still enjoy life.

He was reminded of the little boy he had been at eight. It seemed as though it were only yesterday. A new teacher in the school had praised his story; she had not looked at the faults in his essay. It had felt like dawn dew on bare feet. But nevertheless, he had wondered how many errors he had made.

How can time have slid so through my fingers so quickly? he wondered. *Life is an hourglass in which the opening in the wasp waist wears through the years out. The older I got, the more hours and days escaped like powdery silver sand through the meshes of my experience. As if time makes ever larger jumps, from one recollection to the next one. Without the perspective of the innumerable events between then and now standing by in my memory, the past looks like the distance between the beach and the morning sun rising out of the sea. My life looks like an arbitrary summary of impressions, floating on the surface. Or is it routine that, like weeds, have choked my consciousness of time? And are my memories, coming to my perception, still real thoughts? Or do they just come and go, as no more than rags, connected by associations and elusive as bats? And go on haunting my sleep as lifelike experiences in a clear and defenseless subconscious?*

CHAPTER 25

About seven o'clock in the morning, Tom regained consciousness. He shaved, took a bath, and tuned his clothing to a five-day stay in a chic world: a smooth jacket-combination, a striped shirt and a new tie.

He called for a taxi and let himself be taken to the New World Therapeutic Center.

After climbing a number of steps, he stood before a stately double door. He pulled at a chain and a bronze lion head came down; a heavy gong boomed through the building.

After a minute the heavy doors receded back. A man of about seventy in a grey doorkeeper's uniform invited him inside, took his suitcase, put it in a corner, and asked Tom to follow him.

Paintings were hung at eye level on the walls of the broad corridors. Every five meters deep, oak doorposts with carved doors were deeply sunk in. Dark marble reflected the royal light cast from heavy cast-iron chandeliers. Tom felt confused and numbed by the kaleidoscope of impressions.

The doorkeeper knocked on one of the doors and opened it after a woman's voice had called, "Come in!"

The furnishings in the room that Tom had entered showed a simple taste. On a background of olive-green walls two etchings were hanging. In a corner was a table with three easy chairs around it. In another corner was a mahogany desk.

A very blond woman of about forty in a black silk dress was sitting behind the desk. Face cream, eye shadow, red lipstick, and an eye for perfection of detail had converted her into a beauty. Self-assured and tall in her pumps, she formed a welcome with her arms and helped Tom through his bewilderment with a smile. "I am Mrs.

Baanders. I hope we can offer you a useful and pleasant time with us."

She showed him to an armchair and sat down across from him.

"What do you want to drink?" She pushed a button.

A young girl in a black skirt and a white blouse appeared and Mrs. Baanders ordered two coffees. The girl withdrew, faintly inclining her head. Two minutes later she was back with a silvery tray. She put the tray on the table between them. Mrs. Baanders thanked the girl with a lovely smile. She served the coffee from a silver pot and presented some cookies on a crystal plate.

Tom felt faintly tense.

Mrs. Baanders encouraged him with a smile. "You don't need to be worried; you are in expert hands here. And everything we do will be discussed with you beforehand."

Tom thought this was reassuring.

Mrs. Baanders drank elegantly from her coffee cup. She directed her eyes for a moment to an imaginary point in the room and said, "Tell me about yourself."

"About myself?"

"Your health symptoms."

"Did you read the forms I filled out?"

"Please tell me again."

Tom hesitated, and looked for words. "You read about my work in the forms, I suppose."

"It doesn't satisfy you?"

"I have the impression that I am getting worse. I read reports and minutes without knowing what I am reading. I nearly choked on the piles of paper about innovations and reorganizations. Nobody can explain to me what the purpose of all that paper is, but everybody thinks it necessary. I run after the eternal developments. I was starting to feel useless and superfluous. I can't sleep. I am in a spiral: I am too tired to sleep, and the tiredness gets worse from lack of sleep. But the worst of all is the pain in my chest."

Tom kept silent. He had loosened up more than he had intended to.

Mrs. Baanders explored her fingertips. After a while she looked up. "I hope we can help you. But I have great confidence in Mrs. Van Zon who will lead the sessions. She is a skillful therapist."

Tom nodded. "We shall see," his eyes said.

Mrs. Baanders's face relaxed to form a satisfied trait around her mouth. "I am sure you'll be all right." She rose. "I'll show you the hall of mirrors."

She took him through the stately corridors he had come through to the hall his imagination had already anticipated. The picture in the pamphlet appeared to be an austere reproduction of the reality. Tom's eyes had to get used to the dazzling reflection from an overwhelming quantity of neon lights in an endless row of mirrors along the walls, creating a round hall with a cross section of about twenty meters into an endless brightly illuminated space. Everything in the room reflected light.

Even Mrs. Baanders needed time to recover. She inhaled deeply in before entering. She took him to the middle of the hall with the controlled pride of an insider towards a layman.

Tom had to get used to the illumination and the splendour.

Mrs. Baanders left Tom some time to recover. She beamed with pride as he looked drunk with astonishment. She showed him a set of fifteen alcoves behind the mirrors. "Our hypnotic sessions take place there, led by our highly qualified therapists," she whispered, as if they were attending mass. "Unfortunately I can't show you now, as we have patients here constantly."

They left the hall of mirrors.

"At two o'clock in the afternoon, Mrs. Van Zon will come and pick you up for your first session. She will put you under a light hypnosis. Actually it is more a physical relaxation. You will be able to think more clearly than normally. On the screen in front of you pictures will appear. Then you will slip away in a dreamy condition. Screen and dream will flow together. You'll dream and the therapist will allow you some time for that to occur. And after that you can discuss your dream with her."

After her explanation Mrs. Baanders asked Tom to follow her. "I shall show you to the suite you will stay in."

The luxury of his five-day accommodation seemed beyond Tom's means and position.

Mrs. Baanders seemed to guess at his thoughts. "Many prominent people also come here," she told him. "But would you excuse me now? If you wait here, you'll be fetched for the lunch shortly."

Mrs. Baanders left him alone with his overwhelmed thoughts.

Tom dropped into an easy chair and tried to calm his stirring mind.

Just before two o'clock, Mrs. Van Zon came for Tom.

She was a beautiful woman. A massage with scented oil had given her face a gloss of youthful health. Light blue daydreaming eyes. Her golden, faintly waving hair left a slender woman's neck for the greater part uncovered. She was well and carefully dressed: a red blouse over a tight skirt of light blue denim. She wore some silver rings and bracelets. She gave Tom a slim hand with red varnished nails on long, slender fingers. "Hello! I am Clare van Zon. Mrs. Baanders probably told you about me."

"Yes, she did. I am Tom Corda."

"May I call you Tom?"

Tom nodded.

"Please, call me Clare. Would you come with me?" She smiled kindly.

Chatting about the splendour of the hall of mirrors, Clare van Zon led him straight to one of the alcoves. She invited him into a comfortable armchair that looked a dentist's chair. Diagonally above him, hung a great screen. In the background Tom heard a calming babble of heavenly electronic music.

The therapist sat down to his right, a little higher than Tom, so that she could see him and the screen. She smiled down at him. "You seem a little tense," she said in a friendly tone. "You don't need to be worried!"

Tom smiled back.

"It doesn't matter; I'll let you relax."

What must she think of me? Tom wondered.

"Lay your arms on the armrests. Let it all just happen."

After a short pause she left one part of his body after the other strained and then relaxed.

A deeply warm whispering voice accompanied him.

Tom slid slowly away into glorious peace. His mind was very clear.

"You'll see pictures on the screen and you can quietly let them sink in. After a while your eyes will close. Then the pictures will melt into dreams."

Tom saw hazy figures on the screen loom up out of a foggy realm of shadows and slowly develop into human beings. He saw an old man with a mitre on his head and a cope, stitched with gold, over his shoulders. He had a staff in his right hand. Behind the old man was a Jewish rabbi with a skullcap on his head, wearing a black cassock and with a seven-branched candlestick in his right hand.

After an indefinite period of time Tom heard a Muslim scribe praying. The recitative singing of the man and his nasal-sounding voice made Tom drowsy. His eyes closed.

The old man with the cope remained in Tom's dream. The man rose from his throne and strode in a stately fashion in a procession of clerical and secular leaders through the hall of mirrors that was now a rich and colossal cathedral, veiled in a churchly twilight of stained-glass windows with sanctuary lamp and candlelight. From an endlessly far background, Tom heard the lightly plucking harp sound in the hypnotizing voice of Clare van Zon, in a peaceful harmony with the munificent rest he was undergoing. She encouraged him to enjoy what he saw.

As her voice died slowly away he saw the procession striding toward a gold font with gentle organ sounds in the background. Next to the font he saw Hélène Van Dam with a child in her arms. When he looked up he looked into her eyes. She went to meet him at the font. The man with the mitre and the cope came to him. On his old face was a tired, earnest expression. Tom saw that at the top of his staff there was a large character D in gold.

The old man anointed his forehead with oil. He then put white powder on his tongue.

Tom wanted to cry, but the powder prevented that.

The old man poured water out of a gold bowl over his forehead and spoke solemnly: "I baptize you in the name of...the father...the son...and the holy...authority."

The clerical and secular leaders came to stand around him, looked down at him and mumbled magical words.

Then they resumed their procession.

Mr. D was in front, with the mitre on his head and the gold staff in his right hand.

His secretary followed after him.

Tom wanted to say that she shouldn't leave him there, but his mouth was stuck down by the white powder.

Then he heard the voice of the therapist with its velvety timbre. It seemed as if the sound came slowly at him from a distance. "I believe you had a nice dream." The words sang in his ears.

Tom rubbed his tongue and moistened his lips. He remained in a rosy and peaceful rest. It felt as if his body slept on but his mind was miraculously clear.

He told the therapist about his dream and he was surprised that his voice sounded so clear. It seemed as if he heard himself talking in his dream.

"I don't know," he completed his story, "where the pictures ended and where the dream started."

"A surprising dream!" The voice of Clare van Zon said thoughtfully.

"Yes, surprising indeed."

"We shall take our time. Perhaps the dream will show something of its meaning."

Free from space and time in his light hypnosis, Tom heard and felt the therapeutic velour in her voice. And as he had a feeling of being rocked in a floating dream world, his head nodded yes.

Clare smiled. She allowed him his thoughts.

"It was as if I saw everything in a great mirror," Tom said.

Clare raised her eyebrows. "We are going to drink a cup of coffee," she decided. "First, I am going to get you out of your hypnosis." Using a yoga-awakening ritual, she pulled Tom slowly out of his clear slumber. When he, awake and rosy and still deliciously relaxed, looked up at her, he saw a friendly, pensive face.

After the coffee she let him take his place in the chair again.

"Are you still thinking of your dream?"

"No."

"Okay!"

Clare van Zon took him for a second time into a peaceful rest and then into a slight slumber that gave him, at the same time, a clearing consciousness. She laid her hands on his shoulders and massaged his skin and the underlying muscles.

He felt the last bit of tension slip out of his shoulders.

She allowed him some time to enjoy the rest he felt in himself.

"Are you thinking of anything special?" she asked after a while, in a whisper.

"This is an unknown experience and I've no words for it."

"Shall we go back to your dream?"

Tom took his time. He felt gloriously relaxed and he was at the same time surprised about his clarity of thought. He knew also that he could say what he thought. "The baptism," he began, "and the white powder...the man with the staff put on my tongue..."

"What would you tell me about that?"

"I ate it out of his hand."

"Oh!"

"It tasted sweet."

That evening Tom sat in the room that was his for five days. It was quiet, quieter than he was used to.

Pieces of thoughts haunted his head. He realized suddenly that he had been seamlessly interwoven with Medimarket and that he had unconsciously tuned himself to expectations in The Concern. He had floated on the daily waves of routine in the system. His responsibilities, woven in formal and informal expectations, had not weighed too heavy.

He shook these thoughts off and sank away into unconscious.

After an hour he started awake. He got undressed, took a shower and fell asleep.

"The Concern would manage equally well without me." Stirring his coffee, Tom looked with filmy eyes at the therapist.

"What do you mean?"

"I am not indispensible there."

"So?" She furrowed her forehead in question.

"I won't be missed."

"How do you know?"

"I am a nonentity in that capital world."

"Maybe there are people in that world who appreciate you."

"Maybe."

On his last afternoon they went for a long walk.

They walked for kilometers without saying a word. They just enjoyed the gentle spring weather.

It was Tom who broke the silence. "When you laid your hands on my shoulders it was an unknown feeling for me. It seemed as if an antenna, one that had turned inwardly for years, became loose from old rust. As though my feelings did not need to be on the defence any longer."

She laid an arm round his shoulders.

They went on walking.

"I haven't breathed so deeply for years. I don't know whether this is the effect of the nature or of the relaxation exercises."

"Both," she answered; "and because you now live following what your heart tells you."

He stood still. "My heart...I haven't thought about my heart for a week!"

"Then it didn't bother you either."

"Could my heart complaint be caused by stress?"

"I don't know."

"Then I should resign from my job at The Concern. What would they think?"

"They would look for somebody else."

He shrugged his shoulders.

"Tom, listen to me. We are far from The Concern here, far from the epicenter of stereotypical thinking. You should regularly refresh your thinking and feeling by walking in nature."

"I think I need that; all life in me was extinguished."

"Now and then all of us fall into autopilot. And we need a whole life to discover ourselves."

CHAPTER 26

The minutes of the last meeting were more stubbornly piloted through the assembly then the chairman wanted. As always, he had firmly resolved to keep the discussion short, to prevent items from the previous meeting getting a second life. But in spite of his intentions, the minutes were gone through with a fine-tooth comb, although everybody knew that they would be filed away in the archives.

Tom abstained from commentary, to avoid increasing the proliferation of opinions and misunderstandings.

"Ladies and gentlemen, I propose approving the minutes of the last meeting." Lak kept the time for reactions short, so the hesitation of Vinnie de Haas could not be activated. He beat his wooden hammer on the table. "I confirm the approval of the minutes of the previous meeting."

The chairman then announced the next item on the agenda, the item Tom had been waiting for.

"Three months ago the president of the board of governors gave me the order to have the management of one of our business connections investigated, the pharmaceutical company in Benares, India, and to evaluate our trade with that company."

Tom let the rest of the introduction by the chairman go by him. He was thinking of what he had to say himself. He resolved to defend his advice to the board of governors tooth and nail, in spite of a lack of evidence. *And I shall tell them what I did there.* He did not realize that his intention to make an impression made him a little too tense for a good fight. Clare van Zon had helped him get better with her relaxation therapy; Tom hadn't felt so good for years. But her advice was now forgotten.

"I found Mr. Corda willing to make inquiries on the spot."

Invited by the chairman, Tom started to talk about the approach of his inquiries.

"First, I discovered who the owner of the company is. The man is called Amal Maya. Maya is a rich and powerful man in the town and for miles around. He has a great influence in both political and societal events. I therefore took steps to contact him as soon as possible. It turned out, however, to be quite difficult to make contact with him; but with much patience I succeeded in making an appointment. I got interviews with both Amal Maya and Ram Mayumdar, the manager of the company."

Tom mentioned what he had discussed with the two men and which aspects he had given attention to during his investigation. He told them which steps he had taken, and that all that steps had yielded no results and this was due to a total lack of cooperation from the owner and the manager of the company. He argued that because of that lack of cooperation, he had no trust at all in Maya's business. And he announced that in a confidential report he had clarified to the board of governors, that if Medimarkt was to go on purchasing the products of Maya's business, they could get into great trouble, for reasons he could not, much to his regret, tell at the meeting. He ended his argument with the announcement that he had advised the board of governors to abandon the purchase of products from the Indian company. He thanked everybody for their attention and looked expectantly around the circle.

He saw, however, only blank faces.

He had not expected applause; well, some respect or appreciation. It produced a feeling of forboding. He began to wonder if he had said something stupid.

The chairman broke the silence. "Your consideration is extremely interesting. But before I give my opinion, I should like to offer the opportunity to the other members of the meeting to react on Mr. Corda's words."

There was something deadly in the kindness of Lak's voice.

Nobody reacted. The chairman then decided to do something about it. "Mr. Huls, can you approve of Mr. Corda's conclusion?"

James Huls straightened up. He looked around for a moment and then addressed the chairman. "Thank you, Mr. Chairman. First I would like to state that I didn't get the opportunity to study Mr. Corda's report to the board of governors. That doesn't, however, prevent me from making a marginal note about his argument."

His eyes rounded the circle to make sure that everybody was listening to him. He cleared his throat and went on. "Mr. Corda rounded off his inquiries with a far-reaching conclusion without giving us any valid arguments. His conclusion was based on the fact that he could not inquire into things that the board of governors would have inquired about. It could be that Mr. Corda doesn't sufficiently realize that this concerns an extremely profitable business relationship. Therefore, there must be very important reasons to end such a relationship; I can't deduce any such reasons based on Mr. Corda's argument."

Huls aroused an intent expectation from his listeners by inserting a silence.

"Mr. Chairman, ladies and gentlemen. Every investigation has to start from the question what the financial importance for The Concern might be. Therefore, with respect for Mr. Corda's work, I would like to see his inquiries carried out further."

Huls looked modestly around the circle. Then he went on, "I would have liked to offer Mr. Corda my help; but my diary was already more than full. However, I am willing to give Mr. Corda advice in the event of further inquiries."

"Thank you, Mr. Huls, for your much appreciated comments."

Nobody reacted to Huls's words.

Lak needed some time to think about how he could get the discussion going. Huls's argument had not invited discussion.

Huls filled the lacuna.

"Mr. Chairman, I thought about a possible solution to this problem."

"He is shameless," Tom thought, as Huls told about his possible solution.

But instead of reacting to Huls' words, Tom drifted, by means of a web of associations, unconsciously and out of control, into a lively daydream. In that dream he saw the voluminous Huls as a little iron ball between countless other little iron balls, caught in a giant magnetic field by a magnet under plate glass. In that magnetic field there was a continuous, nervous motion of the mass of tiny balls that all inclined to a now and then changing point. The little balls grouped themselves, as commanded, in greater and smaller connections. Groups of balls melted together. Balls that hung back, as if looking for the why of it, were forced into the same direction. Some little balls could free themselves from the magnetic force and live their own lives, in the margin of the magnetic field.

The predictable world of the magnetic forces held Tom's attention for a while. That's why he didn't hear what Huls had been saying. But he did hear how Huls rounded off the proclamation of his message.

"I have therefore ordered an inquiry in my department into the most profitable possibilities. Although this inquiry hasn't yet been finished, I am cautiously thinking of a new emission of shares, the sale of which we can use to fund the acquisition of Mr. Maya's company.

Tom realized that Huls in his enthusiasm had floated so far away that he had launched a proposal to take over Maya's company. He shook his head and tried to concentrate on the meeting.

Huls had taken his message to its climax.

Tom felt paralysed by the air Huls had spoken with. He even began to ask himself if he had done his inquiry well enough.

Sandy Kamat came in. "Good afternoon, ladies and gentlemen! I have a delicious cup of coffee for you."

Her unconstrained voice brought Tom back to reality.

Lak ruffled, looked up.

"Do you want me to wait?" Sandy asked him.

"No, you don't need to..." Lak decided to make the best of the situation. "Ladies and gentlemen, I would suggest a short break."

Nobody said a word as they got their coffee. Only Bill Mocker said, "Thank you very much!"

Tom nodded, with a sad smile, and got a smile back.

Sandy did not seem to perceive the silence. She went around with her coffee pot and had a kind word for everybody. Little stars in her eyes seemed to defy the weight of their work.

After the coffee, the chairman reopened the meeting.

Bill Mocker asked if he might have a word.

"Mr. Chairman, Mr. Corda has in my opinion sufficiently clarified that there are good reasons, maybe unclear to us, to end the ties with Maya's company. I propose therefore to respect his advice to the board of governors."

The reaction of the assembly was an indignant muttering.

Bot broke prevailing confusion. "On what grounds does Mr. Mocker think that he can respect Mr. Corda's advice to the board of governors?" The certainty of his tone made his question a rhetorical one. "None of us can form a judgment about this. I therefore propose leaving the judgment to the board of governors."

There was nothing to bring up against Bot's arguing.

The chairman came to Bot's aid and said, "The board of governors is quite able to decide independently; so I propose that we wait for their decision. Besides, I can inform you that the board is thinking about suspending a decision, pending further investigation."

Wordless agreement buzzed round the table. Agreement in the interest of decisiveness was usual in The Concern.

"Ladies and gentlemen," the chairman went on, "the board of governors will ask Mr. Corda to again travel to Benares to have another attempt at getting access to the information we need. Mr. Corda can undoubtedly rely on the expert advice of Mr. Huls."

Lak's words were a complete surprise to Tom. He nodded, a little flabbergasted. "I am, of course, willing to do anything to gain a better insight into Maya's business. But I will once again point out to all of you that Mr. Maya did not show any willingness at all to grant me inspection into the management of his company."

"Can that lack of willingness actually be reconciled with Mr. Maya's reputation?" Charles Bot asked. "I can tell you this—I got this information from a quite reliable source—Mr. Maya is known as a charming person."

"He is charming and clever," Tom answered.

"Then I hope that you can make it clear to him that it is also in his interest that we get a good insight into the state of affairs of his company, Mr. Corda."

Tom nodded.

"I declare the meeting closed!" Lak tapped his hammer on the table.

CHAPTER 27

It was seven o'clock on Friday night; time to usher in the weekend. Tom pulled the curtains shut, isolating Vera and himself from the outside world, in the shelter of their house. He had uncorked a bottle of red wine, had peeled the potatoes and cleaned the vegetables. Vera had cooked. Tom set the table and lit a few candles.

This allocation of tasks had grown through the years: she cooked; he was the cook's mate.

They took their time eating; a luxury they only permitted themselves on the weekends.

After the meal they did the washing-up together. She washed; he dried.

As Tom finished wiping the last plate, he grabbed at his breast. His face was ashen and twisted with pain. His eyes reflected a wild, helpless agony, as if the ground under his feet was sinking away.

Vera was just in time to break his fall.

Seconds passed before she could make a decision. She called Frank, their neighbour.

Frank dialed the emergency number.

The waiting time was endless. But when the ambulance came, time sped up again.

Vera sat in the ambulance at Tom's feet. He had a cap over his mouth and nose. His collar and his tie had been loosened. His eyes gazed at the roof. The agony had clung on to his face. She did not know if he was unconscious. He was a stranger to her, a vulnerable stranger. She did not dare to touch him; his vulnerability had paralysed her.

A male nurse administered him oxygen and followed the twirling lines on a screen.

At the hospital she was invisible. They wheeled him in hurriedly. A door closed so that she could not follow them. She hesitated for a moment and then went to the counter.

The man behind the counter was on the phone; he nodded at her kindly.

She chose one of the hundred empty chairs that were placed around a closed buffet. High windows, in combined play with the faint interior lighting, made the darkness outside intense and ominous. It created an evening atmosphere of desolation in the empty hall. With the marble tile floors and the empty corridors leading to the hall, it gave her a lonely, homesick feeling. She was hardly conscious of the work of art, painted in fiercely contrasting colours, which hung at eye level in front of her: an anatomic cross-section of a human being. And she didn't even see the mosaic next to the painting; it depicted Odysseus and his men in a vessel before the island of Aea. She did not see the enormous subtropical plants in the corners of the hall. A man in white went hurriedly past her, a sheet of paper in his hand.

A chaotic bunch of questions raced restlessly through her mind. *Will they come and tell me what's going on? Will they fetch me? Do they actually know that I am here? That I am Tom's wife?* She didn't dare to put into words what was passing through her mind. Fright had her in its grasp, a fright that was more oppressive than half a year earlier, after his first heart infarction. She realized now that all this time she had been afraid of a repeat; unconsciously she had been convinced that a second time would be fatal.

And now that second time was here.

A pulp of wild, unguided feelings smothered her brain. The atmosphere in the hospital felt like that of a church during an evening service: solemn, magic and mysterious. A world of contrasts: illness and health; initiates and laymen; death and life.

Under the influence of the atmosphere, her thoughts floated towards churches and crematories. She and Tom had become occasional churchgoers during their twenty-nine years together, mainly for marriages and funerals.

She saw herself sitting in the church, alone, in front of a full church. Alone with Rose. And Bart, Rose's friend.

Throughout her childhood, faith and church had been one and the same to her; the church with a watercolour future in heaven. She remembered the baroque atmosphere of the church of her childhood, unworldly, courtly, full of drama, a place where life and death merged together. Even then, that church had been strange to her, but this was a strangeness that was an essential part of her childhood world. She had gone to church with her parents until she was fourteen. In the countless hours she had spent there, waiting for the end, she had made a game of fancying sheep or cows in the bent backs before her. She had wondered why people let themselves be compared with sheep.

Vera's memories went on to a moment when she was loading her shopping from the supermarket into the boot of her car. She had been in the early thirties. With a head of lettuce in her hand, she had asked herself then, *Why do I believe in this after all?* She had put the lettuce into the boot and had gone for a walk in the woods. *Then I began to get confidence. In the world, in creation, in myself. I released myself from all those certainties. But the supermarket has become church now...*

A man in a white suit with a file in his hand walked past her and intruded into her memories. His goal-orientated walk told her that the man was an insider in the hospital. The man approached the counter.

"This is Mr. Corda's file," Vera heard him say to the man behind the counter, "for Dr. Falcon." The man in the white suit continued on his way.

Vera ran after him. "How is my husband?"

"Oh! You are Mrs. Corda? No, I can't say anything. I am sorry, ma'am! Dr. Falcon will tell you everything. Good night, Mrs. Corda."

She went back to her chair, her eyes directed at the corridor the man in the white suit had come out of.

She remembered now the distant atmosphere from the last time they had been here. A nurse had advised her then, with a polished kindness, that she should have confidence in the doctor. It had been all right with Tom then. They had taken him to the coronary care area and catherized him. A few weeks later he was back at home, with the warning "Rest!" and a box of pills.

Her heart beat as she saw Dr. Falcon approaching. Intuition told her it was him. He walked up to her. He looked serious and thoughtful. She tried to read the message from his face. She didn't dare to ask, whether Tom...

"Please, take a seat, Mrs. Corda."

"An American," Vera thought.

The man had a balding crown; the rest of his hair was grey. *He must be about forty,* Vera thought. She sat down, her eyes on the physician.

"I'll tell you as honestly as possible how your husband is; I think it's the best way," he started.

The physician's preliminary words were a prelude to disaster to Vera.

"Good?" she squeezed out of her throat hoarsely.

"I can't tell you very much yet. We have to make our judgements based on the first symptoms. We are going to carry out further investigations. But I must tell you that your husband's condition is not good. Immediately after being admitted here, he had an attack of hyperventilation. Besides that, he has a heart rhythm disorder we could barely get under control. Such a disturbance is not abnormal in the first hours after a heart attack. A lack of oxygen in the brain could be a consequence. But fortunately we were able to calm his heart. We have taken him to coronary care. We'll keep an eye on him over the next few days." Waiting for her reaction, Dr. Falcon noticed Vera's expressive face and the sad, gentle features round her mouth.

Vera could only stammer, "But..."

Falcon laid his hand on hers; she relaxed a little. "I am sorry, Mrs. Corda, that I can't tell you more..., can't give you better news."

They were silent for a while. He looked shyly at her hands and her face; she looked to the front of her.

"Can I see him?"

"Okay! But you should know that he is on a monitor. We are going to check his heartbeat and his breathing. And he will not notice you; he is asleep. We should not excite him, Mrs. Corda."

Three weeks later Vera sat in her house, a novel on her lap. A mist of stilled grief lay over her face. Her dark brown eyes appeared to reflect an eternal question. Her fringe lay casually just above her eyes. Large round, silver earrings marked her strong personality. A silver chain encircled a slender neck. She wore a dark blue skirt and a pink blouse.

Her slender fingers drummed on the armrests of the easy chair she sat in.

She did not know how often she had already began to read the same words. She sighed and raised her book again. But the words she read did not reach her mind. The recollection of the fatal moment on that Friday night and of what happened after that dominated her thoughts. Hoping to find some distraction, she kept trying to read. But she did not succeed. After two lines it flashed through her mind that there was a coloured wash to do. She rose to put the laundry into the machine. Going through the kitchen, she saw the coffee machine and she remembered that the machine needed cleaning, as the coffee had started to taste nasty.

Ten minutes later was she back with her book, but as associations came, mostly uninvited, her attention wandered immediately away. When her taste buds came to life, she looked in the fridge, cut a piece of cheese, and took up her book again.

But her restlessness kept itching at her. Already three weeks. From the moment Tom had grasped at his breast, her feelings had been adrift ever since. She walked around her house, dropped onto a chair, rose again, switched the TV on, looking for some contact from the outside; but the only result had been waste of time.

She couldn't get herself to commit to any activity and being alone paralysed her. A song started to sing in her head and invited her to hum along: "It's time to say goodbye." She couldn't get the words out of her mind.

She laid her book aside. She understood that it could not release her from her restlessness.

CHAPTER 28

"Mrs. Varma speaking."

"Good morning, Shakti! It's me, Amal."

"Amal?"

"Yes, Amal Maya."

Oh, Mr. Maya." Shakti didn't know what had happened to her. *Does he pretend that I am his friend? Does he perhaps think that I like...?* She couldn't finish the sentence even in her thoughts.

"Shakti, I have something nasty to tell you."

"Something nasty?"

"I shouldn't tell you this over the phone."

"How then?" Shakti was too upset to react adequately.

"Shall I come to you?"

"Well...okay." She gazed in front of her with the receiver in her hand. *What does that man want from me? Something nasty...Has he changed his mind? He promised me that he would protect Sudhir. What else could he mean?*

She rose and went to the kitchen. "Ragu, Mr. Maya is coming to see me. Would you stay around, please?"

"Of course, ma'am! And I'll leave the door ajar."

"That is good." Shakti knew her servant would not talk to anyone about what his ears or eyes picked up inside her house.

"Shall I make tea, ma'am?"

"Good, Ragu. He will like a cup of tea, I suppose. And I would like to have something in my hands."

Ragu reacted with a knowing glance.

"Will you show Mr. Maya in when he arrives?"

"Yes, ma'am."

Shakti went back to the living room and searched for a novel in the bookcase. *He should not get the impression that I am waiting for him. But on the other hand, I cannot take his hope away as long as he has Sudhir in his power.*

After half an hour she saw Maya's car. The chauffeur got out and held the door open for his boss.

When there was a ring at the door, Shakti made herself comfortable and started reading. She heard Ragu open the door. "Good morning, sir," she heard Ragu saying.

"Good morning, I have come to see Mrs. Varma."

"I shall ask her if she can receive you. Who can I say you are?"

"I am Maya. She is expecting me."

Ragu knocked at the door.

"Come in!"

"There is somebody to see you, ma'am, a man named Maya."

"Let him come in, Ragu." Shakti aimed herself at her novel again.

She did not look up until Maya was in the room.

Then she rose. "Good morning, Mr. Maya. Please, have a seat."

Maya greeted her in his way, his fingertips touching each other under his chin.

"Would you like a cup of tea, Mr. Maya?"

"Yes, please." Maya, who had expected a more enthusiastic welcome, was a little disappointed. *Her manner does not indicate that we had a cosy dinner together last week. And I don't see anything of the admiration she showed me then either; then she even found it difficult to call me Amal, because of my position. And now she pretends that I am just anyone.* It made him a little uncertain. He wondered if he could address her by her first name. *Women are whimsical beings,"* he comforted himself, *but perhaps she's had a bad day. Or she is a little upset because of the nasty message I talked about by phone. Oh well, it must be that!* Maya's uncertainty dissolved quickly with the explanation he had found for Shakti's lack of enthusiasm.

"I'll ask my servant to make tea for you."

Shakti went to the kitchen and left Maya alone with his thoughts. *To make tea for you? Is she going to let me drink tea alone?*

Shakti didn't come back immediately.

Where is she? Perhaps she is afraid of the message I've announced? By talking about a nasty message I must have scared her. I should have known it; I've enough experience with women. But even I can make a little mistake; I know myself well enough to admit that. Or perhaps she is impressed? I must assure her that she can rely on my protection…I shall start with that. If she knows that I am going to support her, it will put her at ease. She must again see me as the generous Amal Maya, who uses his power to serve mankind.

Shakti came back into the room. "My servant has the tea almost ready." She sat down, and picked up the novel she had been reading.

"Do you know this novel, Mr. Maya? *The City of Joy, written* by Dominique Lapierre?"

"No, I don't. You will understand that I do not have much time for reading novels."

"Yes, I understand."

"What is it about?"

"It is about Hasari Pal, his wife Aloka and their three children. A farmer's family. They lose everything and move to the city to make a new living there."

"I respect people who risk such a venture as looking for a living elsewhere."

"Then you should read this book. These people find a living in Kolkata."

"Interesting."

"Hasari has found work there as a horse."

"As a horse?"

"He earns a living in Kolkata as a rickshaw runner. There is no other possibility for him."

"A rickshaw is a good means of transportation in a big city. A good solution for people who can't afford to own a vehicle."

"It is a good solution for those people."

"As I said, I've not much time for reading. I can't permit myself to spend time on those sorts of books in any case. I've got more important things to do."

"You are right; reading this book would be a waste of your time."

Ragu came in with a tray of tea and some sweets. He put the tray on the table and asked if his mistress needed anything else.

"Thank you, Ragu. Is Mr. Maya's chauffeur with you in the kitchen?"

"No, ma'am, he preferred to stay in the car."

"Okay."

"I owe you an explanation," Maya said when Ragu had left the room. "I instructed my chauffeur to wait in the car when I have a meeting; the car is too precious to leave alone. Besides, I can't permit my chauffeur to pass his time with other servants; that would only lead to senseless chatting."

"I would not know what these men would have to talk about, Mr. Maya."

"That is just what I mean; I don't know either."

Shakti presented her guest with a plate of cookies. Maya took one and put it into his mouth.

The cookies didn't distract him from the subject at hand. "I always know what my servants do, madam." Maya couldn't yet bring himself to use her first name; her reserved behaviour kept him from doing so.

Shakti felt his internal conflict. *I must keep the power in my hands,* she thought. *He may imagine himself to be superior; he may feel himself to be as powerful as Durga's tiger, but I decide the limits.*

"You have a certain right regarding your servants, Mr. Maya," she answered politely. "You pay them for their services."

"Exactly, madam. They have, therefore, their obligations to me. Besides, where would they be without me? Perhaps they would be beggars. Or have to pull a rickshaw, if they could pay for such a thing. But, as I have already said, it is good that there are rickshaws for certain ranks of the population."

"For people like us, Mr. Maya; we have no vehicle either."

"Then you will understand what I mean."

"Yes, I do, Mr. Maya."

There was silence for a moment.

"Shakti."

Shakti didn't show the least bit of emotion.

"Last week I offered you my protection."

"I have not forgotten that."

"You can rely on it. I keep my promises."

She held her breath. His words seemed to be meant as an introduction to something, perhaps to the message he had announced. But they seemed to hold a dark threat.

Amal Maya laid his left knee over his right one, put his fingertips together under his chin, and looked at her. The glitter in his eyes disappeared as he saw that she looked straight into his eyes. He aimed his look at the plate of cookies. He understood that the story he had prepared would not suit the situation anymore. He searched for words. "Yes, I will keep supporting you, whatever happens."

"What will happen?"

"Don't worry," Maya answered in a friendly way, "I'll do everything I can to avert the danger."

"What danger?"

"There is danger lying in wait." Maya had to look for the correct words to express his message. "A great danger, I am afraid. But I can keep it under control. I ask you to rely on me."

"How can I rely on you, if I don't know what sort of danger we may be facing?"

"I shall explain." Maya resumed an easy attitude; leaning back, knee over knee, fingertips together and little glittering stars in his eyes.

That glittering was far from reassuring to Shakti. She had to take pains not to show her fright. She knew intuitively that he was playing with her as a cat plays with a mouse.

"You know your secret is safe with me. Nobody will ever learn from me what your husband did. I promised you and I shall keep that promise. I'm a man of honour."

"And the danger?" Shakti forced the words out of her mouth.

"Totally unexpectedly, a new problem has arisen."

The glittering in Maya's eyes had disappeared. "The man who delivered the kidney at the time, the kidney your husband transplanted illegally, is demanding money from your husband—hush money. He threatens to reveal the secret if he is not paid five hundred American dollars."

"He is blackmailing my husband?"

"Yes."

"Who is this man?"

"I am afraid I can't tell you."

"Does Sudhir know who he is?"

"I don't think your husband got the name of the donor at the time. That was unimportant; the donor was a poor devil."

"When must the money be paid?"

"I can ease your mind for the moment about payment; I advanced the demanded amount to the man. If I hadn't, he would have made the transplant in question public. I had to pay immediately. I had after all promised you my protection, hadn't I?" The look in Maya's eyes was now a little conceited.

"Did the man phone you?"

"He wrote me a letter."

"Can the man write?"

"Somebody must have written the letter for him."

"Why did you get that letter, and not my husband?"

"I don't understand that either. It could be that he sent it to me, as he knew that I could use my influence to procure him the demanded money."

"Could it be that the donor doesn't know my husband's name? He was under general anaesthetic, wasn't he?"

"I also thought of that possibility."

"Then I am still left with the question of why the man wrote the letter to you instead of to my husband. How did he know you had something to do with it?"

"I had nothing to do with it. The only thing I can say is that the letter was not addressed and was found in my mailbox."

"What did the man write?"

"He demanded five hundred American dollars, and wanted the money to be paid that same day at five o'clock."

"The same day? When was that?"

"Two days ago."

"How did you pay the man?"

"Cash."

"Did he come to you?"

"No. He mentioned a place where the money could be handed over. If that did not happen, the story would be published."

"Did you send somebody with the money to the meeting place?"

"Of course not! I did it personally. I did not want anybody else to be involved."

"Did you speak to the man?"

"Yes."

"What did he say?"

"He approached me when I arrived at the agreed location. He asked if I was Mr. Maya. I said that I was. He asked me if I had got the letter. I affirmed that I had. And after looking around suspiciously, he broached the matter of the money."

"And you gave him the money?"

"Of course. What else could I have done? Should I have put your husband's name and reputation at stake?"

"Did you drive to the meeting place in your car?"

"I ordered my chauffeur to park the car two streets from the place mentioned in the letter. My chauffeur knows that he must stay in the car."

"When do you expect the money from us?"

"There is no great hurry. You know that I will help you."

"Five hundred dollars is a lot of money. We will need some time to get that amount."

"I will not rush you or cause you trouble. But if it takes too long, you could think about a loan. In that case, I could mediate for you."

"I will talk about it with my husband."

Maya looked relieved. "Do you know, Shakti, that I think this must be very annoying for you. I didn't sleep last night worrying about it."

"I appreciate your sympathy for our situation."

Maya said nothing more and looked silently in front of him.

Shakti was afraid that he had heard the irony in her voice.

"Would you like another cup of tea?" She tried to thaw the icy atmosphere.

"No, I still have work to do."

"My reaction was perhaps a little cool. I was a little disappointed; I am sure you understand. It's not only a matter of money—someone else has knowledge of that transplant, and I'm afraid that he will demand more money in the future."

"That's not impossible," Maya answered, "but don't forget that I shall support you."

"I will not forget that." Shakti made sure that her voice sounded reliable.

Shakti called her friend Sarásvati that evening. "Sarásvati, I need to come over for a little talk. Is that okay?"

"Of course!"

Shakti didn't take any risks; she did not exclude the fact that Maya could have ordered a tap on her telephone. He had connections everywhere.

One hour later, she rang the door of her friend's parents; home.

"Do you like working for Maya?" Shakti asked sympathetically as they sat in the living room.

"So far, I am doing well. The work is simple. And Maya behaves decently. The other staff members deal with me respectfully; my job is obviously held in great respect. It's a position of confidence."

"Sarásvati, I have a question. Last week, did you see a letter in Maya's mailbox? One without an address or a sender's address?"

"No...Why do you ask?"

"You didn't see a letter in which someone threatened to publish a certain story unless they were paid an amount of five hundred dollars?"

"No!"

"You do take all mail out of the mailbox, and you read all the letters don't you?"

"Yes. I told you. But why all these questions?"

Shakti ignored her friend's question. "Did Amal Maya leave his house two days ago at about five o'clock in the afternoon?"

"Two days ago? He wasn't in his office then. I would not forget that as I enjoy being alone at work."

Shakti looked at her friend seriously. She then told her about Maya's visit and about the blackmail.

"If that letter had been in the mailbox, I would have seen it. If Maya had taken the letter out of the box before me, he must have had a reason for doing so. In other words, he must have been expecting something in particular."

"Is there only one mailbox?"

"As far as I know, there is only one."

"So, in all likelihood, he probably never received a blackmail letter. But suppose he had gotten one, could he have gone to a meeting place to deliver the hush money?"

"I cannot exclude that. But I can't imagine that Maya did intercept a letter. I even wonder if he can read."

"That is the impression that I received from you before."

"So Maya made the story up in order to get money from you and to play the part of benefactor all at the same time."

"It looks like it."

"What are you going to do?"

"I don't know. I can't use your information against him."

"And if you ask him if you may see the letter, he will be indignant, as it will look like you don't trust him."

"The only thing we can do is ask him for an extension of payment. That means that I must restrain myself again."

CHAPTER 29

Tom lingered at the table, his morning newspaper between the remains of his breakfast. Through the years the thick Saturday paper had grown to be a fixed component of his breakfast. That's why the sound of the phone was so penetrating and unwanted.

He picked up the receiver.

"Mirabelle speaking."

That's the very limit! He bit the words back in time.

"I heard the bad news from James. We were awfully shocked. And we feel very sorry for you."

"Thank you for sympathizing with me."

"We do. But this is not a thing to discuss over the phone. I would like to come to see you."

"Vera is not home."

"No problem," Mirabelle said kindly, "I am coming to see you."

While giving Vera an alibi he had implicitly kept himself available.

The telephone call reminded him of the interview with Dr. Wiersma. "We still give you six months..." Tom saw the scene in his mind for the hundredth time:

Erik Wiersma, one of Falcon's assistants, wearing a white, loose-hanging coat was sitting behind a too-large desk. With a deadly serious expression on his stiffened face and his eyes directed at his fingers, he had uttered a barely audible, sigh of relief after delivering his message. Then he had, stealthily, gauged Tom's reaction.

He had gone to the hospital for a routine check, as he had said to Vera. She had wanted to go with him, as with his earlier visits; but he had told her that it was no more than a routine visit. That's what he had told himself as well, more than once. *Well, it's only a routine check.*

But deep in his heart he had already known the verdict. Without the judgment of an expert he had been able to keep the truth away. Hope and desperation had taken turns in his heart. He had struggled with his unguided feelings. Through a mist in his mind he had been thinking of taking his leave of Vera and Rose. He had tried to imagine how it would be to never see them again. He had looked at the young man who taken his first steps into cardiology. He had, for a number of seconds, been mesmerized by the clicking of his ball point pen on the desk. Meanwhile, he had wondered if the young man had anything to give. *He molds his bad-news message into a standard formula,* he thought, trying to hold the irreversible reality at a distance. But he had realized as well that he was clutching at straws. As though numbed by endorphins, the pain of the inevitable truth had only been active at a strange and unreal distance.

To break the stalemate and the oppressive silence he had asked the young physician his first name.

"Erik." Embarrassed with the situation and surprised by the simple question, Erik had tried to cover himself with professional reserve.

"It is difficult to deliver such a message, isn't it?" Tom had said. "Is this your first time?"

"Yes, my first time." Erik's voice had sounded hoarse. "And it is not easy for us either..."

There had been a profound silence.

"Shall we make a new appointment?" Erik had suggested after a few lingering moments. "In three weeks?"

Tom had had no inkling of what the point would be as he felt that he had just been written off. However, he had resignedly agreed.

As neither of the two had anything further to say, Tom had quickly left.

A deadly tiredness had overwhelmed him and consciousness of the absolute end had flashed through his mind. *No more springtimes; no more newspapers at breakfast; no more chatting with Vera; Rose growing up without me.* All sorts of daily pleasures he now saw as an eternal farewell. He would never again see the people without whom his life was no life at all. Never again! He had seen a leaden, gloomy, death for eternity.

He had wandered aimlessly through the corridors of the hospital. Outside he had seen a man and a woman of his age arm in arm, talking to each other. Envy and anger had spiralled through his dull mind. He felt alienated from them, like an extraterrestrial being. He had stared after them in a mist of thoughts, life walking away from him. A feeling of being shut out had chained him to the place where he was. The world around him was not his world anymore. His life had become a strange dream.

He had wandered on, unconscious. His ego had been numbed. He had floated in a vacant sleepwalking, timeless daze, until he became conscious again. *Vera must be worried.* He had felt guilty, because he had left her at home. He had fooled her with this "routine check" talk, but he had fooled himself as well. He shuffled despondently to the train.

Looking for an activity and to escape from an atmosphere that suffocated words before they could be said, he had proposed a short walk with her.

On the streets he had been overwhelmed by the unreal mood of someone who sees others celebrating a carnival and who can't understand the exuberance of the party-goers. The world had passed him by. They had walked but were ill at ease and separate. The sun had shone inappropriately. A group of young people passed by, their laughter had sounded shrill to his ears. The world had been totally indifferent to their experience.

Later at the table, he had tried to congratulate her on the food; but the words had stuck in his throat in a muddy desperateness.

When they had finished the meal, she had suggested that he take a seat while she did the dishes.

So, the time of pampering begins, he had thought. Knowing her, she would slave until his last heartbeat.

"But I will not yet be banished to an easy chair," he had said. "Please, don't break the familiar daily patterns by placing me in an exceptional position with the privileges of a terminal patient." Then he had recovered his feelings. "Listen, Vera, for as long as I can, I will take part. Please, treat me as normal?"

She had cried. Awkwardly he had put an arm round her shoulders.

She had washed. He had dried.

She had asked how the interview with the physician had gone. His thoughts had gone back to the waiting room, where his foreboding had already given him an insight into the verdict. "When he came to fetch me, I just knew. I saw it in the look on his face and by his attitude. It is strange, but it soothed me."

The light indignation on Vera's face had degraded his remark to a powerless bromide.

A flash of the absolute reality had followed the bromide. He had closed his eyes. Vera's hands had fallen still. With a bent head she, too, had a similar ruthless flash. He dropped the tea towel.

The gloomy cloud floated over.

She had gone on washing and he had wiped the dishes dry.

That evening they had fetched the outside world into their house and had watched a film on TV. But the film had turned out to be boring and banal. Not believing that zapping would bring anything better, they had switched the TV off. Sitting silently, they had dragged themselves through the evening; an evening that was nothing but tense and uneasy. The matters that really concerned them were too painful to talk about.

Tom let Mirabelle in.

Her hair style looked chiseled. The skin of her face had the transparency of a water colour. Reflective sunglasses concealed her dull eyes. Her smile was artificial. She was thin and fragile. She looked pleadingly sweet.

She embraced Tom as if he were a statue. She inspected herself for minutes in front of the mirror in the hall.

As Tom went to pour the coffee, she took the pot out of his hands.

"The day after my birtday I called in a psychiatrist," she reassured Tom as they sat together after their coffee. "I know now what was going on with me." Mirabelle clarified that she had been the victim of certain people around her. "I've one weakness: I am too good. But now that my psychiatrist has shown me what happened to me, I know what I've got to do."

Tom looked outside to get some inspiration for a reaction.

"You must feel very lonely now..."

The sudden change, of course, wrong-footed Tom. "Sometimes..." he answered clumsily.

"Sometimes? It must have been a shock for you?" Her voice sounded as if she didn't trust her own feelings.

"No. Actually I already knew before..."

She nodded in an understanding way.

Tom realized, with a mix of irony and sadness, that he was still useful. "If I need help, other people will know they are indispensable."

"I'd like to help you, Tom."

"To help? How?"

She looked at him, not understanding.

"Are you still depressed?" Tom asked.

"Depressed? Do you know what you are talking about?"

"No. But as an ordinary layman, I thought that the last time we met you seemed rather depressed."

"My psychiatrist did not use that word."

"I suppose that he has a better view than I. But you didn't radiate happiness either."

"I felt a little down. I already told you how it was caused. But now that I've got an insight into the circumstances which I fell victim to, there is nothing wrong anymore. I am still, voluntarily, in consultation with Hans."

"Hans is the name of your psychiatrist?"

"Yes. So you don't need to worry about me. I should be ashamed to talk about my little everyday problems with you, in your situation. I came for you."

"Can we talk about something pleasant?"

"Oh, of course! If you find it difficult to…"

They drank their coffee in silence. Pleasantry could not be commanded.

Do people, knowing that I am a terminal patient, still see me as a normal human being? Tom asked himself. *Could they still talk normally to me? Would they still ask me around for a drink?*

"Did Vera go out?"

"Yes, she went out for some shopping."

"She left you alone?" It sounded friendly.

Tom looked at his hands. He hesitated for a moment. Then he decided to do what he should have done much earlier, to say what he had on his mind.

"Mirabelle, I thought you beautiful once; when Charles received his royal honour."

Mirabelle gazed, flabbergasted, at Tom for endless seconds. She started to shiver. Slowly her face grew dark red. Her hands clung together. It looked as though she was struggling not to cry.

Tom saw rage bubble up in her and then he knew why he had thought her beautiful: it had been that rage, that honest rage. She had always joined in the games played by the important people with sweet smiles and refined words, but she had suddenly completely changed. When the other people had placed their attention on Charles Bot, Tom had seen the flaming anger on the face of Charles's wife, an anger that came straight out of her soul. An anger that stuck heartrendingly out against the well-formed manners around her. At that moment he had seen her as she was. It had given him a warm feeling.

And now there was that anger again, as though it might finally be aired after all that time.

While her anger searched for a way out—in the wild look in her eyes, in her clenched teeth, in the rude gestures of her hands—Mirabelle looked for words. Finally they came, jerking and faltering, out of her mouth. "A decoration, matching his rank in the name of the queen. The consolation prize for me was an expensive bunch of flowers in cellophane. The anger of a whole life flared up in me. I should have thrown the flowers into the face of the boss of The Concern, who had handed them to me, but I did not have the courage. I let myself be taken in by decorum for the umpteenth time; by men in perfectly tailored suits, and women entrenched behind their make-up; by solemn, hollow words; by the looking up and the looking down. As one of the subordinates in the career pattern of the decorated Charles Bot. And in his peacock pride he put my stupefaction down to the deep impression the whole show had made on me. Even though I was drugged by humiliation, I heard all those people drivelling on. But I did not have the guts to voice my anger."

Mirabelle's first tears became lost. "Looking back, it was good that I didn't do it," she sobbed. "If I had aired my feelings, I should have belched out the hatred of all the years of that la-di-da waffling. They would probably have seen me as a psychopath and knocked me out with the sedatives of their condescending pity."

Tom stared at Mirabelle. "I am astonished at your...I didn't know you at all."

She burst out laughing through her tears. "Excuse me for getting so angry..." She cried soundlessly.

Tom hesitated. Then he went to sit next to her and put an arm round her shoulders.

She looked for her handkerchief and started to say how angry she had always been with her husband and his work. "But I only realized this when they gave him that decoration. Now you, of all people, are the one whom I vent it on, when I came here to help you!"

"You couldn't have helped me better."

"The first thing I'll do when I go home is tell my husband what I should have said much earlier. He will probably not understand it; but I need to do it for my own sanity...Tom, I hope I did not annoy you."

"This was the first time that you did not."

She hesitated. "Tom, I think you are tired. We'll discuss this another time. Okay?"

When he had closed the door behind Mirabelle, Tom poured himself a drink.

With the glass in his hand, he stood himself in front of the mirror. "Yes! I am still a normal human being."

CHAPTER 30

Sarásvati came out of her room at the same time as Ajay Khosla pulled the door to Maya's room closed behind him.

As she saw him she turned her head to the side on reflex. She realized that if the man saw her here, he would tell his boss that it was her who had discovered the children in the pharmaceutical factory, and she knew for certain that Maya would silence her forever. She pulled her sari, which she usually wore just over her crown, further over her head.

She heard Khosla's footsteps coming closer. She held her hand on the door handle to prepare herself for the confrontation. It would be too conspicuous if she entered her room again. She thought for a moment of covering her face, as a Muslim woman approaching a strange man, but that would attract too much attention.

Then she got an idea. She dropped the paper she had in her hand on the floor and bent down to pick it up.

Khosla saw the paper as well and went to pick it up for her. Their heads were ten centimeters from each other. She didn't dare to look. She would have to thank him then for his attentive behaviour, but she would not betray herself. With all her attention on the paper which he handed back to her, she murmured an excuse. She felt Khosla looking at her. She bent her head so that the end of her sari fell over her face.

He stood upright now and was ready to go on, but he hesitated.

She hesitated as well and remained sitting on her heels, with a bent head, looking at the paper in her hands.

Then she saw him walking away. She waited, afraid that he would look back.

He looked back.

Ajay Khosla had the idea that he had seen the woman before, but he didn't know where or when.

Sarásvati went back into her room. Sitting behind her desk, she tried to consider her position, but she could not think quietly. *He recognized me; I saw it, I felt it. Why did he hesitate so long before he went on?*

She waited, frightened and tense, for a phone call from Maya. She calculated the time Khosla would need to go back and tell of his discovery to his boss. *Then Maya will not wait anymore,* she thought, *he will take no risks. How will he render me harmless? He asked me to dinner...*

A feeling of nausea overcame her as she thought back to his slimy look. She had been about to go home. He had called her back and had said, "Sarásvati. I think we should go out for dinner, don't you agree? In order to get to know each other better. The atmosphere in the office is not suitable for learning about each other's personal backgrounds; and that is quite important, isn't it? Especially if people work together as intensely as we do, don't you think so?"

She had wanted to say something, but the words had stuck in her throat. She had felt his inspecting look on her naked upper back. She had been inclined to run away, but she had controlled herself. She had seen his self-satisfied smile. Her brain had searched for a convenient answer. If her words left a little chink of hope he would push the door further open. But if she injured his vanity, it would turn against her.

She had a flash of inspiration and stammered, "Mr. Maya, you may allow yourself much in your position, but I am committed to a marriage vow." She had been shocked by her own words, but was surprised to see pride shining on his face.

"Sarásvati, you see things very clearly. I can indeed allow myself to take such liberties. I should like to share the privileges of my position with you. Don't forget: I can easily do something about that marriage vow."

"I respect my father's decision, Mr. Maya."

"I assume that you respect me as well."

She had thought she recognized a subtle threat in his voice. "I respect you too," she had answered hurriedly. "That's why I can not accept your invitation. You deserve better than a woman who, with a marriage vow, would allow herself to go out with another man."

"Sarásvati, I have already told you: you see things clearly. And you understand me very well. That's why I gave you this job. I need someone next to me who understands me, somebody I can exchange views with at my own level, for I feel lonely in my position. Therefore I want to get to know you better. But perhaps we must wait for a better occasion."

She had not contradicted him.

Sarásvati controlled herself, more or less, when the telephone rang.

"Sarásvati, would you come in, please?"

She was the only one on Maya's staff who was asked to come; other employees received an order. But his kind invitation did not make it any less threatening to her.

She covered her back and her arms. She pulled her sari until it was over her forehead. She was frightened as she heard Maya calling, "Come in, please!"

Now it's going to happen, she imagined. *Khosla will be there.*

She opened the door to Maya's room, but remained standing. She didn't dare to look up.

"Take a seat." Maya showed her a chair in front of him.

She sat down. She saw Maya's face through a mist. His voice came from far away. She was surprised that Khosla was not present.

"Did you discuss the payroll with Avih Shah?"

Sarásvati was startled back into reality. She remembered now that she had been on the way to the housekeeping manager. When she had seen Khosla coming out of Maya's room, her plan had vanished with fright and confusion. She had not thought of the payroll anymore. *What can I say now? That I forgot?*

"Mr. Maya, I am sorry; I have a terrible migraine. I can do nothing anymore. Therefore, I forgot the payroll."

"I need that payroll now!"

"I shall arrange it immediately." She rose and staggered slightly to convince him of her migraine.

His look penetrated into her back.

He looked after her musingly. *How can I approach that woman,* he wondered?

When Sarásvati got home that evening, she heard the telephone ringing. She picked up the receiver.

"Sarásvati, can you make some time free for us?"

Hearing Tom Corda's voice relieved her. "Of course! I didn't know you were in Varanasi."

"I am on sick leave. I came here with Vera."

"Sick leave? Is it anything serious"?"

"No. I'll tell you later."

"Okay! Are you coming here?"

"Is something wrong?" Tom asked because of the hesitation in her voice.

"I saw Khosla. He was in Maya's house."

Tom and Vera were heartily received by Sarásvati and her parents, Umesh and Amrita.

When Sarásvati had made tea for them, she told them about Khosla. "Khosla must have recognized me; and Maya must already know that it was me who discovered the children in his factory."

"You can't stay there," Tom said.

"I warned her not to accept the job Maya had offered her," Umesh answered. "I reproach myself now that I did not forbid her. But now she cannot resign; Maya will find her. I know Amal Maya."

"Do you?" Tom asked.

"There was a time I supposed I could understand him. I saw him as a man whose beachcomber's look confined his horizons. As a man whose need ate ever further around itself, like a fire. But now I see that ruthlessness is threatening my daughter's life."

"I can't understand people like Maya at all," Vera said. "How can a man do this to children? How is it possible that a human being lacks any feelings, even for children?"

"Poor people are, in Maya's mind, beings of a lower species," Umesh said, "and so are their children. People who have nothing are nothing. They are there to be used, and when they are not of use, they must stay away from him. It probably never occurred to him that these people can feel pain or grief."

"This is an unsatisfactory explanation to me," Vera sighed.

It is indeed, Umesh thought.

"How can a human being be so unfeeling, and act like a beast of prey?" Vera went on.

"Can we imagine ourselves in a predator's mind?" Umesh asked.

As everybody was silent, Sarásvati surprised them by continuing. "I must operate carefully, because I am playing a dangerous game," she went on thoughtfully.

"What do you mean?" asked her father.

"Tomorrow I will tell him what I saw in his factory and I'll ask him to save the children. I shall pretend that he knows nothing about it. He can then play the part of a generous benefactor, which is how he likes to see himself."

"Do you think you will succeed?" Tom asked with concern.

"He is stupid enough," Sarásvati said, to put Tom's mind at ease, "and I shall use my female charm in support of it."

"And if he sees that as an encouragement?"

"I have been able to keep him at a distance up to now. I hope I can do it tomorrow too. The main problem is keeping the balance in the game without wounding his vanity; a vanity that asks to be flattered and doesn't leave room for anyone to ignore his advances. But as he has an explanation for every refusal that spares his vanity, there is a chance to escape. Maya doesn't believe that a woman can maintain resistance to his charms. He has filters in his ears. Those filters have protected me until now, and I hope they will tomorrow as well."

Sarásvati did not tell her parents that she was taking secret self-defence lessons. It was important that Maya remain ignorant of that fact. Apart from that, she realized that her self-defence must remain verbal; for if she ever had to floor Maya with a hip throw, his vanity would be irreparably dented. And he would seek serious revenge on her, for Maya would not tolerate his vanity to be so affronted.

CHAPTER 31

Not one hour passed without Parvati thinking back to the moment she had taken Chinky to her room. After bringing her back into the den, about two o'clock in the morning, she had gone to bed. She had lain awake staring into the darkness. Her mind was clear, more than she had ever thought possible.

The girl had, only for a split-second, opened her eyes and gratefully looked up at her. That short flash had made a deep impression on Parvati.

The look in the girl's eyes—Parvati realized it immediately—had been the start of a basic change in her life. In a mysterious way the girl had awoken a deep confidence in her. Parvati could not remember when she had ever felt so self-conscious and so happy and so peaceful. Her life would not pass her by anymore as it had done since her marriage. From now on, she would take her life in her own hands.

She was also thoroughly aware of the task she had taken on herself with her promise to rescue the girl.

After an hour, she had fallen asleep. She slept a deep sleep and one that brought her an exceptional dream:

In the temple of the god Shiva, she had seen the corpus delicti of her husband's crimes carved on a candlestick: a penis, shriveled and wrinkled. An orange ribbon had been wrapped round it. Her husband came in stumbling and grabbed at the bloody genitals. But at the moment he caught it, his neck was caught up in a snare. A snare, the symbol of earthly attachment, as Parvati knew. Then Shiva's wife appeared, the goddess Parvati, who spoke to the shriveled genitals with a chilly sound in her voice. "This is the last time you will stiffen, in death! Before you pass on to decay."

In the dream, the earthly Parvati, had sat before Shiva's statue, cross-legged, without the least emotion, and she had promised him solemnly that she should rescue the child.

Chinky was set to work in the kitchen. At night, she slept with Lila in the shed behind the kitchen.

Parvati was happy with the limited freedom that the child now had. She immediately started to direct herself on Chinky's recovery. She looked after her as well as she could. She could now direct her love and care on both children. She would, as much as possible, set right what her husband had done to wrong them. In particular, she would do everything she could to help the girls to recover their self-respect.

Lila tried to make the life of her new friend more agreeable too. She knew from her own experience what Chinky had gone through and what she still had to do.

Chinky, on her part, quickly found out that Lila was also a victim of the man who had dragged her into his bed. She saw Lila being fetched. And Lila was always very upset when she came back.

The fact that both were victims of the same man forged a strong friendship between the two girls.

Parvati shared in that friendship; and the girls found an ally in her.

Since the night Parvati had pronounced her holy promise to Shiva, all her life and thoughts were aimed at fulfilling that promise. She explored every situation and, step by step, she worked out a plan. She was aware that she had to free herself from her husband's power, if she ever could execute her plan. Freeing herself from his power also meant getting him under control. For if Amal Maya should disappear or die she would not only be without any power, but also without any rights. A widow has no rights, she knew, less than a married woman anyway. The Maya family would send her away without any wrinkles on their conscience, and she would not get even a rupee.

Only my sister-in-law, Bindu, would support me, but the words of Bindu are only the words of a woman.

A week after her dream, the man whom she had earlier seen with Maya and Sarásvati paid her a visit. Sarásvati had told her the man's name. Intuitively she had known that this man could play a part in looking for Chinky's parents. She had sent Kailash to arrange an appointment with the man.

Chinky had been in Maya's house for six months when an occasion to help Parvati's slowly ripening plan began to stand out. Even before Chinky's arrival in the house, Amal Maya had devised a new pleasure. In the evenings, after he had finished some glasses of beer or whisky, he thought it amusing to send for his wife to come into his office and to let her give account for the work that had taken place that day. The first time Parvati had wondered what he wanted from her, but after that first time she knew. *He wants to emphasize my subordination; he wants to humiliate me and enjoy my fear.*

The first time she had been anxious. But after the night Chinky had come into her life and she had made her promise to Shiva, Parvati had begun to gather more and more courage. So she had finally conquered her fear of her husband.

To Maya, however, she had remained the shy, submissive being that had willingly let him banish her to the kitchen. She had decided to join in his game, and she had patiently waited for the moment she thought suitable to show him who she really was.

CHAPTER 32

Parvati straightened up as a servant knocked on the door of her room. It was ten o'clock in the evening.

"You are expected in Mr. Maya's office, ma'am."

"Would you tell my husband that I am busy; he must have some patience."

The servant was fiercely shocked. He withdrew in a hesitating manner.

He was back within five minutes. "Mr Maya is terribly angry. He orders you to come immediately!"

Parvati would not burden the servant with a second message to her husband; he would, as a substitute, undoubtedly get Maya's anger. She knew that Maya's last vestiges of reasonableness would be drowned in his alcoholic rage; she knew that Amal was already undoubtably very drunk.

"Okay! I am coming," she reassured the servant. "No, you don't need to join me."

She gathered the things she thought were needed and bound them, under her sari, round her waist.

She went to her husband's office and inhaled deeply before, without knocking, opening the door and entering. She went to his desk, took a seat in front of him, and looked him straight in the eyes.

"Well! You may say what you have to tell me!" She was perfectly quiet.

Amal Maya gasped for breath. His face darkened. He threatened to choke on his rage. He could not utter a word. He had already been terribly angry that she had defied his order; but his wife's calmness and the fact that she had taken a seat without his permission, made him furious. Why didn't she creep around like a terrified, little rodent?

Parvati, however, was not the least impressed.

Maya looked in his mind, which had been fuddled by alcohol, for an explanation for his wife's unusual behaviour, but every attempt to think was stiffled by his drunken rage. He began to feel uncertain. Somewhere deep in his heart stirred the fear that his power over the world around him was beginning to falter. He clung convulsively to the armrests of his chair.

Parvati saw him sitting on his throne as his head almost exploded with rage. She also saw the coat of arms of the Maya family, painted on the back of the throne. She looked into his eyes and kept on looking into those eyes, with a deep disdaining look.

He tried to avoid her gaze, but her self-confidence hypnotized him. Anger and confusion fought in his head for priority. Never before had someone defied Amal Maya; and of all people, it was his submissive wife who was doing it now. It was an unreal, bad dream. He pushed himself, with bulging eyes and foam at the corners of his mouth, up from his throne. He pushed it backwards and tottered in her direction. His eyes looked bloodthirsty.

Parvati rose quietly and let him advance on her.

Her quietness and the penetrating look in her eyes provoked him most of all. *Why doesn't she go into her shell so that she can undergo her punishment?*

Parvati's smile, however, expressed mockery and disdain. She maintained direct eye contact.

He tried to avoid her look, as it made him uncertain in his drunken fit. But his anger only got worse. He tried to think of what he should do. Without realizing it, he tried to strike her. He missed.

This stirred up his rage still more. He grabbed for the chair she had sat on and raised it into the air, to let it come down with an uncontrolled force on her head.

Parvati evaded the blow. The chair, not broken in his speed, jolted Maya out of his drunken balance.

Although his fall was slightly broken by the plush carpet, nevertheless he passed into blackness.

Two minutes later, when he began to regain consciousness, he felt the sharp tug of a headache.

His wife had pulled his belt out from his trousers and had used it to bind his wrists together behind his back. Besides that, he had a rope around his neck and his ankles were bound together with the other end of the rope, so that when he stretched his legs, he tightened the rope and strangled himself. He lay on his belly, his hands behind his back and his lower legs pushed upwards, like a seal on the beach.

Parvati went to her husband's desk, fetched a bunch of keys out of a drawer, and shut the three doors to the room. Then she put his throne next to her husband and sat down on it. She let her slippers slip from her feet and waited for what would happen next.

It took Amal Maya some time before he realized that he was his wife's prisoner and completely powerless. He still wondered whether or not this was a bad dream. Then he screamed.

She put her right foot on the rope between his neck and his ankles, thus stifling his voice and threatening suffocation.

Then she let out the rope again.

He shouted again. But once more he felt the rope tightening round his neck. His shouting died away into a rattling sound.

After a third attempt it began to dawn to him that she would not give him a chance to sound the alarm.

He tried to put his fuddled brain into action and to concoct another plan. But his uncomfortable position, the alcohol, his headache, his rage, and his terror prevented him from concentrating. His brain, however, did comprehend that his wife would not obey him anymore. He swooned away into a fuddle, as it was all too much for him. Then he dropped onto his right side, hoping to find a little more relief.

Parvati took the rope between his neck and ankles and pulled him back onto his belly. Then she sat down again on her husband's throne, her foot standing by.

After less than a minute, Maya started to squirm and to groan.

Just for a moment Parvati tugged at the rope with the big toe of her right foot, to remind him that a shout for help would be relentlessly punished.

She felt relieved now that she felt herself to be free after more than twenty years of humiliation. Amal Maya had no power over her anymore. It was now her turn to command him. She had resolved to ignore even the least inclination toward mercy.

"Why are you doing this to me?" An indignant sound reverberated in his voice.

"Because of all the suffering you have caused me and other people. But especially because you stole children from their parents and misused them in such a beastly manner."

As a flat pebble skims over the water, so Parvati's words grazed along Amal Maya's dank and hazy brain. "I always treated you well, didn't I?" he wailed, full of self-pity.

"Treated me well? You banished me to the kitchen, and used that opportunity to have sex with other women and to rape innocent children!"

"If you let me go, I'll make love to you tonight."

"I won't make love to a beast of prey!" she cried indignantly. "Do you really think I could tolerate your indolent body against mine?"

The grimace on Amal Maya's face could not grow more painful; he did not know how he could react to the insulting words of his wife. His charm had never been in doubt before and it had certainly never been so brutally violated.

"What do you want then?" he asked.

"I want the keys and the code to the safe."

"Never!"

Parvati put her foot on the rope which tightened and cut off Maya's breath.

Maya perspired. He had the feeling that his head had expanded and was about to explode. His agony got worse. There was now a double threat: she was playing with his life and she also wanted his possessions and his secrets. Nobody knew the code and nobody knew where he kept the keys. He kept his money in the safe, as he didn't entrust it to a bank. The safe contained bars of gold, precious jewels and trinkets as well as important documents. He kept confidential minutes of meetings with his companions that should never be read by anyone, and cassette tapes of secretly recorded interviews; this was so that if he ever got into trouble with one of his companions, he could blackmail them. The safe contained more secrets than his whimsical imagination could concoct. The safe, his alter ego, was even better locked up from the outside world than his own thoughts. Amal Maya shivered at the thought that someone other than himself should ever open his safe. Nobody would ever know the double-secret code of the safe. *"That will never happen!"*

Parvati pushed with her toe on the rope and kept it tightened for a bit longer. She took care that he did not suffocate; if he died, she could not execute her plan. She looked down at him from the throne.

Maya needed more time to recover his breath. The cold sweat was stuck to his body. His face betrayed his agony.

Parvati looked on impassively.

When, after some minutes, he did not show any signs of indulging her demands, she put her foot on his head and pushed his face into the thick carpet. The carpet smothered his whining.

After that punishment, Maya began to cry.

"Don't think I'll take pity on you! Why should I pity a predator that never had the least bit of pity for other people?" She pushed his face into the carpet again.

Amal Maya could only groan.

"The keys!" she commanded.

He shivered.

"The keys!"

"Never!"

She pushed her big toe on the rope.

His crying was saturated with self-pity. But, in spite of the strangling reality giving him no way out, he did not give in.

Parvati went on punishing him. She was astonished at herself, and by the fact that she felt no pity at all.

I shall never give up my treasures and my secrets! Maya kept thinking.

But the pain of the discomfort became unbearable, and the strangulation time after time exhausted him and made him desperate. He yearned for just a few seconds of rest.

But Parvati didn't allow him the least respite. Now and again she put her foot on his head and let him bite into the carpet, or she tightened the rope to cut off his breathing.

Amal Maya saw, for a moment, his life passing by him. He saw and felt every detail of the sadness he had caused other people. He passed through the hunger and the thirst, the loss, the homesickness of the children he had ordered to be kidnapped. He saw himself raping Chinky and Lila, and he felt their desperation and saw the agony in their eyes. That one moment seemed to last for an eternity.

Even Parvati did not know how long she had sat on his throne before he surrendered.

"In the bottom drawer of my desk," he sobbed in a choked voice.

"How can I open the drawer?" she commanded, her foot on the rope.

"With the key that is behind the painting of Durga."

Parvati fetched the painting from the wall and took the key. Immediately she sat down on the throne again and touched the rope to remind him that she was still there. Then she went to the desk and found the key.

"Where is the second key?" She touched her foot on the rope.

"In the second bottom drawer," Maya groaned.

Parvati put the keys in the keyholes of the safe and turned them around twice.

"The code!" she commanded.

He hesitated.

She put her foot on the rope.

He gave up the code. Sweat was on his forehead. His eyes were broken.

Parvati tapped in the code and pulled the heavy door open. She was, for a moment, taken aback by the splendour she saw there. But she pulled herself together. She took a cotton shawl from under her sari, pulled it through her husband's mouth, and tied it tightly behind his head. Maya's wailing changed into a muffled, nasal rattling.

CHAPTER 33

The consulting room in the hospital was striking in its firm, straight lines and fiercely contrasting colours. Cornflower blue window frames were built into fine brickwork. The curtains were bright yellow, as was the wooden panelling. The table and the chairs were made of chromed steel. There were two copies of Toorop paintings in sober frames hanging on the wall. Two huge palm trees stood in glazed crockery pots on either side of the door to the corridor. The room breathed an atmosphere of hygiene and efficiency.

Vera's feelings, faintly frozen in fear and uncertainty, were not warmed by it. Tom had already become used to the friendly functionalism; after his second heart attack, he had stayed for a couple of weeks in the hospital.

Dr. Falcon had invited them for an interview. He shook hands with them and introduced his assistants. "To my right is Dr. De Vries, and the man on the left is Dr. Wierts. Mrs. De Vries and I are cardiologists and cardiosurgeons. Dr. Wierts is a trainee cardiologist. And next to Dr. De Vries is Dr. Wanders; he is an anaesthetist." The four physicians wore white suits.

Erik Wierts had a tanned face and contrasting blond hair with too-light eyebrows. Under his nose was a thin little moustache. He sat staring at a file and had not yet looked up. He gave Vera the impression of insensivity. *But perhaps he is not able to show his feelings,* she corrected herself. But he seemed so formal to her that she could not imagine him having a first name. "Erik," Tom had told her.

Wanders, a man with blond curls and striking glasses with thick frames, did not have a file. He sat looking at the people round the table in a relaxed manner.

Marianne de Vries, blond as well, peered over small glasses that were set on the point of her nose and smiled encouragingly at Vera and Tom. She tried to talk with them, but the effort flagged into a clumsy game of questions and answers.

Vera fought with a strange mixture of fear and sadness. She had tried to resign herself to the idea that Tom had no more than a few months to live. But nevertheless, hope simmered inside her; she had not stopped looking for little cracks in the reality she could not accept. When their G.P had dropped the word "transplant," into the frame her hope had flared up.

"Mr. and Mrs. Corda, we invited you for an interview, a very important interview, but an interview you could also experience as problematic." Falcon was formal in choosing his words, but his eyes and his voice showed a warm affection. He paused for a moment to find the suitable wording for his message.

"You have had an eventful few months already, and the future also promised to hold some concerns."

He hesitated for a while before going on.

"We are going to make a proposal to you. We thoroughly realize that this proposal could raise questions and that the decision we ask from you may be particularly difficult to make. Both for you, Mr. Corda, and for you, Mrs. Corda. Apart from that, it is not easy for us to weigh the pros and cons either. I ask you therefore to see this interview as an exploratory talk."

Tom looked with a great question mark on his forehead at the physician in front of them. The announcement by his G.P. that Falcon was thinking of a transplant had confused him, when he should have been happy. But he had become more or less familiar with the thought of dying, and now he needed some time to get used to the possibility of new twist: a new, unexpected chance. To his friends and neighbours he was terminal; for some of them, he did not even belong in this life anymore. And to his friends in Benares he had also made his farewells.

Vera felt uneasy; she expected Falcon to announce a transplant. Her eyes went tensely and uncertainly along the four people on the other side of the table. She took Falcon to be about forty, and the other three to be in their early thirties. It occurred to her that two of them must have been born about the time of her and Tom's marriage; Wierts must be still younger. They could have been their children. This casual thought did not help her to feel the proper respect due to them because of their functions. She knew of course that the hospital was not a world of gods and subjects anymore, as she had experienced in her youth; but she kept finding it difficult to see medical specialists as normal fellow men, especially now that they were depending on them.

"You know, Mr. Corda, that your condition is quite grave." Falcon waited for several long seconds. "We did an ultra-sound scan and we tested your blood. The great quantity of enzymes, set free in your blood, is an indication of disorders in the heart muscle. We discovered that a part of the muscle tissue has died off, and by means of an electrocardiogram we mapped the place and size of the damaged area. By doing this, the consequences of an earlier heart infarction are highlighted as well. The medical officer at Medimarket had already stated high blood pressure and an irregular heart rhythm, although this was admittedly not alarming. Your G.P. had prescribed some weeks of rest and had given you the advice to take a walk every day. Your wife stimulated you to do this. Your G.P. wanted to try treatment without medicine. Physicians have different opinions about this."

"Some believe only in medicines, whereas others try to convince the patient that he should adapt his way of living." With these words, Marianne de Vries gave her view; she agreed with the G.P.'s policy.

"But you will understand that we must give you medicines," Falcon continued.

"Mr Corda's standard of living is important," Erik Wierts replied. "He has a busy job; he is a manager in a concern, as we all know. An organization in which one manager creates work for the other ones; where people are always hustling and never have time for a coffee break."

"Like in our hospital," Willem Manders replied laconically.

"And now?" Tom asked.

"What we can do next? We already told you that balloon angioplasty or an operation on the coronaries wouldn't make sense. Vascular surgery would also not bring any improvement, as a great part of the heart muscle tissue has been eliminated. Restoring coronaries can bring the blood supply back, but without a properly working ventricle, it would be to no avail."

"Does that mean that things look black for me?" Tom wrung the words out of his throat.

"A donor heart is the only possibility. To be honest, without a new heart you will not live longer than three or four months."

It was deathly quiet in the room.

"Actually you knew this already, Mr. Corda; but now that we are confronted with an important decision, I think it desirable to describe the situation once more."

Tom could read on Falcon's face that the man found it difficult. He needed a long time before he was able to speak, then he spoke soberly. "Our G.P spoke also of another heart."

The physicians kept silent. They knew that Tom Corda and his wife were about to receive a message that would be difficult to digest.

"So you are thinking of a transplant?" Vera whispered in a hoarse voice. She thought her tongue was paralysed.

The silence in the room was tense.

"You mean the heart of somebody who has died?" Tom looked fearfully around, from one face to another. He read compassion on the faces, but nothing that could give him any hope. "The heart of a dead...?"

"Another heart—but not from a dead person."

The silence was frightening.

"Not from a dead person?"

"In view of the long waiting lists there is no real chance that a suitable heart will become available. Therefore we are cautiously thinking of the possibility of xenotransplant."

Because of his work for Medimarket Tom knew what it was about, but in spite of all fuss, he had seen the phenomenon as the hobby of woolly scientists. Now, however, he was convinced of the real sense of it. "Xenotransplant?"

Vera voiced the thoughts that were running through her mind. "You mean the heart of an animal?" She shivered.

"Of an animal, yes."

"An animal?" Vera's hands searched for a hold on the table. Her eyes saw only hazy figures around her. Her mouth hung half-open. She remembered that Tom had told her about Pigor, where people did research into the possibility of transplanting animal organs into human beings. She had shrugged her shoulders then. *Does it make sense to make a fuss about such idiocy* she had thought? *Why worry about* these *scientists who don't live in the real world.*

As he consciously observed their reactions, Dr. Falcon quietly went on. "Xenotransplant already has a long history, Mr. and Mrs. Corda. As long as we can look back, human beings have made use of animal material, for example for food, for clothing, for medicines. Until recently we were not, however, capable of transplanting something from an animal into a human being, in order for it to stand in for a disfunctional organ or a part of it. There were two important obstacles that seemed, for a long time, insurmountable."

Tom seemed numbed by a delirious dream.

Vera heard Falcon talking, but she seemed to have found herself in an unreal world where the physician's words buzzed round her head as though they were a cloud of insects. "Xenotransplant? You mean the heart of...?"

"Of a pig." Falcon looked straight into her eyes.

She looked at him, astonished. "A pig?"

"Yes. A pig."

Vera gazed vacantly ahead. It was as if her thoughts were floating in an endless space far from her.

Tom seemed totally unconscious; he stared vacantly at a useless ashtray.

"It has not yet been done. That is to say, your husband would be the first human being to be implanted with a pig's heart. Heart valves of pigs have been transplanted into human beings, but a whole heart, no. This would be the first heart transplant where a pig's heart would be implanted into a human being." The physician's words sounded businesslike and seemed to float around the room. They certainly didn't get through to Vera's conscious mind, although every word had registered in her brain.

Marianne de Vries did not know what to think. She had read about experiments with animals; about a monkey that had lived for a few days with a pig's heart. She knew that Pigor had researched the possibility of implanting pig's hearts into human beings, but it had remained an academic phenomenon to her. Now was she supposed to assist in transplanting such a heart? She had wrestled with the idea since John Falcon had presented the proposal to her. Deep in her heart, she had hoped that Tom Corda would refuse. *But what shall I do if he says yes? Is it not my duty then, as a physician, to cooperate?*

"We are getting ahead of ourselves," Falcon went quietly on. "I emphatically stress once more that this interview has an exploratory character and that it only concerns a proposal."

Nobody reacted to Falcon's words.

"Let 's take some time to think about it," Falcon said quietly. His words could not reduce the tension round the table.

"A pig's heart in Tom's body?" Vera's words were aimed at nobody in particular; she spoke as though she could only talk to an imaginary sounding board. Indignation and sadness marked her face.

"I realize that we have taken you by surprise, Mr. and Mrs. Corda. The idea must be strange to you. Nonetheless, this is not totally new. We have already replaced bad heart valves of a human being with pig's heart valves, and successfully!"

"But a pig's heart!" Vera shouted. "Why a pig's heart?"

"The heart of a pig, of all animals, looks most like that of a human being."

Vera's face was deathly pale. She couldn't think clearly anymore; snatches of thoughts ran through her head, wild thoughts she had no hold over. She was paralysed and could not utter a word. Her eyes looked dull. She sat there as if drugged.

Falcon and his colleagues had no antidote to the paralysing silence.

After what seemed like a long time, Vera slowly pulled herself upright. "Dr. Falcon, tell me honestly." Her tone was surprisingly clear. "If you had a sick heart; if you knew that you only had a few months to live and that they would put a pig's heart into your body, what would your decision be? Would you decide to die, or would you allow them to put a pig's heart into your body?"

"I would choose a pig's heart." There was no hesitation in Falcon's voice.

Vera was confused by his tranquillity and definite tone. Somewhere in her misty mind whined a shadowy doubt. *Was it so strange to have a pig's heart in a human body? Am I making a problem out of nothing?*

"The heart is no more than a pump," Falcon explained.

"No more than a pump? I am sorry, doctor, that I think it strange."

Marianne de Vries smiled kindly at Vera. "It's quite normal that you take this seriously. Many people would probably think as you do if confronted with this problem. It's quite normal that you have objections. We realize that this is a very difficult choice for you and your husband. We don't expect you to come up with an answer immediately. I remind you again that this is just an exploratory interview."

Vera did not immediately react; she was considering Marianne de Vries's words. Then she said, "Choice? Can we choose, then?"

"That is what makes it so awfully difficult, for you, and for us as well. If we want to save your husband's life, we have no other possibility. The choice is: a pig's heart or death."

"I would miss him so much."

"We understand that," Wierts replied.

Vera wondered if he did.

"And a donor heart? I mean, from a human being, a dead person." Tom was finally able to say something.

"The offer of donor hearts is limited, as I have already told you. You would be on a waiting list—a long waiting list, too long."

There was another long silence.

"And an artificial heart?"

"The medical technique is not that far advanced. You could only live for a couple of hours with such a heart."

"But can such a heart,…of a pig…, be implanted into a human being just like that? Into me?"

"Not just like that. The heart of a human being and the heart of a pig have, anatomically, much in common. But in spite of that resemblance, much research was necessary to make such a transplant possible. There were two great obstacles to be surmounted."

"Obstacles?"

"The first obstacle was the human being itself," Falcon continued. "Our bodies won't bear organs or parts of organs of other animal species. So the human body rejects the strange organ; white blood corpuscles and blood proteins destroy the strange organ. Much research has been done into the reactions of rejection between different animal species. As you know, human beings are, in a biological view, animals as well."

Falcon could not perceive how his words sounded to Mr. and Mrs. Corda. They half-sagged in their chairs, their faces were without any expression, as if they were lost in a ghostly emptiness. He hesitated for a while, but then decided to go on. "Scientists have made the organs of the animal transgenic by applying a human gene onto the surface of pig cells, by which they will be rejected less quickly. That human gene produces a human protein, thus reducing the risk of acute rejection."

"You told us about two important obstacles," Vera said. She had a vain hope that she could postpone the horrible dilemma. *How can we make a choice? It is perhaps better to leave the decision to Tom; it is his body, his life, isn't it?*

His life? She corrected herself immediately. *It is our life! And how can I leave this inhuman decision to him?*

"I indeed mentioned two important obstacles," Falcon went on. "The second obstacle concerns the chance of infections. Micro-organisms like bacteria, viruses, and parasites can be transmitted from animal organs to a human being, and there is the risk that once infected, one human could trigger an epidemic of that disease. But the chance that human beings will be infected by an implanted pig's organ is negligible. Donor pigs are bred under sterile conditions, and are tested for all possible infections."

Vera had a feeling like terrible jetlag, as though she did not fit into time and space. It felt as if all order in her body had changed into a pulpy mass. She was weary and she felt an amorphous emptiness in and around her.

Tom put his hand on her arm.

Vera did not notice it. There was a mysterious mist in her soft, sad eyes. The people in white coats felt sorry for her, but they were helpless as well.

Falcon broke the silence. "Mr. and Mrs. Corda, we all realize this is an impossible situation and you have an incredibly difficult choice. I hope we can help you to reach the right decision. We know it will not be easy."

CHAPTER 34

Sarásvati sat behind her desk as there was a knock at her door. "Come in!" she called.

As the door opened, she saw Ajay Khosla in the doorway. Sarásvati could not move.

"Is Mr. Maya in his office?" Then he changed his mind. "It is you isn't it? Do you work here? How is that possible? Does Mr. Maya know, that you...?"

Sarásvati tried to pull herself together. "Yes, he knows. And Mr Maya is always late on Tuesday mornings."

"Oh! I had forgotten...Would you tell him that I'll come back?" Khosla looked at her impertinently, grinned and turned on his heel.

Sarásvati gazed at the closed door. *I am too late. I knew I should have told Maya yesterday. But he was drunk, very drunk. If I tell him now, now that Khosla has seen me here, he will know that I am just covering myself; he is smart enough...This will be the end for me. I'd better go away immediately; I've nothing to lose anymore. I must be quick, for Maya will be here any moment.* She looked at her watch. "He is late," she stated. "He is always later on Tuesdays, as he visits the temple of Durga; but he has never yet been as late as this. Perhaps he was drunk last night," she mused.

Depending on the quantity of alcohol he had drunk, Maya was often late the next morning; sometimes very late, and sometimes he did not arrive at all. If he was late, he usually had a hangover. She avoided him then more than usual for fear that his bad mood would explode. "Amal Maya is a mean drunk," people said. "When he is drunk, a thunderstorm hangs over his head."

Sarásvati, however, thought that the alcohol did not change his character, but that he merely lost control of his behaviour when he was drowned in alcohol.

I must hurry, Sarásvati thought. *If Maya has a hangover, and when Khosla tells him—in that condition—that it was me who discovered the children in the factory, then there will be no hope for me.*

She had scarcely started packing up her personal things when there was another knock at her door.

I am too late, was her first reaction. She pulled herself together. "Come in!" she said.

A servant entered. "Mrs. Arora, can you tell me how Mr. Maya is?"

"Mr. Maya? How do you mean? He's not arrived yet; he will be here shortly."

"Mr. Maya's was taken to a hospital last night," the servant replied. "Didn't you know that?"

"No, I didn't know. What is wrong with him?"

"I don't know. Nobody knows. His wife called his chauffeur in the middle of the night to drive him to the hospital. She is not yet back. Nor is Maya's chauffeur."

"Which hospital did they go to?"

"I don't know, ma'am."

Sarásvati sat down behind her desk. She needed half a minute to make a decision. Then she called the nearest hospital.

"No. Mr. Maya hasn't come in here."

She called three other hospitals only to discover that Maya had not been brought to any of them.

Sarásvati called Avih Shah. "Do you know which agent was on duty on the gate last night?"

The police officer, who was fetched there by a servant, told her that Mr. Maya's car had come through the gate between three and four o'clock. "His wife was sitting next to the chauffeur. I don't know if Mr. Maya was in the car. I didn't know he was ill."

I shall have a look around, Sarásvati decided. She realized that she might bump into Khosla, but she took the risk.

There was no sign of the chauffeur anywhere, or of the car. Sarásvati went to the kitchen to see if Parvati had come back yet, but learnt that she had not yet returned. It transpired that the two girls who worked in the kitchen, Lila and Chinky, had disappeared as well.

Before Sarásvati left the kitchen, a man came up to her. He greeted her. Sarásvati recognised him as the man who had come to give her the advice to accept the job Amal Maya had offered her.

"I came to tell you that you don't need to be anxious. But I would advise you not to tell anything to the police if something unsual should happen."

"Thank you, Mr...?"

"I am Kailash Anand, ma'am; I am the cook in Mr. Maya's house."

"Well..., thank you, Mr. Anand; I'll keep quiet."

Sarásvati went back to her room. She called the police station but nobody there knew anything about Mr. Maya's disappearance. "No, we have not received any reports of an accident involving Mr. Maya's car," the police officer on duty said, in answer to Sarásvati's question.

Half an hour later, Sunar Chand called her. "You called the police, Mrs. Arora?"

"Yes, I did," Sarásvati said. "I am worried about Mr. Maya's disappearance."

"I'll look into it. When I know more, I shall call you." Chand was very attentive.

After work, when Sarásvati shut the door of her room behind her, Maya's chauffeur called her.

"I was ordered to take Mr. Maya to the hospital," he told her falteringly. "Then Mrs Maya instructed me to get a stretcher for Mr. Maya, and when I came out, I saw the car drive away."

"The car drove away? Who drove it away?"

"I don't know. I am afraid they have been kidnapped."

"Was Mr. Maya ill?"

"Yes. He was lying on the back seat, under a blanket."

"Where are you now?"

"In a village fifty miles from Varanasi." Then the connection went dead.

With her chin in the palms of her hands, Sarásvati sat staring at a point on the wall in front of her. "Fifty miles from Varanasi," she repeated to herself. "And why did he break the connection? Did he run out of money? Or was it just a bad line?" She shook her head. "Why should I be worried about Maya's chauffeur? He can look after himself. But where is Parvati? And her husband? And the two girls? They must have been kidnapped. It is possible that there will be a ransom demand." Sarásvati gazed sightlessly at the point on the wall.

She decided for a second time to go home.

But before she could reach the door, police inspector Chand was announced.

Sarásvati was frightened. She was not looking forward to being alone with Chand. *Why didn't he just call back, as he said? Does he know something in particular?* She did not have much confidence in the police officer.

Chand knocked. She opened the door and offered him a seat. He placed his chair in front of hers.

Embarrassed by the situation, she asked him if he wanted a cup of tea. Sunar Chand said that he would like tea.

She was glad that she could occupy both her eyes and her hands on the task.

"Do you have any news?" she asked.

"No. Nothing. We visited the hospitals in the surrounding area. But no Amal Maya has been brought into any of them. That is why I am here. I hope to learn more. Can you perhaps tell me anything?"

"No."

"Did Mr. Maya, or his wife, leave a letter perhaps?"

"There is nothing on his desk. His private rooms are shut, I suppose, as is his wife's room."

"Are there no keys for those rooms? Could I have a look in them?"

"I shall ask Mr. Shah."

Nobody had a key to Maya's private rooms, but the police inspector was able to gain entry into Maya's wife's room.

"Perhaps I'll find there a clue to explain why they have disappeared, and why the two girls have disappeared. I presume there is a link between these disappearances."

As Chand drank the hot, sweet tea, he secretly looked now and then at the young woman before him.

Sarásvati paid a lot of attention on her tea. Her face was composed. *Let him drink his tea quickly,* she thought, *and then he can go. Or does he want me to go with him?*

As though he had read her thoughts, he asked, "Would you show me Maya's wife's room? Being a man, I don't like to go into a woman's room alone, more so as I do not actually have any right to go in there without permission."

"You have the consent of the house-steward."

"That's true. But in any case..."

"I'll join you, if you insist."

Parvati's room was pleasant but was a bit disordered. There was a suitcase on the floor that turned out to be empty.

"It looks like she left unexpectedly," Sunar Chand noticed. "She has not taken her suitcase with her."

"Perhaps Mr. Maya felt sick and asked her to take him to a hospital?" Sarásvati conjectured.

"Did they have contact with each other?" the police officer asked.

"I don't know. I didn't pay any attention to it."

"Is it not strange that he asked her...?"

Sarásvati waited for the rest of the question, which did not come.

"There is no trace of the girls, either," the police officer went on, as if he had meant nothing in particular.

"No."

"May I see Mr. Maya's office?"

"As you wish."

"That chair's got a broken leg."

"Oh! Visitors always sit on that chair."

That is not usual for Mr. Maya, Sarásvati thought. *When something is broken, it must always be repaired immediately.*

"I've sat on that chair a couple of times." Chand looked around the room as he said this.

After a short silence he asked, in a way that made it seem that he did not think it important, "Do you know what's in the safe?" As he studied the painting of Durga, he looked casually to see how Sarásvati reacted to his question.

"No. I suppose…documents. Actually, I don't know."

Sunar Chand felt relieved. She seemed to know nothing.

"It's a pity that we cannot gain access to Maya's private rooms," Chand said before he left. "If Maya and his wife do not turn up, I'll ask for permission to break in. Maybe those rooms will tell us more."

CHAPTER 35

For years, Pigor has been engaged in research into the possibilities of xenotransplant. Pigor is a daughter company of Medimarket, your employer." Dr. Falcon intended to discuss the decision Tom had to make.

"I was not involved in it, Dr. Falcon."

"What do you think of this research, Mr. Corda?"

The physician's question reminded Tom of the conversation between Huls and Lak he had overheard by chance on his first day at The Concern. After Medimarket had taken over Pigor, Tom had understood what Mr. D had meant by "experimental subject," but then it had been a distant problem. Only after the interview with Falcon and his team had he realized that he had been a pawn in Mr. D's game. All along he had been viewed as a potential guinea pig.

"I've never gone deeply into it," Tom said, dodging the question. "I saw it as no more than an expensive hobby."

"And now? Do you still see it as an expensive hobby?"

"Now it is a nightmare." He saw the white coat of the physician at a distance, and his words hung in the room.

Falcon understood his patient needed time to come to a decision. Just for a moment he was overpowered by doubt, influenced by the uncertainty of his patient. He had been involved in Pigor's research as a medical consultant. It had been a scientific experiment for him; but it had not yet really dawned on him that there would ever be a human being, a human being like himself, who would actually be implanted with a pig's heart. Only now did the scientific experiment have a human face. The physician shook his doubts off.

"Mr. Corda, I believe we have overwhelmed you."

Tom tried a smile.

"The heart is only a pump, Mr. Corda."

Those words kept stalking through Tom's head. *The heart is only a pump.*

"Mr. Corda, I'll ask Mrs. van Zon to have a word with you."

Tom gazed in front of him, without realizing what the physician had said.

"He needs time to make such a decision," Clare van Zon said.

"Time is a commodity that he does not have much of anymore," Falcon replied quietly.

"How do you mean?"

"We cannot wait much longer. His condition is only getting worse."

"Can you do this just like that, Dr. Falcon? I mean, is this allowed?"

"The minister is positive about our project, and he suspended the moratorium on the project at the advice of the Ethics Commission of the National Health Council."

"Does the minister think it ethically acceptable?"

"The risks are now sufficiently under control for the minister to give us a once-only concession for a xenotransplant. The minister sees the operation as a scientific project and he is even willing to pay for the costs of the operation. The question has also gone through the parliamentary mill. So there are no legal problems."

"How do you think people will react?"

"I don't know! We only know about the reactions of the Royal Society for the Prevention of Cruelty to Animals. For the rest, we don't know how the operation will be received in the country."

"So the question as to whether the transplant will be done or not must be answered by Mr. Corda?"

"Yes. From now on he is the only one who can put a halt to the operation."

"Dr. Falcon, you ask me to talk to a patient and help him make a decision about a medical surgery that I can't accept myself."

"It is his decision. Not yours."

"Of course! But I must say that I've never thought my responsibility as elusive as now. I don't know if I can approve the project in good conscience."

"Your conscience is not under discussion."

"I know I am not responsible for the decision to be made. But I don't yet know how I should handle this."

"It's not so dramatic, Mrs. van Zon. There have already been pig's heart valves put into human beings before, and there have also been liver patients treated with liver cells of pigs."

"But replacing the organ of a human being, an organ that is so essential as the heart, with the heart of a pig—I cannot get my head around it. I will talk to Mr. Corda, but I will respect his decision if it is 'no'."

"Of course!"

In her daydreams Clare embroidered the old legend of the Thessalic centaur. She had already imagined Tom as a pig-man; but she had quickly pushed that thought away. She wondered what the influence of a pig's heart might be on the life of a human being. She had no idea. Who in the world did?

During the evening meal she had discussed the problem with her husband, Joe.

"What actually is your problem?" Joe had asked her. "If the man survives the operation, and if the new heart is going to function well, what do you have to make a fuss about?"

Clare couldn't find an opening for an exchange of thoughts or feelings with her husband. The gap between them was broad and deep. For him it was a mere matter of replacing a component. For her, the heart was an essential part of a human being, forming a oneness with the whole being.

She wrestled with the question of whether Tom Corda would still be Tom Corda after the operation until deep in the night. *Will he become another person? Or will he remain the same, only with a healthy heart and a unique experience richer? Or would he essentially change? Would his nature change? His character? Would his intelligence and his emotional life change? Would the harmony in his reasoning and emotional life be disturbed? And what of his spiritual qualities? Would he become more materialistic?* Clare shuddered at her thoughts.

In the media she had seen no more than the bare medical-technical deliberations. The ethical question had remained limited to the question of the risks of losing physical health and the possibility of infections.

Am I an exception? she wondered. These were questions nobody could answer. She sympathized intensely with Tom and Vera because of the brutal conflict they were involved in. She had already discussed the problem with Vera; Vera thought as she did. But Tom was still confused; he had not yet realised fully what was going to happen to him.

Clare and Vera had another chat now.

Vera had poured them coffee. Clare sat at the window. Vera sat with her back to the wall.

"What do you think?" Vera said to open the conversation.

Clare put her cup on the table. "It is a horrible dilemma. I even wonder if medical science can confront people with such a choice. But I understand, of course, that otherwise the physicians would just have to accept the death of the patient. Medical-technical developments can result in terribly difficult choices for patients."

"It's an impossible choice. But a choice we can't avoid any longer, now that we are confronted with it. We have to choose, don't we?"

It was quiet in the room. The two women stared ahead.

"Clare, what would you do if you were in Tom's situation?" Vera's voice sounded soft, but resolute.

Clare hesitated. "You asked Falcon that as well."

"Now I ask you. You must realize that the confrontation is much more direct to Tom than to you. It remains a supposition to you. But try to imagine yourself in the life and the situation that you will be dead in three months, unless you choose a pig's heart to be put in your body..., that unless you did this you would have to leave of your husband and your daughter..., that you would leave

your friends forever, that you could not do your work anymore...,
that you would have to drop all your ambitions and plans..."

Clare felt uneasy. "I would of course talk about this to Joe. I couldn't make such a decision by myself. Joe would probably say, 'Do it!' But if I'm honest...I believe that I should prefer to die, although I don't know what I would do if I really had to choose. Now I say, if it concerned only me, I would say no, but for my daughter...I don't know."

"One of the doctors spoke about improvement of the quality of life. Probably he meant better breathing, being less tired. Will Tom experience it also as a better quality of life?"

"I've no idea, how Tom..." Vera gazed mistily ahead. As she spoke, she talked more to herself than to Clare. "I should prefer to die than to live with such a heart, but all the same...I hope that he will say yes. I would miss him so." She went on looking in front of herself. Her eyes glinted with a silent sadness.

Clare felt helpless. The only thing she could offer Vera was a sounding board, with a hollow sound to her own feelings, and an arm round her shoulders. But she doubted if she could give her and Tom the feeling that they were not alone. *Is it possible to share someone else's sadness in such a miserable situation?* she wondered as she biked home? *Vera has already weighed the problem so intensely that I don't know how I can make it clearer to her. And the dilemma remains, also after the possible operation. Would I have decided otherwise? It will be a lifelong dilemma for Vera. And what it will mean for Tom, I have no idea.*

CHAPTER 36

A head began to stand out over Tom's sleepy eyes. It was some time before it dawned on him that the head belonged to Sister Mermaid.

Her fiercely red lips and her varnished hair style had converted her into a rejuvenated old woman. She looked a little sour, but that didn't strike Tom as anything strange, as she always looked a little sour.

"Mr. Corda, you must wake up. Mrs. van Zon is coming to see you at nine o'clock."

"What time is it?"

"Seven."

Long after the nurse had left the room, Tom began to look back at his life. In the past weeks with nothing to do, he had already discovered that there was more life on earth than he had been aware of—and life in himself, as well. He had begun to realize that feeling and tasting the moment, living without looking back or ahead could be worthwhile. *I am going to enjoy my life with the new heart more than I did up until now. I am going to pay more attention to Vera and Rose. I've scarcely seen them in all these years.*

Tom didn't realize that he was making a decision.

There was a knock at the door. Clare van Zon entered. She hesitated for a while, and then she approached the bed.

Her hair was wet and curly, as if she had just taken a shower. A red cotton shirt hung to just above her knees. She wore a little coat of purplish damask over a black silky blouse. Fifty-plus glasses hung on a string round her neck. Tom thought her smile beautiful.

"Dr. Falcon asked me to talk with you."

"Have you come for my decision?"

"Falcon thought you were finding it difficult to…"

"That's true. But…I think I am going to say yes. You know? It's a difficult decision. I had already resigned myself to only having four months to live. But I'm going to attune myself again, to a new life, although it does give me sort of Lazarus feeling."

"How do you mean?"

"There are people who have already taken leave of me. I wonder how they will react now."

"And how are you going to react to them?" Clare never dodged reality.

"I don't know. People in the terminal phase of an illness are 'deceased-to-be'."

"All of us are." Clare realized too late that her reply was senseless.

"People in a terminal phase lose the illusion of immortality."

"We all know that we shall die, although we are not yet convinced."

"Perhaps you must face death to be convinced," Tom answered.

"Do you wonder how people will regard you when it turns out that you will not die after all?"

"Yes. I wonder if people will see me as a normal human being, as one of them."

"Are you afraid of being written off in their eyes? Not of this world anymore?"

"I am afraid some of them will avoid me."

"You can show them that you are still a normal human being."

"A normal human being? After the operation?"

"Why not?"

"The same Tom Corda I am now?"

"The same Tom Corda. With a lot more experience."

"How do you know? Nobody has ever had this experience before."

"That's true. I don't know either. I only think so," Clare answered quietly.

"To encourage me."

"Yes."

"But you don't believe it yourself. I can hear it in your voice."

Clare hesitated. "You are right, Tom."

"Now we can talk."

"Now that I've said what I feel."

"Exactly! I don't need a therapist; I need an honest person."

"I shall try."

"I've already made a decision. I'll do it for Vera and Rose; I will not leave them alone. So there is no other choice."

"You'll do it for them?"

"Yes. Otherwise, I wouldn't."

"So deep in your heart you would not."

Tom wrinkled his forehead.

"I am sorry. I shouldn't have used that word."

"I shall do it for them. But don't tell them."

"Are you sure? You know the alternative?"

"The alternative is four months to live. Compared to that, it shouldn't be a problem for me."

"I think your decision is courageous. I do hope that you realize the consequences of your decision."

"I've no idea. Nobody has."

"And nobody can help you..."

"In making this decision, no."

"So I am here with empty hands," Clare said.

"It doesn't matter what you have to offer."

"Do you still want a talk with me?"

"Of course! You are important to me as you are."

CHAPTER 37

Sarásvati could not make herself work. The disappearance of Maya, his wife, and the two girls kept occupying her mind. As she looked for a clue for the umpteenth time, the phone rang.

"Miss Arora, Mr. Thapar, Mr. Maya's chauffeur is back; he wants to see you."

"Would you send him to me?"

As the chauffeur knocked at her door, she bade him welcome. The man looked as though he had not slept for a week. His clothes were torn and dirty. He did not smell fresh. His hair was a wilderness.

Sarásvati offered him a seat.

Invited by Sarásvati, the man started to tell his story. "Last Tuesday, in the middle of the night, Mr. Maya was taken ill. His wife asked me to take him to a hospital. I got dressed and drove the car to the main entrance of the house. There I was given the order by Mrs. Maya to put some suitcases into the car. Five suitcases. When I got to the car with the last one, Mr. Maya was lying on the backseat. I drove as fast as I could to the nearest hospital. But when we arrived there, I was ordered to drive on to another hospital. So I drove on. We drove to the center of the town and from there we went in a westerly direction. As we reached another hospital, she ordered me to stop the car and to ask at the reception area for a stretcher. I went inside. There was nobody at the reception, so I went outside again. I was just in time to see the car driving away. I waited for a while, expecting the car to come back, but it did not. I went back inside to call the police. I asked the receptionist if I might make a call. I was told that I could but that I would have to pay for it. However, I had no money. I told the man that my boss and his wife had been kidnapped and that I had to inform the police. He didn't believe me. So I started to walk in the direction of Varanasi. I've been walking for about an hour—the sun had already risen—I was tired, hungry and thirsty. I stopped at a restaurant, where I was told that I could make a call and get a dish of food if I did the dishes. I called the police, but the officer who answered me thought it was a joke. Then I called you. But halfway through the conversation, the connection was broken."

Sarásvati needed some time to digest Lal Thapar's story. She looked for clues in the story.

"Had you taken the ignition key when you went to the reception of the hospital?"

"Yes, ma'am. Here it is."

"You had put five suitcases into the car?"

"Yes. Five large suitcases."

"Into the boot?"

"No, between the front and back seats. There is a lot of room in Mr. Maya's car."

"Who put Mr. Maya into the car?"

"I don't know."

"Did his wife tell you what was wrong with Mr. Maya?"

"No. She only told me that it was very bad and that I should drive as fast as I could."

"Was Mr. Maya unconscious?"

"I don't know. He was lying under a blanket."

"His wife was sitting beside you in the car?"

"Yes, ma'am."

"And did Mr. Maya say anything?"

"No, ma'am."

"Did you see anybody else round the hospital?"

"I saw a man walking there as we arrived. He looked a little strange. But I didn't pay any attention to him; I only thought of Mr. Maya. When I came out of the hospital the car was almost out of sight, and I could not see who was behind the wheel. But I think it must have been that strange man."

"Mr. Thapar, there were two young girls working in the kitchen, Lila and Chinky. The girls disappeared at the same time. Did you see the girls anywhere?"

"No, ma'am."

"Well, Mr. Thapar, it seems to me that you'd better get some sleep now and take a few days off. Until Mr. Maya comes back, your services will probably not be wanted anyway."

"Thank you, ma'am."

"Another thing, Mr. Thapar. You'd better not tell the police what you told me."

"I shall tell them nothing, ma'am."

When the man had gone, Sarásvati looked at the duty roster to see which servants had been present on the Tuesday night in question. She asked the men to come to her room, and asked them if they had noticed anything out of the ordinary. One of the servants told her that the evening before Mr. Maya had summoned his wife to his office, and that she had told him to tell Mr. Maya to wait for a while. But when Mr. Maya had become angry she had gone to see him. That had been the only thing that was a bit strange.

Could Parvati have put Maya into the car without anybody else's help she wondered? *Such a delicate woman? But I could be mistaken...And the two girls? Could they have helped her? And where have they gone?*

Two weeks after the disappearance of Amal Maya, his wife, and the two girls, a man delivered a parcel to Sunar Chand's house.

"Who is it from?" the police officer asked the man.

"I am not allowed to tell you; it's a surprise," the man answered.

Chand went inside with the parcel and opened it. He found a cassette tape, a list of names of companies, two keys, and a letter.

Mr. Chand,
I wish for all the children kidnapped by you and your friends to be taken back to their parents.
Brace yourself as you have been allotted an active part in this.
You can expect more orders from me shortly.

*Furthermore, I advise you to stop the investigation into the
disappearance of the people from Amal Maya's house.
If you do not understand this letter, then I advise you to open
Maya's safe with the enclosed keys and with the code ciphers
mentioned under this letter.*

*P.S.: I have put certain measures in place in case something
should happen to me or to my courier.*

The letter was signed: *"Durga Sahayan"*

Sunar Chand was deathly pale.

The list with the names of the companies the sender had
enclosed was enough for him to know that the woman who had sent
him the parcel had information at her disposal, information that
could be incriminating to him and his friends. Kidnapped children
worked in all those companies, children who had got there through
him and his partners.

"Who is Durga Sahayan?" he asked himself.

With trembling hands he took the cassette tape out of the
wrapping paper. "I must know what it is." He put the tape into a
recorder and listened anxiously. Only snatches of the conversation
were clear to him:

"Where did you get that woman from?" he heard Puttilal
Kakkar saying.

And then he heard Amal Maya saying, "and his secretary chose
to receive safety and certainty here with me. And the job I gave her
she would not have got anywhere else."

"Is it only the job she chose?" Sunar Chand was shocked to
hear his own voice.

"You should ask her; there are more women looking for my
protection."

Then Chand heard nothing more.

With the sound of Maya's conceited voice reverberating in his
head—the man he detested, but to whom he was tied to by all sorts
of illegal involvements—his brain went feverishly to work.

This is no proof, he thought, although he knew better; for he understood that the person who had sent him the tape must have still other conversations on tape. Chand remembered exactly what had been discussed during that deliberation with Maya. A nun wanted a license for building a school. They had known how many American dollars would come in for that school. They had agreed on a plan to demand ninety thousand rupees, the equivalent of the dollar amount, as slush money.

But much worse than that, they had discussed the employment of vagrant children and the kidnapping of children out of the slums. Sunar Chand was overwhelmed by a wave of nausea.

What sort of trick is Maya playing on me? Chand tried to think of which part Maya would be playing in the game, but he didn't have a clue. *Maya had better not think that he can come through this without being punished himself,* he hissed! *And the list of companies is no proof...But it can not be made public either.*

Sunar Chand had already suspected that Maya had secretly taped their conversations, in order to be able to control his partners, if necessary. But he had not expected that Maya had done this for another purpose—the purpose of destroying him. Chand now understood that this had been Maya's intention. Maya had tricked him in order to ruin him.

Chand realized that somebody from their circle was informed and had evidence against them. There was now an elusive threat hanging over his head. He did not know how much incriminating information this woman had, but he was convinced that it was enough to destroy them. *If Durga Sahayan is indeed a woman; maybe it is Maya himself and he is working under a pseudonym,* Chand thought. *Is Durga Sahayan Maya? Or is she cooperating with him?* It looked as if Chand was stuck in a nasty situation.

He lay awake for hours that night. The children they had kidnapped and whom they had sold kept on haunting him. A morbid growth of associations spun a web of questions and assumptions through his brain. He kept asking himself why Maya had passed on such information to Durga Sahayan. *Assuming that Durga Sahayan is another person. But he will destroy himself as well. I advised him to destroy all incriminating evidence, but Maya brushed my concerns aside with his slippery smile. Or was he planning this all along? I wish he would turn up! That would provide me with a little handle on the situation. But what can I do now? I must stop the investigation; otherwise, that woman—or Maya?—will not spare me…And she advises me to open Maya's safe. But when Maya turns up, he would prosecute me for that…He's playing a game with me…as I can only open his safe with judicial authorization. But I'd better keep the judge out of this.*

Sunar Chand was tossing and turning, and the problem kept going through his head until the sun had risen high.

While he got dressed in the morning, a strange thought occurred to him. *Could Miss Arora, Maya's beautiful secretary, have something to do with his disappearance?* But he changed his mind immediately. *Why would she have warned me then, when Maya and his wife disappeared? Or was she merely doing that to put herself above suspicion? Could Durga Sahayan be her alias? Perhaps Miss Arora is Maya's darling. Did she tape our conversations? Would Maya use her in his dark games? Would he use her to keep himself out of range?*

The longer Chand thought about it, the more he was convinced that Maya's secretary was Durga Sahayan, and that she had sent him the parcel in question. *Why was I so stupid? I should have persisted in asking the man who delivered the parcel for his name.*

Chand decided to pay Sarásvati Arora a visit.

Where are the two girls? Sarásvati thought inadvertently of the boot of the car. She shivered. *Parvati would never put them into the boot. Or could she have smuggled the girls out in this way? Could she have used Maya's illness as a means to release the girls? But they could have suffocated…On the other hand Parvati must have known what she was doing.*

Another thought dawned on her. *Could the girls have been under the blanket? And not Amal Maya? The chauffeur did not see Maya under the blanket. And in that case, Maya must have been in the boot. Who put him into it? None of the servants had helped Parvati, nor had the chauffeur. Is Parvati so strong that she could do this by herself? Maya would not have got into the boot himself, I suppose. Besides he was ill.* Sarásvati thought of the five suitcases the chauffeur had put into the car. *Maya can't have been in those suitcases…?* Sarásvati shivered again. *I must stay sensible. I can't believe that Parvati…Or could it have been Kailash Anand who helped her? I am going to talk to him.*

A moment later, Sarásvati thought, *If Maya did not have the keys to his private rooms with him, then they must be somewhere in his office.* She decided to look for the keys. *I will not be interrupted by anyone, unless by Maya himself, if he comes back—or if he is in his living room or his bedroom. But I must take the risk, if I want to learn more.*

She shut the door to the corridor of her own room before entering her boss's office. She checked the locks on the doors to the waiting room and the corridor, and then searched the desk drawers. She was surprised to find them open. *Maya locks up everything when he leaves his office. This could mean that he had no intention of going away,* she thought. She found three keys. Then she went through her own room to the corridor, looked around to see if she could see anybody, and entered Maya's private rooms.

The second key fit. She turned it, and looked to the right and the left before opening the door. She entered the room which had the splendid view on the Ganges. However, she didn't pay any attention to the holy river. She looked around to see if Maya was in one of his rooms and, as she didn't see him, she shut the door to the corridor.

There were some dirty glasses in the living room, and half a bottle of whisky, alongside a dish with bits of mouldy food on it. Otherwise, she saw nothing out of the ordinary.

A quick look in the bedroom did not show her anything in particular either, except disorder and an unmade bed.

After looking around, she left the rooms. She cleaned the door handle with the end of her sari.

In her boss's office, she cleaned the keys and put them back. Then, just before she went back to her own room, she was struck by an ominous feeling; her blood congealed. She shivered. Yet she had no idea why. She shrugged her shoulders. *"I must keep control."* She shook the fear from her, looked around, and went back to her room. Then she decided to visit Kailash Anand.

"Mr. Anand, can I have a word?"

"Of course, Miss Arora! How can I help you?"

"First I would ask you not to tell anybody what I am going to ask you."

"If I could not keep a secret I could not work here..."

"Mr. Anand, did you notice anything in particular about the night Mr. Maya and his wife and the two girls disappeared?"

"What do you mean by 'anything in particular'?"

Sarásvati smiled.

"I mean, did you see anything related to the disappearance?"

"Unfortunately I can't tell you anything. But you needn't be worried."

Sarásvati understood that Kailash Anand knew more, but was not at liberty to say anything. She greeted him and started to return to her room. Suddenly Sunar Chand was standing in front of her. She thought it annoying that the police officer had seen her with Kailash Anand.

Chand, for his part, was surprised to see the man who had brought him the fatal parcel in Maya's house, in the company of Miss Arora. He had no further doubts. *She is Durga Sahayan. She is the woman who ordered that man to bring me the parcel.*

"Were you friends with Maya's wife?" Sunar Chand asked Sarásvati with a charming smile.

"Me? No. I hardly knew her. I talked to her once or twice. Why do you ask?"

You underestimate me, she thought.

Chand ignored her question. "What did you discuss with her?"

So I am being interrogated, Sarásvati thought.

"I don't remember. It wasn't personal. Oh, I remember! I needed some information about the people who were working in the kitchen."

Sunar Chand was frightened. The two girls who had been kidnapped and who had disappeared worked in the kitchen. Could Miss Arora have discovered something?

"You still have that information?"

"Mr. Chand, tell me please, what do you want?"

"I am sorry, Miss Arora. The only thing I want is to learn more about the background relating to the mysterious disappearance of Mr. Maya and his wife."

"And of the two girls," Sarásvati completed his answer.

"Of course! But you will agree that Mr. Maya and his wife play the leading roles." Chand paid attention to Sarásvati's face. He wondered if her remark was an insinuation about the kidnapping.

"That depends on which side you look at it from."

"What do you mean?" Chand asked worriedly.

"Nothing."

"If Mr. Maya and his wife and the two children have disappeared, they must have had a reason. Have you any idea what sort of reason?" Chand asked.

"No. I only try to think logically."

"Did Mr. Maya ever talk to you about his wife?"

"No."

"Does he love her?"

"You know as well as I do."

"But I am asking you."

"Mr. Maya is interested in the kitchen, as food and drink is prepared there; his wife works in the kitchen."

"Can you explain to me why they left together?"

"I learned that she wanted him taken to a hospital."

"They didn't arrive there. Could it be that they have gone somewhere else?"

"Anything is possible."

"Is it possible that they have been kidnapped?"

315

"That's also possible."

"I had hoped that you would know more."

Sunar Chand decided not to ask her about the man in the kitchen. He was convinced that she wouldn't tell him anything relevant. But he was convinced that she knew more, much more. *I would like to ask her about her relationship with Amal Maya,* Chand thought, *but then she will know that I suspect her; she is smart enough. And she's got a lot of information about me...*

He rose.

Sarásvati rose as well.

"Mr. Chand, I hope you don't think I have something to do with the disappearance."

Sunar Chand thought for a while. "I don't think you do." He went to the door.

It is absolutely clear now, he thought. *Miss Arora is Durga Sahayan.*

CHAPTER 38

You'll be given medicines to help against the rejection of the new organ," Dr. Falcon told Tom.

"What sort of medicines, doctor?"

"Cyclosperine. Cyclosperine is a fungal product. You'll get thousand milligrams twice a day. That medicine is supposed to suppress the immune response of your body against antigens. So they undermine, more or less, the immune system. Therefore, we'll keep you in quarantine for a while after the operation, to keep the risk of infection down as much as possible."

Tom wondered if the medicine would not only suppress his immune response, but also his aversion response. Aversion made him shiver as he lay at night peering into the darkness; an aversion he could not overcome. He had said yes, but it had been a yes for the sake of the two people he loved more than his own life.

"What about an artificial heart?" Tom knew it was not an option.

"The artificial heart is a hope for the future. Besides, it will never come up to the quality of a natural heart."

"I am finding it hard to accept the reality of the operation."

"I understand. It's a major operation. But…you'll be in a deep sleep. And when you awake, you'll be in an insulating tent in a room where you will be treated most carefully. The anaesthetist and I shall keep you under strict supervision. All contingencies will be elaborately discussed. We will be watching you every minute, as this operation is something new. Besides, the news will go around the world; that will influence us as well, so that we shall try still more to succeed."

"I hope that my name will not be world news."

"No. Nobody other than the members of our team will know your name."

"It would make me unhappy, if people were to know that...you know what I mean, doctor."

"Don't worry, Mr. Corda!"

That night Tom lay restlessly in his hospital bed. Now and again he dozed off, but he was almost immediately frightened awake by a dream that kept teasing him; three dancing underwater beings in white coats approached him. The beings turned out to be strange figures in butcher coats, with knives in their hands. Their faces grew larger and greedier, and morphed into magnifying glass faces. The friendly smile of a thick woman in a nurse's uniform contorted into a false sneer as she tied his wrists and ankles together. Two other figures pushed an iron bar between his wrists and his ankles, and hung the bar from two chains over a fire. The white coats danced in a macabre shadow play around him.

"Release me," Tom tried to cry, but they had shut him up. Nevertheless, he felt nothing.

"Are you frightened, Mr. Corda? You don't need to be afraid!" Sister Mermaid's voice washed over him out of the water dancing world. Her friendly, shrill voice, her false eyelashes, and her laquered wig slotted themselves easily into his dream.

After a while the room had another décor. Tom didn't know if he was in an operating room or in an old country house full of Mafiosos, who were going to perform experiments on him. His nocturnal images flitted across his brain. He lay in a steel bed in a white room. A spotlight was directed on his chest. A man in a white coat came up to him. Dark-rimmed sunglasses covered his eyes. His black hair had given way to half-baldness. The man had a black moustache. Tom recognized Amal Maya by his smooth smile. Maya came nearer. He had a file in his left hand, with 'Tom Corda' written on. A stethoscope hung out of a pocket of his coat. Maya kept his hands together under his chin. Tom saw a camera in Maya's hands. He unbuttoned Tom's pyjama jacket to take a picture of his heart, then he burst out laughing. "We need a photograph of your heart," he explained. "We must check if my heart matches with yours." Then Falcon and Satori appeared. Falcon in a green suit, a green cap on his head, a green mask over his mouth and nose, and green gloves on his hands. Satori in green clothes with a green mask over her mouth and nose as well. She went to the other side of Tom's bed. Falcon gave instructions. "Pass me the knife, please?"

Satori handed the knife over. "I've just sharpened it."

"Okay! There we go!"

"Wait a minute, John! Which heart do you want to put in: the pig's heart or Maya's?"

"Maya's heart is anatomically more like Tom's. That decreases the risk of rejection."

"I wonder," Satori answered. "The pig's heart is more social; that will fit better."

"A social heart? The heart is only a pump."

"I know, but I would prefer the pig's heart. Tom will have less chance of reaction than with Maya's heart. A pig is not a predatory animal."

"I think Maya's heart is better."

"You are the boss. But I warned you. Where is Maya's heart?"

"In the safe."

"The safe is locked."

"Then we will use the pig's heart all the same."

"We must take care that Tom remains himself," Satori said.

"Of course! We'll only put another heart into his body; the rest remains the same."

Tom suddenly sat upright in his bed and discovered after some delay that he had been dreaming.

"You can't sleep, Mr. Corda?" Sister Mermaid's voice came out of a world that was both nearby and far away.

Tom lay down, muttered a little, and slipped back into a restless sleep.

Falcon came to see him.

ED MOOLENAAR

Tom asked him a question he had already thought about many times. "Doctor, how can the new heart work if all the nerves have been cut off?"

Falcon started to tell him with a friendly smile. "The heart is an organ that can generate the electric stimulus for contraction by itself."

"Does that mean that the new heart can work by itself?"

"No. The new heart needs fuels, oxygen, and nutrients. But it doesn't need to be stimulated by the brain to start its work."

"So that means that the new heart is less connected with my body than my own heart..."

"You could say that. There will be no nervous connections between the new heart and the rest of your body. But for the rest, it will be your own heart, and it will just be a part of your body and will work as such."

Two nurses in white suits came to prepare him for the operating room. While they were pushing his bed along the corridor, Tom saw the ceilings passing over him. The ceilings formed part of the unreal world he had already lived in for days. His eyes were half-closed. His hands clutched the edges of the bed.

The swirling flood of thoughts did not leave him any time for fear. Time and space evaporated along with the figures in white who were buzzing everywhere. The encouraging smile on the face of one of the nurses went floating along in his dream like a butterfly. It didn't dawn on him that he had been taken into the operating room. Now he saw light green coats floating before his eyes, and saw stressed smiles above him. It was quite clean in the room. And silent. No words were spoken. There was no sound. Tom closed his eyes.

But three wild men suddenly appeared behind his eyelids, above him. They wore white butcher coats and wooden shoes. They had daggers in their hands, and flourished their weapons.

Tom opened his eyes. The figures he saw now looked friendly and full of sympathy. He decided to keep his eyes open.

A young nurse brushed the sweat from his forehead.

Dr. Falcon's voice sounded as if it was coming from a pulpit. Tom didn't understand what he was saying.

After the operation, Falcon and his staff retired for a little rest and a cup of coffee. They had worked diligently for hours. Now they were proud; they had finished an adventurous undertaking. Their tiredness was overcome by a feeling of victory. "Good work and a masterly example of teamwork!" Falcon praised his colleagues. They reflected on the job they had done and their feelings grew gradually slightly euphoric. They even had the conviction that the problem of the lack of organs had been resolved forever.

After half an hour Falcon looked at his watch. "I am going to see the patient," he said. "Do you want to come along, Bill?"

The anaesthetist brushed his mouth clean with his hand, greeted the other colleagues, and accompanied Falcon.

They found the patient as they had left him. He looked fine. The two physicians were satisfied and proud.

On their way back to the coffee room some journalists stopped them.

"Dr. Falcon, may we ask you some questions?"

"No more than five minutes."

A man, who had presented himself as correspondent for a national newspaper, started the unexpected press conference.

"Has the operation been successful, doctor?"

"Judging from the early signs, yes."

"Congratulations, doctor! Can you tell us something about the patient? Is he an adult? A man or a woman? And how is he now?"

"The patient is, under the circumstances, all right. Next question."

The correspondent grinned.

A radio journalist asked, "Dr. Falcon There were no human hearts available?"

"No, sir."

"Dr. Falcon, would a pacemaker have been possible?"

ED MOOLENAAR

"Our patient would not have benefited from a pacemaker."

A young woman wanted to know what Falcon thought of the fact that an animal had been sacrificed to save a human being.

"Do you know how many offerings are made daily for the meat on our plates?" he replied.

The woman took no notice of the physician's counter-question. But she did want to know if the donor pig had been a boar or a sow.

"I can't tell you that," Falcon answered.

"Can you tell me then," the young woman went on, "how old a pig can become?"

"You know that here on our planet that is also inhabited by humans, not many pigs live to be old. But a pig that's not destined for the slaughter—for example, a pet pig—can live to around twenty, twenty-five years."

"How old was the donor pig?"

"I can't tell you."

"What I want to know," the woman went on, "is how does the heart age? Does it age like that of a pig, or does it age at the rate of the creature it is put inside? The age of the patient who received the heart would, in this respect, be important. But I shall not ask you for the patient's age; I understand that you are not going to tell me this."

"I appreciate journalists who don't ask questions which they know they will not be answered. As to your other question, we have no idea about that. We have no prior experience."

"Thank you, doctor."

CHAPTER 39

A faint sound came out of the strange, deep crypts of his subconscious. Muttering noises floated away. He heard the voice of a young woman, "Congratulations...the operation has been successful..."

The voice sank away. "...operation..." The word whirled through his brain like fluffy snowflakes. Tom had no idea what had happened, where he was, who he was...He drifted back into a black hole.

Other faint thoughts made their way through to him. "...a hollow muscle, as big as a fist...it's only a pump." The words resounded, echoing as through an endless, hollow space, dancing like butterflies looking for freedom against a pane. *Who said that? Or did those words come out of my mouth?*

He heard the voice again,"the operation has been successful..., Mrs. Corda."

Vera is here. Tom fell back into nothingness. It was pitch-black. Only faint, flat waves of slumbering consciousness simmered through his brain. He had no idea of time or of where he was; he didn't even realize that he existed. At the moment he started to regain conciousness, he dozed off again.

A shock went through his body, a painful shock. He shrank together. His face contorted. With the pain came the watery notion of his existence. The pain flew back.

A new shock. A stab of pain. Sharper now. The notion grew that there was something...something outside of himself..., then... a deep, dark nothing.

A strong undercurrent brought a new wave and he found himself swept along. He felt unsafe, threatened. He groped around..., something to do with his body. He could move.

There was another wave. Quite strong now. The waves came more frequently.

Why won't they leave me alone?

The congestion grew more serious. He felt for a support but didn't find it. Then he felt himself lying on something soft. It was warm and cold. He folded himself together, to find some protection from the emptiness around him. His ears caught something. A cry...out of his own mouth...

I feel lonely, desperately lonely in this mysterious, endless space.

He heard footsteps...wheels..., pointed wheels. A strange mixture of sounds...He felt himself borne on the wind. He became dizzy. There was a whiny feeling in his gullet. It felt as if a ill, sour air wanted to press itself through his throat, but couldn't find a way out.

He felt a sharp pain round his temples. Tiredness clung to his body.

His eyes had to get used to the light. He closed them and then opened them again. He noticed faint, shadowy figures against the light. One of the figures bent over him, offered protection against the fierce light. There was a face, a shadowed face. And ears, sticking-out ears. There was talking..., words...

Rags of memories skimmed along his brain. Then he knew; *I am a strange being.*

Tom awoke. He looked around. He lay under a transparent tent. Round the tent were white walls and white, drawn curtains. The ceiling was white as well. A night light at the head of the bed deepened the mysterious atmosphere in the room. Rubber tubes came out of the wall. Tubes ran out of his body as well.

A nurse sat reading on the other side of the room. A nurse with a varnished wig. There was no sound at all. It was all as mysterious as the night. In Tom's head the faint notion of what had happened began to filter through. He looked at his hands unwittingly. He turned around. *Nothing in particular...I want a mirror.*

His look went from the corners of his eyes to wander through the room, passively, without thoughts..., to the reading nurse. His eyes closed, opened again. He had no idea of where he was or what time it was. It didn't interest him. Only his face. *I want to see my face.* He fell back into a light slumber.

Then he was frightened awake again.

"Sister!"

"Mr. Corda, what is it?"

"Sister, would you bring me a mirror?"

"A mirror?"

"I want to know what I look like."

"You look very well, Mr. Corda..., at least, considering the circumstances..."

"Circumstances? What do you mean?"

"You've undergone a serious operation, Mr. Corda. Besides, you'd better calm down. It's only a couple of hours ago that you..."

"Sister, please! Will you bring me a mirror?"

"Okay! But then you are going to sleep. Deal?"

"Deal."

Rubber gloved hands pushed a mirror through an opening before his face. His face was unshaven. He looked as if he had been out boozing for a whole night. *Not extremely intelligent...,* he thought before he dozed off. But it was, all the same, a human face.

The revolution in medical science got half of the news time on TV. The interviewed minister of public health was extraordinarily enthusiastic, and he congratulated the physicians who had done the difficult job, the scientists who had made this operation possible after the research of many years, and the anonymous patient. Cardiologists and biologists might also throw their lights on the medical backgrounds of the operation.

Marketing agencies could report that 94.8 percent of the people were of the opinion that animals might be sacrificed for the use of human beings, if that could save a human life. And 43 percent of the population turned out to be afraid of unknown infections. Thirty-one percent were convinced that the implanted heart would not be rejected, while a majority of 64 percent had answered that they didn't know.

A current affairs program was dedicated to the operation. Mrs. Wondering, professional broadcasting ethicist, was invited to discuss the event with the chairman of the Ethics Commission of the Health Council, Professor Brick. Mary Burgers was the hostess.

"Professor Brick, would you give us your view on this remarkable operation? Do you think it justified?"

"I can be quite short, Mrs. Burgers. There are a lot of people who need a new heart. There is an enormous shortage of heart donors. Now there are scientists who have discovered how a pig's heart can be used for this purpose, without unacceptable risks. It is self-evident to me that we must make use of this possibility in order to save human lives."

"Mrs. Wondering, do you agree with Professor Brick?"

"I agree with him when he says that there is a great shortage of hearts. I don't agree with him that this should be a justification to transplant animal organs into human beings."

"It is, of course, not a justification in itself," Brick replied. "My commission has thoroughly studied the investigations into the risks of infection and the possibility of rejection. The commission considers both problems sufficiently under control to think xenotransplant acceptable."

"So you think xenotransplant acceptable, if the medical problems alone can be resolved?" Mrs. Wondering asked.

"If human lives can be saved, yes."

"Also if that means that different sorts of creatures become mixed?"

"I don't see this as a problem."

"And if the human being changes in quality as a result of this transplant?"

"What do you mean?"

"I mean, if the nature of a human being changes. If something of the pig's nature goes with the strange heart into the human being, for example something of its character, of its qualities. My question is, is human integrity at stake here?"

"For me the heart is a pump, Mrs. Wondering. The heart just does its work, like the pistons in the motor of a car."

"So for you, the heart is not an essential part of who you are," Mrs. Wondering concluded. "Without your own heart, with a strange heart, you would be entirely yourself as you are now?"

"Yes."

"Nobody knows what the consequences of such an operation are going to be," Mrs. Wondering objected.

"That's right," Brick answered. "We can only discover this by trying."

"Experimenting with a human being, to see how it will turn out?"

"Can science work without experimentation?"

"Experiments can be useful; the question is: can we experiment at any price?"

"In this case the price will be reasonable. I think you can compare a heterogeneous heart with an artificial leg."

"An artificial leg has nothing of the nature of an animal," Mrs. Wondering said. "It is an artificial product and is no more than an appliance, in substitution for the lost limb."

"Is a pig's heart more than an appliance?"

"The pig's heart will take over essential functions in the human body. It is going to be an integral part of the body, whereas an artificial leg remains a substituting help. One can loosen a prosthetic leg at any moment. It doesn't become an inseparable part of the body. But the pig's heart does. The question is, will it ever be a human heart?"

"So for you the heart is more than a pump?"

"Yes. My heart is an integral part of myself. I don't have a body and I don't have a heart, no more than I have a soul. I am my soul, I am my body, I am my heart."

"Can we actually pass a judgment on this?" Mary Burgers asked. "Can we decide what is good or wrong?"

"The creator of the intelligent design has, in the earthly paradise, apparently applied a new link in our brain, by which we are supposed to be able to discern good and evil. And in the course of history there were often figures who knew what was good and what was evil, and who could convince masses of people to follow them as well. But daily reality dishes up questions we just can't answer. Moreover, we always make it more complicated. By learning to implant a pig's heart into a human body, we have created a new dilemma as well. A dilemma that poses new ethical questions." Mrs. Wondering nodded kindly at her opponent.

"But," Professor Brick resumed, "if I lose a leg, I can learn to live with that loss. That is to say, I can become myself with that loss. And after some time I can get a prosthesis which I have to learn to live with, and to become myself once more. I am convinced that in that situation a prosthetic leg is an added value."

"So am I," Mrs. Wondering answered.

"And couldn't I learn to live with a pig's heart? Couldn't I learn to accept myself with that heart too?"

"You would have to revalue that heart up to the level of a human heart, to your own heart, to an essential part of yourself."

"And you are saying that I would not be able to do this?"

"I don't know. We have no experience with the implantation of animals' hearts into human beings, except for the baby in the United States who lived for a couple of days with the heart of a baboon. How can we know what an animal's organ in a human body might mean for that human being? For his self-experience? For his experience of integrity? Nobody knows."

"Therefore we should ask the person with the pig's heart for advice," Mary Burgers rounded the discussion off. "The Anonymous Receipient."

CHAPTER 40

Themes Anonymous Recipient. Could that possibly be Tom?"
Frank Sturing had been listening to the discussion on TV
between Professor Brick and Mrs. Wondering.

"Tom? No...Or...? Why do you think of Tom?"

Tineke Sturing was indignant about the casual remark, made
by her husband. But there was some doubt in her voice.

"He had a heart attack, didn't he? Vera told us that he had
been taken to the coronary care centre."

Frank had dialed the emergency number that Friday night two
months earlier. When the ambulance left with Tom and Vera, he
and Tineke had waited for Vera's return. Vera had come back in
a taxi in the middle of the night and they had invited her in for a
drink. But after that night, Vera had told them nothing more.

From the moment the xenotransplant had been given
attention by the media, however, Frank had started to speculate
enthusiastically.

"Anneke had a talk with Vera last week." Anneke was another
neighbour. "Anneke thought that Tom was doing well. It had been
critical in the first few hours, but they had got there in time."

"And that doesn't mean that Tom got that heart. He is not the
only one who has had a heart attack."

"Of course not! But he would have been an ideal candidate for
it."

"How do you know? What do you know about heart
problems?"

"Well..., I've got a lot of experience," Frank answered,
sheepishly grinning.

Tineke knew what Frank meant. She pinched her eyes closed and saw behind her closed eyelids his short love affair shatter into little stars.

Tineke then paid attention to her cooking, as she knew Frank to be a gourmet. When they sat down to dinner, her thoughts strayed restlessly to Tom Corda and his heart. She could not concentrate on the meal. Only when her plate was empty did she realize that she had not been enjoying it. She wondered if Frank had given more attention to the results of her cooking.

But Frank seemed also to be thinking about his neighbour's heart rather than his dinner "Be serious!" Frank resumed when his plate was empty. "A man of between forty and fifty years old, I read in the paper."

"That was what was assumed."

"A serious heart attack," Frank went on, "and isn't it strange that nobody has seen Vera since the operation?"

"Anneke thinks she is staying at the hospital."

"Well, she is right; if I had to get such a heart, I would avoid other people as well," Frank said.

"But you don't know if it is Tom! How can you say that?"

"Of course I don't know, but I mean that..., if I..., well..., I can't even think about it! I would rather die. The patient could choose between a heterogeneous heart or death, they said on TV. I shouldn't want such a heart in my body."

"You were not facing that decision."

"I know. But nevertheless! No, I would rather want to die than...the heart of a pig! I've even heard that people with a donor heart—a human donor heart—change in character. They start to look more like the donor. Their tastes might change. Not only related to food and drink, but also concerning music...and women. Think about that! The heart of a pig!"

Tineke thought of her dream of the previous night.

She had been at a wedding, where men and women in Tyrolean costumes danced to an inaudible waltz. A man with a thick red head and an enormous belly had pulled her with his short fleshy arms to the dance floor. They waltzed around without touching the floor. Six boys in white coats and chef's hats on their heads had carried in a suckling pig on a great dish. The dead animal lay on its back in a jelly bed, with pink crepe paper round its deathly pale little paws. Little silly eyes threw a fatal look at her. Her dancing partner grabbed a plate and a knife and pulled her to the dead pig. He cut into the white flesh of the dead animal and dug into it with his thick fingers. He grabbed the heart out of the body and threw it onto her plate. She then saw the grinning face of the man change. His eyes narrowed, and the look in his eyes was empty, absent and passive, as if the pupils registered stimuli from outside without looking; a spiritless look. Anxious eyes, submerged in flesh. Ashen white eyelashes accentuated its defenseless innocence. His cheeks filled up and his cheekbones increased. A lengthened nose, curled at the end, and runny nostrils. A sagging chin. His ears hung down like flaps. The man came to her, the pink paper of the suckling pig round his wrists. He sniffed good-humouredly at the heart on her plate, then he grabbed her with his garnished paws and they danced on.

"Do you believe that a person with a strange heart is going to be different? A different human being?" Frank disturbed the dream memories of his wife.

"Me? Well, no..., I don't think so. There are no nerves connecting the new heart to the body."

"But the new heart pumps the blood through that body!" Frank replied. "Five litres a minute; that is more than two and a half million litres in a year."

"But blood is not made in the heart."

"Of course not! But the heart is where oxygen and nutritious substances are added to the blood."

"That oxygen and those nutritious substances don't come out of the heart," Tineke replied.

She realized now that she was defending Tom Corda.

"That's true, but I would know all the same how the heart influences the body. And..."

"And?"

"If one gets a pig's heart." Frank looked with glazed eyes over his empty plate. His hands trembled as he filled his glass.

"What do you mean, Frank?"

"If one's tastes could be influenced or changed by a new heart, and if that heart is a pig's heart..." Frank's face grew ashen. He looked as if he had swallowed a spoon of *chilli sauce.*

The telephone rang.

Tineke picked up the receiver. "Hello, Anneke! Have you already heard the news about Tom?"

"That's what I wanted to tell you. Vera called me. She told me that it had been a very hard time for them, but Tom's condition is steady now. They must wait of course; but there is hope again."

"That's fine. We were seriously worried about him, the more so as we had heard nothing at all. I am happy for Tom and Vera that it's going better now."

Six weeks later it was Frank's birthday. Besides Vera and Tom, Anneke and Roel were invited. Frank's mother was already there. They sat in a circle behind their coffee cups.

Tom enjoyed being back amongst his friends.

"Was it a major operation, Tom?" The engaging smile of Mrs. Sturing matched the warm sound of her voice. That's why Tom was convinced that there was no hidden meaning in her question. After his operation he had developed a sharp ear for hidden meanings in concerned questions, but he had prepared his answer.

"The operation itself could have been worse. The coronary arteries had become choked. They first tried a balloon angioplasty, but that didn't succeed. So it became a bypass."

"And are you going to be O.K now?"

"Very well. I can do more now than I ever could. I breathe like a top-level athlete, and I can walk for miles."

"The doctors today are very capable, compared to the time when I was your age. Fortunately, I've never had problems with my heart."

"A bypass is no great feat, Mother. Nowadays they can replace the whole heart," Frank told his mother.

"Yes, from deceased people. You think I know nothing!" Mrs. Sturing replied. Her tone showed that she felt underestimated by her son.

Frank's remark had shocked Tom. He looked casually at his neighbour, but saw his face only through a mist. Through that mist he saw Frank's eyes grow, and he saw them change into looking-glasses. In those looking-glasses something strange began to appear: little, silly eyes...and a nose growing longer...and wrinkled...

I am going crazy.

"Who wants another coffee?" Tineke broke through Tom's thoughts.

Everybody did.

The conversation became more and more cheerful and chaotic. Frank and Roel launched their sometimes suggestive remarks and duelled as usual in subtleties.

Just like in days gone by, Tom thought.

By and by he felt more and more comfortable, although he was still weighing his contributions to the muddled discussions. *I shall have to learn to live with it,* he thought. *That's what they said in that TV program.*

Clare van Zon had taped the discussion on TV for him.

You can learn to live with it, just like with an artificial leg. With an artificial leg one can become oneself again...I must become myself again... I've been trying my whole life, but now I must start all over again.

He spilled coffee on his trousers.

There was a silence suddenly in the room, an embarrassed silence. All eyes were directed at Tom.

He was aware of his centripetal attention. He began to grow warm.

Mrs. Sturing laid her hand on Tom's.

After a few long seconds, Tineke broke the silence. "It doesn't matter, Tom. I spilled coffee too last night, on my sweater. Come, I'll clean it in the kitchen."

Tom knew she had invented the story about her mess to distract attention from him. He felt inclined to hug her. And he realized immediately that the feeling was still there; it left him feeling relieved.

In the kitchen he tried to hide his tears with a towel.

"I hope I can help you," Tineke said shyly, "and if you want to talk about it...,I..., well, wash your face a little."

CHAPTER 41

Good afternoon, Mrs. Corda. My name is Smulders. I am a journalist for Mystery Magazine. Mrs. Corda, I beg you not to resent me for ringing your doorbell without announcing myself in advance."

Vera studied the man on the doorstep curiously. He was in his forties with a balding head. He spoke with a posh accent and with a honeyed tongue. He wore a dark blue suit, a white shirt, a red tie, and black, polished shoes. His sticky smile was acquired rather than natural. His complacent look revolted her most of all. His little eyes and the calculating features of his face told her that the man had not come unselfishly.

"I can hardly resent you anything, Mr...?"

"Smulders."

"I can hardly resent you anything, Mr. Smulders, as long as I don't know what you've come for."

Smulders permitted himself an assessing look at Mrs. Corda. He did not immediately react to her words. Then he decided to start with an introduction. "May I pay you a compliment on your splendid garden?"

Vera did not feel like chatting about her garden. "What do you want, Mr. Smulders?"

The man understood that Mrs. Corda did not appreciate his compliment. He felt uncertain for a moment. He tried to think of another introduction, but couldn't find one. He could think of nothing other than to start on the matter he had come for. "Mrs. Corda, your husband was in a hospital for some time, wasn't he?"

Vera's reserve changed to distrust. A relay of questions ran at a crazy tempo through her head. *What does he know? Has there been a leak? Or is he just fishing? Is he looking for the person with the pig's heart, and is he just throwing out a feeler, hoping that I will betray myself?*

It cost her enormous effort to keep her self-control and to feign genuine astonishment. "Mr. Smulders, what do you actually want from me?"

"Well! Nothing, madam. I thought...er...your husband was in a hospital, wasn't he?"

Vera looked at the man as if he were an idiot. "Sir, I don't know who you are, but perhaps you can tell me now what you've actually come for." She was really angry now.

"Well...er...to be honest, Mrs. Corda, we think your husband underwent a heart operation, and..."

"And what?"

"And got that heart."

"Got that heart? Which heart?"

"The pig's heart, madam."

"The pig's heart? My husband? Sir, what do you actually think? The heart of a pig! Do you know what you're saying?" Vera saw the man grow uncertain, which led her to believe that he knew nothing.

"My husband, the pig's heart? Where did you get that from?"

"Didn't you see it on TV, madam? Or didn't you read it in the papers?"

"Of course I read about it! But what has my husband to do with it?"

"Am I to take it that it was not your husband?"

"My husband? Where have you got this nonsense from for heaven's sake? Who sent you actually?"

"Nobody, madam. I only thought that...you see? Your husband can earn a lot of money if..."

"Earn a lot of money? Sir, what are you talking about?"

Vera knew now for sure that the man had gambled. She decided to finish the game to her advantage and to let her opponent bite the dust; she hated the man.

"If it wasn't your husband, will you please excuse me, madam?"

"Excuse you? Where did you actually get such a stupid idea, to ring randomly at doorbells to ask such idiotic questions?"

"It wasn't just anywhere, madam. I mean...your husband was in a hospital, wasn't he?" the man stammered. His face grew redder and redder.

"And you have never been in a hospital, I suppose? Or are you going to pay a visit to everybody who has been in a hospital?"

Vera saw the man squirm. She vented her anger with some relief.

Smulders realized that he could not convince the woman of his good intentions, so he started to withdraw carefully. He moved backwards...

Vera kept looking at the man. Only when he was on the sidewalk did she decide to end her punitive actions. But immediately after she closed the door, she looked for support on its inner side. She stared vacantly ahead. She breathed deeply to relax herself. Only now did she feel how the confrontation had moved her. A flood of feelings and thoughts she had no words for overwhelmed her. *This is what I've been afraid of all the time,* she realized, *that there would be a leak and that journalist would jump on it, if one can call that sort of person a journalist. I am glad that Tom wasn't here; he would have become mad from the distress.*

Vera was afraid. She was aware of the danger of a leak and of their vulnerability as well. *If it ever got out, we would be at the mercy of the gossip press, and that man Smulders would show no mercy...*

Vera did not tell Tom about the incident, although she couldn't stop thinking of it.

She could not expel Smulders's face from her mind. She couldn't get to sleep that night. The after-images of the stalking gossip journalist and his slippery shampoo commercial face kept haunting her. She switched on the reading lamp over her head and started to read. But the more she tried to read, the louder Tom's snoring became.

He woke up and saw that she was awake. "I had that dream again," he said.

"Dream? What dream?"

"This has been the third time that I have had the same dream. I walked into the hospital through a revolving door. A revolving door with large mirrors. And the mirrors turned ever faster. I saw an old sow with long drooping ears...and little empty eyes...dull foggy lights...and a hairy pink skin...and a sagging battery of teats...The animal's eyes had a passive, inward look...and the mirrors kept turning...until I awoke."

Tom related his dream in such an absentminded way that Vera wondered if he was really awake. She caressed his shoulders.

Tom turned onto his back and stared with veiled eyes at the ceiling. His voice sounded hoarse as he spoke. "I can't get accustomed to it."

Vera had the feeling that a wall had been built between them, a wall of impotence, of an inability to put things into words. "We accept you as you are...," she said.

"You do...and Tineke does...I talked to her today. I told her."

"How did she react?"

"She cried. She took my hands. You know how she is. She said that it did not make any difference to her...that I was still the same Tom. She hoped that I could learn to live with it."

CHAPTER 42

*D*o I still love Vera? The question kept whining through Tom's head. More than once he had thought back to the day he had first met her. The first time he had seen her with her melancholy eyes, brilliantly reflecting her soul, he had fallen in love on the spot. Her face radiated a warm interest. His love knew no reserve. His soul celebrated the discovery of perfect love. It was light in his head and light in the world around him. His blood bubbled with energy and an enormous, bright feeling washed over his reason. He breathed life in like a child. Vera was his life; all the rest was background.

But the happiness of the time they had been together seemed now to be cut off; a phenomenon from a former life. *Do I still love her?* he asked himself. *Like I did before the operation, when I was still normal? Is it still love that I feel? Or am I only attached to her? Has the mild sadness in her eyes been an omen?*

The mist in his eyes had been a mist of love. But now, in the dark silence of the night, he wondered how pigs saw things. He knew that the pig's vision was foggy. This was the reason that he had told nobody about the mist in his own eyes; not Clare van Zon, not his G.P., and not even Vera. He thought about having his eyes tested by an optician in another town, one who didn't know him.

His thoughts went back to Falcon's consulting room. "Your body seems to have accepted the heart, Mr. Corda."

"My body?" he had asked.

"Yes. I think we've won the fight."

"The fight between my body and the heart," he had whispered. "Can my body want different things to what I want myself?"

"You have not yet come so far with your mind, Mr. Corda."

"My mind?" He had become confused. "Does my mind feel differently than my body?"

Dr. Falcon had not understood his reaction. He had been glad and proud after the operation was successful. But now he was a little disappointed that he was not getting the appreciation from his patient that he had expected. But he had controlled himself, lest he should show his irritation.

But Falcon also realized that his professional skills were limited. "Mr. Corda, we are in territory here where I can't help you. I can only confirm that your body is reacting to the new heart better than we expected. You are healthy in terms of your heart function. But if you have mental problems, I advise you to talk to Mrs. van Zon as she is a psychotherapist, so she can help you better than I can."

Tom had sat gazing vacantly at Dr Falcon's hands while his own hands felt aimlessly along the edge of the table. He had drowned himself in stunning self-pity.

But there had also been a shadow over his conscience: his feeling of dissatisfaction with his attitude toward Falcon. *Why am I not grateful?* he had asked himself. *The man saved my life, and he did everything he could for me. Without him I would be dead. And there is even more; yesterday I walked for two hours with Vera under a lovely springtime sun, without getting tired, a thing I haven't been able to do for years.*

"I am very grateful, of course. I hope you can understand that. But the idea…I can't become accustomed to it…I realize what you did for me, but…I am sorry, doctor."

Falcon had looked at his patient, not understanding. *How can he react this way to such a breakthrough in science* he wondered? He thought back to the headlines in the World's press, to the news conferences and the interviews, to the lectures he had given at some American and English universities, to the three honorary doctorates that would be granted him. *How is it possible that this man isn't dancing with joy and gratitude?*

Nonetheless, the physician was able to bring a smile to his face. "Mr. Corda, you should present your problem to Mrs. van Zon. I am convinced that, with her help, you can learn to get used to the idea."

The next morning his gloomy reflections had, with the darkness, more or less ebbed away. But Tom knew they would come back.

Two weeks later, Tom had made a fire between a number of little boulders on their garden terrace. In the evening, he, Vera and Clare sat silently round the fire. The mild summer night was perfect for a barbecue. The meal had been light and tasty. And they were in a good mood because of the wine. In the twilight of the stars in the open sky they were, helped by the fire, in the mood that meant they were experiencing time as lasting for ever. They felt a dreamy eternity as the fire radiated a living light and a promise of timelessness. The angrily and irregularly flickering flames and the glowing hollows they surged out turned to quiet astonishment. The meal, the stars and the fire had harmoniously banished the daily worries to the far background.

Tom had not yet thought of his new heart.

"In my view, Prometheus did not only steal the fire from the gods, but timelessness as well." Vera stared dreamily ahead. She didn't seem to realize that the words had come out of her mouth.

Clare nodded in approval, her eyes fixed on the fire.

Tom poked the fire with a stick. The silence was not disturbed.

After an indefinable time, Tom broke the silence, "I had a dream tonight..., a wonderful dream." The words seemed to have escaped from his lips, and were addressed to the flames.

Vera and Clare looked up.

Tom went on staring into the flames.

The two women saw his face that was capriciously lit up by the flames. His mind seemed to stray to the unfathomable depth of the fire. The relaxed atmosphere invited a story. The two women needed only to wait.

"I dream almost every night."

"You dream almost every night?" Clare's question sounded like an encouragement.

"That's why I know it's true…, the heart is more than a pump."

Vera and Clare kept waiting.

Tom stared vacantly into the fire, unaware of the presence of the two women. His timid whispering increased the tension.

"I was lying on my side on a steel grid in a low, dark pigsty. The grid was over a manure cellar; the black dung of the last hours stinking in it. I inhaled in the sweet and rancid ammonia air. I lay alone in that sty. I smelled and heard two other pigs; but we couldn't see each other, as there were high walls between the sties. The sties were cleaned and disinfected three times a day. I could not sniff; the only thing I smelled was manure and disinfectant. Besides that, I had a ring through my nose. I grunted only to make contact with the other pigs; for the rest, there was nothing to grunt for. It was always dusky in the sty; there was no day or night. When the men in their white coats, masks over their mouths, and their rubber gloves and boots came to clean the stocks, they shone their fierce flashlights on me and blinded my already hazy eyes. One of the other pigs grunted, always friendly; but the sow on the other side annoyed me with her screaming. I don't know why. The loneliness, the lack of attention, and the ring in my nose made me feel depressed. In the attic, two yards over the grid, between a criss-cross of tubes, was a little, rusty, square hatch. Once I saw that the little hatch opened, quite slowly. It started faintly, then more fiercely. It was threatening. I saw a square, dark hole. After a while, something slipped out of that hole. It was small, hairy, dark, quick and elusive. I was paralysed with fear. The hairy thing fell out of the hole and kept hanging from the bars of the grid over the manure cellar. Then it climbed out of the cellar and came to me. It crawled over my belly. Then it took a knife, cut my belly open, and clawed my heart out of my body. Then I saw the face of the hairy thing—Maya's face. He smirked and ran away with my heart."

Vera looked anxiously from Tom to Clare. Clare laid her hand on Vera's. She looked at Tom with a mixture of disbelief and compassion.

Tom's eyes were aimed at his hands.

"Tom, have you ever been there?" Clare asked after a long silence.

"Where?"

"In the pigsty at Pigor."

"No. Why?"

"Do you know somebody there?"

"No."

"Tom, what do you think of having a talk about it tomorrow?"

"About Pigor?"

"Yes."

"I can't live with it."

"With your dream?" Clare van Zon replied, with a sympathetic smile at Tom's words.

"Dream?"

"The dream you told us last night."

"Me?"

Clare understood that she had better change the subject.

"Tom, is it the new heart that you cannot live with; is that you want to tell me?"

"Yes."

"What about the medication?"

"The medicines work well…, worked well."

"You are not taking them anymore?"

"No."

"Have you discussed this with Falcon?"

"No."

"Do you want the heart to be rejected?"

"Yes."

"Why?"

"I have the feeling that I am not myself, that I am not Tom Corda anymore."

Clare van Zon did not immediately know how to put her respect for his feelings into words.

"And I am afraid."

Clare laid her hand on his. Tom let the pleasant warmth sink in. It helped him to go on.

"I am afraid that people will discover it...and are going to see me as..."

She caressed his hands.

"Actually, I am convinced that they already know, but they will not tell me...That makes it worse still; the idea that they are sparing my feelings. That they are tolerating me."

"Are you saying that in your view, they don't see you as one of them anymore? That they don't see you as a normal human being?"

"I am not normal."

Clare swallowed down her shocked reaction. "Tom, can you tell me why you don't see yourself as a normal human being anymore?"

"I am partially human, partially..."

"You perceive yourself like this?"

"Yes."

"Tom, for a couple of months you've had another heart. Do you think yourself to have been changed by that? Essentially changed?"

"Yes."

"That is your perception."

"I see it also in the eyes of our friends."

"What do you see in their eyes?"

"I see it hazily, of course...I see everything hazily..."

"What do you see in the eyes of your friends?"

"I see dull, passive eyes and..."

"Do your friends know about your new heart?"

"They don't officially know. They know it under the skin."

"Are you sure?"

"Yes. They try to protect me. Or they try to skirt around the tricky subject."

"If they are real friends..."

"How many friends feel up to the risk of the painful truth?"

"People need time to get used to strange phenomena, to become able to think it normal...and...good."

"I shall never think it normal."

Clare would not get bogged down in a discussion. Her opinion was not relevant if she was to help Tom; he should reflect on his own feelings. She caressed his hands again, quietly, and tried to start again.

"Tom, do you think that Vera is treating you in the same way?"

"Yes. Vera is the best woman in the world, but..."

"But?"

"I've become a strange being in her eyes."

"Do you mean you have no contact..., no real contact with her?"

"I know how she thinks about me. But she does not want to hurt me."

"Do you also see the little things you are afraid of in her eyes?"

"I haven't looked into her eyes..."

"Are you afraid of what you will see in her eyes?"

"Yes. But I would rather want her just to say it; then I would know where I stand. But the uncertainty!"

"The uncertainty makes it worse still."

"It is torture!"

"Tom, what do you think of having a talk between you, Vera and me?"

"Seems to be a good idea."

CHAPTER 43

"Of course you are welcome!"

As Sarásvati set the receiver down after these hearty words from Shakti, she suddenly felt terribly alone in her office. She would have liked to unburden her heart, but was cautious about talking on the phone.

Sarásvati was scared. She had, however, no idea of what. The atmosphere felt mysterious, ominous. It was as though her thoughts fluttered through and round her head, driven in and out by an unpredictable wind, like in a dream. Although she didn't know where Amal Maya was, he was more horribly present than ever before. She thought her fear was ridiculous, but she could not free herself from it. She could not get herself to work, either. Besides, she did not know what to do, as there were no orders to carry out. She wondered if Maya would approve if she did things on her own initiative.

"I really do not need to worry about that; I'd better be gone before he comes back anyway. When Khosla tells him his story, my life won't be worth anything anymore, if I am still here." She started to search her desk drawers for personal things she had not yet put into her bag. But a shrill ringing broke the smothering silence. It shocked her fiercely, as though she had woken from a ghastly dream.

It was a few seconds before she could pick up the receiver.

"Good afternoon, Mrs. Arora, Chief inspector Chand speaking. Unfortunately I must interrupt you. I have a judicial order to search Mr. Maya's house. I hope I can rely on your cooperation."

"Of course, Mr. Chand!" She was too surprised to offer any other reaction.

Chand arrived with eight police officers.

He asked Sarásvati for all the keys to all the doors, chests or drawers in the house, if she knew where to find them.

"I only have the keys to my own room, my desk and my chest."

"Unfortunately, I am obliged to search your room as well," he said shyly. "And your bag," he added, when he saw her bag, open, on her desk.

She gave Chand her keys.

The chief inspector gave instructions to his men. Two of them should look for clues in Maya's office. Another was ordered to search Sarásvati's room, supervised by Chand. The five other men should search the other rooms in the house.

Nervously pacing up and down, Chand waited for what his men would report back to him.

"Would you unpack your bag, madam? I beg you to excuse me, but I must search everything."

Sarásvati took the things she had put into her bag out of it.

Chand secretly hoped to find a hint of her involvement in the mysterious disappearance of Maya, his wife, and the two girls. Khosla had told him that she had discovered the children in the pharmaceutical company and that had confirmed his conviction that she had played an active part in the drama. *I am convinced that she is conspiring with Maya; otherwise, she would have been eliminated by him,* he argued to himself.

"Why have you put these things into your bag, Mrs. Arora?" Chand asked.

"What do you mean?"

Chand ignored her question and continued searching her personal things.

The men who had searched Maya's office came to report to their boss that they had found nothing in particular. The only thing they had found were three keys. Chand ordered them to try those keys on all the doors in the building and to search the respective rooms.

When the men had gone, Chand confided to Sarásvati, "I have a judicial order to open Mr. Maya's safe." As he said this, he watched her reaction.

Sarásvati was surprised. "Have you got the keys and the code?"

"Yes," Chand answered. *The woman is a good actress,* he thought. *She always was. Maya couldn't have a better assistant in his conspiracy.*

In the meantime, there were a number of questions running through Sarásvati's head. *What does Chand know? What does he expect to find in the safe? Why is the safe so important to him? Why is he afraid of the safe? How did he get the keys and the code? Did he actually really get a judicial order?*

Chand entered Maya's office. Alone. He locked the door from the inside.

Sarásvati understood that Chand would tell her nothing about the contents of the safe.

Chief inspector Sunar Chand had beads of sweat on his forehead while he was in Maya's office. Without Maya's consent and without the order of a judge, he felt like a burglar. He checked to see if all the doors were locked; he did not want to be interrupted when searching the safe; least of all by Amal Maya. He looked around, and then took the keys Durga Sahayan had sent him out of the pocket of his uniform jacket. He searched for the letter with the code figures. He was extremely tense. He breathed deeply before taking the four steps to the safe.

Sunar Chand thought back to the times he had seen Maya watching over his safe like a Cerberus. In an exhibitionistic mood, Maya had once opened the safe in Chand's presence and had allowed him a superficial look inside.

Now Chand had a foreboding that he would uncover an important secret.

What game is Maya playing with me? he wondered. *And what game is the woman in the next room playing with me?*

Chand turned the keys. He felt the bolts moving. That intensified his tension.

He read the code with trembling hands, then he typed the code figures in.

He turned the spoked wheel to the left as far as he could.

He stood upright and closed his eyes, before he could pass on to the final action.

Just before he pulled the door of the safe open, he smelt a faint but strange odour. He hesitated.

Then he pulled the heavy door open.

He sprang back immediately, terribly frightened. A body had tumbled out of the safe, with the woe stench of carrion. A stifling stench of rotting flesh swamped the whole room in no time.

To protect himself, Chand covered his mouth with one hand and pinched his nose with the other. He closed his eyes; it was too much for him.

When he finally opened his eyes, he saw the body of a half-dressed man. The skin of the face and the naked lower part of the body was black, swollen and cracked here and there, as if it were sun-dried river clay. Little white creatures crept out of the half-open mouth and crossed through the swampy havoc that had been his moustache toward the nostrils. They continued to swarm there, doing their cleaning work and converting the body, millimetre by millimetre, into the unbearable stench that was filling the whole room. A mousy culture of bacteria had been formed round the anus. The man's wrists were tied together behind his back with a belt, and his ankles were joined with a rope, the other end of which formed a noose round his neck.

Pinching his nose and with a hand over his mouth, Chand bent forward and discovered the body was Amal Maya's. The chief inspector emptied his stomach over the body. Then he fled to the door, his hands over his mouth and nose. Chand had forgotten that he had locked the door. He looked wildly in his pockets for the key.

Then he opened the door and appeared deathly pale, in Mrs. Arora's room. He smacked the door shut and fell onto the two-seater sofa that had not yet been used. He searched in one of his pockets for a handkerchief. He wiped his forehead and his mouth. He looked at Sarásvati wildly, who stood in front of him. He stared at her like a fool.

Sarásvati was too perplexed to ask questions. But she knew there was a dead body in Maya's office; for a wave of the horrible stench had escaped from the room with Chand.

Chand needed several minutes before he could speak. "Please, call the police office!"

After Sarásvati had made contact, she gave the receiver to Chand.

"Send four men to Maya's house immediately! They should bring protective clothes with them, and gas masks, and a body bag, and a stretcher!"

Two hours later, Chand announced the departure of himself and his men.

Before leaving he said to her, "You are playing innocent, but I know more than you think."

She stared at him with an open mouth.

"What do you mean?" she stammered.

"You know very well what I mean."

Sarásvati became angry. "Mr. Chand, are you accusing me? I demand that you withdraw that accusation."

Chand knew that Durga Sahayan, *alias Sarásvati Arora*, had evidence against him. She had also written that she had taken measures in case anything should happen to her or one of her co-workers. Chand had not forgotten that. He concluded that he had better back down.

"I beg your pardon, Mrs. Arora. I lost my self-control for a moment; I recant my words."

The astonishment on Sarásvati's face was veiled by a sad smile.

That smile was, for Chand, the umpteenth indication that she was Durga Sahayan, and that she knew more about Maya's death. *I've been mistaken,* Chand thought. *She did not conspire with Amal Maya; she was fighting against Maya and against us. She is more dangerous than I thought.*

Sarásvati's vague foreboding that the safe would unveil something about the mystery of Maya's disappearance had been right. She shuddered to think of it. She would not stay in her room, next to the room with the safe. She took her bag with her personal things, left her room hastily, and locked the door. As fast as her sari permitted, she walked to the gate, and looked there for a motor rickshaw to take her to Sudhir's and Shakti's house.

CHAPTER 44

Vera and Tom had spent their holidays in France. They had gone back to the village where they had spent their honeymoon. They had been curious about how they would find it after so many years.

They had, however, hardly recognized the old village. Many buildings were refined antiques, tuned to the masses of tourists. People they had met in the old days were either dead or had left. They had met only a couple of business people, expensively dressed men and women, some of them with polished smiles on their faces. There were dozens of restaurants and shops with endless amounts of mass-produced articles for sale.

In the center of the village was a huge restaurant, with pre-processed food complying with the presumed human fear of strange cooking.

The village has no heart anymore, Tom had thought, *as little as I do.*

They had fled into a forest for a long walk, to shake off the tourist feeling.

The day after coming back from France, Tom was standing in the queue in a bank, waiting to cash a cheque. There were eight people ahead of him and three people behind him. He was in a hurry.

The counter clerk, however, did his work with ruthless accuracy. He had no eye for the people in the long queue before him. The man had a black beard, black eyebrows, black hair, and a black skullcap on his head, and his suit was black too.

When it was Tom's turn, the man didn't see him, either. When Tom took the money in his hand, the dark eyes of the man were, just for a moment, aimed at Tom's fingers.

He noticed my fingers. I saw his eyes. He knows that I am not kosher!

Tom fled from the building. He felt himself once more to be sinking away in a swampy feeling of being something eccentric. *I am an exceptional phenomenon for the archives of medical history,* he thought. He looked at his nails, without seeing the notes in his hands. *I've changed, he knew. Still worse, I am changing. Sneakily changing. And I see everywhere mirrors in people's eyes…, telling me who I am…, what I am.*

Vera sat on her chair; her hands lay before her on the table. She stared vacantly ahead. Tears freed themselves from her eyes. Clare offered her a tissue. Vera did not see it.

Clare carefully introduced her proposal. "Tom feels uncertain about what you think of him."

"I know. But I am uncertain as well. Since Tom told us about his dream in the pigsty, I've had my doubts. I even wonder if that dream has something to do with the past of the pig. I know it's insane, but…"

"To be honest, I've also played with that thought. I've even thought about making a trip to Cambridge, to see the situation there. I want to know for sure that the dream has no grounding in reality."

"It would relieve me."

"Then I shall do it," Clare decided.

"Thanks!"

"How is Tom now?"

"He can be deeply depressed. And he has absences, as our family doctor names them. He can be absent for hours, not aware of anything. Then he sits in his chair or he lies on his bed without doing or saying anything."

"You are afraid, aren't you?"

"I am terrified. The depression and absences are frightening. Sometimes I think…"

"It is difficult to say it?"

"...that he got more than a heart..."

Clare laid her arm round Vera's shoulders. "Could it be that he experiences your terror as losing his most basic pillar? You are the most important support in his life. Your confidence in him is indispensable."

"I blame myself that I am unable to help him."

"That is your experience?"

"His experience as well."

"Vera, I can hardly imagine that a marriage between two people, who have loved each other for years, can be ruined only because each attributes to the other an incorrect image of him- or herself."

"How can I make that clear to him?"

"What do you think of a talk between the three of us? I can maybe play a mediating role."

"I am willing to do anything I can to free him from his strange ideas."

"When I came home after the operation, I had the feeling that I was a visitor in my own house. It was all known to me, but known from a former life."

Tom did not look up at the two women who sat with him round the table; he kept looking at his hands.

"You had been away for a couple of weeks, Tom. And you had had an impressive experience. You had became familiar with a new world, the world of a hospital. That's perhaps why you've come to see yourself and your surroundings in another light."

"That's true. The heart attack, the panicked admission to the hospital, the decision that had to be made, the operation, the follow-up care. And the terrific people I got to know there. Vera had decorated the room when I came home. There were flowers from our friends. But..."

It was quiet in the living room.

"My feelings were confused; there is no unity, no oneness anymore...in what I feel. And my eyes have become misty..."

Vera and Clare looked at him, concerned. Tom didn't see it.

"Tom, your world has changed, as you perceive it. And you are worried about that."

"Yes..."

"Vera is worried as well."

"I know."

"Vera is concerned about your ideas and your fear, not about changes you think there are."

Vera nodded in approval.

"You can't talk about it, since you can't accept yourself as you think you are."

"I shall never accept."

"And as you cannot accept your—imagined—changes, you suppose Vera cannot either."

Tom shrugged his shoulders.

"Tom, do you think you'll have less difficulty with accepting changes if you don't talk about it?"

He could not answer her.

"Do you think Vera has less difficulty if you don't talk about it?"

Tom did not react. He could feel that Clare and Vera understood his struggle. Tears came to his eyes, the first tears since his former life.

Vera laid her hand on his. That was enough to free his tears.

When the crying fit had more or less passed, Tom felt a relief he had not felt for years.

"The tension bothers you, Tom, doesn't it?"

"Yes."

"Do you get the feeling that you are not like other people anymore?"

"I am not one of them anymore. I don't know how to say it. Sometimes I can't make heads or tails of it. It is as though I am playing in an orchestra, but don't understand the music. I feel no harmony. I can't follow the rhythm. I have the feeling that I don't fit in here anymore."

After Tom's story about his dream, as they sat round the fire on the garden terrace, Clare van Zon had already considered going to visit the pigsty Tom had dreamt about, to see it on-site. Now that she knew Vera had toyed with the same thought, she was determined: she would have a look at Pigor in Cambridge. She would convince herself that Tom's dream had nothing to do with reality. She could not really believe that the dream memories of the pig had nestled into Tom's subconscious and gone on to live in his dreams. *It can't be true that the life of the pig continues, with the heart, in Tom Corda's life,* she tried to convince herself.

But her mind was not really at rest.

She telephoned the managing director of Pigor. She introduced herself and asked for an interview.

She took the first plane to London Heathrow and went from there by train to Cambridge.

A young woman named Mary opened the door. Mary took Clare to the director's room.

The director welcomed her courteously and introduced himself as Marc Jones.

Mary offered Clare a drink.

"What can I do for you?" Marc Jones asked. He told his guest about the work of the company.

"Mr. Jones, have you ever been visited by one of the employees of Medimarket?"

"I don't know why you want to know this, Mrs. van Zon, but I can tell you that two members of the governing council of Medimarket have been here. Those visits were part of the preparation for the takeover of our company by Medimarket. Pigor is a daughter company of Medimarket, as you probably know."

"Have you ever had a visit from one of the other employees of Medimarket?"

"No."

"Has one of the employees of Medimarket visited the sties of the pigs?"

357

"Absolutely not, Mrs. van Zon! Visitors are rarely admitted into the pigsties, and only then with my permission. We want to prevent any infection. Except for me, the research team, and the people from the cleaning service, nobody goes there."

"Have pictures of the pigs or of the sties ever been published?"

"Never! We don't want publicity. As far as I know, pictures have never been taken there."

"Mr. Jones, you know that some months ago the heart of one of the pigs was implanted into a human being."

"Of course I know. The heart of Napoleon."

"Napoleon?"

"That was the name of the pig that provided the first heart to a human being."

"What sort of pig was it, Mr. Jones?"

"Napoleon belonged to the Yorkshire family.

"Did Napoleon have a ring in his nose?"

"Yes. The pigs must remain sterile, and therefore they get a ring through their noses to prevent them smelling the grid of the manure cellar, which would increase the risk of infections."

"What else do you do to keep the pigs sterile?"

"The pigs and the sties are cleaned and disinfected three times a day. But Mrs. van Zon, may I enquire as to why you are asking all of these questions?"

"Mr. Jones, I am going to tell you this in confidence. The person who got Napoleon's heart has had inexplicable dreams."

"May I suppose that this person is in therapy with you?"

"Yes. But I can't tell you any more."

"Not about the dreams?"

"I am sorry, Mr. Jones; professional secrecy."

"I understand. You want to know more about the source of the dreams?"

"Yes. In my client's interest, I want to know for sure that the dreams have nothing to do with the donor pig."

"How can I help you with that?"

"I would like to see the sty Napoleon lived in."

Mr. Jones hesitated. "I already told you, Mrs. van Zon, that happens only rarely."

"I hope to help my client by doing this, Mr. Jones. He has been helped with the heart, but other problems now threaten. I hope that I'll be better able to help him if I know the whole situation."

"But Mrs. van Zon, you are not going to suggest, are you, that there is a connection between Napoleon's sty and the dreams of your client?"

"I cannot and will not suggest that, Mr. Jones. I only hope to determine that there is no connection."

"Mrs. van Zon, I'll give you permission, on the condition that you observe the regulations of the company."

"For my client, I'll do anything."

"Okay!"

Mr. Jones cleared his throat. He went on to explain what would have to happen before Clare would be able to approach the pig sties. "You'll have to undress completely, and then you'll be disinfected. After that, you'll be dressed in sterile clothes. I'll make sure that the correct size will be provided."

Clare nodded in approval.

On the way to the sties, she started to ask some questions about the Pigor pigs.

"Do you have other pigs, Mr. Jones?"

"We still have one, Squealer."

"So you named them after the pigs in *Animal Farm?*"

"Indeed! We also had Snowball, but she has been sold to a hospital in Italy, for the liver cells, to clean the blood of liver patients. We got the impression that Napoleon and Squealer did not like her. The two pigs became much quieter after Snowball went."

They approached the pigsty shed.

In one of the changing cubicles, Clare undressed herself. Then she went from the changing cubicle to an adjoining shower cubicle, where water mixed with a disinfectant streamed over her. After the shower, she found a white suit, white boots, white gloves, a white hat, and a white mask in a third cubicle.

When she came out of the cubicle, Jones, also dressed in white, was waiting for her.

Jones showed Clare the room where only Squealer still was. Squealer had just been cleaned.

Clare felt pity for the animal, which apparently was in pain, and tried to cough away an annoying itch in his mouth and nose. High walls separated the sties from each other. The ceiling was so low that Jones could barely stand upright. Clare was a little smaller.

"The tubes you see over the sties," Jones said, "have been put in to suck out the air, and the other tubes blow clean air into the room."

When they came to the middle sty, Jones stood still. "This is the sty Napoleon was in." Jones shone his torch over the sty.

Squealer, in the next sty and already nervous, was frightened by the light and started to squeal. The pig did not seem to like people in white suits or the fierce light of the torch. Nonetheless, the animal was curious enough to come and look. With an introverted look in his dull little eyes, the pig was especially interested in Clare. The animal sniffed her passionately.

Jones smiled shyly.

Clare looked curiously at the attic over Napoleon's sty.

"Does that hatch screech?"

Jones looked at her, astonished. "It could; it looks rather rusty. But it hasn't been opened for years." Marc Jones thought her question rather strange.

Clare was silent. She kept looking at the hatch. Then she looked attentively at the grid over the manure cellar for a while.

After a couple of minutes, she proposed, "Shall we go? I've seen what I wished to see."

They went through the sluice again, to find their own clothes in the changing cubicle. Then they went silently to Mr. Jones's office.

Mary offered the guest a meal before she got on the train, but Clare was too restless to accept the invitation. She wanted to go back home as soon as possible. She had found out what she had come to find out. She felt, however, deeply unhappy. She had secretly hoped that Tom's dreams had nothing to do with the past of the pig, Napoleon. But any way she tried, she could not see Tom's dream as separate from the heart of Napoleon.

CHAPTER 45

Ravi sat cross-legged on his mat and looked at his wife's face. It was marked by a hard and poor life, a life full of struggling and misfortune. But he knew there was a warm affection under the faintly wrinkling skin of her face. She radiated inspiration, harmonizing with a warm-sounding voice. Mild and relaxed features round her mouth betrayed a flavour of irony. Ravi admired the deep glow in her melancholy eyes, expressing distress. Her head was wrapped in long, silver-black hair. Ravi called her Asha-ji, or beloved Asha.

He thought of her struggle for years and years against a cruel nature and against exploitation by other people; an exploitation, born from timeworn traditions, given rank through an endless row of generations. But she had fought still more against the rooted mind of servitude. From her early childhood she had worked in her parents's house and in the field, so obvious that it had struck people around her only once. Only as she had lain on her mat with an aggressive fever, had they missed her. But a week after that everyone had forgotten it again.

Asha had inherited an attitude of natural servitude from her mother and forebears, inherited from generation to generation, and she had learned to be alert to the needs of men and children. Her own ambitions had been strange to her. She had been an instrument in other people's lives.

But, as a primeval feeling, a germ of individuality had nestled deep in her soul, and she had wrestled herself up out of the grey valley she had lived in. She had gained courage and strength, step by step, and had formed an invulnerable confidence out of her resignation. She had fought herself free from the whims of the waves of general and impersonal thinking, from *the* faith and *the* belief, from powers that were inclined to suffocate original thought and feeling in human beings. Her ever-resigning, dull anxiety had matured to an understanding smile. Her confined vocabulary did not decrease her wisdom.

Once she had told him that the nuns had put her on the track to discovering what she was worth. Free from rusted patterns of thinking, reducing women in the slums to drudgers, she had been able to deepen her own conscience to a natural and reliable compass. She had, with a growing insight in following paths and wrong paths, bit by bit, discovered a feeling of a sense of life. And stumbling and scrambling up from under the ballast of a forced surrogate, she had discovered the qualities she had in herself. She was now independent of stereotypical views. All the same, she felt herself, more than in her former life, united with the world around her.

Ravi looked at his wife. As there was only a tiny flame coming from the oil lamp and a hole in a wall, he could hardly see her. He loved his wife and he knew that she loved him.

The dusky interior of the hut with its mud walls and earthen floor looked more like a stable than a living room, but what was the difference for poor people? The atmosphere was warm and relaxed.

Chinky had been home for three days now.

Ravi thought back to the time their daughter had been kidnapped. He remembered the empty, soulless eyes of his wife. Her life had been no more than a faint heartbeat and an invisible breath. She had been a wounded animal. Her grief had been unreachable by other people; nobody had been able to share it. But as her companion in misfortune, he had known the chilly caverns of her experience, desperate and grey as a tomb, when their child had been stolen from their life. Until Radharana's heart-warming visit, the spiritual force of Krishna, in their nightly dream. After that night they had, step by step, recovered themselves and each other.

Ravi, who had grown up with ups and downs to become a mild, wise man, excelled in simplicity. Kind, silver-grey eyes and strong lines round his mouth reflected an aura of old nobility. In his view, truth could better be found in the smile of children's eyes than in theologian's seriousness.

Ravi and Asha had grown intensely close, with heart-warming feelings towards each other. They knew, without words, each other's intimate secrets. They understood each other with a look, a gesture, and a sigh. Sometimes their eyes met each other's.

Ravi's train of thought was disturbed by a rickshaw. Then he saw Durga coming.

They welcomed her heartily and invited her to sit down and to drink a cup of tea with them.

After talking for a while, Asha told Durga that Chinky could not tell them about her experiences in Maya's house. "I am very happy and grateful that she came back to us," she said, "but I keep wondering what she went through there."

Durga looked at the two people she had learned to love. She decided then to tell them what she knew. "Dear Asha and Ravi, I understand that you have questions about what happened to Chinky. But you must know that it will be very painful for you, if I tell you about it."

"The questions," Ravi said in a hoarse whispering voice, "have haunted us since Chinky disappeared. They have never been out of our minds. But we can't express them."

"You have had so much grief already that I find it difficult to tell you. But on the other hand, I will not leave you with such unanswered questions. I will not leave you with this horrible uncertainty any longer."

Ravi and Asha stared fearfully and silently downwards.

Durga told them about Amal Maya. She told them everything she knew. She even revealed the terrible fact Maya had often raped their daughter. In the meantime, she kept her eyes on the two people before her. And she was relieved when Asha's tears began to flow freely. She took the hands of the two people she loved and she cried with them. She held their hands until one of them was able to react. "How can a human being so misuse and violate a child? Our child!"

Considering the hoarse cry of despair from Asha, Durga kept silent. She laid an arm round her shoulders. Then she told Chinky's parents that she had been horribly scared and that she had felt helpless.

"But when I met your daughter, I discovered strength in myself; I discovered that I could overwhelm my terror. And from that moment on, I did everything I could to help the girls. I've asked them to tell me everything, again and again. Only in this way could I give them the feeling that they didn't need to despise themselves because of something that had been done to them against their will. We talked about it for many hours. I decided to distance myself from Maya. I no longer see myself as Mrs. Maya. I have taken another name, my maiden name. And I changed my first name too; I am now Durga instead of Parvati."

Asha and Ravi were appalled and stared into the distance.

Durga felt guilty, as if she had torn the deep wounds of these people wide open. And she felt ashamed, because her ex-husband had caused all this. "I am very sorry that I told you this," she said.

Asha laid a hand on hers. "It is good that you told us. The tearing pain of knowing is not as bad as the eternally whining pain of ignorance and uncertainty. We know that pain too well."

They remained sitting together.

After a long time, Ravi broke the silence. "And Maya? Where is Maya now?"

"Maya is in the place where his heart had already been for a long time," Durga answered softly.

CHAPTER 46

After some conversations with Clare van Zon, Tom Corda still had doubts about his new heart, but he could more or less accept it. He had also decided to go to Benares, although he had already taken leave of his friends there. But he felt an urge to go back to them there and by going back, he hoped to find some rest there. But most of all, he had an indefinable feeling that he had to go to finish some important unfinished business.

He was sitting in the lounge of the Central Hotel in Benares, from where he had a nice view of the restaurant. He looked quietly around and enjoyed "people watching" and seeing what was going on in front of him. A man in waiter's clothes spread all sorts of fruits on a bed of ice cubes, and bumped the cubes into a smooth iceberg for preserving the attractively displayed fruits. The man's colleague was adding up numbers with a pencil stump at the cash desk. The boss gave instructions to a boy on how to clear the tables and clean them.

Alongside Tom, there were five other guests in the lounge. The other guests included a man and a woman in their sixties from a South-East Asian country, who sat facing each other at a table. Two tables further along were two Indian men, involved in a fierce, tangled discussion, smoking beedies. In a corner sat a European businessman, writing something.

Tom looked fascinated at these people, who each came from different places in the world, but who were together in this place without even really seeing one another. This was one of the reasons that he loved Benares: the endlessly changing compilations of completely different worlds that attracted or rejected each other, or just lived at cross-purposes. A town where all colours of the world came together.

His eyes became attracted to a new figure that was now at the entrance of the hotel. He saw a woman there, a beautiful woman, graceful and self-confident. It struck him that the woman was somehow familiar. He did not, however, see immediately who she was.

Pausing at the entrance, the woman looked around, saw him, and came over to him.

Then he saw who she was. "Parvati?"

"My name is Durga Sahayan."

Tom looked at her, not understanding.

She ignored his reaction. "I've something important to discuss with you."

"With me?"

"Yes."

"How did you know that I was here?"

"I know a great deal about you. You were shadowed when you tried to investigate Maya's company. I have the information he collected. And Sarásvati told me that you were staying at this hotel."

"She told me yesterday about your mysterious disappearance and about your husband's death."

"Maya is dead. And I am back, as you see. Lila is staying with me and is going to school in Mirzapur. Chinky has been returned to her parents. The two girls have become bosom friends."

The questions in Tom's eyes elicited a smile from Durga.

"After Maya's death, I was able to close off my old life. I started a new life, as Durga Sahayan. My maiden name was Sahayan. Durga is my pseudonym. Maybe you know that the goddess Parvati appears also in the form of Durga. I would like to ask you to have dinner with me. I should like to renew our acquaintance."

Tom looked surprised.

"I have absolutely no associations with Maya anymore. I have broken from that past, from Maya's world."

"What do you mean?"

"In Hinduism, *maya* means illusion. I have shaken that *maya* world off; I want to be myself, and to judge on my own feelings, instead of thinking only what I am supposed to think. I want to follow my own will. I want to learn to know myself, learn to know what I wish in my deepest heart."

"That is what Satori told me."

Tom remained looking at the woman before him. *If she disappeared with Maya, he thought, she must know more.*

"Were you really the woman I saw in Maya's house?" he stammered.

"Yes, I was."

"Have you changed? Or didn't I see you well?"

"I have become another woman."

After they were seated at a table and were enjoying their *biryani* with rice and nuts, Tom was so impressed by the way that she was acting that he felt that he couldn't ask questions about Maya.

But Durga guessed his thoughts and started to tell him without being asked. "From the moment I met Chinky, I made plans to deliver myself from Maya's grip."

Durga took time to find the right words to use to continue her story. In the meantime, she washed food debris from her right hand in a bowl of water.

"Looking back on that last night, I believe that I gained my strength by thinking of the children and of what Maya had done to them. But it was more of a supernatural force that helped me. Sometimes he sent a servant to bring me the order that I had to go to him and account for what I had been doing in the kitchen. He always drank whiskey. His self-satisfaction fermented as the alcohol in his body. He enjoyed humiliating me. He let wait me for minutes standing in front of his desk, while he completely ignored me. And I was afraid, too afraid to be able to say what I really thought of him."

Durga smiled and went on. "When he had made wait me long enough, he asked me some senseless questions. My answers were never good. And if it began to bore him, I was sent away like a dog. I knew that he had ordered the kidnap of children, for profit. I knew that he abused young girls. I knew that he deceived people. I knew everything and I did nothing. I was afraid. Maya enjoyed my fear and he encouraged it. I hated him as I have never hated another person. I hated him for his blind self-satisfaction. I hated him for being indifferent to poor people's feelings. He ironed every wrinkle of compassion out before his feelings had a chance. He suppressed his own feelings, afraid of recognizing other people's misery; what he didn't know, he didn't need to feel. He disdained poor outcasts, to excuse his behaviour. Wealth and power were his criteria for humanity. Poor people were no more than flies on a windshield. But he was poor himself, as he could not share his wealth. His heart was in his safe. Durga was his favourite goddess—Durga, who controls the human ego by riding a tiger. He had no idea of what that meant. I despised him. But deep in my heart I despised myself as well, as I did not fight back. All the years we were married, his dominant behaviour carried me away. I only complained. In this way, I unconsciously supported him in maintaining his power. Actually, I was a victim of *maya,* as he was; a victim of illusions. This state of affairs lasted until Chinky came into my life.

"One evening, after Maya had raped her, I took Chinky into my room to look after her. Then I made a remarkable discovery. When I had the child in my arms, she opened her eyes. She looked at me, just for a brief second. In that moment, I saw what I had to do to break Maya's power, by overwhelming my own fear. I promised to take the child back to her parents. I knew by intuition that I would have to cross the borders of my own familiar world to get more self-confidence. And there came a moment when I felt myself to be stronger than Maya.

"In the meantime, I had been exploring the conduct of Maya and his accomplices. I discovered that Maya had important information in his safe. I had to run risks, but these just exhilarated me. I planned and prepared my actions carefully. I searched Maya's living room and his office, using the keys of the servant who cleaned the rooms. A watchman saw me coming out of his office. The watchman came up to me, to check what I had been doing in there. I said to him that Mr. Maya should not be interrupted, and he believed that Maya was in the office.

"Maya ordered me to come to him three times more, and I played along. I controlled my feelings of anger. But I became more and more conscious that my lack of defense irritated him. I did not offer him the resistance he needed to prove himself. And the more self-confidence I gained, and the more conscious I became of my pretended submission, I came to realize that my submissive attitude made him furious. He despised me for that. I could understand that contempt. I remembered a scene on the streets: a police officer beat up a poor outcast with his baton. That policeman grew angrier as the poor man fell on his knees and begged for mercy. The policeman behaved like a dog, getting aggressive by smelling fear. I saw that same anger in Maya's eyes. I realized that I had the power to provoke him. I even took pleasure in it. I felt that he was looking for a counterbalance, but couldn't find it. Maya began to waver.

"When my attitude—after playing the game three times, I had had enough of it—suddenly changed into indifference, he was confused. He felt that he had lost his control over me. The last time he ordered me to come to him became his ruin."

Durga told Tom what had happened that last time. "I knew I could eliminate Maya, as he was drunk; his courage came out of a bottle. But he helped me once more by losing his balance."

Tom looked impressed.

"In the weeks leading up to it I had bought six suitcases, with the help of my friend, courier and servant, Kailash Anand. Two suitcases packed with my personal things were ready in my room. I took these suitcases and three empty suitcases to Maya's office. The sixth suitcase I left in my room. I loaded the contents of the safe into the three empty suitcases. Amal Maya was lying knocked-out on his belly but could see what I was doing out of the corners of his eyes. He remained unresponsive though. He had only a dull faraway look in his eyes. By giving up his treasures and secrets, his world and life had collapsed.

"When I had loaded the contents of the safe into the suitcases, I put his throne back behind his desk. I put the chair he had wanted to hit me with against the wall; a leg was broken off. I hung the Durga painting back on the wall. At that moment I hesitated, wondering if I should carry out my plan. But I had to. I would not run the risk of Maya making more children unhappy. Besides, if he survived, he would have manipulated the media and I would have been a scapegoat. Being forced to destroy Maya was the most difficult task in my process of overcoming myself. In spite of everything he had done, I felt pity for the bastard at my feet. But he was unconscious and scarcely breathing. I dragged him into the safe—into his alter ego—and locked it. I washed my hands. I didn't feel the least bit of satisfaction.

"I called Kailash and gave him instructions. He woke Lila and Chinky and told them that they should wait. Then I called Maya's chauffeur and told him that his boss was seriously ill. I ordered him to drive the car to the entrance, to take the suitcases to the car, and to put them between the seats in the car. And, after that, to get Mr. Maya to the car and to take him to a hospital.

In the meantime, Kailash got the two girls and ordered them to lie down on the back seat, under a blanket.

When the chauffeur came to the car with the last suitcase, I told him that Mr. Maya was already in the car."

Tom's thoughts strayed between admiration and disbelief. Durga's story about Maya's elimination and the calmness she had told it with asked much from his comprehension. He looked at her, quite astonished.

She waited quietly for his reaction.

But Tom wasn't able to react.

"The chauffeur sat down behind the wheel," Durga went on. "He was driven by blind fear. I sat next to him. The police officer standing guard at the gate jumped to attention. The chauffeur drove as fast as the traffic allowed. There was not much traffic at that time of night. After an hour, we arrived at a hospital. I ordered the chauffeur to stop and to ask at the reception desk for a stretcher.

The man got out and went to the entrance of the hospital. When he had gone, I got behind the steering wheel, started the car, and drove off. In the rear-view mirror, I saw the chauffeur come out and stare after the car.

"Before I married, I had often driven a car with my father next to me, in the evening when there was not much traffic on the streets. I had carefully watched what the chauffeur had done and had fixed that in my mind. It was a huge American car. I drove slowly and falteringly, but the car rode. Then I told Lila and Chinky that they could come out from under the blanket. They had only been in a car once before, when they had been kidnapped. They sat now in the splendid car, and they could look around and be at ease.

"I drove on, slowly and carefully. A driver behind us became irritated, but I didn't pay any attention to him; I needed all my attention to get through the traffic without a collision. After driving for a couple of hours we reached a town. I drove to the center and looked for a hotel. It was seven o'clock in the morning. A servant in livery came out to welcome us. I asked him for rooms for several nights. The man bent his head and promised me that he would arrange it. After half a minute, he came back with another servant, also in livery. They took the five suitcases inside for us.

"The two girls did not know where to look. They wandered about as in a dream, through the expensively tiled corridors with their doors of splendidly painted woodwork. The two servants walked ahead of us with the suitcases. They carried them into a lift and bowed their heads, then used the stairs to go up. They waited upstairs for us and bowed again.

"Chinky asked why the servants bent down for us. 'We are rich,' I answered. The girls did not understand that.

"One of the servants invited us to follow him. He opened a lacquered red door. He gave me the keys. He brought the suitcases inside. I gave him a tip and he bent his head again. When I had closed the door behind him, I looked at the bashful girls. They could not say a thing. Without knowing it, I had chosen the most expensive hotel in town. I sat down and invited the girls to sit next to me. They needed some time to get used to the situation. They had never slept in a bed; they had only known Maya's bed. I laid my arms around their shoulders. We sat there for a while. Then I explained to them that they deserved this, and that the suite had been paid for with money obtained at their expense.

"Chinky started to cry, and so did Lila. At that moment, the tension became too much for me. We sat there crying together. After that, I let the girls enjoy a warm bath, and then I ordered a delicious dinner. We slept until the next morning and then we went out shopping. I bought the finest clothes for the girls and for myself."

Tom was silent.

"I wanted to share this story with somebody," Durga said. "I do not know anyone else I can trust with the story. I do not want to burden Sarásvati, as she is chief inspector Chand's number one suspect. I think it better that she knows nothing for the time being."

"But you hardly know me," Tom answered.

"I know I can trust you."

"But you could be arrested and charged with murder," Tom whispered, afraid that someone would overhear him. "Then you would go to jail for years."

Durga smiled. "I took precautions, with help of the incriminating material I got from the safe. There are some people who have an interest in covering up this event. I have the impression that since Chand discovered Maya's body in the safe the whole business has been hushed up. I am corresponding with Chand under my pseudonym."

Tom was too surprised for a reaction.

"Sunar Chand is one of the men who wants to cover up Maya's death. I sent him the keys and the code and I advised him to open the safe. I copied a part of one of their conversations on tape and sent it to him, so he knows the information from the safe is in my possession. I wanted him to know this. The taped conversations between Maya, Chand and Kakkar are my biggest asset. I ordered them to release all the children they kidnapped, and to accommodate those children in a SACCS refugee center, the South Asiatic Coalition against Child Servitude, in Mirzapur. The SACCS fights against recruiting children and when children are recovered they try to discover where they were taken from."

Tom needed some time to digest this information.

"I also found something for you in the safe." Durga produced a bundle of letters and gave it to Tom. "This is the correspondence between Amal Maya and the general director of Medimarket. They wrote to each other. Maya made a lot of money trading with Medimarket, and so Medimarket also benefited greatly. Maya would have earned much more money if he hadn't been eliminated. He convinced Mr. Drover that he had set up a foundation to help children to find work; the Maya Foundation. But the foundation was no more than a notory's deed. He indeed helped poor children to get work, but he did this in his own way. Mr. Drover promised him that he would support the Maya Foundation. But Mr. Drover must have heard a rumour that there was child labour in Maya's pharmaceutical company, because he wrote this letter to Maya."

Tom took the letter Durga showed him.

Dear Sir,

It has come to our attention that the produce of your pharmaceutical company from which we obtain great quantities of medicines is based upon child labour.

We, the Governing Council of Medimarket, have no objections in principle against child labour; we understand that poor families cannot manage without this form of income.

The problem becomes, however, more complicated if it concerns child slavery. The rumours we heard do not, unfortunately, exclude this.

You should know that in our country child slavery is taboo. The Governing Council of Medimarket will therefore point out to you that, if the rumours about child slavery in your company rest on truth, we don't want to take any responsibility for the possible involuntary production of medicines by children.

We hope that you can and will convince us that the above mentioned rumours are not correct. You could give Mr. Corda, who will soon be paying you a visit, a guarantee in writing that there is no involuntary child labour used in your company.

I would like to remind you, perhaps unnecessarily, dear Mr. Maya, that the possible circulation of the rumour that medicines sold to us, which have been produced by children's hands without payment of wages, would seriously harm Medimarket's current spotless reputation.

Therefore, a guarantee in writing that the products of your company are made and packed in a respectable way is, from a publicity point of view, of the highest importance.

Finally, I should inform you that Mr. Corda has not been acquainted with this problem.

Yours sincerely,

D.W.G.H.M. Drover,
President of the Governing Council and General Director of Medimarket

"Until recently nobody in Medimarket knew the name of the owner of the pharmaceutical company in Varanasi; at least I thought so," Tom said. "But apparently the big boss knew it, didn't he? He knew it all the time. This letter proves it."

"If you will come with me, I shall show you what else was in the safe."

When they had arrived at the hotel suite, Durga showed him three suitcases. She opened one of them. The case turned out to be full of money. Durga looked at it joylessly.

"I shall pay back the dowry to my father, with interest for all those years," she said. "I shall pay Lila and Chinky the wages for the time they worked for nothing, also with interest. And they have the right to reasonable compensation for the wrongs done to them. So do their parents. I shall use the rest of the money for freeing other children who have been kidnapped by Maya and his accomplices."

Then she opened the second case. This case contained jewels, ornaments, silver, gold and diamonds. Durga looked at it in a disgusted way.

"It is magnificent," she whispered, "but it has been greedily and ruthlessly scraped together. This golden necklace was once my mother's; it was part of the dowry when I got married. The chain lay in the safe all those years, where no one could enjoy it. Maya made it dead by possessing it only. He enjoyed the control he had over it; if he could enjoy anyway."

In the third case were documents, incriminating papers, and twenty-four cassette tapes.

"With this material I can help the Bonded Liberation Front," Durga clarified. She told Tom about the man who had set up the organization. It fights against child slavery, and had already freed many children.

"That's it!" Durga closed the case and looked sadly ahead.

CHAPTER 47

Waiting for Dr. Falcon, Tom saw Sister Mermaid. She came to him and shook hands with him. "How are you feeling now, Mr. Corda?"

"Well...pretty fair, sister."

"So, not too well!" Sister Mermaid decided.

"Eh...to be honest, I've had a little difficulty...accepting the new heart."

"If you find it difficult maybe I could help you."

"Could you?"

"I completed my Therapeutic Touch training last month. Therapeutic Touch, or T.T., is a way to exert a positive influence on negative feelings, with the help of the invisible field of energy every human being has around himself."

"I am willing to do anything to be free of this nasty feeling... and from that humming..."

"Humming?"

"In my head."

"Well, shall we make an appointment?"

In the consulting room Tom distinguished the strong scent of lysol with some other perfumes he could not name. He recognized also the penetrating odor of tar and nicotine from the three cigarette butts that had found a soulless end in a dirty ashtray. He saw Sister Mermaid as if through a mist. That's why her cosmetic aura did not strike him. He had already become used to her artificial social worker's jargon. Actually, he did not know why he was there; he wondered why he had made an appointment with the nurse.

The scent of the cake before his nose pleased him. He smelled coffee as well. After his operation, he had not liked coffee anymore. But he realized that the cake belonged with the coffee. He liked cake.

"Do you want a cup of coffee, Mr. Corda?"

"Yes, please!"

The nurse cut four slices of cake. When she had poured the coffee, she presented the dish of cake to Tom.

He wanted to take a slice, but his fingers were somewhat swollen. He unintentionally pinched two slices together to form one thick chunk. He hesitated.

Sister Mermaid smiled carefully.

Tom took the chunk of cake and licked his fingers clean. The therapist examined him. Tom picked up the cake with his fingers and put the half of it inside his mouth. The nurse seemed a little uncertain. Tom looked at her.

The fact that Mr. Corda had accepted her help gave the nurse a good feeling. She could, however, hide that feeling.

Sister Mermaid decided to open the conversation. She coughed shyly and started using Tom's own words.

"Mr. Corda, you've had a little difficulty accepting the new heart?"

Tom thought for a moment. "Yes. Well, you see...?" The flavour of the cake dispersed his thoughts. He saw the nurse vaguely, as if from far away. And he saw her eyes, her reflective eyes...

"I have a strange feeling inside. Sometimes I wonder who I am...,what I am..."

Sister Mermaid, seeing the passive look in the empty eyes of her client, did not feel at ease. But as she noticed him staring at the cake, she knew how to react. "Do you want another slice of cake, Mr. Corda?" she asked worriedly.

"Yes, please!"

When Tom's mouth was empty she started once more. "Mr. Corda, you said you had a strange feeling inside?"

"Yes, strange and incoherent. How shall I put it? Sometimes I don't know what I am feeling. My head swims then...and at night, in my bed, there is often a humming sound in my head."

Sister Mermaid grew more and more uneasy. She looked anxiously at the man before her, who seemed lost in his own empty dreams. He stared through her with a myopic look.

After a while, Tom began to realize where he was. His look became clearer.

I must do something, the therapist thought, *but what can I do? This fits in with none of my treatments. Besides, this man makes me nervous.* She walked back and forth in the room. It was oppressively quiet in the room, so she switched the radio on. She heard a waltz. The music relaxed her a little.

Then, without thinking, she asked, "Do you like dancing, Mr. Corda?"

Tom got up. He placed his arms forward.

The nurse went to stand between his arms, placed her left hand on his right hip, and her right hand found his left one. She breathed deeply, closed her eyes and started to dance. Tom let her lead. He tried to put his feet down in time with hers.

He smelled her perfume. He felt her thighs and her hips. The woman appeared to be able to rouse a strange, dreamy desire in his subconscious. He felt a delicious warmth in his lower belly, and his blood was rushing. His heart beat faster; he forgot that it was not his heart.

Sister Mermaid had not expected her client to press her so tightly against him. She became unusually aroused, but she was also panic-stricken. As a therapist, she did not enjoy the strange feeling, and decided that the feeling was not delicious.

"Mr. Corda, would you try to follow my rhythm, please?"

"Rhythm? It's all confusing, the music and the dancing." The cosy warmth in his belly flowed away.

Instead of that warmth, a memory grew in his mind, a memory from a former life: a faint melancholy memory of waltzing with Vera. A memory of waltzing in a perfect harmony with the everlasting

381

music, a memory of overwhelming togetherness with the laws of gravity. But that miraculous memory faded away immediately because of the heavy work he had to do now. He moved laboriously, as if dragging his feet out of mud. The music sounded fierce to his ears and Sister Mermaid drove him on.

The music and the forceful hands of the nurse drove all memories of his past life away. Sister Mermaid went on trying to lead by pressing his hip and pulling at his left hand. For her, it was a heavy chore as well.

"Mr. Corda, will you adjust your rhythm to mine?"

"I shall try."

There was sweat on his forehead. He had an understanding that all rhythm had deserted him. He began to feel stranger and stranger. *I am an outsider, unable to feel the rhythm of daily life. I am not myself anymore. How could I be? I belong to two different species: I am a human-pig being. Can a two-species being ever be at one with themselves? I must try to become myself again. But then I would not have to dance; for dancing is rhythm, the rhythm of life. I must develop a new system of thinking, like Napoleon and Squealer and Snowball from Animal Farm. They had a complete system of thought.*

Sister Mermaid gave up. She had cramp in one of her calves.

CHAPTER 48

Tom lay on a hospital bed gazing at the ceiling. He had taken off his jacket and his tie hung loosely round his neck. Sister Mermaid looked at him worriedly.

She had come to realize that she could not help her client with music and dance, so she had decided to switch to a treatment she had learned in her T.T. training. She cleared her throat to get Tom's attention.

"It is not unusual, Mr. Corda; there are other people who hear voices."

"I don't hear voices, Sister; it's humming."

"Humming can be a particular form a voice expresses itself through."

"But where does it come from?"

"People sometimes hear the voice of a dead person they had a strong bond with."

"But why the humming? Why no voice?"

"The dead person could be confused. Perhaps he has not yet found peace in his new condition, or cannot accept the fact that he has passed over."

"As he has been killed?"

"That is not impossible."

Sister Mermaid kept the palms of her hands together in front of her mouth and closed her eyes. She meditated.

Then, after a few long seconds, she went on. "Mr. Corda," she said, with a therapeutic intonation in her voice, "you don't need to be worried. What you hear is not abnormal. You are not abnormal either. You are exceptional."

"I don't want to be exceptional. The humming is exasperating. It's exhausting."

"It's not always pleasant. So I propose that we look together to see how you can learn to cope with it."

"To cope with it? Can't you put me out of this misery?"

"I would rather teach you to accept that voice, or, as you say, the humming. I mean, you should learn to fit it into your life, so that it will bother you as little as possible."

"I can't imagine that it will not bother me anymore."

"When I say fit it into your life, I mean that you will get the upper hand over that voice, instead of the other way round."

"I hope you are right."

"Trust me, Mr. Corda."

"I shall try."

"So let's begin. First, I am going to help you to relax."

Tom looked askance at her.

"You don't need to be afraid, Mr. Corda. You are no longer alone with that voice, that humming. We are now going to listen together." Sister Mermaid switched a CD player on.

Tom heard soothing, monotonous background music, like in the auditorium of a crematorium.

The therapist sat down next to the bed, so that she could see Tom's face. She looked at him and smiled. Then she started to speak in a velvety voice. "Keep lying comfortably, arms along your body. Good!" Then she was silent for a while. She looked at him in a friendly way. "You are still a little tense, aren't you? No problem. I am going to help you." After a short rest, she made him relax with the help of some yoga exercises.

Tom slipped slowly away into a pleasant physical languidness. Every activity seemed to be banished from his mind. Thoughts came, but he remained completely passive. He felt more relaxed than he could remember. He heard no humming. The soothing sound in Sister Mermaid's voice danced in his ears.

There was, however, no time to enjoy it, as he slipped away into a dream and saw Sister Mermaid's eyes grow. He was drawn by those eyes, and he could do nothing but look into them. He saw in those eyes, mistily indeed, the reflection of a smooth, long nose with two dark holes in it, and around that nose grew little white hairs. He saw little dull eyes with half-closed, weary eyelids. He saw ears hanging down like great shells. And he heard, quietly at first, then louder, an anxious humming. His relaxed face became tense.

Sister Mermaid's voice tried to reassure him. He heard her quiet, faintly muffled voice whispering, "Tom, you have crossed a border. You've broken the species barrier. You're going to live in another world. You lost something, but you got something back."

The words of the therapist needed some time to get through to Tom's mind.

"You are going to live in the world of two species, the world of centaurs, sphinxes, sirens, and mermaids. You are a unique mythical creature; I would call it a susanthropos. The natural laws that apply to human beings don't apply to you anymore. You are endowed with the qualities of two species. That makes you an exceptional being. I'll take you to that other world, a world that is tightly connected with the world of the gods."

There was a silence, a silence that left room for the voices; voices only perceptible to the nightly audience. Tom heard growling, neighing, bleating, laughing. He heard a pandemonium of human and animal voices. It seemed as though time was eternally turning round one and the same moment. The voices quickened.

Tom felt the therapist's arm around his waist. Then they were lifted up and turned around in a tornado of voices. The tornado carried them along and they floated through the space, without any effort.

Tom saw now a mermaid, slender and elegant, floating through the air and through the water, carrying him along with her, defying time and space. The laws of nature did not impede them. The moon was reflected in the water of the sea that was deep and full of mysteries. There was a windless silence. The air was clear. The sun was still behind the long, faintly bowing line of the horizon, but sent its first mild beams in advance. There was an island far away. Around that island hung a hazy veil, low over the water which, quietly rippling, promised an eternal rest.

The mermaid and Tom floated in the serene atmosphere of the world around them, over the endless water to the island. There was no time, and space was endless. The sun started to break away from the horizon. The mysterious island on the horizon in the twilight of the morning was mirage and reality.

The calm current put them gently and noiselessly onto the beach. There was rest and peace. Tom didn't even hear the leaves of the trees rustle. The trees turned out to be part of a gigantic, impenetrable forest. A discrete, noiseless wind played a game with the sun, the water, the horizon, the island and the trees; a bewitching game in a shimmering air over a smooth, clear sea.

Tom and the mermaid floated toward the forest, without touching the ground. They arrived at a huge tree on the fringes of the forest. Irresistible women's voices began to free themselves from the silence. The voices grew louder and louder. Tom and the mermaid floated further. Branches and bushes gave way to them. The voices followed them. Tom underwent the miraculous events in a mood of drunkenness. The splendid, compelling women's voices sounded so beautiful that he got back an old feeling—the longing for beauty.

They reached at an open place in the forest. Falcons flew over them, falcons as big as grown-up people. Tom heard their voices, heavenly women's voices. The voices had tempted them to the open place in the forest.

Then he saw pigs, squealing, coming from all directions. They ran around on their short, thick legs. One of the pigs, a gigantic animal, came to Tom and sniffed him. The animal gazed at him with empty, hazy eyes, reflecting innocence from under faint eyebrows. The animal seemed to wonder if Tom was nearby or far away. His long upper jaw was full of little grey-white, bristly hairs. His small lower jaw hung like a white, hairy sack of bacon under it. At the end of his flat, slippery, wrinkled nose were two small, shiny holes. Tom felt that there was something peculiar in the air.

The largest of the falcons alighted on the pig's back. The bird began to speak to Tom in a language without words. Tom understood that he was welcome on the island. He wondered what the falcon wanted from him. The bird took off and rose. It remained hovering in the air.

Tom saw now a beautiful woman above him, carrying a spinning wheel from which she created splendid musical sounds. And she sang with her tempting voice a song that entranced Tom. She radiated an enormous strength. Then, defying gravity, she descended, as a mysterious heavenly being. She went on singing her song in a dizzily high voice. The voice was irresistible and aroused a deep and intense desire in Tom. His heart beat in his body. The miraculous, compelling voice swelled, with the other miraculous voices, slowly until it dominated him completely. His heart beat wilder and wilder, raged furiously.

"The sirens!" the mermaid whispered.

The beautiful woman with her seductive voice, who must be a goddess, had kindled an ardent desire in him. His heart hammered fiercely against his chest. When she held a white, fragrant flower before his nose, he lost his heart to the beautiful woman with the golden voice.

The siren granted him a fetching smile and she sang and played on her spinning wheel. When she had sung her song, she laughed a sparkling laugh.

Tom enjoyed the happiness he felt and had thought to be impossible. He enjoyed the feelings he had fancied dead; his sense of beauty, his sense of rhythm and harmony, his love for Vera and Rose. He even thought the mermaid beautiful to look at. He had the feeling of breathing life and energy in a timeless, primeval dance. Deep in his soul he had always longed for this freedom. *This must be the eternal happiness,* he dreamt.

CHAPTER 49

Sister Mermaid had been working for more than twenty minutes to bring Tom Corda back to consciousness. During her treatment he had sunk into a deep sleep. In the meantime, she had observed a strange phenomenon. Her patient had a quite peaceful expression on his face, as though he was in a trance. The nurse had even thought of a near-death experience, and had thought he might have entered the tunnel to see eternal happiness.

Then, as the peaceful expression disappeared from his face, Tom Corda had sunk deeper into his sleep. The nurse began to fear that her patient was going to die.

Sister Mermaid was afraid. The fear that her job was hanging in the balance continually had to be lulled to sleep. She worked harder and longer than other nurses, as there was not much to enjoy beyond her work. By working more than was asked for, she could convert her uncertainty into indispensability. The nurse also knew that the hospital management overlooked the Therapeutic Touch she had exercised once before, as they saw it as harmless.

But now that a patient might die during her T.T. treatment, she felt her position wavering. After trying to resuscitate him for a quarter of an hour, it began to dawn on her that the patient was in coma. She decided to call Dr. Falcon.

When Falcon heard the name of his patient he did not hesitate. In two minutes he was on the spot. He saw at a glance what was going on.

"To coronary care!" he commanded.

He wheeled the bed with Tom Corda to the door. "Sister Mermaid, you must help me!"

They ran with the bed to coronary care. Sister Mermaid was numb. She acted as though she was in a trance.

"Sister, you are going to assist me. We can't wait until a coronary care nurse has been called."

They moved the bed into the coronary care room.

"Sister, we must get him on the respirator!"

The doctor gave her a mirror. "Will you take a look to see if he is still breathing?"

Sister Mermaid saw a faint trace of breath on the surface of the mirror.

In the meantime, Falcon had connected his patient to the respiration apparatus.

It was barely visible, but Tom Corda blinked his eyes. One minute later he opened his eyes.

"Sister, we have him!"

Sister Mermaid fainted. As she fell, she took the mirror along with her. It broke on the floor into a thousand pieces.

John Falcon didn't see it. He looked at the peaceful expression on Tom Corda's face. Then he saw Sister Mermaid, who was scrambling to her feet between the scattered pieces of the mirror.

CHAPTER 50

Tom Corda lay staring at a spotlessly white ceiling. The walls of the sickroom were equally spotless and equally white. Over his bed hung an almost empty bottle. Next to his bed a tube for oxygen emerged out of the wall. On the other side of his bed was a steel chest. Nurses had put a vase of white flowers on it. They had come from a woman who had been there to visit Tom while he was in the coma.

In the morning, Tom had woken up from his coma.

Dr. Falcon had decided to keep him in the hospital for several days. His blood pressure had been a concern, and the physician had prescribed a larger dose of Captopril.

Sister Mermaid had given Tom a suppository to help soothe the pain.

All this made his shadowy, wandering thoughts merge together with light-headed dreams. The dreams were mysterious veils of mist, close by and dizzily far away. Unreal, twisting patterns on the white sickroom ceiling, filtered by the lashes of his nearly closed eyes, joined in the dreamy game. A polar cap with faint shadows, without any life. The endless white plain relaxed him and brightened his mind; reconciled him with his limited earthly life which he felt was merging into a sea of eternity.

Then the polar field changed into a broad stream. Floating on the water, Tom grabbed for a beam stuck in the bank of the stream, and floated on. But the stream was merciless and a wave struck his last hold out of his hands. He looked around and saw circles forming on the water, increasing circles. The sun created an endless panorama of brilliant rainbow colours inside the circles.

Absorbed in the splendid colour game, Tom thought himself to be a colourful bubble in the circles around him. He enjoyed his beauty and wanted to grow. The colours around him faded away; everything became black and white. The bubble grew, and...

Ruud Lak and James Huls were next to his bed. They looked serious. They were quiet in a strange way.

"The whole network has already emigrated to the sun," Lak said with a cautious smile. "We have to postpone our holidays for a few days. Mr. D needs us. Merger problems..."

"There must be people to earn a living," Huls finished Lak's words.

Huls usually thought digitally. His world was a world of ones and zeroes. He thought—if it could be called thinking—in pairs of categories. He classified the world consistently in two opposite sorts. So for him, there were people who worked and people without a job. As there were also developed countries and developing countries. And also democracies and dictatorships. One part of mankind was politically left, and the other part was politically right. And for Huls there were homosexuals and normal people. As there were people who were terminal and people who were just going on to live...

Sister Mermaid brought an extra chair and asked if the gentlemen wanted a cup of tea. Ruud Lak declined very courteously. James Huls joined him.

Sitting on both sides of the bed, the two men made some careful attempts at conversation. Tom got the impression that they had not come for him; but because visiting a colleague in a hospital was the done thing. He would not, however, join in the game of social duties and, because of the suppository, he did not try to master his languidness. Without being aware of it, he floated back into his own dreams. It was not long before his eyes closed. But in spite of this, the exchange of views of his visitors reached, more or less, his mind. It concerned everyday things at The Concern.

To Tom, however, it seemed like they were talking about another planet. He stared, now and then, with half-open, empty eyes at his visitors. He regulated his breathing in a sleeping tempo, loud enough to be heard.

"James, how is the Maya Foundation doing?" Lak asked.

"The Maya Foundation is doing very well; we have collected a lot of money."

"Has that money already been paid into the account of the Indian foundation?"

"No. We got an inkling that there was a little problem..."

"What do you mean?"

"The owner of the company we were trading with turned out to be the man who had set up the Indian Maya Foundation. But that man suddenly passed away, and his foundation has no direction anymore. Mr. D will wait until the Indian foundation has a new director."

"Our own foundation also seems to be without a leader...since Mrs. Bot has ended her presidency."

"Mrs. Bot informed Mr. D in writing that she would immediately end her presidency. The reason has not been revealed, but there are rumours that she thinks the whole business is an illusion. You know the woman is being treated by a psychiatrist?"

Lak and Huls looked silently at Tom. They had the impression that he had somehow reacted to this news.

But after a short silence, Ruud Lak started on another subject using whispering tones. "It is not easy to have to..."

"No...and he is still rather young," Huls agreed.

Tom was astonished. *They think that I am going to die...*

"It's sad for his wife as well," Lak said.

"Yes, indeed! But fortunately she will have no financial worries."

"The pension will, at any rate, be sufficient to live on."

After a short pause, Huls made another contribution to the subject. "And what do you think of Mr. D? It must be a great disappointment for him, if he...For a long time it looked like his plan would succeed."

"Yes, quite a nuisance for him. But Mr. D is not a man to hang on after one failure."

Tom was dumbfounded.

After another short rest, Lak switched to a higher level. "It will be our turn too in the end."

"I hope it will end quickly," Huls replied. "I shouldn't like to look at it for months."

"It would not be mý choice either," Lak mused carefully.

Tom saw between the cracks of his eyes the serious looks of the two men, as there was a rest again, before another subject began.

"We should take leave in the first weekly meeting after the holidays," Lak stated.

"We can use point four of the agenda for that. You should leave that point on the agenda for..."

Tom's anger disrupted the regularity of his sleep-breathing. *So they are going to write me off...*

The two men were on the alert and inserted another pause.

After a while, when he thought Tom was in a quiet sleep, Lak started again in a muffled voice. "I've still to look for a replacement."

"I thought you had a substitute."

"That's a temporary solution, a young man without a university degree. I must think of someone for a permanent appointment."

Tom froze. *Permanent! I am out! Forever! They don't need me anymore. I am superfluous. I have been pushed aside. I am exchangable.*

Blocked by anger and a sudden tiredness, Tom lay as if floored in a boxing ring. His breath caught.

The conversation between the two men kept hanging in the air. The silence in the room was loaded with a sense of guilt. Tom saw through his half-open eyes the fright on the faces of the two men. But he should not be able to bear their apologies, so he ignored what they had talked about. He left them hanging between fear and hope with the question, "Could he have heard our talk?" He increased, vindictively, their uncertainty with a defying silence.

They were silent for a long time. They looked at their watches more than once.

Tom wondered why the two men had written him off. *Do they know something that I don't? Have they heard somewhere that I'm going to die? Falcon did not tell me that...I must ask him...tomorrow. And if it's true, I must discuss the funeral with Vera. "Just imagine that one of these men would praise me to high heaven...*

He left off his reveries. *If I fall asleep, they will have an excuse to leave without a word.* He kept his eyes open.

James looked at Ruud; he seemed to expect a signal about leaving from him. But Ruud was too decent and would leave in style.

Tom tried to imagine how the two men, who had their standard codes for meeting people and who knew the routine of the eternal daily life, were experiencing this situation.

An anxious feature round Lak's mouth betrayed his urge to escape. James Huls controlled himself better; he was not really interested in the sick man in the bed. Sympathizing was something strange to him. He just did his duty. But he wanted to leave as well. His only problem was how to close the visit in a dignified way. He looked at his watch for an excuse.

Finally, it was Lak who took the lead. "I think we should go..."

Tom appreciated that Lak did not make up an excuse.

The two men shook hands with Tom and wished him a speedy recovery.

Tom saw their departing backs and the controlled hurry in their departure.

As he was dreaming about the first weekly meeting of The Concern after holiday, and of point four of the agenda that would be devoted to his departure, Tom thought, *I hope that I'll be there.*

But then his eyes strayed to the white ceiling again, and the ceiling changed into the water of a mountain lake in a sunny, wintry daybreak. The lake radiated a peaceful rest. Tom saw himself clearly reflected in the depth of the crystal-clear water. A peaceful feeling washed over him, a feeling that he was part of nature. His ego lost itself in the existence around him. It felt as though a harmonious singing and dancing was in him. It felt as if bubbling champagne was sparkling in his soul. And in the depth of the lake he saw Satori. He knew, *Satori means enlightenment.*

Vera came in. She saw his radiating eyes. She laid her hand on his.

"You heard everything, didn't you?"

"Yes. I heard them. I was waiting at the door."

"So you heard them talking about my replacement."

"Yes. And I saw the pain on your face."

"They have written me off. That hurt me. But I think it's over now."

GLOSSARY

Ambassador is a car that has been produced in India since the 1960s.

Asha(ji) To indicate that someone is favourite or beloved, the letters "(d)ji" are added to the first name.

Avidya   The absence of vidya. See: Vidya

A dowry is a gift of the parents of the bride. About eight hundred years ago, in the time of the predatory raids and lootings of Mahmud of Ghazni and his gangs, it began to change. To protect women, and especially their chastity, against those gangs, widows were shaved bald or even burnt with the dead body of their husband. The women had to remain sati or suttee, chaste. Therefore, the burning of widows is called suttee as well. Young girls were protected against the loss of their virginity before their wedding by giving them at an early age in marriage. Parents even paid a price to the parents of the bridegroom to prevent untimely loss of their daughters' virginity. This became later the dowry, which through the centuries often deteriorated into a vulgar trade between the fathers of the bride and the groom.

Beedi is a cigarette made out of a sort of leaves.

Benares is a (holy) city at the river Ganges (the Indian name = Varanasi).

Betel is a leaf of a plant that, spread with lime and filled with different sorts of ingredients, is eaten after a meal. But it is often used for chewing as well. It has a faintly soporific effect. It is harmful to the health. In the long term it can eat away at parts of the mouth and the teeth.

Brahma is the universal soul or spirit that exceeds time and space and that expresses itself in the form of the creator Brahma, the protector Vishnu and the destroyer Shiva.

Brahman/Brahmin See Caste

Caste (System)is a rigid system of religious/societal classes that since the 1950s is officially forbidden. The Hindu society was (originally) divided into four castes: 1. The Brahmins (teachers and priests); 2. The Kshatryas (warriors and governors); 3. The Vaishyas (traders); 4. The Sudras (farmers and hand workers). These castes are subdivided into sects, which mostly are called castes as well. For example, the Takurs (landowners), a sect in the caste of the Sudras, are also named the caste of the Takurs.

Chai is the Hindi word for tea. This tea is cooked for a long time with lots of milk and sugar. Many people earn a living from it.

Chapati is unleavened bread in the form of a pancake. One takes a piece of chapati between the fingers, takes with it some rice, vegetables, etc., and brings it to the mouth. People eat without knife or fork.

Dhoti is a loincloth, worn by men.

Durga is another form of Parvati. See: Parvati.
Durga is mostly represented as the goddess that rides a tiger, as a symbol of controlling the human ego.

Ganesh is the god of happiness. The god with the elephant head. Son of Shiva and Parvati.

Ganges is the holy river which, particularly in Benares or Varanasi, Hinduistic pilgrims come to bathe in. (in Hindi it is called Ganga).

Gangama is Mother Ganges

Hijra is a eunuch

Holy (Phagua) is the Hinduistic New Year

Kafi is coffee

Kshatryas see: Caste

Krishna is the eighth incarnation of the god Vishnu

Kurta is a white, mostly cotton coat that reaches to the knees and is worn over white cotton trousers

Lakshmi is the wife of Vishnu and goddess of welfare

Maharaja is a former native sovereign who governed a part of India

Marnikarnikaghat is one of the places on the Ganges where bodies are burnt. A ghat is a number of steps along the river. The ghats were a gift of the British to the Indian people.

Maya is a Hinduistic concept that means illusion.

Muezzin is a man who calls the Muslims to prayer from the tower of the mosque five times a day.

Mumbay the Indian name for Bombay.

Namaskar is the daily greeting (to a more important person).

Namasté is the daily greeting (to an equal or less important person).

Neem Tree Indian people clean their teeth with a little branch of this tree.

Orwell, George *Animal Farm*, Penguin Books, London, 1951.

Outcasts Descendants of people who, in the far past, have violated certain caste rules and become outcasts or untouchables.

Parvati is the wife of Shiva. Is honoured as a particular beauty. She appears also in the form of Durga.

Radha(rana) is the inner or spiritual force of Krishna.

Rickshaw is a bicycle to which a little car for two people is coupled. It is used for transportation of people in the city.

Rickshaw Wallah is a rickshaw cyclist.

Rupee is the monetary unit in India.

Sarásvati is the goddess of wisdom. The origin of the beauty of the human voice is attributed to her.

Satori is a Buddhist concept that means resting point in the swing between opposites; or a vital feeling of the here and now. It also means to see one's own nature as a part of something great. It is also (Buddhist) enlightenment.

Shakti is the goddess who gives significant, female life force.

Shiva is destroyer and, paradoxically, renewer as well. Forms with Brahma and Vishnu the very important trinity in the Hinduistic world of gods.

Soedjata is the woman who brought Buddha a cup of soup, while he fasted. She convinced him that he should eat it, as he would help nobody if he would die of hunger.

Sudras See: Caste

Tandoori-Chicken is an Indian dish of chicken that can be eaten in every Indian restaurant.

Tica is a little round dot on the woman's forehead, a symbol of spiritual seeing. In daily life often a beauty dot.

Tray-Tea is tea with milk and sugar separate.

Vaishyas See: Caste

Varanasi (Benares) (Holy) city at the Ganges

Vidya is literally: spiritual seeing. Vidya (and the opposite of it, Avidya) is described in one of the Upanishads, the Mundaka Upanishad. The Upanishads are a part of the Veda, the Hinduistic Vedic scripts. One can exercise Vidya by freeing oneself from the influence of material circumstances.

Vishnu is the protector. Forms with Shiva and Brahma the trinity of important gods in Hinduism.

Made in the USA